"Born storyteller Ian W[...]
terrifying trip-of-a-lifeti[...]
depths of the exotically [...]
excellent fantasy thriller[...]
  Tanith Lee

"Adventures in a nightmare citadel – a story that hits
the ground running and doesn't let up."
  Liz Williams

"The elements which constitute this novel may be
familiar – a vast, stratified community, a ragamuffin on
the run, criminals and officials vying for supremacy –
but Whates's assured prose, slick pacing and inventive
imagination make for a gripping read. His first novel is
the work of a born storyteller."
  The Guardian

"Brilliantly inventive."
  SFX

"It is his characters who live through the story and
make the reader need to know just how it's all going to
pan out, human characters who may seem familiar but
then there's that one thing, that shifted alteration that
changes the world and changes the reader too."
  Michael Cobley

"All in all, it is an excellent book. The city is almost a
character on its own. One of the best creatures is the
demon hound, a spider-like beast that can influence
the minds of weak people. I give it 5 out of 5."
  Gnostalgia

IAN WHATES

City of Light & Shadow

THE CITY OF A HUNDRED ROWS
VOL. III

ANGRY
ROBOT

ANGRY ROBOT
A member of the Osprey Group

Midland House, West Way
Botley, Oxford
OX2 0PH
UK

www.angryrobotbooks.com
A hundred reasons to live

An Angry Robot paperback original 2012

ISBN 978-0-85766-190-6
eBook ISBN 978-0-85766-191-3

Printed in the United States of America

9 8 7 6 5 4 3 2 1

ONE

Stu hated this place with a passion; it gave him the creeps. Typically, he'd drawn the short straw and the responsibility of carrying out the day's final inspection fell to him. *Inspection?* Of what, for Thaiss's sake? Weren't nothing here except a load of stiffs. Literally. And it wasn't as if they were going to cause trouble for anyone anytime soon.

Bone flu victims, row after row of them lined up along the floor side by side and then piled up on top of each other when there weren't no more room on the floor; each one as dead as the next.

There was something eerie about seeing a human body encased in a sheath of bone, like some hard-case method of embalming, let alone the couple of hundred that occupied the vast hall Stu was charged with patrolling. Especially when you considered that they'd all been alive just a few days before. And the bodies kept coming; more and more brought in every day.

The one saving grace was that you couldn't see their faces, which meant you could kid yourself these weren't people at all but just great big dolls or statues or something, newly made and waiting to have their faces painted on. That's what Stu did, that was how he coped.

This late inspection though, when there was no one else around – just him and the stiffs – he didn't like this, not one bit. It was easy to let your imagination run wild, to believe that these ominous figures with their knobbly off-white coatings weren't dead at all but were only sleeping, waiting to catch some poor soul on their own.

If it were up to him the stiffs would have been burned straight away, the lot of them, or buried, or whatever it took to get rid of the breckers. Course, nobody ever asked for his opinion, and the doctors, they wanted all the victims stored so they could study them and try to work out a cure. All well and good he supposed, but did they really need *this* many?

This inspection was going to be a quick one, and to hell with regulations. It was dark. The wan illumination that much of Thaiburley benefited from during daylight hours – thanks to an ingenious system of mirrors, crystals and glass tubes leading from the walls – had disappeared with the sunset, and this area didn't merit electricity, it wasn't posh enough. Nor were there any oil lamps lit here in the hall. What use did the dead have for light? So all Stu could call on was his big black battery powered torch. He hefted it in his right hand, reassured by its solid weight; a useful weapon if need be.

He strode quickly down the central aisle, swinging the torch from side to side, its beam playing across the dull white surfaces of the bone-encased bodies. Halfway. That was as far as he intended to go. The torch could reach the rest of the way from there. He'd play the light along the back wall, take a quick look to make sure everything was all right, and then get the hell out of there, job done.

Two more steps and he reckoned that was about far enough. So he stopped… which was when he heard the cracking sound. A sharp, loud *snap*, and it had come from his left and a little ahead. He whipped the torch around, cursing as the beam flickered, but it steadied again almost immediately. Nothing. Just the same gnarly effigies of human form; there was no sign of movement and he couldn't see anything obviously out of place. He stood there, conscious of his heart pounding and of his own heavy breathing, too loud in all this stillness. So what was he supposed to do now? Any further investigation meant stepping out among these things, and he was hanged if he was going to do that. Ignore it, that seemed the best option.

No sooner had he reached a decision than the sound came again. He jumped, nerves frayed. It had been closer this time, almost at his feet. Stu shone the torch at the nearest bony cadaver. Had it moved, just as the light reached it? His feet shuffled a few steps backward. Was that a crack? He craned forward despite himself, leaning down for a closer look. Yes, definitely a crack, running down the side of where the face would be, from the top to the chin.

Then came the loudest sound yet, like an explosion, as the figure split completely, ripping apart. The small crack expanded all the way to the body's groin and the two halves gaped wide. Light streamed from the resulting gap, causing Stu to stumble backwards, shielding his eyes. Squinting and looking through the cracks between his fingers, he watched as something stirred and a figure began to emerge from the calcified body.

Stu hadn't got a brecking clue what this was, but he knew they didn't pay him enough to hang around and find out. He turned and bolted for the door, dropping his torch in the process. But he was too slow; far, far too slow.

Assembly Member Carla Birhoff entered the grand hall and paused, casting her gaze around the room one final time before the first guests arrived. Her aim was not to focus on anything in particular – every detail had been scrutinised and approved according to her exacting standards during previous inspections and she now felt confident that each individual element was as perfect as it could be. No, it was how those components fitted together that concerned her at this stage, the assemblage which she had so meticulously planned. Her gaze, therefore, swept across the room, taking in the whole that was the sum of its many parts.

First impressions were paramount. The entire décor had been chosen with this one view in mind and geared towards maximum impact. She would greet her guests here on the mezzanine level, causing them to pause at the top of the small flight of steps that led down into the room proper. Then, as they turned to descend those steps, the whole vista opened up before them. She was determined that it should wow every single one of them.

And it would. It *would*.

White table cloths – one traditional detail she had insisted on, though the potential starkness was alleviated by fine, wide-mesh, golden-brown gauze which flowed from the middle of each table to cover roughly two thirds of its area. At the very centre sat an arrangement of bright red berries nestled among autumn leaves and pine cones, while flecks of gold leaf had been sprinkled over the web like gauze, causing it to sparkle. The fanned napkins before each place setting matched the golden brown of the arrangement, and the stylish chairs were wooden framed, boasting deep burgundy upholstery. Small gifts in gold boxes awaited each lady when she arrived at her seat: tiny khybul sculptures – predominantly birds and fish. Simple pieces certainly, mere tokens, but all those in attendance would know the value of khybul and appreciate the cumulative price of so many pieces, no matter their size.

The evening's seasonal theme was picked up again in a display that dominated the long wall directly opposite the stairs. A cascade of gold, brown and russet veils tumbled from ceiling to floor, transformed by artfully directed air currents and clever lighting into the wild rush of an autumnal waterfall. The illusion was completed by brown drapes gathered and pinned to the wall in imitation of rocks around which the veils flowed.

Another treat awaited guests at the bottom of the stairs. In order to find their appropriate seats, they would need to consult the table plan which stood to their right. Proudly displayed on a glass plinth beside the plan was Carla's latest acquisition: by far the largest, most intricate, and breathtakingly beautiful khybul sculpture she had ever seen. Here, depicted in sparkling crystal, was an exquisite representation of Thaiburley itself. The straight walls of the city seemed to erupt from a base of rugged rocks, shooting upwards to culminate in a dazzling array of delicate spires, chimneys and crenulations. The design cleverly encapsulated the spirit of Thaiburley's wondrous roof, while the walls of the piece were marked with the suggestion of tiny windows and even, here and there towards the top, a balcony or two. And if the ninety-odd floors of the City of a Hundred Rows were not all here, who would quibble? None could dispute that this was an inspired work and that the unknown artist had captured the spirit of Thaiburley in all its grandeur.

The piece had been far from cheap but Carla didn't begrudge a single penny. As soon as she clapped eyes on the sculpture she simply had to have it. Others might own khybul figures but none had anything in their collection to rival this.

Determined that no one would miss its magnificence, she had arranged for lights to be embedded in the glass stand, which then shone up through the sculpture and caused the whole piece to glow, while the tips of the spires sparkled with fairy light.

On the wall above and behind the crystal city hung a large painting, almost lost against the sculpture's magnificence. It was by the artist Arielle, once feted as the greatest painter of her generation. Completed more than two decades earlier, the picture depicted a ball, a lavish function much like the one about to commence. All present were evidently having a wonderful time. Faces glowed, smiles beamed, pale golden and deep burgundy wines flowed, the women were elegant and beautiful, the men dashing. Vibrant colours leapt from the canvas and it was hard to imagine that anyone involved had a care in the world. As you studied the painting, your eyes were inexorably drawn to the figure at the very centre of the composition: a woman, so young, so beautiful, so unmistakeably Carla.

She had always loved this painting, for its vibrancy and the pure joy of life it expressed, as well as the memories it stirred and the emotions it evoked, yet she hadn't looked at it for some fifteen years; not since the scandal. Arielle had once been Carla's closest friend and then her bitterest rival. Look at them now. The once celebrated artist had disappeared, her reputation sullied and her work forgotten, never to be seen in polite company again, while Carla had gone from strength to strength, becoming a respected member of the Assembly – the administrative body of Thaiburley's government – and the darling of the Heights' social circuit.

Carla looked at the painting again. In truth, she would have been hard pressed to explain the whim that had caused her to take it from storage for this, her big night, except that it seemed fitting somehow that the painting should be present as she reaffirmed her position as society's queen; not as a centrepiece, no, but in the shadow of something even more beautiful, acting as a faded reminder of rivals vanquished and glories past.

Her gaze finally reached the stage to her far right, where the multi-stringed duoharp was already in position, the great chordophone resembling a stylised heart. Its twin opposing soundboards met at the base, where they converged on the central pillar of polished wood and gleaming metal embellishments before sweeping upwards and outward like wings. Identical curved necks connected the rounded shoulders of the soundboards to the pillar's crown.

The instrument was to be played by the Gallagher Sisters, said to be among the finest musicians in all Thaiburley. The dark haired girl – older and prettier than her sibling – was already in place, studiously tuning her half of the harp, but the seat opposite her was empty. Carla felt a flash of irritation that both girls weren't ready and she was about to call out when the blonde, sour-faced one hurried over to take her seat, licking her fingers and chewing on something, as if having snatched a bite to eat before the performance.

Carla pursed her lips. She was tempted to take the girl to task but in the end decided to put it down to artistic temperament. Instead she returned her attention to completing her survey of the room, which ended with a glance down at her own dress. Commissioned from Chanice, one of the Heights' hottest designers, the gown featured a beautifully arranged skirt of layered silks graduating from autumnal russets at the bottom to shimmering scarlet at the top, matching the bodice. The dress was so artfully cut that the skirt avoided being billowy while still drawing in tightly at the waist to emphasise her slender figure. Carla had studied herself from every angle before coming here, and was confident that she looked fantastic. Scarlet could be an unforgiving shade, one she probably wouldn't dare risk in another five or ten years, but she felt bold tonight and knew she still retained enough of her youthful glamour to get away with such audacious display. While she could, she would.

Finally satisfied, Carla allowed herself a small smile. Everything seemed in readiness; soon the great and the good of Heights' society would be here to pay her tribute. She would accept their compliments with an appropriate degree of grace and modesty, of course, while privately secure in the knowledge that she had earned each and every plaudit.

An hour later found Carla in her element, meeting and greeting, sharing a few words with this couple, a sentence or two with another and a joke with the next, before flitting away to greet a late arrival. The Gallagher Sisters were playing divinely, though as more people arrived and the volume of conversation grew louder it was becoming increasingly difficult to hear them unless you were standing right next to the stage. Not that it mattered. The fact that Carla had secured their services when others had failed to do so was reward enough.

She handed a barely touched flute of finest Elyssen champagne to a waiter – she had been holding the glass for far too long and the wine had lost much of its chill and fizz – and took a fresh one, savouring a sip of cool dry effervescence before the customary smile slipped back into place. She laughed politely at the end of someone's anecdote, a tale she'd only half been listening to. The smile was one which had been perfected over many years: the expression of a hostess who knows her evening is a success and is confident that it will only get better. In the corner of her eye she saw white jacketed waiters circulating with what should be the final trays of warm canapés. It would soon be time to usher the guests to their seats for the meal. Glowing comment had already been made about her khybul sculpture, most pleasingly from young Xyel, a pretty little thing who saw herself as something of an emerging rival to Carla. Poor deluded girl. Her Summer Soirée had been pleasant enough but she still had a lot to learn. Carla reserved a special smile for her.

A ripple of polite applause ran through the section of the room closest to the stage as the Gallagher Sisters finished their latest piece – surely the penultimate one of their set – and Carla noted waiters returning to the kitchen with empty salvers. She looked across and caught the maître d's eye. He nodded, to show that he was on top of the timings. If things continued to run this smoothly, she might even be able to relax a fraction and enjoy herself during the meal.

It was a little thing really in the context of everything else that was going on: the scream that heralded such a dramatic change of fortune for Carla and all those present. Most wouldn't even have heard it. The only reason Carla did was because she happened to be at the top of the small flight of steps, at the spot where she'd greeted the guests, and so was close to the door. The scream came from outside; high pitched and unmistakeably a woman's. Conversation on the mezzanine level died and for a second there was a bizarre contrast between the silence to Cara's left and the continuing hubbub from the rest of the room to her right.

When no further indication of disturbance came, those closest to Carla resumed talking, with a shrug of their shoulders or a knowing rise of the eyebrows, and muttered comments such as, "Kids!"

Jean, the maître d', had moved across to speak to the doorman, but nobody seemed concerned and Carla was about to dismiss the incident as a minor glitch soon forgotten, when the doors burst inward and Hell strode through the opening.

The first figure was merely a giant, towering above Jean and the doorman. The latter tried to block the intruder's way, but the burly man was picked up and tossed into the room in one motion, crashing into a knot of startled guests. The maître d' was simply brushed aside.

More than one scream rent the air now.

Further figures were pressing through the doorway behind the first. One or two had human features but most seemed composed of nothing more than silver light, dazzling to look upon. All were of similar stature to the first. Carla gaped, unable to rationalise what she was seeing. She couldn't move, didn't know how to react. She was supposed to be the perfect party host, ready for any eventuality, but not for *this*.

Several things then happened at once, snapping her out of her paralysis. The tall windows which dominated the wall opposite the stage shattered, seemingly all at once, sending shards of glass raining down on those nearby, and more of the silver light giants strode through the broken windows. This registered only at the periphery of Carla's awareness, her attention focused elsewhere. She stared in horror at the shimmering figure who reached out towards Jean while the maître d' was still recovering from his brush with the first giant. As a glowing finger touched him, a cocoon of light enveloped Jean's body and he froze, all except for his face, which took on an expression of wide-eyed horror that swiftly transformed into one of excruciating agony; eyes screwed shut, mouth thrown open as if screaming, though Carla couldn't hear him. It was a moment she would never forget, as if every tortured line of Jean's face burned itself into her retinas and hence into her memory. A second later the expression was gone, vanishing as his face exploded. No, that was wrong, the process was less dramatic. Jean's face, his whole body, seemed to simply drift apart. One moment there was a shape within the glow that was recognisably Jean, the next nothing human stood there at all. In the brief instant before the glow which had surrounded the maître d' faded, Carla watched a cloud of russet flakes drop towards the floor like ruddy brown rose petals.

The glowing silver giant was no longer silver or glowing. It now looked like Jean.

Only then did Carla grasp the full horror of what was happening here; only then did she realise their doom.

She stumbled away in a daze, with no clear idea of where she was going, just the certainty that she had to get away from these creatures. Somebody bumped into her, causing her to stagger, and she was abruptly aware that pandemonium had broken out and that everyone was trying to get away. The thin veneer of politeness, of etiquette, had been abandoned, to be replaced by the drive to survive. Men, women, young or old, it didn't matter; all were screaming, fighting, pushing and elbowing in their desperation to reach the stairs and escape. Never mind that more of the creatures waited below, a whole cordon of them, herding folk towards the stage, instinct still drove people to flee the most immediate threat, and a bottleneck started to form at the top of the mezzanine stairs.

For those at the back there was no hope of escape. The silver giants moved implacably forward, killing with a touch. The ones that had already adopted a semblance of human form simply killed. The crowd discovered new levels of desperation. Carla watched an elderly woman, resplendent in diaphanous gown and diamond jewellery, knocked from her feet and trampled by her fellows, with no chance of recovering.

A small part of Carla's mind remained detached, refusing to accept any of this as real. A symptom of shock
perhaps, but that small corner of sanity brought her
hope. She realised that the stairs which those all around
her were straining towards offered only temporary
respite, that even those who reached them would still
be trapped. Then her gaze fell upon the door, off to one
side, evidently overlooked by everyone. The kitchens,
deliberately designed to lead off the mezzanine to ensure that a supply of freshly chilled champagne was
always on hand during greetings and that diners could
fully appreciate each new dish as it was paraded down
the stairs prior to serving. She started to forge her way
in that direction, moving across the flow of panicked
people. She prised a woman's chest away from a man's
back and inserted first an arm and then her whole self
between. Moving against the human tide proved to
be an unexpected advantage. While others were faced
with a wall of backs and had nowhere to go, she could
slip through – with a little persuasion. Somebody dug
her in the ribs with an elbow, someone else struck
her shoulder with bruising force. She ignored the
minor flares of pain and kept going, focussing only on
that door.

Doubtless she *knew* these people, many of them
would be her friends, yet terror and desperation had
converted their faces into those of strangers. She
pushed, kneed and fought with the best of them, forcing a passage, closing her vision and her mind to
everything else and refusing to think about how close
the death-dealing giants were coming.

She was nearly there, with just a few more people to fight through, when it happened. In her eagerness to find sanctuary she overstretched across intervening legs and feet. Somebody trod on her gown, her beautiful gown, tearing it, and she was jostled as she tried to bring her trailing leg through. Carla stumbled and tripped, falling heavily onto a man's knee and then the floor. Desperately she tried to pull herself along, no longer keeping track of the number of bumps and bruises. Somebody stepped down on her calf and she cried out, barely hearing her own voice above all the screaming and the shouting, which suddenly seemed to intensify.

A woman to her left, oblivious to her presence, looked about to repeat the act of stepping on her but this time in stiletto heels, when she froze and her body began to glow. Carla scrambled away, pulling her legs in frantically, determined not to touch that nimbus. Within seconds the woman imploded, disappearing in a cascade of rusty flakes, some of which fell onto Carla's exposed arms and legs.

She lost it then. All rational thought deserted her as she opened her mouth and shrieked and writhed and kicked, not even aware that she had broken through the crowd of people until the door to the kitchen loomed before her nose. She pulled it open and half-rolled half-crawled inside, to collapse, her body wracked with sobs.

Heat washed over her. The lights were still on but the kitchen was deserted, the cooks and waiting staff having presumably fled. The rich aromas of cooking, which normally Carla would have breathed in deeply and relished, now only made her feel nauseous. She reached up to grip the harsh metal edge of a table, pulling herself to her feet, and stumbled across the empty room towards the service door. Two thirds of the way across, her stomach heaved and she was forced to double over, throwing up onto the floor. It seemed an age before the retching subsided and she could move forward. Not even pausing to find water and wash the sour taste of vomit from her mouth, she finally reached the door, thrusting it open and staggering into the corridor beyond.

She stopped to draw in fresher, cooler air, amazed at how muted the noise from the ballroom had suddenly become. From out here the shouting, the screaming, the sounds of people being slaughtered, it could almost be mistaken for over-enthusiastic revelry. Almost.

There was nobody else in sight. Part of Carla was glad, conscious even now of what a mess she must look and relieved that there was no one here to see it, but guilt immediately swept such concerns away as the implications sank in. Surely others must have escaped? She couldn't be the only one; but, if so, they were already long gone. Not that she could blame them.

Carla took a deep breath and braced herself. It was time to forget that she was Carla Birhoff, celebrated socialite, and remember that she was Assembly Member Birhoff. Her city needed her.

She wriggled her feet and kicked off the impractical shoes that still somehow clung to them, gathered up the skirt of her ruined gown, and started to run; a somewhat shuffling gait perhaps, but it was the best she could manage – the greater part of two decades had passed since she last attempted to move this quickly. As she ran, she bent over to spit out the taste of sick from her mouth, all decorum forgotten. Such considerations seemed no more than petty affectations in the light of what she had just been through.

Carla determined to find the city watch, to alert the Kite Guard, to rouse the Assembly, to mobilise the Blade. The people of Thaiburley needed to be warned, they had to be told the unthinkable truth, that the Rust Warriors had returned.

TWO

Tom couldn't breathe. Coldness enveloped him, pressing in on his chest, sapping warmth from his body and strength from his limbs. Bitter chill nipped at his cheeks and hammered at his ears and forehead, to set searing pain dancing behind his temples. He tried to suck in air and found only icy water – more cold, this time drawn inside his body. He was drowning.

Frantically he thrashed, straining to reach the surface which had to be somewhere above him. Yes, there! His head breached the boundary between the elements and he emerged gasping and spluttering, dragging his arms out of the water.

"Tom!" Someone called his name. He blinked, wiping his eyes and face with clumsy numbed hands. A name fell into place: *Mildra*. She was there, wrapping something around his body. Instinctively he grasped it, finding soft warmth which his fingers sank into as they fastened on the swathe. A towel, all fluffy and soft and warm. Mildra was trying to wipe his face with one corner of it.

"Come on," she said, placing an arm around his shoulders and urging him to stand. "Let's get you out of there. He was sitting in the water, he realised. Was it really so shallow? Felt much deeper when he first came round. *Of course* it was shallow, this was the ice tank.

He was shivering violently now, his legs mere pillars of ice. In fact, he'd lost all sense of feeling from the waist down and needed to lean on Mildra for support while he half-clambered and half-fell out of the submersion tank.

"Thaiss," he muttered, forgetting himself for a moment, "Why the breck does it have to be so cold?"

"The cold is an essential part of the process," said an older, strangely accented woman's voice. "As you well know."

Looking a great deal healthier than the gaunt figure that he and Mildra had revived just days before, the living goddess strode towards him. She was moving a lot less stiffly as well. Her long silver-grey hair had been tied back so that it fell past her shoulders in a ponytail, while the pale blue one-piece she'd worn during her centuries-long sleep had been replaced by a much darker black-blue outfit with white trims. Combined with the serious-looking black boots she wore, the effect was very much that of a military uniform.

"Doesn't m-mean I have to l-like it," Tom replied, his teeth chattering as shivers coursed through his body in violent spasms.

"Like?" the old woman said, pausing to stare at him with arched eyebrows. "Whoever said that you or indeed

any of us has the luxury of *liking* whatever role life
allots us, hmm?"

"No-nobody," he conceded. Whatever this walking
fossil was – aged human, eternal goddess, the living
dead, or ancient spirit in human form – she could
learn a thing or two from Thaiburley's Prime Master
when it came to teaching methods, that much was
for certain.

Tom automatically lifted first one foot and then the
other, allowing Mildra to slip soft furred and instantly
warm garments over his feet, drawing them up his
legs. Realisation of two things struck him simultaneously. The first being that this was a Thaistess waiting
on him as if she were some servant girl, the second
that he was stark naked.

Fortunately the numbing cold and assorted distractions had prevented the otherwise inevitable
reaction to having a woman he was attracted to so
close to his exposed genitals – evidently "frozen stiff"
was merely a saying, at least in this instance. Even
so, he reached down hurriedly to grasp the hem of
the soft-furred one piece garment with both hands,
his fingers thick and clumsy, still tingling with the
return of circulation.

"Thanks," he told her, "I can take it from here."

She raised her eyebrows and showed him a hint of
a smile, a welcome reminder of the friend he knew.
In recent days such glimpses had become all too rare.
Tom didn't really understand what had changed between him and Mildra, but there was no question that
she was acting differently towards him. They had

grown so close during the long trip from Thaiburley
to the icebound Citadel of Thaiss, a closeness that cul-
minated in their intimacy in the meadow of flowers
just days ago, a memory which still burned fresh in
Tom's mind. A real bond had formed between them,
one which had proved strong enough to survive any
embarrassment over indiscretions provoked by the
flowers' aphrodisiac pollen, but which seemed to
have frayed dramatically since they arrived here. And
he had no idea why.

Images assaulted his mind's eye as he straightened
from pulling up the clothing. A bewildering array of
memories not his own, their sudden eruption causing
him to stagger, disorientated for a moment.

"Are you all right?" Mildra asked, steadying his
arm.

"Yes, I'm fine," he assured her, pulling away, embarrassed by his feebleness and reacting before he
considered how this might look to Mildra. "It's just all
these things that keep swirling around in my head,"
he added, suddenly afraid that his actions might distance her still further.

The old woman, whom he still had trouble thinking of as the same goddess to whom so many temples
had been raised in the City Below, was beside him
now, looking into his eyes and frowning, though
whether with concern or disapproval he couldn't be
sure. "Give it time," she told him. "Your subconscious
will already be working on coherency, pulling the
various fragments of imposed memory together." She
was walking away again, saying over her shoulder,

"Another session or two, three at the most, and it wil
all fall into place, you'll see."

Tom didn't bother trying to mask his horror, turning to Mildra and mouthing *three at the most*? This had
been his second stint in the ice tank and he'd hoped
it might be the last.

The Thaistess grinned and gave Tom's arm a reassuring squeeze before hurrying after her goddess
who had to be the most unlikely, not to mention
sprightly, deity Tom ever expected to meet.

Since their arrival and the old woman's awakening – she really did seem to be the Thaiss of legend
despite Tom's reservations – they'd been kept constantly busy, driven by the goddess's conviction that
Thaiburley stood on the brink of disaster. To Tom i
felt as if he were being shunted from one teacher to
the next, his life a constant round of lessons. Back
in the city it had been the Prime Master, then on the
road their self-styled leader Dewar set about teaching
him how to use a sword, and now that he'd reached
the river's source as instructed a whole new load of
lessons were being pummelled into him, even more
difficult to understand than the old ones. What was
it with everyone wanting to educate him all of a sudden? He'd done fine with breck-all learning up
until now.

The ice tank was part of what Thaiss described as a
"crash course". While he was submerged and all but
unconscious, information was fed directly into his
brain – weeks of concentrated lessons crammed into
hours. Quite where the cold came into things he

wasn't sure, but Thaiss assured him it was essential, slowing bodily functions and focussing the mind. Who was he to argue with a goddess? She claimed that only by being subjected to the ice tank could he hope to absorb the wealth of intimate detail needed to save the city.

Him? Save Thaiburley? Ridiculous. Yet she insisted that he was the city's only hope. Tom had always found it hard to accept the Prime Master and others telling him he was special back in Thaiburley, but now here he was half a continent away hearing much the same thing. Maybe all these folk really did know something he didn't; though, if so, shouldn't he *feel* special in some way? Instead he continued to think of himself as an ordinary street-nick swept up in events he didn't fully understand, things that some-one like him had no right being a part of.

Apparently, one of the Prime Master's motives in sending him on this journey was the hope that Tom might grow into his abilities and responsibilities. He *had* changed, he knew that; maturing in all sorts of ways, though not perhaps in the directions his mentor had intended – memories of the flower meadow crossed his thoughts again. Therein lay the worry that niggled away at his innermost thoughts and fuelled his self-doubt. Tom was afraid that even after all he and Mildra had been through he was still going to disap-point those who believed in him, that he was destined to return to Thaiburley a failure rather than the sav-iour people anticipated. He winced as a new montage of images cascaded through his thoughts. He'd be a

brecking knowledgeable failure though, that was
for sure.

Tom didn't follow after Mildra and the goddess,
not immediately. Instead he sat by himself, allowing
the last of the cold and the damp to seep from his
body, leached away by the wonderfully soft clothing
Thaiss had provided, which somehow absorbed
moisture while remaining dry and warm against his
skin. As he sat there he did his best to assimilate this
most recent torrent of knowledge, determined to follow the advice the goddess had given him first time
around by relaxing and allowing the memories to
come to him rather than chasing after specifics – a
habit which experience had taught him brought only
frustration.

If he could start making sense of it all now, perhaps
he could get away with just one more session in the
ice tank rather than the two or three Thaiss had so
casually suggested. In a strange way, the bits and
pieces he was already able to glean both increased and
decreased his awe of their host.

Assuming that all these images and history were
true, Thaiss and her brother genuinely *had* been responsible for building Thaiburley. Tom witnessed vast
machines of impossible size straddling peaks and
canyons. Monstrous drill bits hewed into the face of
a mountain, while beams of raw energy melted and
blasted away rock that had withstood the elements
for millennia. Tom knew that he was witnessing time
compressed, that the work of months passed before
his mind's eye in seconds, the years in minutes. As he

watched, the city of Thaiburley steadily took shape before him.

It wasn't just machines doing the hard graft. Armies of workers in bright orange overalls swarmed over everything like ants, and there were others: figures in powder blue gowns who were often there, directing and organising. The robes might have been bulkier and longer than he was used to but these could only be arkademics, or their forefathers. On a couple of occasions he saw these blue-robed figures take a more active role. A small group of them would stand together with hands raised, and from their palms energy poured out; blinding light that disappeared into the now honeycombed depths of the mountain. He had no idea to what purpose this energy was unleashed but it was impressive all the same. Was that really an example of what the founders could do? Was that what *he* could do if he only knew how? The idea seemed absurd.

Seeing history compressed like this brought home just what a colossal undertaking the building of Thaiburley had been, and as he watched the city take form Tom felt awed that anyone would ever attempt such an undertaking, let alone succeed.

He caught glimpses of Thaiss several times, and of her brother; once even, a fleeting view of a Jeradine, its presence a surprise. What part had the bipedal reptilians played in the founding of Thaiburley? Thaiss looked younger – confirming that this was no "eternal goddess". She aged like everyone else, if a good deal slower.

In the final scenes, as the City of Dreams he recognised began to emerge from the face of the mountain with miraculous speed, Thaiss became a constant feature – an observer in the foreground, overseeing the work, often grasping a staff as tall as herself, the crown of which ended in a cylinder of what appeared to be swirling energy. Never static, the staff's top broiled and flashed, a stunted pillar of light ranging from gold and orange to red, bound within clasps of silver metal. Beyond these clasps, there was no obvious container to hold this writhing of light.

The intertwining energies were mirrored in a far larger object which Tom witnessed being installed towards the end of construction by two of the monstrous machines working in tandem. With the roof still only half formed, a huge column was lowered with great care into what looked to be the centre of the city. Scale wasn't always easy to judge, but it seemed to Tom that this column was two or three times as wide as a man was tall and longer than any twenty men put together. He had no doubt that this was the core, the heart of Thaiburley which the Prime Master had spoken about, the element that the arkademics and the healers and the seers and even Tom himself drew upon when using their talents. Despite the hulking size of the two great lifters involved, there seemed a great delicacy in the way they handled this kaleidoscopic pillar, as if it were something immensely fragile. Looking on, Tom couldn't escape the feeling that the changing patterns of colour and shape the column displayed had some underlying purpose, that they represented communication of some sort, albeit beyond his understanding. It seemed to him that here was something alive, and caged.

The column disappeared in short order, lowered into the heart of the half-sculpted city. Within a handful of breaths Thaiburley was finished. The City of a Hundred Rows stood proud, all new and gleaming and beautiful.

Tom had grown up knowing that his home was vast, and had gained some sense of just *how* huge the night he ascended the walls, but seeing it like this brought home the full scale of the place for perhaps the first time in his life. He felt humbled at the thought of the ambition and effort that had gone into the city's founding, but he was also vaguely troubled. As yet these memories had no context. He still didn't know *why* Thaiburley had been built or how long ago all this had happened. That was the problem with this form of forced but disjointed learning; it lacked logical progression. As a result, the more he discovered the more the questions mounted, a great heap of them gathering to taunt him.

Chief among these were questions about the goddess. He'd seen Thaiss and her brother enter this world through a great rent in the sky, a slit that glowed with light at its edges, a light that glittered and twinkled like illuminated jewels as the gap widened to accommodate their passage. It was like a long vertical rip in a curtain being prised apart – that was the only way Tom could think to describe it. There had been nothing regal or divine about the appearance of the godly pair, no slow descent on a raft of clouds, no celestial spirits to herald their arrival, no choir singing of their glory, just a stepping through from one place to another. It was obvious that Thaiss and her brother had come from *somewhere* else, but Tom had strong reservations about just how heavenly either their place of origin or they themselves might be.

This wasn't a riddle he was likely to solve here and now. Besides, when all was said and done, he reckoned the pair's divinity or lack of it didn't really matter. After all, they came from another realm, had knowledge far beyond that of anyone in this world, could perform miracles, were worshipped, and had been around for centuries. As definitions of gods went, that would do for Tom. It was only his innate curiosity that made him determined to find out more.

With a flash of insight, Tom wondered whether this might be the cause of Mildra becoming more distant. Perhaps it had nothing to do with him after all but went deeper than that. If she'd begun to suspect, as he had, that Thaiss and her brother were not in fact the divine, omnipotent beings that religious doctrine painted them, wouldn't that affect her profoundly? After all, it was difficult enough for him to adjust to the idea of their being mere flesh and blood, and he'd never believed in them as gods in the first place. How much harder must it be for someone whose life had been dedicated to serving the goddess?

Was that it? Was she suffering from a crisis of faith? He resolved to try talking to her when circumstances allowed. He knew he'd have to choose his moment carefully and that, even if he did, she might not be willing to discuss the matter, but he had to try.

Tom stood up, reckoning he'd spent enough time collecting his thoughts, and followed in the wake of the two women. If his feet dragged a little, it was only because he knew that his arrival would signal the start of another lecture from the goddess, intended to bring the latest jumble of submerged knowledge into focus. All well and good, but what was the point in cramming his head full of all this history, when whatever threat Thaiburley might face was bound to be in the here and now?

Tom couldn't help but worry about what was happening back home while he was cooped up here in the frozen north. Were things really as bad as the goddess claimed?

"I'm coming with you."

"No you're not."

"I know I might seem old and crotchety to a young whippersnapper like you, but I can still swing a sword with the best of them."

Kat sighed. This wasn't the first time they'd had this discussion. "Shayna, *Shayna*, this has nothing to do with your age or your ability to hack people to death with a sword, I *need* you here." While she'd need the very best warriors the Tattooed Men could field for her trip into the Stain, despite her protestations, that wasn't Shayna.

"Course you do. You're about to go traipsing off into the most dangerous area of the under-City, a wasteland stuffed full of monsters, wild beasts and creatures we haven't even got a name for, oh, and you're intending to beard the most villainous fiend of the lot in its own lair… so naturally you need your *healer* to be somewhere else. Have you any idea how ridiculous that sounds?"

When she put it like that, yes, but Kat wasn't about to be swayed. "It's not my *healer* I need here, it's you. Someone has to take charge while I'm gone, a person the men will look up to and respect; someone they'll listen to without question, someone I can trust to begin carving out the territory the Tattooed Men both need and deserve. If we don't make our move now, when everything down here is still in flux, we'll miss our chance."

"Pfff…" Shayna pulled a face. "You could ask any one of half a dozen to do that. I'm the only real healer among the lot of us." Kat had rarely seen her so worked up. "Answer me this: what happens out there when one of the men gets their guts torn open or loses a limb? How are you going to feel when you watch one of your friends bleed to death, knowing that I could have saved him if you'd brought me along? You need somebody in charge back here, no question, but you need *me* out there!"

Kat shook her head in exasperation. "Were you this much of a pain to my sister?"

"You bet I was when she was wrong; every single time."

Kat glared at the older woman. She never imagined that leading the Tattooed Men on her own would be so trying. "Out of everyone," she muttered, "I thought I could always count on you for support." She regretted voicing the thought as soon as she'd said it, knowing that what emerged sounded like the frustrated mewling of a petulant child; not exactly the image she was going for.

"You can," Shayna assured her. "In front of the others I'll toe the line and back you up every which way, but, at the same time, when it's just the two of us don't expect me to hold back. I'll let you know whenever I reckon you're making a god-awful mistake and being a stubborn ass about it, like now."

Kat grinned. "Thanks."

"You're welcome."

It wasn't as if Shayna didn't have a point, but in truth Kat *was* worried about her. The healer was the oldest of those who'd survived the Pits and she'd done little fighting since they'd emerged, protected because of her talent rather than her age but protected nonetheless.

The Stain was unknown territory, shunned because it was feared, feared because it was deadly. Kat simply didn't want to put Shayna at risk by including her in the expedition. She was too valuable, to the group for her healing abilities and to its leader as a friend.

She took a deep breath, knowing that what she was about to say might jeopardise that very friendship. "I'm sorry, but no. You're too important, too valuable. You're going to stay and take charge of things this end."

"You're making a…"

"I've heard your arguments and taken them into account, but I've made up my mind."

"Then you haven't been listening closely enough."

"Shayna!"

"I know, and don't worry, I'll behave myself in front of the others as I promised, but you're still making the wrong decision for all the wrong reasons." There followed an awkward pause. "I can see I'm wasting my breath, though. So…"

With that the older woman stood up and moved away, leaving Kat to ponder whether she was right. Maybe, and if so this doubtless wouldn't be Kat's last mistake, but it was hers to make; not Shayna's and not Chavver's, not anymore. Kat sighed and got to her feet. In the Pits, when she was a kid, it had all been so simple. Leading the men as they fought wild animals or sometimes each other had come naturally. She and Chavver were the best fighters and the best tacticians, with an instinct for how to handle situations that she could never have explained in words. Leadership devolved to them as a natural consequence. Having them in charge meant a better chance of surviving the bouts for everyone. Out here in the real world things were invariably more complicated. There were so many other things to take into account, and Kat was increasingly concerned that she simply wasn't up to the task, not on her own.

She wondered whether her sister had ever suffered from such misgivings. If so, she never showed it, not even in the Pits. Perhaps she had after their falling out, when Kat was banished from the Tattooed Men, but Kat suspected that even then no one would have known.

The two of them might not have been close in recent years but she still grieved for Chavver. She missed her sister's certainty, yes, but above all she missed *her*.

No turning back though; this was a new age. Chavver was gone and the Tattooed Men were now looking to Kat to make the decisions. One of which she was about to announce. Straightening her back, doing her best to project the sort of confidence Charveve had always shown, Kat went to call the men together, to announce who would be going with her into the Stain and who would be staying here with Shayna. She knew that they'd all be hoping to go, which said something about those who comprised the Tattooed Men; though whether it reflected on their bravery or their foolishness was another matter entirely.

As Kat stepped out of the small room she'd adopted as an office, she bumped into an increasingly familiar uniformed figure. This was the man who had saved her life but she was determined not to allow that fact to rule it. At any other time she might have been glad to see him, but not now. There was business to be done, business that didn't include him; so her response to his unexpected appearance was curter than it might have been.

"You're a day early,"

"Technically, just half a day," the Kite Guard replied, "since we're due off first thing tomorrow."

Was he thick-skinned or just plain thick, she wondered. Surely her tone must have warned him now wasn't the time. "Exactly, which isn't today, so why are you here?"

He shrugged. "Everything's ready my end, so I thought I'd fly over to check on how you were getting on and perhaps have a quick discussion on how we're going to deploy tomorrow."

Kat stared at him in disbelief. "*Deploy*? We're the Tattooed Men, not some unit of your precious Guard. We'll deploy as I say we will."

"All right, I just thought…"

"Well don't!"

"Fair enough, bad idea, forget I ever mentioned it." He held his hands up defensively. "Now that I *am* here, is there anything I can do to help?"

"Actually there is."

"Excellent, just name it."

"Fly on back to where you came from and make sure you're not late tomorrow morning."

He looked startled, as if she'd slapped him. Kat relented, reasoning that the last thing she wanted to do was antagonise the man who'd be leading the authorities' part of the expedition at her side. Besides, he was kind of cute. "Look, Tylus, don't take offence, but I've got a lot on; Tattooed Men business, you know? And the only thing that's going to stop us being ready for the morning is interference, no matter how well-intentioned. So for now, just breck off and leave us alone. All right?"

He opened his mouth as if to say something but then shut it and nodded, before trying again. "Understood. I'll see you tomorrow." With that he turned on his heel and strode off, a little stiffly.

Kat lingered for a moment, watching him go. She still couldn't make up her mind about this Kite Guard captain. Her reaction to him was a jumble of conflicting emotions. He was a lot older than her but handsome enough in a clean cut sort of way; dashing even in that dark blue uniform, and she did owe him her life. He was also from the Heights, another world – one she never expected to come into contact with and was a little in awe of, truth be told – added to which he was an agent of authorities she'd never fully trusted; the people who, ultimately, had sanctioned the Pits. Or at least turned a blind eye to the place for far too long.

She smiled ruefully at her own indecision: part of her was attracted to this Tylus while another part wanted to look up to him, as if he were the older brother she'd never had, but there was a neediness about him that undermined that image and which she found just plain annoying at times. She shook her head in frustration. Perhaps after they'd been in the Stain and she'd seen how he acquitted himself under pressure her opinions and feelings would crystallise into something more certain.

Mind you, she wouldn't be at all surprised if there were a few among the Tattooed Men thinking in much the same way about her own leadership. Now there was a cheery thought.

Tylus left the Tattooed Men's makeshift headquarters cursing himself for an idiot. Why in Thaiss's name had he gone over there? Just because *he* had some spare time on his hands didn't mean that Kat would. Of course she'd be busy. All he'd achieved was to irritate her.

How was he going to look her in the eye tomorrow? Only one way to deal with this: ignore the whole embarrassing incident and pretend it never happened. He'd be formal and polite, making it clear that his interest in her was purely professional, and the fact that she was the most intriguing package of a bewitchingly pretty, slender, feisty, agile, dangerous and extremely capable young woman he'd ever come across meant nothing to him whatsoever.

Maybe he could even convince himself of that while he was at it.

He'd been intrigued by Kat from the first moment he encountered her – when they'd both been scouring the streets independently searching for the same killer – and his fascination with her had only grown since he'd plucked her from the air by the grand conveyor. He saved her life that night, at no small risk to himself, and it seemed to him that she wasn't always as grateful for that as she might have been. He stopped himself, a little dismayed at the proprietorial nature of his own thoughts. He didn't *own* the girl for Thaiss's sake.

Not being in the mood for petty distractions, he flew high to avoid any stones which a strong arm or a catapult had been known on occasion to launch his way when he strayed too close to the under-City's rooftops. Chasing down and scaring the living daylights out of the nick responsible could be fun when he was in the right frame of mind, but not today.

In brief moments he was dropping towards his destination, cape extended between his torso and outstretched arms, shedding momentum as he adjusted his shape, swinging his body from the horizontal until it hung beneath, ready for landing. His feet touched the ground, knees bending to absorb the last dregs of momentum.

Tylus stood straight and found himself in the shadow of a towering stadium – the Pits, infamous home of gladiatorial blood sports and birthplace of the Tattooed Men.

The irony of the situation hadn't escaped him. Here he was at the very place that had shaped Kat and made her into the person she was, and tomorrow he would be striding out beside her, leading a dozen of the toughest warriors the under-City had ever known, warriors fashioned by these very same Pits.

Knowing the dark history of this theatre – which is what it had been, in effect – he still had some misgivings about making the Pits his new place of work, but he had to admit that the Prime Master had probably chosen wisely. Training facilities were already in place, as were any number of attendant buildings formerly used for housing the Pit Warriors and all the support personnel required to run the facility. Of course, much of the place needed to be gutted and some of it rebuilt, but work on that had already begun and this was better than starting from scratch. All in all, it was the ideal location for the new Kite Guard

Training School. There was a pleasing sense of ironic justice in seeing the site of so many evil deeds turned into a facility for education, an establishment that might actually give something back to the under-City's society.

Tylus' thoughts switched for a moment to his parents, his mother in particular. Specifically he recalled the bitter sweet moment when he returned to the Heights sporting a captain's stripes. The squeal of delight and look of incredulous joy on his mother's face when he'd spoken of his unexpected promotion would live long in the memory. Not merely a single step up the career ladder, but a leap all the way from mere officer to captain in a single bound. Tylus was quite certain neither parent had ever imagined they'd see the day. His father's chest almost visibly swelled with pride, while his mother immediately began planning a reception at which to announce and celebrate the occasion, insisting he should attend. It was at this point Tylus revealed the second part of his news. He was to be stationed in the City Below. The speed with which expressions changed was almost comical, and the looks of dismay his words evoked were at least as memorable as his mother's initial yelp of joy.

Knowing her, he suspected his mama would still organise her reception, albeit in his absence – he had neither the time nor inclination to attend – and he had little doubt that discretion would come into play, with some judicious editing of his tidings ensuring that only the first part was ever reported and celebrated.

His reveries were interrupted by the approach of a stocky, solidly built figure in the mud and clay uniform of the city watch. Tylus recognised him immediately.

"Everything in order, sergeant?" he called to the craggy-faced man.

"All on schedule, sir. Had to give one of the foremen a right rollicking over some missing materials, but I think he's learned his lesson."

"Good. You'll keep an eye on him, I take it."

"Of course I will, sir."

Tylus was still getting used to that – being called "sir", particularly by a hard-bitten veteran like Sergeant Able. This was the man who had refused to provide any help when he'd first arrived in the City Below, before grudgingly lending him Richardson, the runt of the department, in what was undoubtedly intended as a joke but proved to be an inspired assignment. Despite that unfortunate beginning, Tylus liked Able. He was essentially honest – well, as honest as any officer of the watch down here was likely to be – hard working, resourceful and, for want of a better word, able. Exactly the sort of man the Kite Guard was looking for.

He beckoned the sergeant to follow him into the cabin which served as his temporary office until the permanent one was fully refurbished.

"Still don't know what I'm doing here," the sergeant muttered once they'd stepped inside.

Tylus didn't reply, instead opening a cupboard and taking out two glass tumblers and a bottle of ten year old Atlean whisky. Not the best vintage, but it would do. He poured two generous measures of the amber spirit and passed one tumbler to Able, picking up the other himself before dropping into his seat behind the desk.

The sergeant grinned – an unintentionally sinister expression – and raised his glass. "I've worked for many a worse officer, mind, but that doesn't alter the fact that I know breck all about flying!"

"That's not what I want you for," Tylus assured him. "The Guards will already have been taught everything they need to know about flying and gliding and fighting on the wing up-City. Little point in us bringing them all the way down here only to go over the same old ground again. What we're aiming for at the new school is a short, sharp shock, a course designed to show them what it's like to do *real* police work in some place where the streets are dirty and mean, where the miscreants don't recognise moral codes and won't show an officer respect simply because he's sporting a fancy cape and a puncheon."

Able snorted. "Well, I can do that all right, but do you really think a bunch of toffee-nosed cloud scrapers from up-City are going to pay any attention to the likes of me?"

"It'll be up to us to make sure they do, sergeant. Don't worry, I've already had a few ideas along those lines."

"Good, cos I'd hate to think I was wasting my time. Can't help feeling I should be out there now, helping to rein in the new gangs that are forming and moving into the old street-nick territories rather than kicking my heels watching a load of labourers at work. The watch is stretched thin enough as it is."

Tylus had to stifle a grin. He knew full well that the canny sergeant was still keeping his hand in, that a stream of officers and runners were constantly coming to and fro, bringing him updates and carrying off his orders. Tylus couldn't blame him. He had learned firsthand just how hard pressed the watch was down here in the City Below, and it wasn't as if any actual teaching would start for weeks yet. There was hardly enough here at the moment to keep both Able and Richardson occupied, so he couldn't begrudge the sergeant his dedication.

"That's one of the things we'll be doing before long – supplementing the watch with Kite Guard patrols. Just imagine it, hunting someone through the Runs with watch officers on the ground and Kite Guards in the air, working together in a coordinated search."

"Now that would be something worth seeing," Able conceded.

"Look, bear with me on this. I know it's a bit frustrating at present, but in a little while I'll have you rushed off your feet. You'll look back on these quiet days with wistful fondness. For now, though, all I ask is that you oversee the building work and make sure there's no slacking while I'm off in the Stain chasing monsters."

"Yeah, well, good luck. I don't mind admitting that I wouldn't swap places with you on that one, not for anything."

Able drained the last of his whisky, placed the glass down firmly on Tylus' desk and took his leave. "Time I went to check on that foreman again, just in case he thinks I've forgotten about him."

Drinking alone had always struck Tylus as a uniquely morose pastime, and he was tempted to abandon what remained of his own whisky once the sergeant had gone, but after the way he'd humiliated himself in front of Kat earlier, he decided to make an exception just this once.

No sooner had he taken a further sip from his glass than there came a smart triple rap at the door. Startled, Tylus hurriedly cleared the two glasses and the bottle away into a drawer, before calling out, "Come."

Even as he pushed the drawer shut he felt bemused by his own actions. After all, he was in charge here, and if he wanted to have a drink in his own office, why shouldn't he? Yet he still felt like a kid caught with his hand in the cookie jar, which was ridiculous, particularly as he knew full well whose knock that had been.

Another figure dressed in the brown and orange of the city watch came in, this one taller and considerably younger than the sergeant. Tylus felt a certain degree of pride at how far Richardson had come in a very short time. Oh, he knew the man himself deserved most of the credit, but Tylus felt he'd played his part in giving the young officer a break and inspiring the man's burgeoning self-confidence.

Whereas Able always wore the mud and clay as if born to it, not so long ago Richardson had looked anything but comfortable in his uniform, as if the collar perhaps chafed a little and the trousers were a tad too tight at the groin. Tylus had seen that awkwardness disappear bit by bit during the time he'd been here, and today there was no sign of it at all as

Richardson strode into the office and stood before his captain. This was a man on a mission.

"Yes, Richardson?"

"I wanted to ask you a favour, sir."

Sir? Richardson never remembered to call him sir. "Go ahead."

"Well, ehm… I was hoping you might stand beside me, sir. You see, I'm getting married."

Tylus couldn't have been more surprised if Richardson had declared himself to be a Jeradine in disguise. "*What*…? Congratulations! Who's the lucky girl? No, doesn't matter, I'm not going to know her in any case."

"As a matter of fact you do, well… you've met her at any rate. It's Jezmina, the girl who used to run with the Blue Claw, the one I took away from the station to work for my sister."

"Jezmina? But she's…" *just a kid*.

"Young, I know. But we've been spending quite a bit of time together lately, what with her bein' at my sisters and all, and, well, she's a really sweet girl and… she's just *so* beautiful."

All of which might be true, but when Tylus thought of the girl the image that came to mind was of a manipulative and opportunistic little strumpet, for all her tender years and innocent expression.

"I'm delighted for you," he said. He managed to keep the smile in place but couldn't resist asking, "How old *is* she, by the way?"

"She doesn't know," Richardson admitted, a little forlornly.

Doesn't know?

"She was orphaned at a very young age, you see, and no one keeps any records of births, not down here. So she might even be older than she looks… I mean she *acts* older than she looks."

No argument from Tylus on that score. Jezmina was certainly far more mature than her physical appearance suggested – she would have needed to grow up quickly to survive on the streets with a pretty face like that – and she knew exactly how to make the most of the elfin beauty the gods had blessed her with. Within minutes of arriving at the watch station she'd had a couple of the officers running around after her with their tongues hanging out. Manipulating men seemed second nature to her, but it never occurred to Tylus that Richardson would fall under her thrall, not to the point of wanting to *marry* her at any rate.

"This is all a bit sudden, don't you think?" he ventured.

Richardson pulled a face. "That's what the Thaistess said."

"You've already been to see a *Thaistess*?" How far had things progressed? How much damage was already done?

"Well, I wanted to check… what with Jezmina being so young, that the Thaistess would be happy to join us before the goddess. If she hadn't been, there are always other temples, other religions, you know."

"And was she?"

"Yes. I mean, she didn't say so immediately, asked me to bring Jezmina in to see her. I left them alone so they could have a chat. Never seen my angel so nervous,

I can tell you, but I kept saying there was nothing to worry about, that once the Thaistess saw how mature and sensible she was, there'd be no problem."

It struck Tylus as far more likely that the Thaistess would have realised how far away from being an innocent maiden Jezmina was and what a savvy and worldly-wise creature had been brought before her, that far from *her* needing protection, any prospective husband was likely to; but he limited his response to, "And was there?"

"No, she did brilliantly; must have done, because afterwards the Thaistess said she'd be happy to conduct the ceremony. So, anyway, as I said, I was hoping you would do me the honour of standing beside me."

How could he possibly refuse without offending this man he'd come to regard as a friend? "I'd be delighted to," he said, with a growing sense of impending doom.

"Thank you!" Richardson rushed forward, clasping the Kite Guard's hand. "That means a lot. It won't be for a few weeks yet, so you'll have plenty of time to get back from the Stain."

Get back from the Stain? What a charming way to dismiss the living hell Tylus was bound for in the morning. He watched the man who'd acted as his assistant since he first arrived in the City Below float out of the office on a cloud of blissful infatuation and sweet delusion. As he did so, resolve hardened. Tylus wasn't about to stand by and let a good man like Richardson be taken advantage of and emotionally disembowelled by a callous and calculating gold-digger, which was all he could think Jezmina to be. It seemed that he would have a very different battle to look forward to when and *if* he returned from the Stain. Wonderful.

THREE

Tylus paced up and down before the row of deep blue liveried figures. Six of them: a sergeant and five officers; his men, at least for the duration of the mission. He recalled the many times he'd been where they were now, in briefings, either standing to attention like this or sitting attentively, never dreaming that one day he'd be the one out at the front doing the talking.

"I don't want to see any discourtesy," he said, his gaze sliding from one face to the next. "We work as a team. Yes, they come from the City Below whereas you're from the Heights. Yes, they look outlandish with their interlinked patterns of tattoos while you look dapper and proper in your pristine blue uniforms, but don't be fooled. These are intelligent and extremely capable men.

"Do you know where we are? Have you any idea what this is?" He swept an arm wide to take in the looming presence of the Pits' amphitheatre, which stood dark and brooding in the sun globes' dawning light.

Nobody responded, heads remained rigidly facing forward.

"Well? Speak up, anybody?"

"The Pits, sir!" the sergeant, Whitmore, replied.

"Exactly right. The Pits, where warriors were pitted against the deadliest animals the world has to offer, where champion fought champion to the death, where life expectancy was measured not in decades but in days and weeks. The men you'll be working beside today are the winners of this darkest of all theatres. They're the ones who survived the horrors of the Pits and walked away to tell the tale. Some of them were there for *years*. So when you look at the man beside you and feel tempted to sneer at his barbaric appearance, at his primitive, unsightly tattoos, just stop to think for a moment. Reflect on the fact that the more elaborate and extensive those tattoos the more bouts a warrior survived, the more he triumphed. Today you will have the *honour* of working alongside some of the deadliest fighters Thaiburley has ever produced, professional killers whose skills were honed in the fiercest environment imaginable. They deserve your respect and by Thaiss they'll get it! Do I make myself clear?"

"Yes, sir!" six voices declared in unison.

Tylus pursed his lips, doubting his stirring words would make a jot of difference. He recalled his own deep-rooted prejudices when he first arrived in the City Below. If asked, he would have denied they existed; only once they were fully dismantled was he able to recognise that they'd been there in the first place. These lads would be no different, however well-intentioned they might be. Their entire upbringing would have constantly reinforced their sense of superiority over those who dwelt in the under-City. It was going to take more than mere words, no matter how stirring, to overturn something as ingrained as that. Only experience could do the job; but experience had to begin somewhere, and these six were about to receive a baptism of fire.

"Sergeant, you and your men follow me." With that Tylus spread his arms, allowing the cape to unfurl. He felt lighter immediately, as if the cloak were eager to carry his body skyward and lift him above the rooftops. Seeing no reason to deny it, he bent his knees and leapt, soaring upwards. Behind him, the other Kite Guards did the same.

There hadn't been time for him to get to know these men properly. He'd been assured they were among the best the Guard had to offer and had no reason to doubt that assessment, but it wasn't the same as knowing the man at your back and being confident of how he was likely to react in a given situation. Still, they had the weaponry provided by the arkademics plus the new slings, which they had evidently trained with, and there was no doubting that his little troop maintained a tight formation in flight. He felt irrationally proud of them as they soared over the rendezvous point just short of the Stain and came in to land in neat order. Surely those waiting couldn't fail to be impressed.

If so, they masked it well.

"About time you got here," Kat snapped.

"Hardly our fault if you decide to be early," Tylus responded.

Tattooed Men were milling around, while half a dozen ebony giants stood statue-still in a row before the crumbling wall of a derelict building. The Blade.

Tylus went to talk with the man who had come to see them off: the Council's newest member, Master Thomas, supposed victim of the apparent murder that led to the Kite Guard being assigned to the under-City in the first place.

"Sorry the Prime Master can't be here in person," Thomas said. "There's a developing situation in the Heights which he can't afford to leave."

"Quite understood," Tylus assured him, while wondering what the situation might be. This expedition was the Prime Master's idea, and from all that Tylus knew of the man it was unlike him not to see a project through.

In truth, he paid little attention to what was said after that – which, in any case, amounted to little more than a wordy "good luck" from what he did hear – his thoughts were focused on what lay ahead.

Kat seemed all business this morning, which made the job of glossing over yesterday's events that much easier. He sneaked a sidelong glance at her as she organised the Tattooed Men. Despite his best intentions, the girl remained impressive and annoyingly hard to ignore.

"Hello, Tylus," a voice said, snapping him out of his reveries.

He looked around to see a woman in arkademic's garb. She appeared to be around his age; her brown

hair worn short – as short as Kat's though not as ragged
and spiky, rather it was well-cut and shaped in a sort
of bob. She had a dark complexion, large almond eyes,
and a slightly plump face, pleasant as opposed to
overtly pretty. In fact, there was something vaguely familiar about that face... then it clicked into place.

"*Issie?*"

She laughed. "It's been years since anyone called me
that, but yes, it's me."

He joined in her laughter and had to resist the urge
to hug her – she was an arkademic after all. "I don't
believe this. It must be, what, ten years... twelve?"

"At least. I haven't seen you since we moved away
and I went to train as an arkademic. Look at you now:
a Kite Guard!"

"And look at you: an arkademic!" He was surprised
and overjoyed. Issie's family had been neighbours and
the two of them had virtually grown up playing with
each other, but he hadn't thought about her in years.
"So what *do* people call you these days?"

"Well, that depends on who they are. Arkademic
Haq for the most part, Isar to my friends, but they'd
both sound a little odd coming from you, so let's stick
with 'Issie', shall we?"

Tylus was grinning despite the daunting task that
had brought them here, delighted by this wholly unexpected encounter.

Kat yelled something at the Tattooed Men and then
said, "When you two have finished catching up, shall
we get going – unless you've got some reason to hang
around here, Kite Guard?"

"None at all," he assured her. "Talk later," he said to Issie, who nodded in response as she was abruptly surrounded by the towering figures of the Blade.

Tylus went to re-join the men, glaring in Kat's direction as he did so, reckoning that if she was determined to stay in this sort of a mood it was going to be a very long day indeed.

Kat and the Tattooed Men were the first to arrive at the rendezvous point. She was impatient, sensing that this was it, the day of reckoning for the monster that had murdered first her mother and now her sister, the callous creature who so casually altered the course of her life without ever knowing or caring that it did so.

She felt well rested and alert, despite getting to bed later than intended the previous evening. As the sun globes dimmed to darkness, she'd slipped away from the Tattooed Men and made her way through the flickering twilight and long shadows of lantern-lit streets to a familiar door. Her knock was answered by an elderly woman, who showed her to a seat by a simple wooden table before making them both hot milky drinks.

Kat had seen little of the apothaker since they parted company in an abandoned warehouse the night she went in search of Brent. She'd never asked what became of Sur Sander, reckoning that it was best left between the old woman and her conscience.

Kat felt a strange kinship with this woman, a connection she found difficult to define. They both knew what it was to be cast out, they'd both known loss, and they shared a common enemy. Perhaps that was all it was. Perhaps that was enough.

On the table in front of the apothaker rested a sheet of textured paper. Though it lay face down, Kat had seen it before and knew that the other side held a vividly rendered sketch of a young woman – Kara, the apothaker's apprentice, slain by the Soul Thief.

"We're going to get her, Mother," Kat said softly. The familiar honorific was one she reserved for few people, but this was one woman who merited it.

"You're going after it, you're going into the Stain?"

"Yes."

The apothaker took a sip from her mug as if mulling this over before replying, "Thaiss guide you then, girl."

No recriminations, no reminder of their failure to hunt the monster down in the streets or the disaster that had been Iron Grove Square, merely a blessing. It reaffirmed Kat's high opinion of this enigmatic, brave woman.

"Thank you. We've got some help this time, from up-City. She won't get away again. I just wanted to let you know." She deserved to know.

The apothaker nodded. "And I'm grateful for your trouble."

Kat couldn't resist saying, "No luck potions for me this time?"

The apothaker shook her head and said, "No, you had my best last time, but..." and her hand strayed to the sheet of paper which she pushed across the table. "Here, take this with you."

Kat stared at the paper, strangely reluctant to reach out and touch it. "I... I can't take this." It was all the woman had left of the girl she had doted on and raised as a daughter.

"Yes you can. Look at it."

Kat did reach out then, taking the corner of the sheet and turning it over. To find herself staring at a beautifully depicted face as anticipated; but this wasn't Kara. The face was rounder, the eyes more intense, the lips a little thinner and the hair shorter and more ragged, spiky even. The image was still striking, but it was unmistakable... "*Me*?"

"I had to draw it from memory," the apothaker explained, "but I always did have a good eye for detail. I'm still not entirely happy with the hair but it'll do."

"It's stunning," Kat assured her. She stared again. "Do I really look like this?" Although she recognised her own features there was a wild beauty in the face as rendered by the apothaker, a defiant splendour which didn't match her own self-image.

"I only ever draw what I see."

Kat wasn't sure what to say. There was a depth of beauty here which she felt embarrassed by, convinced it was more in the beholder's eye than her actual face.

"I'm too old to go traipsing across the Stain, but if you take this with you at least a part of me will be there when you give that bitch what's coming to her."

Kat had to smile. There wasn't a hint of doubt in the woman's voice, no suggestion that the venture might possibly fail.

She lifted the picture from the table and hesitated.

"Go ahead," the apothaker said, evidently anticipating her thoughts. "Fold it up by all means. The image shouldn't smudge."

Kat did as instructed, and then slipped the paper into a pocket as she stood up. "I'd better be going. Busy day tomorrow."

They both got to their feet, the apothaker surprising Kat by coming around the table and hugging her. As they embraced, Kat was very conscious of just how frail the older woman felt, though there was a smile on her face as she stepped back and said, "Give her hell!"

Kat had to suppress a shiver, struck by a sense of déjà vu. These were exactly the same words the apothaker had said to her ahead of the debacle at Iron Grove Square, before Chavver was killed. She could only hope that things would go a little differently this time.

Kat's hand strayed unconsciously to her pocket, fingering the edge of the apothaker's folded picture as she shared some banter with the men. The chosen dozen had been split into three teams of four, each with a specified lieutenant – divisions that would mean nothing until the fighting actually started but which would give them shape and discipline when hell came a calling. This was how she and Chavver had always organised the men, a leftover from the Pits when small groups of disparate individuals had needed to gel quickly into cooperative units to stand any hope of surviving.

The Prime Master hadn't turned up to see them off but another Master had, Thomas, and he'd brought the promised six members of the Blade with him, their dark towering presence impossible to ignore for all that they stood silent. When she'd considered them at all, Kat had always imagined the Council of Masters to be a bunch of ancient and wizened men and women, but Thomas looked to be a good deal younger than that, a man still in his prime. The same was true of the person he brought with him, a slightly stocky, round-faced woman wearing the pale blue robes of an arkademic.

"This is Arkademic Haq," Thomas said. "She'll be accompanying you into the Stain."

"Like hell she will," Kat responded. "Nobody said anything about us taking a civilian in there with us."

"Sorry, I probably didn't phrase that very well," Thomas said, with a grimace and an apparent degree of humility which surprised Kat. "The arkademic isn't here to penalise or handicap you in any way, far from it; she's essential to your mission."

"I devised the whip you see," the woman said, "the one which somebody used against your Soul Thief. I'm attuned to it, drawn to those elements of the whip she absorbed when it struck her. I can feel it even now, pulling at me."

"The arkademic has kindly agreed to help us, despite the considerable risks involved. If anything, you might want to thank her."

Kat scowled. She never had reacted well to advice, especially when it concerned her own behaviour. "I expected the detector to be in a box or something, not in a person."

"Sorry, it doesn't work that way," Thomas replied.

Kat glared at the arkademic, not remotely intimidated by his status. She hadn't reckoned on this. The need to safeguard a non-combatant would change things drastically, ensuring that at least part of their force would have to be tied down, static, prepared to take a hit in order to protect the defenceless.

They hadn't even entered the Stain yet and already their effectiveness was compromised.

"The Blade will take responsibility for Arkademic Haq's safety, so she won't be a burden to you or your men," Thomas continued, as if reading Kat's mind.

Better than nothing, she supposed, but that would still mean restricting the party's most formidable element – the Blade. She shook her head in annoyance at her own fretting. No point in looking for problems before they arose. After all, not so long ago she'd been an outcast with only her wits to call upon. Now she had Tattooed Men, Kite Guards – assuming they ever showed up – *and* the Blade at her back. Whichever way you looked at it, that was progress, and whatever awaited them in the Stain had better watch out.

Right on cue, Tylus and his men came sailing over the rooftops to land in front of her, all neat and pretty and oh so smug.

"About time you got here," she snapped.

The Kite Guards weren't really late, merely the last to arrive, but she was itching to let off steam at somebody and, besides, it didn't hurt to give that

captain of theirs a slap in the ego first thing. With
any luck he might keep his mind on his men and not
let it wander in her direction too often. True, she
might have welcomed his attention another day, but
not on this one. Today she wanted everyone involved
to be sharp and focused. No way was she about to let
the Thief escape her again.

Tylus and the arkademic fell into conversation immediately and were clearly old friends. Kat found herself
studying the other woman, looking for faults, almost as
if she were a rival in some way; which was ridiculous.
Kat made no claim on the Kite Guard captain, nor
would she wish to. Even so… the woman was solidly
built, stocky even, and her face was plain, pleasant at
best. No competition at all.

Kat's impatience was building towards boiling point.
Unless someone was prepared to take responsibility they
could end up standing around chatting like this all day.

"M'gruth, Ox, Half-hand," she called out to her
three lieutenants, "look lively."

Ox, named for his massive shoulders, wrestled with
his harness. Physically the strongest of all the Tattooed
Men, it had fallen to him to carry the most portable of
the "Big Weapons" from the group's armoury. They'd
also brought with them some flechette guns, distributed
between the men, but Ox carried the real artillery. He
was also considerably more intelligent than his hulking
frame might suggest, which was why Kat had chosen
him to lead one of the squads as well. She was confident he could handle both jobs.

Tylus and the arkademic were still in a world of their

own. For all she cared they could stay there and skip
into the Stain holding hands, as long as they moved
their asses in that direction sooner rather than later.
"When you two have finished catching up, shall we
get going – unless you've got some reason to hang
around, Kite Guard?"

"None at all," Tylus assured her.

"Then let's get this over with."

The Blade had yet to speak – she had no idea
whether they *could* speak – but as the Tattooed Men
and Kite Guards started forward, so did they, coming
across to escort the arkademic, who looked a lost and
tiny figure in their midst.

There was no stirring music or grand speech to send
them on their way as she'd feared the cloud scrapers
might arrange – unless whatever Thomas had been
prattling on about to Tylus counted as such. Kat was
grateful for that. They were here to do a job, not perform in a parade.

She studied their destination. A deceptively placid
landscape of rugged mounds and low hillocks. No
crumbling walls – the Stain had never been built on –
and the area didn't look particularly big. The far wall
of the vast cavern that housed the City Below loomed
large, foreshortening the view and creating the illusion
that this visible area of the Stain was little more than
a broad strip of wasteland, skirting the under-City and
separating it from the rock face. Kat knew it to be
broader than that. She knew too that there was more
to the Stain than met the eye. On the far side of this
apparently solid wall of rock lay another cavern, a

darker part of the Stain beyond the reach of the sun globes, a chamber accessible via a couple of fissures that formed short passageways in the base of the wall. She just hoped their quarry resided on this side.

There was evidence of an attempt to contain and isolate the Stain, to shut it away, just beyond the point where the derelict houses ran out. A line of concrete posts as tall as the Blade stretched in both directions. Here and there lengths of wire-mesh fence still linked one post to the next, but even these tended to be sagging and holed. For the most part, the fencing had been pulled down and trampled on long ago. It clearly hadn't been repaired in decades, and, to judge by the Stain creatures Kat had encountered, could never have been more than a token gesture in the first place, a symbolic barrier rather than a physical one. What a waste of effort.

Kat stepped between two vacant posts, leading the group into the one place in all Thaiburley with a reputation even darker than the Pits'.

Tylus was a few steps behind Kat as she crossed into the Stain, each of them followed by their respective groups in twin columns. Issie brought up the rear, flanked by her towering honour guard.

"We need to head a little to the right," the arkademic called out. "Yes, that's it," as they adjusted their course accordingly.

When he first entered the City Below, Tylus had been struck by the pervading smell of stale sweat and decay. He'd quickly acclimatised and had barely spared the odour a thought since, but the Stain revived those memories. For the first time since his arrival he was aware of that off-sour rankness again. He gazed at the territory ahead with a mix of unease and distaste.

For centuries the Stain had been used as the dumping ground for the waste of a city of millions. It might have been left fallow in recent generations, allowing mosses and grass and spiky thorned plants to flourish, lending the place a semblance of wilderness, but the Kite Guard knew that this thin veneer of nature merely disguised the discarded detritus beneath his feet. He was conscious of the ground feeling spongy and soft, in marked contrast to the rest of the City Below, and he tried hard not to think about what he was now walking on.

"Sergeant," he said as way of distraction. "I want two men aloft on a patrol loop, scouting either side of the column as well as ahead and behind, not straying too far but maintaining reasonable distance between them." He'd never seen anything flying over the Stain but it was best to be careful. He'd prefer the men offered two targets rather than one.

"Sir!"

Oddly enough the sun globes, which provided the City Below with an approximation of sunlight and an imitation of the outside world's day night cycle, didn't extend over the Stain. The final pair of vast solar bubbles embedded in the cavern's ceiling lined up more or less above the demarcation of buildings and wasteland, almost as if the city's original designers had never intended this deepest pocket of the cavern to be

populated. Having studied the schematics, Tylus knew
that the under-City's chamber extended beyond the
limits of the rest of Thaiburley. Perhaps that was the
reason. Perhaps whatever had been responsible for in-
stalling the sun globes was so slavishly loyal to the
dimensions of the City Above that it stopped once
those limits were reached. Not that it mattered. The
globes' influence was such that most of the Stain was
bathed in as much light as the rest of this subterranean
world. Only in the furthest reaches, close to the wall,
did twilight's gloom hold sway.

He glanced up to see two of his officers climbing into
the air to take station above the group. They established a slow elliptical circuit, complying with his
instructions to the letter by ensuring they were at opposite ends, one in front, one behind, one passing to
the group's left as the other approached on the right.

Tylus felt an unexpected chill. He'd always thought
there was something inspirational about watching Kite
Guards in flight, that they were magnificent and regal,
but this time the sight struck him as unaccountably sinister. As he watched the two officers dutifully continuing
their circuits, he was reminded of carrion birds circling
above their prey. Not an image he cared to dwell on and
not, he trusted, an omen of what lay ahead.

The rat moved another tentative step forward, its nose
twitching, eyes darting this way and that. The rodent
was cautious, perhaps sensing something wasn't quite
right, though not yet disturbed enough to actually flee.
Scorke held his breath and stayed completely motion-

less, willing the little bundle of flesh and fur to come just a little bit closer.

That's it, you little brecker, only another couple of steps…

At last the cautious critter seemed to decide that the quicker it was through here the better; it suddenly scampered forward to where the hunter waited. Scorke unleashed his attack, striking with a speed that defied the eye, whipping his segmented prehensile tail down and skewering the rat with its barbed tip. The unfortunate rodent gave an alarmed squeak and struggled for an instant, the body apparently not realising it was already dead. Then the venom went to work and all movement ceased.

Scorke brought the still-warm corpse to his mouth, human lips and teeth manoeuvring and then lifting it from the metal spike of his tail until he could throw his head back and swallow, feeding the organic components of his body. No more than a morsel, perhaps, but rats were plentiful in the Stain and this was merely the first of the day.

The rodents were most common closer to the river, but Scorke didn't go near the water. That was where the Bumpy Beetle lived – his name for a creature much like himself, part organic and part machine, but bigger and far more powerful. Scorke was afraid of the Beetle and gave the river a wide berth. There were rats enough elsewhere.

Scorke knew he wasn't bright, that much of his human brain had been beyond salvaging, but it all worked well enough. He was still alive, wasn't he? And he was wise enough to know that people were his biggest threat. His type had been hidden away from the first day they were made because people wouldn't understand, they'd consider the marriage of human parts with those of animals and machine to be an abomination, fit only to be condemned and destroyed on sight. The Maker had drilled that knowledge into them again and again, but the Maker wasn't there to look after him anymore. The man's death had left Scorke facing some stark choices. He wanted to live, but knew he wouldn't be permitted to do so in the streets. So he had fled to the Stain, neither knowing nor caring what became of his fellows.

The Stain was different. The Stain felt like home. The very ground welcomed him. Layer upon layer of compacted rotting detritus covered the hard rock floor, allowing his long sinuous body to slip through and between. He could move unseen, burrowing beneath the surface, and had become an accomplished rat catcher, lying in ambush by their runs and their trails. But rats brought only limited sustenance and now his keen senses detected something far more rewarding: people. People had come into the Stain. Not the streets, not their world, but his, where he could be the hunter and they the prey.

He moved closer to investigate. The primary instincts of hunger and caution warred within him, but still he slid forward. A large group, strung out. They had with them creatures like him but not like him. Towering blocks of darkness, powerful and fearsome. Almost, he fled, but greed whispered to him, tempted him, overriding caution. Greed's seductive voice argued that it wouldn't hurt to stay near, to watch and await his moment, just as he did with the rats.

Opportunity presented itself when the puff bladders struck. A seed dart punctured one of the soft-skinned people, focussing the attention of everyone there. Scorke seized his chance, singling out a large specimen at the rear of the group and moving in for the kill, hoping to make off with his prize before anyone even knew he was there.

"Get down!" Kat flung herself at Tylus, catching him off-guard and hitting with enough force to knock him from his feet despite her smaller frame. She landed painfully, her midriff and thigh slamming into his hip and knee, though she wasn't paying much attention to either at the time. Her gaze focused on the patch of bramble where she'd spotted movement, just in time to see what looked to be a bloated and diseased fruit tear open. Grey-brown mottled flesh parted in tattered fronds and a single long, thin object spat out with explosive force, targeted close to where she'd been standing.

One of the Kite Guards cried out as the missile slammed into him. He collapsed, clutching at his stomach. Blood covered his hands as he tried to pull out the sickly yellow dart protruding from the wound. It was an elongated ovoid, slender throughout but tapering and evidently pointed at either end.

Kat rolled off, bringing her feet beneath her and half rising into a crouch, twin blades already in her hands.

Tylus struggled to his knees. "Thaiss!" she heard him mutter. "Is that thing a *seed*?"

The Blade reacted quicker than anyone, two of them advancing on the unholy bloom. The one nearest to Kat raised his right arm and pointed. An ebony spear which must have been part of his forearm shot forward, punching into the fruit or whatever it was and shattering it into a score of flying fragments. The impact elicited a high-pitched shriek, though whether the result of agony or merely escaping air she couldn't be sure.

More of the bulbous fruit were visible now, a whole nest of the things camouflaged among the low growth.

The second member of the Blade now lifted his arm, squirting a stream of liquid at the patch. Wherever the liquid struck it burned, raising a cloud of fumes as the puffed-up uglies popped and wheezed and withered. One managed a parting shot, and a second pus-coloured dart shot out, heading directly towards the Blade. It struck his unyielding hide and dropped to the ground. Instead of lying passive, the thing writhed around like some unwholesome maggot, the twin pointed ends wriggling back and forth as if searching for prey. The Blade pointed a finger and a stream of acid descended to consume the persistent seed.

Kat turned away, covering her mouth and nose as acrid fumes rose from the shrivelling husk.

She turned just in time to witness a new menace erupt from the ground and strike Half-hand, one of her lieutenants. Silvered metal gleamed in the globelight as something resembling a segmented snake leapt up to hit the Tattooed Man in the back. She watched in horror as blood flew from Half-hand's pierced torso and a crimson-smeared metal barb thrust out through his chest.

Kat was running as soon as she saw the thing strike and was upon it in an instant, arriving even as Half-hand sunk to his knees. Dropping one sword, she grasped the other in both hands and swung it against the metal tentacle with all her strength. The blade bit, finding purchase between two of the plated segments. At first Kat thought it wasn't going to cut clean through, though she struck with enough force to pull the barb fully out of Half-hand, who slid off the tip to collapse face down. She tugged anew and the blade came clear, while the severed barb dropped to the ground and the truncated limb waved in the air, spilling what looked to be blood.

A wailing sound split the air and the creature's head poked up above ground, loose earth and clumps of grass tumbling off it like water. Kat froze for a second, shocked at how human the face looked. That fractional pause almost proved her undoing. Two rapier-like blades flashed towards her, one from either side. She leapt, twisting and spinning, seeing steel flash past her face a hair's breadth from her nose and feeling the other blade cut the air close to her leg.

Kat landed, rolled, snatched up her discarded sword and went on the attack, blocking a clumsy strike from one blade and moving inside its reach to clash with the second. These were different from the barb she'd hacked off, broader and with longer – edged weapons or tools whereas the barb had been all about stabbing – more scythe than sword. The limbs that supported them differed as well. These were less flexible and more muscular, with clearly defined joints identifying them as arms or legs. More vulnerable, too; flesh and bone above the ankle or wrist.

Kat jumped to avoid a further pass by one of the blades, tucking her knees up to her chest so that it passed harmlessly beneath her feet. As she came down she thrust – her own swords designed to be versatile, capable of both cutting and stabbing – and felt the point bite home. Again that disturbingly almost-human wail sounded as Kat pulled her sword free, ripping through the creature's flesh. Other Tattooed Men were there now, fighting beside her, grasping and hacking at limbs. They'd pulled the thing almost entirely free of the ground, revealing a long multi-ribbed body which writhed and bucked as the creature tried to escape back into the muck beneath them.

She saw a pair of the Blade move forward, but she didn't want that. This was Tattooed Men business. "No!" She held out a restraining hand, sword still clasped.

"Finish it!" she said to her men, and caught a glare from M'gruth as he grappled with a limb while struggling to avoid getting stabbed, which seemed to say "What the hell do you think we're trying to do?"

Then someone found the creature's head with a heavy blade, landing a blow that took half its skull away. The fight was over, as suddenly as that. One spasm, which sent scythe-tipped legs thrashing dangerously, and then it lay still. The Tattooed Men stood in a ragged circle around its elongated, improbable corpse, panting and staring at each other. The creature looked to be an unholy blend of man, machine, scorpion and snake.

"The Maker's work, do you think?" M'gruth asked as he came up to stand beside her.

"Maybe." She could well imagine that madman conjuring up something like this during a particularly dark period. Her gaze turned to the prone form of Half-hand. One arm seemed to be reaching out towards her with the hand that boasted the two absent fingers – the source of his nickname.

"I was standing beside him in the arena the day he lost those fingers," M'gruth murmured, evidently following the direction of her gaze. "He took on a snow devil with nothing but a knife and his naked fist."

Kat grunted agreement, remembering the awe and excitement that bout had generated even though she hadn't witnessed it or been a part of it. "He saved more than just his own life that day."

Half-hand's lifeless body acted as an uncomfortable reminder of her own mortality, one which only strengthened her resolve. It had taken the deaths of Chavver and the others who fell at Iron Grove Square to bring home to Kat a harsh fact. There was no one to replace them. No matter how formidable the Tattooed Men might be in terms of the City Below, their numbers were finite and dwindling. They had to change, *had* to settle down, or the Tattooed Men were doomed to disappear. Her thoughts turned to Shayna, whom she'd charged with starting that process in her absence. She hoped the healer was having an easier time of it than they were here. One thing she was certain of: not even Shayna could have helped this time. Half-hand's injuries were too severe.

"We'd best be moving on," M'gruth said.

Kat nodded. They couldn't spare the time to tend to the dead. All being well the bodies would be here later when they came back this way – assuming they did, assuming that the Stain didn't claim them all, but she wasn't about to dwell on that cheery prospect. Tylus had other ideas, wanting to use slings suspended between two of his airborne officers to ferry the dead out of the Stain, but Kat persuade him to reconsider.

"You're here to pursue a mission," she reminded him, "not split your forces to act as body boys for the rest."

He agreed, though he didn't much like it. Nor did she for that matter. Half-hand deserved better, but then again, so did they all.

The Prime Master listened impassively to the latest reports. Jeanette, Thaiburley's senior physician, sat beside him. She had been as intimately involved in the efforts to stem the spread of bone flu as anyone and the Prime Master saw no reason to exclude her; besides, he valued both her company and her opinion. Verrill, the man making the reports, had been captain of the Council Guard for the best part of five years. The Prime Master had watched him develop from enthusiastic over-achiever to consummate professional with a certain degree of satisfaction and pride – the man had been his preferred choice for the position. He both liked and respected Verrill and knew him well enough to realise that the reports were proving as difficult to deliver as they were to listen to. The captain's demeanour and expression remained neutral and wholly professional, but the slightly raised pitch of his voice gave him away.

The reports made grim listening indeed. Much of Artists Row had been sealed off – all those unaffected having been evacuated long ago. As many as could be, at any rate. No one knew how many Rust Warriors were bottled up down there. The Blade held them at bay. There were similar if smaller "quarantined" areas in the Residences and throughout most of the Heights. If he could assemble the Blade in strength, he could take the initiative and purge the Rust Warriors from any given area, but he daren't. That would leave too many other sectors of the city exposed. The Council Guard and even the Kite Guard had been mobilised, equipped with weapons treated by the arkademics to be effective against Rust Warriors; but despite their undoubted qualities they weren't the Blade.

For some reason, there had been no reported cases of bone flu in any Row below the Artists, which lent credence to the theory that the blight was in some way a targeted attack, that a malignant intelligence directed events. But who?

He suddenly realised that the officer had finished speaking and was standing a little awkwardly waiting for the Prime Master to respond.

He nodded to the man and smiled – that warm, re-assuring expression that had served him so well over the years; a creasing of the face that told the recipient he was appreciated, that his words were valued.

"Thank you, captain," the Prime Master said. He'd reached a decision as the man spoke and now acted upon it. "Authorise the reassignment of officers from lower Rows. We need more men up here." More targets, more victims, but what else could he do?

"Yes, sir!" With a slight nod, the captain pivoted on his heel and marched smartly from the room, leaving the Prime Master alone with Jeanette. She wouldn't have missed his momentary distraction and now regarded him, concern etched in every line of her face.

"Will the extra men help?"

"Oh yes, they'll help… a little."

Jeanette was one of the many Heights citizens forced to abandon their homes, the Row of Medics being among the worst hit. As soon as they realised that the calcified off-white shells that enveloped bone flu victims represented the pupal stage of a transformation from human to Rust Warrior rather than a clean death, they had destroyed all those stored for research. No easy task in itself; pneumatic sledge hammers, fire, and arkademic talent had all been deployed. Hundreds of pupae were destroyed that way, but many hundreds more had already hatched and new victims were appearing all the time.

"Still no breakthrough, no sign of a cure?" he said, knowing the answer even as he asked.

She shook her head. "I'm increasingly convinced that there *is* no cure, that this isn't a medical problem at all but is talent-related."

He nodded, her words anything but a surprise.

"I feel so useless," she continued. "All those years

of training and dedication, all my skills, and I can't
do anything to help people when the biggest challenge of my life appears. I'm reduced to watching folk
die and making them more comfortable in their final
hours."

"I'm sure that neither those people you and your
staff help nor their relatives consider your efforts to be
useless, not by a long shot."

Small comfort, he knew. Jeanette had been pushing
herself hard throughout the crisis with little concern
for her own health. "You look exhausted," he told her.
"You should go and get some rest."

She guffawed. "That's fine advice coming from you.
Have you looked in the mirror lately?"

"I try not to." The Prime Master knew he'd been
driving himself just as ruthlessly, but he had his reasons. There wasn't much time left to him. He'd already
lost sensation and most of the mobility in his left hand
and the right was only a little better. Before long, he'd
be just one more victim of the bone flu; though he intended to take matters into his own hands before that
actually came to pass.

"I'd better be getting back to my patients."

She rose and headed towards the door, but stopped
part way. "Oh, one more thing."

"Yes?"

"Why are you wearing gloves?"

He hesitated. Almost, he told her, but shied away.
She had enough burdens without him adding to them.
"A skin infection, nothing serious."

She stared into his eyes, not fooled for a second, he

felt certain. "Of course it is. If you want me to have a look at it, or just to talk... you know where I am."

He nodded, once. "Thank you, Jeanette."

She gave a thin, worried smile and left.

For long seconds he simply stared at the closed door, abruptly overwhelmed by a surge of despair. Life was filled with so many regrets.

FOUR

They lounged in comfortable chairs and there were no desks in sight but Tom wasn't fooled for a minute. The goddess, facing them, was the teacher, and they were there to learn.

"How did you first become aware of your talents?" Thaiss asked.

Tom hesitated, needing a few seconds to frame his reply. Fortunately Mildra stepped into the breach, evidently happy to answer first.

"Small things, when I was a little girl. A cut or a bruise... If I closed my eyes and concentrated, I could sort of sense what needed doing to heal them, how the blood vessels could be repaired and the escape of blood staunched, the pressure eased and the skin knitted together. It wasn't ever a conscious process, just something I could do at an instinctive level. When I was older, somebody I cared about was murdered in front of me, and I thought I was going to be next. I was spared, but the experience traumatised me and I went to one of your temples seeking... I'm not really sure what; advice, solace, reassurance... maybe a bit of all those things. A purpose most of all, though; a reason to go on.

"The Thaistess sensed something in me and suggested I apply for the priesthood. She was very persuasive, answering my questions with patience and warmth, smoothing away all my reservations. I took her advice, applied, was accepted, and immediately knew that this was where I belonged. I loved it. For the first time I received formal training in healing and the other aspects of my talent."

Thaiss nodded. "And Tom?"

"Hiding," he replied. "That's all it was. From bigger boys, from market stall holders I'd nicked things off, from razzers who were trying to catch me for doing the nicking, from other nicks who wanted to take from me what I'd nicked, from everyone when I wanted to be alone... but from my mother first of all, when I was really little. I discovered that if I crouched down and made myself as small as I could, and then concentrated, I mean *really* concentrated, I could make people not see me, not sense I was there. They could stand right next to me and never even realise."

"And you never tried to do anything other than hide?" the goddess asked.

"No, not until I met up with the Prime Master at any rate. It never occurred to me that I could."

For Tom, the days spent in the citadel had taken on a surreal, dreamlike quality. Matters that had once been so important to him – Thaiburley, the Prime Master,

Kat – paled and lost their intensity, becoming abstracts, the concerns of another lifetime. The things he learnt in the ice tank and heard from Thaiss's lips began to bleed into one another, individual moments blurring and running together to form one long stream of consciousness and knowledge. Yet he never felt fully part of that flow. This wasn't knowledge he had earned, these weren't memories he had lived through; rather they had been thrust upon him, and while they might be at his beck and call – he could dip in and out of their stream at will – he didn't yet feel that he fully owned them.

During this time, he ate when food was provided and slept when his body required it, though he couldn't have defined when that was. The constant mellow lighting painted the world in pastels and seemed to rob everything of vitality; time moved at its own pace here and the standard compartments of morning, afternoon and night became meaningless.

Tom wouldn't necessarily have said that he enjoyed the sessions with the goddess, but he certainly came to crave them. Curiosity had been one of his defining traits from a very early age, his downfall more often than not, and here was an opportunity to learn so much about Thaiburley and its history. He was like a kid in a sweet shop, greedily devouring every new morsel of information. He would never get used to the ice tank, but welcomed the information each immersion imparted, if not the frustration of trying to assimilate it afterwards. That was why he loved the more physical lessons, the face-to-face talks and lectures. No confusion here; everything was concise and clearly explained.

His life within the citadel settled into a new rhythm and was defined by new parameters: day and night no longer held sway, it was all about lessons and non-lessons.

Mildra sat with him for many of these, though she was clearly not as obsessed as he was. During one where they were both present, she raised the question of their abilities working outside of the city as they followed the Thair's course, wondering whether her theory regarding the river's proximity had any merit.

"No, the river isn't really an issue," Thaiss explained. "Distance *is*, but you can still reach the core a considerable way beyond the city's walls. I'm afraid the superstition about the river carrying the essence of the goddess is just that – perhaps inspired by a lingering memory of where I dwell. But since you were travelling between here and there, it's likely that as you moved out of range of Thaiburley's heart, you were growing closer to this citadel and able to draw on the core here. Had you travelled this far from Thaiburley in any other direction, I suspect your talents would have failed you."

At any other time Tom would have found this an interesting revelation, but he had been bombarded with so much of late, and this followed his final immersion in the tank, when concentration was at its most fractured. He hadn't yet fully mastered the processes stimulating his brain.

Tom had undergone four sessions in the submersion tank by this point – or was it five? – and was feeling ever more disassociated from the world around him.

"I'm worried about what all this is doing to him," he heard Mildra say to the goddess at one point.

A corner of his mind registered that she was probably talking about him, but the rest appreciated that it didn't much matter even if she was.

He still recognised Mildra, but wasn't entirely certain of her significance.

Oddly, the incident which afterwards would stand most distinctly in Tom's mind occurred right towards the end of their stay at the citadel, perhaps because it *was* an end and so marked the imminent return of harsh reality and worldly concerns. Perhaps, also, because he was beginning to get a handle on things by then, coming back to himself and able to connect with what was going on outside his own head.

When not teaching them or answering questions, the goddess spent much of her time ensconced within a curved U of equipment – intricate yet oddly elegant constructs of metal and glass crystal, the latter putting Tom in mind of the khybul sculptures of the Jeradine. She would sit back and stare one moment, then lean forward to press on a pad with fingertips or pass the open palm of a hand over a green light, which would highlight her spread fingers in an eerie eldritch glow. On occasion, lines of opaque writing or strange glyphs would materialise – indecipherable despite Tom's newly-crammed knowledge – hovering in the air before her only to slowly fade or be dismissed with the wipe of a hand. Tom didn't pretend to understand any of the processes involved but guessed that she was communing in some profound fashion.

She would say nothing of her purpose but would come away troubled, or even frustrated. On this particular occasion she pushed herself back and stood up sharply, and the concern etched upon her face was more pronounced than ever. Her eyes met his and she said, "I understand now. I've had difficulty reaching the core and now I know why. Things are worse than I thought. I only hope we haven't delayed too long." Mildra stepped forward, obviously anxious. The goddess's gaze darted between them. "Don't just stand there," she snapped. "Get ready. You must leave. Immediately."

"Why? What's happened?" Mildra asked, a fraction before Tom thought to speak.

The elderly woman rubbed her eyes, suddenly seeming tired and frail. It was the first time since her awakening that Tom could recall Thaiss looking so human. "My brother," she said, "he didn't die."

The words triggered a welter of images and memories for Tom – embedded knowledge he was paying attention to for the first time.

He knew that Thaiss and her brother had come here through some sort of gateway from another world. He knew that they were here by design rather than accident and that they had set about constructing Thaiburley almost at once. The two of them were...

leaders…? Gods? King and queen? He wasn't sure of their exact status, but their intent was to build a home for others from their world – followers or subjects – who became the city's "founders".

"We knew the population would be mixed," the goddess had once explained. "With a large number of native folk dwelling in the city, perhaps more than there were of our own people. Planning for the long term, we realised that the only way to successfully settle would be to integrate – this world was chosen specifically because we *could* interbreed with local human stock." The impersonal phrasing might have made Tom uncomfortable once, but it now seemed perfectly natural. "Obviously our own gene pool would dilute and diffuse with the passage of time, but we severely underestimated to what extent. We assumed that the majority of citizens would always be able to access the core, rather than the minority that are able to do so in the current age. Oh, I appreciate that if you add all the arkademics and medics and talented together they amount to an impressive total, reaching into the thousands, but in terms of Thaiburley's overall population that's still a tiny fraction. We never foresaw integration to that degree, which was short-sighted of us and is one of the underlying reasons for the current predicament."

That particular lecture seemed crystal clear in Tom's memory, yet still he couldn't have sworn that it wasn't something learned in the ice tank.

There were so many things Tom didn't understand. It seemed that every piece of knowledge he gained merely opened the door to more questions. Perhaps that was the very nature of knowledge – it certainly seemed to be judging by his recent experience. The frustrating thing was that he might even have the answers to some of them without being able to access them yet. Rather than attempting a futile chase through the labyrinthine maze of unassimilated memory he strived to be patient as the goddess had advised, but it wasn't easy.

This resolve didn't stop him from mulling over the most pressing issues and wondering. He justified the exercise by telling himself that it might stimulate related information to surface. Chief among these nagging questions was why Thaiss and her people had originally come here in the first place. Were they fleeing something, was this world a refuge from some terrible threat? What could possibly threaten those who had built Thaiburley? Besides, the suggestion that this world had been selected seemed to argue otherwise, that this was a planned migration rather than a desperate exodus made in haste. If that were so, might others from their world follow at some point? Centuries had passed in the interim, which presumably made that unlikely, but he couldn't be certain. The next thing that puzzled him was why Thaiburley had been built at all. Was it to impress upon the natives the newcomers' power and establish them as gods? Was Thaiburley to be a seat of government from which these newcomers would rule the world? If so, something had clearly gone wrong. Sibling rivalry, perhaps. Or had Thaiss and her brother built the city purely for altruistic reasons, to improve the lot of the people they

brought with them. The third thing to rouse his curiosity was the falling out between Thaiss and her
brother. What had caused the tension that had clearly
developed between them? At some point the two sib-
lings had fallen out catastrophically, a row that
escalated into a war as each fought for control of
Thaiburley, mobilising armies to battle for their cause.
On each occasion Thaiss had won, causing her brother
to disappear for decades, presumably to lick his
wounds, before he emerged to try again. This he knew,
but nowhere had he caught any hint of the reasons.

The sibling warfare continued sporadically, the intensity of the ensuing violence the only constant. New
tactics were tried by the brother and new defences devised by the sister, with Thaiss emerging triumphant
and Thaiburley remaining under her control, if narrowly on occasion. Tom became increasingly
convinced that the omission of such an explanation
was deliberate. Perhaps Thaiss considered the specifics
too personal to share, which was understandable, but
it did raise the question of precisely how selective the
information he was being fed might be. He was learning so much about Thaiburley's past, but he was doing
so from Thaiss's perspective, and who was to say that
hers was the only valid viewpoint?

Tom's thoughts continued to follow the developing
rivalry that had shaped so much of the world's recent
history. It became clear to Thaiss early on that her
brother was sleeping through long stretches of the
passing decades, preserving his body via arcane means
that Tom didn't pretend to understand. Presumably

the intent was to outlive his sister and claim the city by default if all else failed. So she started doing the same, secure in her isolation here at the Thair's source. Woken to replenish Thaiburley's core at regular intervals by pilgrims from the religion she founded specifically for the purpose – the only people trusted with details of her location – Thaiss slept secure in the knowledge that alarms would rouse her should the city come under threat. So the centuries rolled by.

All this had changed in comparatively recent times, during the Great War which still held such dark memories for the City of Dreams's inhabitants, though it had ended more than a century ago. The city had come close to falling and had suffered appalling damage, but Thaiss's brother had finally been vanquished. Killed. Or so Tom's newfound knowledge insisted. Evidently, this knowledge wasn't without flaw.

"Somehow, he's corrupted the core," Thaiss said.

"The Prime Master said something about the core being damaged during the War," Tom added. The malaise, the sense of detachment that had afflicted him in recent days as he pondered matters internally, was receding by steady degree, like a veil lifting from his mind. What Thaiss was saying fascinated him, stimulating his innate curiosity and helping him to look outward again, focussing on the present.

The goddess nodded. "Yes, more than just damaged, it seems. He's actually imprinted himself on the stack, so that even after his physical form died he's been able to live on within it. Cunning. Twisted and cunning, which shouldn't surprise me in the least. He's been there all this time, establishing himself, insidiously spreading his influence and working against the city from within, erasing records and promoting his own agenda. No doubt subtly at first but growing bolder as he became more secure. His first priority would have been to ensure the core wasn't renewed as scheduled, which would have driven him out."

"But why?" Mildra asked. "He doesn't have an army with which to conquer us now, so what's he hoping to achieve?"

"The downfall of Thaiburley. We might have built the city together but it never became his home. He hates it as he hates me, and won't be content until the City of a Hundred Rows is no more."

"Can he really hope to do that?"

"Regrettably, yes. With the core under his thrall he could bring the whole city down. All he needs is to gain a sufficient level of control, and he's well on the way to doing so." Her gaze fastened on Tom. "You must replenish the core, Tom, restore it so that my brother's influence can be flushed out once and for all. Thaiburley is doomed if you don't, and there's not a moment to lose."

Tom nodded, now fully focussed as the gravity of the situation registered. He couldn't help but note that things always seemed to depend on him, no matter how hard he sought to avoid them.

"But how can we possibly get back in time?" Mildra asked.

Her words triggered memories of the long days they'd spent travelling to the citadel and the treacherous terrain that now stretched between them and Thaiburley.

"Oh, I don't think you need worry about that," the goddess assured them. "The return trip will take no time at all. Tom will make sure it doesn't."

"I will?"

"Certainly. You've seen how the Prime Master moves around the city, haven't you?"

"Yes…" Tom admitted, cautiously.

"Anything he can do, you can do. Your genetic make-up is closer to pure founder than anyone's in centuries. The core will respond to you in every way possible."

"Maybe, but I don't know *how*."

"No, but I do."

The goddess reached forward and touched the centre of his forehead. The fingertip felt warm on his skin, but otherwise nothing changed. There was no spread of warmth as from a healer's touch, no shift of perspective which he might have been anticipating… nothing at all.

And yet – *and yet* – Tom blinked. Suddenly he *did* know. In fact it was so obvious he felt as if he'd *always* known. "That's all there is to it?" he asked.

"Yes."

One thing still bothered him. "The Prime Master can only move between specific points in the city, but it feels as though I can go anywhere."

"You *can* go anywhere, and so could he, at least in theory."

"Then why…?"

"Convention. The Prime Master was taught that his talent could only take him to specific points, so he expects to reach only those points. As a result, he *can* reach only those points. You, on the other hand, are unburdened by any such preconceptions."

Tom laughed. "If the founders could do this, why did they even bother with stairs and the clockwork lifts and that elevator thing when they built the city?"

"Because even in the early days there were far more of this world's native people in Thaiburley than there ever were founders. We established the city as a haven for our people, not to be a prison. We knew that if they were to survive they had to mingle with local races rather than stay aloof from them, so the city was always intended to be multicultural, to become a focal point for this world, for the native races and founders alike."

"With the locals acting as servants and labourers," Mildra said, surprising Tom with her candidness.

"Not entirely, but yes; initially it fell that way for the most part. We knew, though, that the situation was only temporary. Inevitably over the course of generations bloodlines mingled and racial distinctions blurred."

"Is that where the levels verse came from?" Tom wanted to know. The familiar words ran through his mind:

From the Streets Below to the Market Row,
From taverns and stalls to the Shopping Halls,
From trinkets so cheap to exclusive boutique,
From the Cloth-Makers' Row and people who sew,
To haberdashers, tailors, and upward we go...

"A way of making sure everyone would know their place even after all this blurring?" he continued.

"Perhaps," Thaiss conceded. "That wasn't something we did. That confounded rhyme seemed to spring up spontaneously. I awoke from one of my first sleeps to discover that in my absence the levels verse had established itself throughout the city. I've no idea where it originated, even. A very powerful meme, though obviously."

"A what?"

The goddess shook her head impatiently. "Never mind; a term from another age. You have to realise that so much time has passed…" For a moment it seemed to Tom that the goddess was speaking more for her own benefit than for his and Mildra's. "The periods of sleep have meant that over a thousand years have been and gone since Thaiburley was founded. I don't think either of us planned this far ahead. You probably don't appreciate how unique this is, for a city to stand for such a length of time virtually unchanged, neither expanding nor contracting. I sometimes think Thaiburley should be called the Eternal City rather than the City of Dreams.

"However, it won't be standing for much longer unless we get a move on."

Tom started, fiddling with his shirt and shifting his feet. He realised that he'd been standing still, almost in a trance while Thaiss spoke, lost in the imagery of her words, which resonated with so much of his assimilated memories.

"You'll need this." The goddess held out his old

backpack, the same one that had accompanied him all the way from Thaiburley.

Tom took it without query, though he was wondering *why* he'd be needing it.

Thaiss then offered him a squat cylinder, perhaps a little longer than a man's forearm and half again as broad. She held it in two hands, with a care that bordered on reverence.

The tube itself was a thing of beauty. Fashioned from leather stained a rich reddish brown, it was banded at intervals by strips of gleaming brass which also formed a rim at either end. As Tom took the container he saw a multiple, fragmented image of his own face reflected in the brass, distorted by its curvature. The cylinder had a very obvious lid at one end – snug-fitting and sealed by two studs – and a leather strap so that it could be carried by hand or perhaps attached to a belt. As Tom first laid hands upon this beautiful object he felt a tingle dance along his arm.

"Pure concentrated core material," the goddess said. "Shielded, contained, but you can still sense it, can't you?"

Tom nodded, his mouth suddenly dry, as he contemplated what he was being charged to carry and deliver.

"Open this only once you're physically standing in front of the core, and when you do, point it straight towards the core. Do you understand?"

Again Tom nodded, not trusting himself to speak.

"If the container is opened under any other circumstances, the results could be catastrophic."

Great. No pressure, then; just what Tom needed to hear.

As he placed the cylinder carefully into his rucksack, having to manoeuvre it a little to make it fit, Mildra reappeared, without his having realised she'd even gone.

She was dressed once again in the full green robes of a Thaistess. It was odd seeing her like that again. It had been easy to forget she was a Thaistess at all for much of the journey here, she'd become simply Mildra.

She evidently noted his scrutiny and held her arms out, displaying the robe. "This seemed the appropriate thing to wear, given that we're going home."

Tom nodded, realising that she was right. He lifted the rucksack and slipped the straps over his shoulders, shrugging a little until the cylinder settled into a comfortable position.

Thaiss appraised them both and smiled, as if happy with her work.

"Go, my brave children, go and save our city."

Tom braced himself, hoping this would work, but before he could do more than begin to focus Mildra spoke up, interrupting his concentration.

Early in their relationship with the goddess, Mildra had expressed concern for Dewar, the man she and Tom had been forced to abandon in the lee of a ruined Thaissian temple on the final leg of their journey to the citadel. Their erstwhile leader had apparently been in a coma and neither of them felt happy about leaving him behind, but they couldn't see any other choice.

In response to their concern, Thaiss's eyes had glazed over for a few seconds, as if staring at some distant point. "Don't worry," she had then said. "I've sent him warmth and done what I can to heal his mind. It bears many scars from traumas old and new, but these should all trouble him a little less when he awakens."

The implication that he *would* awaken came as huge relief to Tom, who held himself responsible for many of those scars, at least the more recent ones.

Now, as they prepared to leave, Mildra asked the goddess to check on Dewar again.

After a glaze-eyed instant, Thaiss declared, "There is no one at the temple site."

"What?"

"Surely that's a good sign," Tom said quickly.

"The man has clearly left, hopefully of his own volition," the goddess said.

"*Hopefully*?" Mildra raised her eyebrows, as if to suggest she'd expected more.

"Child, you've done what you can for him; *I've* done what I can. This one man is no longer your responsibility. Your only concern now should be for the safety of the city that birthed you and all who dwell there."

"Dewar will be fine," Tom said. "He's a survivor, you know that."

Mildra nodded and favoured him with a tight, unconvinced smile. "*We* left him there, Tom."

He hardly needed reminding. "I know."

His anxiety must have shown, because her smile changed to one of reassurance and she reached across to squeeze his hand. It was a testament to how nervous

Tom felt that he barely noticed. This was it. He was about to take them across half a continent in the blink of an eye, a journey the like of which he'd never attempted before.

He closed his eyes. Not essential, but he wanted to rule out any distractions.

"Remember," Thaiss said, "picture the person you most need to see, hold that image and focus on it."

The Prime Master. But why was he finding it so difficult to picture the man's face? He'd seen it often enough. Stature and general shape of the face, yes, he had that, but the details were proving more difficult to visualise than he ever would have imagined. What colour were the eyes – brown? Blue? He could only hope such detail didn't matter, that what stood before his mind's eye would prove enough. Satisfied that this was as clear as he was likely to manage, Tom began to reach out as the goddess had taught him. It was an odd sensation, not the flicking of some mental switch, more a flowing of thought, a sluggish slide that swiftly became a surge and then continued to gain momentum, pulling at his mind and at his inner self.

It was working! Tom could sense his body beginning to shift, moving in concert with his mind and spirit. He felt triumphant, elated. *He* was doing this. He was taking them back to Thaiburley, avoiding all the walking and the climbing and the days of sitting on boats that had brought them here. Nobody else was doing this, just him.

Despite his best efforts, his concentration waivered for an instant as he was swept away on the wave of his own success. In that instant his thoughts turned briefly to the people he missed and would now be able to see again. Foremost among them, he thought of Kat.

The man came awake abruptly; instantly alert, as if something had disturbed his sleep. He felt chilly, but not excessively so. He kicked out, disturbing the cloak which covered him. The fur on the outside was stiff with frost as he pushed it to one side – a woolly board moulded to the shape of his own body. Not just frost, snow. The sudden movement disturbed a large long-necked bird, which squawked and hopped back in alarm before taking to the air properly and sailing away on broad, splayed wings. A vulture, a carrion eater.

Cold assailed him, nipping at his cheeks and nose, emphasising how insulated he'd been beneath the cloak. Snow topped the rocks and the crumbling walls around him, while the air had that bright crystal clarity which only winter brings and his breath billowed in cooling clouds.

Suddenly ravenous, he examined the small parcels that had rested beside him in his slumber, tearing open the packaging to discover dried meats, a wax-sealed truckle of a creamy white cheese, a bar of stale, crumbly cake and a small stack of travel wafers. The meats went first, teeth tearing and mouth swallowing the salty toughness before taste had a chance to blossom. His throat was dry, the swallowing difficult. No drink had been left among the provisions so thoughtfully provided for him, but the abundance of snow rendered that immaterial. He clawed up a handful of whiteness and brought it to his mouth. The cold made his gums ache but the cool melt water trickling down his throat soon eased the rawness.

Bites of tangy cheese and chunks of dry bread interspersed with more scoops of snow followed, and soon he began to feel human once again. Hunger sated for the moment, he stood up and took stock. The wind howled through the ruins like a chorus of restless spirits but the sky held few clouds and there seemed little threat of any more snow for the moment.

He remembered these ruins and dimly recalled the fight that he had interrupted here, but he had no clear memory of what happened next. Despite this he felt well, surprisingly so. In fact his thoughts seemed clearer than they had in a long while, as if the long sleep had helped heal the darkness in his soul, a malignancy that had been festering for more time than he cared to think of.

He knew what had to be done, what should have been done a long time ago, and the lack of doubt or confusion was a revelation of a sort he would never have expected, particularly here, on a barren snow-swept mountainside, among the ruins of a derelict Thaissian temple.

The cloak he reclaimed, dusting off the crystals of ice and rubbing and rolling it to break the stiffness before slinging it around his shoulders. The remains of the food he abandoned for the rodents and the birds to pick over. His course was clear, his immediate destination certain, and there wasn't far to go.

He didn't head north, the direction the quest would have taken him – the boy and the Thaistess were long gone by now, their fate no longer his to influence; he dismissed them from his thoughts. Instead he turned to the southeast and set off towards the nearest town, the settlement of Pilgrimage End.

He was Dewar, and he had things to do.

FIVE

"She's definitely in there," the arkademic confirmed, opening her eyes. The fact that the woman then gave an involuntary shudder, as if touched by an unexpected chill, was all the convincing Kat needed.

They stood a little removed from a ruined building – the first they'd encountered here. Tylus identified it as the remains of a monitoring station, built not long after the city's founding, when some regulation of the Stain was still being attempted. The building had clearly once been a tower, its circular shape evident in the ring of stubby brickwork that remained, though it had long since collapsed. It sat there now like the tattered stump of a fallen tree or perhaps the stubborn remnants of a rotted tooth.

They had reached the ruin without any further incidents of note. A rat the size of a spill dragon had briefly confronted them, though it looked as startled by their presence as they were by its and had soon turned and scurried away. A little later, a thick tentacle had whipped into the air, falling just short of one of the Kite Guards soaring above it before dropping back into the undergrowth. They'd given the relevant area a wide berth and seen nothing further of the creature or plant responsible. Other than that, things had been uneventful.

The crumbled tower sat in a slight depression, as if the ground had sunk a little beneath its weight, though Tylus insisted otherwise when Kat commented to that effect, claiming that much of the detritus they now walked on would have settled after the station was built.

The most disturbing aspect of the place was that no grasses or brambles or even moss had risen to claim it; the brickwork looked old but clear, as if it were too unwholesome for even the vegetation that flourished here to grow on. No, forget that. The most unsettling thing about the place was that the arkademic reckoned the Soul Thief was hidden somewhere inside it.

"You're sure?" Kat had asked on their arrival, not willing to risk any error where this was concerned.

The woman had nodded. "Positive, but my long sight can confirm it."

Kat had never heard of long sight but was willing to bet the clue was in the name. If half the things rumoured about arkademics were true, this one doubtless had all sorts of tricks and weird abilities up her sleeve.

Arkademic Haq closed her eyes. Kat watched closely, waiting for something else to happen – an aura, a shimmering – some indication of arcane manipulation, but she was to be disappointed. Everyone stood waiting, even the Kite Guards were grounded by mutual consent, nobody wanting to go too close and risk alerting their quarry.

Oddly there was no real sense of anticipation or excitement, which Kat would have expected to feel, just a general air of impatience, though maybe that was just her. A minute or two dragged by before Isar returned to herself and gave the confirmation they'd been waiting for.

Now Kat began to get excited. "Right," she said, preparing to address the men.

"Kat...?"

What did the blasted arkademic want? "Yes?"

"Your swords, they won't touch it you know, they won't do any real damage." Kat knew, but that didn't mean she wanted to be reminded of the fact. "I can attune them," Isar continued.

"Nobody touches my swords."

"I won't need to."

Kat glared at the older woman. "If you do anything to damage them..."

"I won't, I promise. This will simply establish a resonance between your blades and that part of my whip which the Soul Thief absorbed. I doubt it'll give you enough to kill or even to seriously injure her, but you should be able to hurt her."

Kat smiled her dark smile and, without saying anything further, whipped out her twin blades and presented them. The arkademic reached out with both her hands spread, holding them palms downward just above the proffered swords, as if the weapons were braziers she could warm herself over on a chill winter's night. Again Kat watched closely but was disappointed. There was no glow, no spark of light, nothing overt to indicate anything at all was happening. A few seconds, that was all it took, before Isar looked up and smiled. "There."

"Is that it?" Kat said. What was the point of being an arkademic with all these wonderful talents if you couldn't be flash about it from time to time? Isar nodded, evidently happy with herself.

Kat's smile was sweeter this time. "You couldn't do the same thing to the darts carried by our flechette gunners, could you?"

"Certainly."

Once that was dealt with, Kat quickly organised the Tattooed Men, though it took longer to get everyone in position than she'd have liked. The attack would come from five sides; one aerial and four at ground level. Two members of the Blade remained close to Isar, while the balance formed one groundside attack force; the Tattooed Men provided the other three, with Kat taking over the leadership of Half-hand's squad. The Kite Guards would attack from above, though quite what use they'd be or how they'd cope if the Soul Thief decided to go after them remained to be seen.

Tylus seemed confident enough. When Kat tried to warn him what they were about to go up against he gave a knowing grin and said, "Don't worry, we've got a few surprises of our own."

Smug bastard. Kat shook her head, tempted to say more but seeing no point in her fretting; she'd just have to trust that the Kite Guards really were capable of keeping their end tight. Maybe the sheer presence of so many flying things buzzing around would keep the Soul Thief groundside where Kat and the others could get to grips with the monster and settle things once and for all.

Finally, M'gruth's squad were in position; they'd skirted around to the far side of the ruin and so had further to go than anyone else. Kat raised one sword above her head and twirled it – quite impressively, she thought – giving the agreed signal. Everyone started forward, their wide circumference constricting rapidly. Kat got a real kick out of knowing that the Blade had just moved into action at her command. Who'd have thought it?

The earlier flat tedium of inaction was forgotten. As they closed in on the Soul Thief's layer, Kat could feel the excitement ratcheting up with every stride. Surely the bitch had to be aware of them by now, or was she so confident of her power that she slept soundly and unguarded out here?

Anyway, who said she was asleep?

The Kite Guards were the first to spot it. They circled above the stump of the ruined building like flies above a rotting corpse. One of them shouted something and Kat didn't need to hear the individual words to catch their meaning. Seconds later she could see it for herself. A black fog had begun to emerge from the stunted building, drifting out to tumble over the edges of the brickwork like liquid boiling from an overheated beaker in some experiment of the Maker's.

The inky mist fell to the ground where it pooled and gathered and started to take shape; a column of darkness which built quickly, facing directly towards Kat.

As the column was still forming and the suggestion of a face within that swirling darkness was still more imagination than actual impression, one of the figures circling above dipped its wing and dived towards the Thief.

"No!" Kat yelled, even as she realised it was Tylus. *The idiot!*

But the Kite Guard didn't plummet all the way down to engage the Thief hand-to-mist as she'd expected. Instead he banked and levelled out, passing a little above the broiling figure. As he came close, something dropped from his belt, a fist-sized package that arced towards the Soul Thief to strike the ground at the foot of the black column. On impact the package exploded.

Kat laughed. A bomb; *the Kite Guards were carrying bombs!*

The sound was deafening. Flame and smoke and clods of grass, mouldering earth and rotted detritus rose up at one edge of where the Soul Thief stood. Its developing form waivered and a shriek of pain or perhaps alarm rose from the mouth, which was now clearly visible.

The shriek was music to Kat's ears. Tylus may have struck before she was fully ready, but she couldn't argue with the results, and perhaps it was just as well none of them had been any closer with bombs flying around. Two more Kite Guards were following Tylus' lead, swooping in and dropping grenades. Kat turned to Tug, the Tattooed Man immediately to her left, and said. "Hit her!"

Tug nodded, braced himself, levelled the flechette gun he was carrying, and squeezed the trigger. A stream of metal slivers blasted from the muzzle, crossing the intervening distance in an instant and scything into the Thief's billowing form just as the two bombs went off one after the other, the sounds buffeting Kat's ears like the staggered beat of a giant's heart. The shriek was constant now, a wail of frustration and pain. They were hurting the bitch.

This wasn't Iron Grove Square. There was no Brent and no would-be street gangsters to intervene. This time the creature whose murderous deeds had shaped so much of Kat's life wouldn't escape. She was going down, whatever it took.

M'gruth's squad had moved in closer, shifting around the tower stub for a better angle. Their flechette gun now joined the fray as another pair of Kite Guards swooped in. Metal darts were tearing into the substance of the Soul Thief from two sides, passing through to chew into the more solid wall behind.

"Careful!" Kat screamed, as the stream of darts from M'gruth's gunner flew through the Thief and past the tower, coming perilously close to Ox and his group who were manoeuvring around the opposite side of the ruin. Good leader that he was, M'gruth had already recognised the danger and instructed his man to stop firing, motioning for him to move around further so that he would only threaten the brickwork rather than his fellows. Kat's gunner continued to keep the Thief occupied as the Kite Guards swooped in.

This pair proved less accurate than their colleagues, their bombs landing a fair bit wide of the target; due in part, no doubt, to the Soul Thief contracting. The smoky column collapsed rapidly into a dense ball which slipped and drifted around the side of the tower towards Ox, trying to get away.

Kat went to yell at Ox but there was no need. The big man had already unslung the equipment from his back, flipped open the tripod with practiced ease and was slipping the cylinders into place. Beside him, a flechette gunner opened up, trying to persuade the Thief not to come any further around the tower after all. Kat signalled her own gunner to stop, to offer their target an easier route back the way it had come.

The Kite Guards were back, two of them stooping for another run, right to left as Kat watched. They were getting cocky; this pair flew lower than any before them. The bombs were dropped, driving the Soul Thief back towards Kat, but this time the Thief was ready to try something different. She attacked, taking the initiative for the first time, funnelling away from the blast and stretching upwards with incredible speed. A strand of darkness shot into the air, as if drawn there by the Kite Guard's passage. It touched a trailing leg of the nearest Guard, instantly solidifying around the man's ankle.

"No," Kat yelled, as, for an instant, the Kite Guard floundered, reaching for the air as if hoping to grasp it and somehow keep himself aloft. Then he was quite literally yanked from the sky.

It all happened so quickly. One moment the Kite Guard was sailing majestically past, the next his cape folded and he'd been brought crashing to the ground. The inky blackness drew on that treacherous tether and used it to flow across, enveloping the fallen Guard.

Kat was already on the move, sprinting forward. The flechette gunners had been caught by surprise. They'd adjusted now but couldn't fire for fear of hurting the fallen man, and the other Kite Guards weren't about to attack while one of their own was at risk. It was down to her. They'd been hurting the bitch, and now it was about to draw the life force from a victim and replenish its energies, undoing everything they'd achieved. Not if Kat could help it.

She didn't give a thought to whether Isar's trick with her swords had worked or not, to whether she could actually *harm* the Soul Thief in any way, she simply reacted. Her arms pumped, sword in each hand in a manner that had become second nature to her, as she closed the gap across the uneven ground. Someone shouted her name but she ignored them. It was just her and the Thief now.

She struck even as she arrived, a crude overhand blow accompanied by a shriek of effort and anger and hate. Her blade bit. She felt a hint of resistance as she drew it through the murky insubstance. The Kite Guard had been completely hidden beneath the Soul Thief, but at Kat's blow the darkness seemed to flinch, pulling in on itself. Kat's other blade followed the first. She struck again and again, in a fighting rhythm that came as naturally as breathing. The Soul Thief shied away from her blades, the Kite Guard evidently forgotten as it came upright, the wheedling yowl of its hurt, its indignity, ringing in her ears. She smelt rot and decay and death. A face took shape in the creature's shadowy form.

"Kat, don't, please… you're hurting me!" Chavver, her features wracked with anguish, pleading, begging. The ghost of her sister, resurrected to disarm her. She'd expected this, steeled herself against it, but still it hit home – a bolt of loss slicing through her heart – but that wasn't enough to make her hesitate. If anything, she increased the tempo of her assault. This wasn't her sister. Charveve would never have begged, she would have died first.

Next the face shifted into that of her mother, looking exactly as memory painted her, as if the passage of time hadn't marked her at all. "Why are you doing this to me… your own mother? All that remains of me is here. Katarina, please don't…" The shadowy face, so familiar from painful memory, plucked at her heart strings, but this wasn't enough to stop her either. The Thief had played this card before and this time around it only made Kat redouble her efforts yet again.

"Kat!" That might have been M'gruth, but she'd pay attention to whatever he wanted later.

Then her blade carried a little too far, or perhaps the darkness deliberately shifted. Her wrist brushed against the Thief, sinking a little into its misty substance where it stuck fast. Kat couldn't pull free.

The face no longer pleaded. Instead it gloated. "Foolish, foolish girl. Come to join your mother and sister, have you?"

Kat's arm felt cold, numbed, and she could no longer hold her sword. She watched the weapon tip from her unresponsive fingers and tumble towards the ground, seeming to fall in slow motion.

She tried to twist, to pull away, but the darkness held her firm. In fact it was pulling her in, picking at her inner being.

It suddenly occurred to Kat that she might die. Strength flowed out of her, drawn along that captured arm. Somewhere deep inside her a savage, bitter laugh threatened to bubble through. What did it matter? What did she have to live for anyway? But she couldn't die, not quite yet; not until the Soul Thief had first paid for all the hurt and misery she'd caused.

Regrets piled one on top of another in her mind. Why hadn't she listened to M'gruth when he called her? Why hadn't she pulled back when it was obvious there was no saving the fallen Kite Guard? They were hesitating because of her, she now realised. Her presence was *protecting* the bitch. Flechettes couldn't fly, bombs wouldn't fall, all because she was in the way.

"Don't worry about me," Kat yelled. "Just kill the bitch!"

That face, so like her mother's, seemed to swell, occupying all the Soul Thief's form. It demanded attention, capturing Kat's gaze and refusing to let her look anywhere else even for an instant.

She felt her soul, if that's what it was – her inner spirit, the very essence of who she was – well up, pulled inexorably forward; a horrible, stretching, wrenching sense of being ripped apart from within, that made her want to retch and shriek at the same time. "No!" she growled through gritted teeth. She couldn't, *wouldn't* let it end like this.

Somebody else was there, at her left-hand side, a presence dimly sensed.

Kat abruptly snapped back to herself, reeling at the sudden return of perspective, welcome though it was. M'gruth stood beside her, clutching a flechette gun, mouth contorted into a scream of savage challenge as he poured metal round after metal round into the Thief.

Kat brought her other hand up, sword still gripped in rigid fist, and sliced through the inky bond that held her other wrist.

She staggered free. "M'gruth... pull back, let the others finish this," she said, her voice lost against the incessant chatter of the flechette gun. He hadn't heard her or didn't want to hear her. He might have come in close to help but his focus was now entirely on the Soul Thief, his face set in a snarl as he played the stream of darts over the creature's twitching, dancing form.

Others were there now, off to one side – Ox and his team, the big man having carried the flame thrower with him. Tripod down and firmly grounded, Ox just needed a clear shot.

"M'gruth, fall back!" Kat yelled.

Then, disaster. In evading the darts tormenting her, the Soul Thief streamed away from the tower. Caught up in the moment, M'gruth followed, tracking her movements with the muzzle of the gun, trigger still depressed and darts tearing through her dwindling body and beyond… to rip into Ox and one of the men beside him. Both went down, gouting blood.

"M'gruth!"

He stopped then, mouth falling open in dismay. The Soul Thief was greatly diminished after the pummelling she had taken, the humped form suggesting that of a hunch-backed old woman as she cowered; but she re-acted first, seizing her chance and flowing towards the stupefied man. Given a choice the Thief always went for talent. She had raided the streets at erratic intervals to harvest the seers and the healers and the other gifted, but evidently when push came to shove she could feed off any life force, as the unfortunate Kite Guard had so recently discovered. Kat ran forward, snatching up her fallen sword in her still-recovering hand and preparing to throw herself upon her nemesis once more. She wasn't about to let M'gruth die, not for her sake; in fact she had no intention of losing *anyone* else to this mur-derous hag.

"Hey, you! Soul Thief! Where the breck do you think you're going, you coward? Come back here and finish what you started."

The nebulous form paused, gathering itself into an upright near-human form. The outline of a face coa-lesced once more as if to encourage the impression. "As you wish," a voice seemed to whisper. The dark-ness flowed towards her.

She braced herself and a smile creased the corners of her mouth. This was it: do or die; her against the Soul Thief. Just the way she'd always imagined it would be.

Then the world tore apart; or at least the air did, quite literally. There came a rippling between the Thief and Kat, a peculiar twisting. Kat shuffled back, was *forced* back, by an intense gust of wind. It only lasted for an instant, the air falling deathly still immediately after, but in that instant two people had appeared out of nowhere.

Kat gaped. "Tom?" And beside him a woman she recognised, a Thaistess, though she couldn't quite recall her name.

"Kat?" He looked as bewildered as she felt.

There was the suggestion of movement behind the two new arrivals. "Look out!" Tom and the Thaistess were facing towards Kat, they wouldn't even realise that the monster was at their backs, let alone that it was coming straight for them.

The distance was no distance at all. Even as Tom began to react to her warning, black mist welled up behind him, as if set to engulf boy and Thaistess alike. Tendrils of night reached forward to encircle both their heads. The woman – Mildra, memory suddenly supplied – froze, her eyes opening wide as if from shock.

Kat was only a few paces away, and wasn't about to stand by and simply watch. With a snarl, she raised her good hand, brandishing her sword, and... flinched.

Searing light erupted from Tom's head, annihilating the fingers of darkness that had been attempting to grasp his skull.

What the hell? Kat squinted, struggling to stare into that light, where she beheld a night black form rear up behind the lad, brightly illuminated by the energy pouring from him. Mildra had fallen over or collapsed, and was now sitting with one hand pressed to the ground for support and the other raised to shield her eyes as she too looked towards that darkness: the Soul Thief.

The Thief had adopted a surprisingly solid-looking form, notably human though ragged at the edges as though flayed. Two protuberances sprung from her shoulders to sweep outwards before fading into wispy nothingness; they might almost have been wings. For an instant only, through screwed-up watering eyes, Kat beheld that form. Then it tore apart, quickly and violently. The raggedness extended, like a multitude of tears in paper swiftly spreading across an entire sheet. One instant there was a recognisable shape, the next it was rendered into a collection of mere strips that disappeared as if swept away by a gale. The brightness died and for a moment the whole world seemed still.

All Kat could do was stare; unable, unwilling, to accept what she had just witnessed.

Both swords slipped from her numb fingers as the truth slowly sank in. The Soul Thief was gone. The bane of her life had just been slain before her eyes, swept away as if it were nothing by a mere slip of a boy Kat had considered a friend.

Tom, now looking like any ordinary kid, turned towards her, smiling broadly.

"No!" Kat shouted.

"Kat, it's all right, I'm not hurt."

"Hurt? You stupid brecking bastard!" She flung herself at him, clenched fists pummelling his shoulder and head.

"Ow! Hey, stop. What's wrong? I thought... will you stop hitting me!" He was backing away, arms crossed in front of his face for protection against the barrage of over-arm blows raining down upon him. Kat wasn't aiming to hurt, not really, he'd have been writhing on the ground by now if she had been. She just needed to hit *something*.

"It was supposed to be *me*," she sobbed. He'd cheated her, robbed her of the only thing that might have brought her some peace, some closure. After a lifetime of hating and hurting, of scheming and dreaming, of imagining the sweet taste of revenge, he'd snatched it away from her. "*I* should have killed her. Not you, not anyone else... *Me*. Don't you understand?" Her one chance of redeeming herself, of making up for her shortcomings and putting things right with her mother and her sister, gone in an instant.

"I... I'm sorry," he said as the assault subsided. "That thing attacked me. What was I supposed to do?"

"I don't know, I don't *care*. I just... Argh!" How could he ever understand? How could anyone? Without saying another word she swivelled on her heel and strode away, fists still clenched, head bowed to hide the tears from Tom, from M'gruth, from everybody.

Tom stared after Kat, exasperated. What was wrong with her for Thaiss's sake? He'd arrived here disorientated, elated that he'd managed his first ever materialisation as more than a mere passenger, to find himself... where? Was this the *Stain*? And before he had a chance to get his feet properly on the ground he'd been attacked, his mind assaulted by the most evil and invasive presence he'd ever encountered. Cold, dank, *horrible*. The mere memory was enough to make him shudder. What did she expect him to do, stand there and let that thing kill him? Of course he'd lashed out.

Quite spectacularly, he had to admit. His talent had never manifested so visibly before. It wasn't deliberate, he'd just been aware of an all-consuming darkness creeping into his head, like a damp, cold cloth, numbing his thoughts and pulling at his very being, as if trying to loosen it and winkle his spirit from his body. Light had been an instinctive response, to counter the dark. Maybe he could work on that, though; he kind of liked the effect.

As for Kat... who did she think she was? The frissing monster was dead. What did it matter who'd done the killing? If anything she should be *thanking* him, not cursing and beating him about the head. Still, he didn't suppose Kat would ever make the first move to apologise; no, that would be up to him no doubt. With a sigh, Tom went to follow her, to explain, but he was stopped by a restraining hand on his arm.

"Don't," Mildra said, her gentle face showing sympathy, concern. "Not yet. Give her a few moments to collect herself. She isn't in the mood to listen to reason right now."

Tom drew a ragged breath and nodded. Mildra was

doubtless right, as usual. He'd wait. So all that followed Kat was his gaze.

Kat walked away from everyone, suddenly desperate for
some space. Ox groaned loudly from behind her and
that almost gave her pause, but she breathed deeply
and kept going. Why was she being so stupid? The Soul
Thief was finally dead. Her mother, her sister, every single person that monstrosity had ever consumed, could
finally rest in peace. If someone had brought her that
news at any other time she would have rejoiced. So why
did she feel so angry now, so *cheated*?

It wasn't Tom's fault, she knew that. Beating up on
him wasn't going to achieve anything – and where the
breck had he and Mildra appeared from in any case?
She glanced back, to catch Tom staring at her. He
looked away quickly as their eyes met. Beside him,
Mildra was already busy, tending to Ox and Petter, the
other Tattooed Man M'gruth's overzealousness had injured. A cluster of tattooed figures stood around her
as she worked. Kat hoped to Thaiss both the injured
men were going to be all right. She'd lost enough
friends of late and had precious few left to spare. Besides, M'gruth would be inconsolable if either of them
died, and he was one of her best lieutenants. She was
going to need him to be sharp and confident in the
days ahead, not distracted and questioning his own
competence. She remembered Shayna's prophetic
words and hoped she wouldn't end up regretting that
particular decision. The Thaistess had better be up to
the task.

Her gaze took in the rest of the group: the Kite Guards, now all firmly on the ground and seeing to their own fallen comrade, the arkademic in her pale blue robes standing close to Tylus, the Blade statue-still in the background...

Sudden realisation gripped her. No, she shouldn't blame Tom, not when there was someone else more deserving. *Where were the Blade?* She set off, jaw set, temper barely in check. It had all been about her, Ox, and M'gruth; fighting the Soul Thief had been left entirely to the Tattooed Men. *Where were the brecking Blade?* Had they just stood by and watched? Had they deliberately done so in the hope that the Tattooed Men would perish or at least take a severe pounding? What were their orders? She was itching for a scrap, sick of people playing games with her life.

"Hey!" she yelled, striding towards the Blade.

The arkademic stepped across. If not exactly blocking her path, Isar certainly made sure she was in direct line of sight. "What's the matter, Kat?"

"Out of the way, Isar," Kat told her. I don't have a problem with you, just with those walking pieces of coal over there."

"Perhaps I can mediate," Isar said. "The Blade rarely speak."

"Rarely fight much either, far as I can see," Kat snapped. Standing beside the arkademic, Tylus looked uncomfortable. Perhaps even a little embarrassed. Clearly he had no intention of getting involved in this if he could help it.

"Ah, I see," the arkademic said. "You're upset because

the Blade didn't get involved in the battle with the Soul Thief."

"*Upset*? Two of my men nearly died just now, still may do, while the mighty Blade just stood around and watched. *Of course I'm upset*!"

"They stayed their hand out of respect for you," Isar said calmly.

"Respect? What the breck are you talking about, *respect*?"

"When the other creature with the metallic legs and sting attacked us from beneath the ground, you didn't want the Blade to interfere but were determined to handle it yourselves. They assumed the same applied here and that you would call on them if you wanted their help."

Kat paused, realising the arkademic might have a point, but that didn't stop her for long. "If I didn't want them to help I wouldn't have included them as part of the attack plan."

"They assumed you wanted them there for containment, to prevent the monster escaping."

Kat scowled, not sure whether to believe Isar or not, but the woman's calm arguments had succeeded in taking the edge off her temper. Even so, the whole thing smacked of justification to her, of making excuses after the event. She glared towards the row of towering figures standing impassively behind the arkademic and raised her voice to ensure they didn't miss her words. "Yeah, well next time we're getting our collective asses kicked by a monster straight from hell, tell them to feel free to pitch in anytime they want."

"They realise their mistake and will not remain un-
involved again."

Kat suspected that this was the closest to an apology
she was likely to get. Brecking cloud scrapers.

She turned away, rudely perhaps; rudely she *hoped*.
Now she supposed it was time to patch things up with
Tom, since clearly he didn't intend doing so. She
looked across to where he stood, his back turned towards her as he talked to M'gruth of all people. Kat
wasn't big on apologising, never had been. Best thing
to do in this instance, she reckoned, was to be all
friendly, make it clear everything was all right between
them by acting as if nothing had ever happened.

Tom couldn't hang around. No matter what was going
on here and how important it might be, his mission
had to come first. One of the Tattooed Men he vaguely
recognised, M'gruth, had been filling him in on what
was happening down here, but it wasn't really his concern; reaching the Prime Master with the core cylinder
was. He looked across to where Mildra crouched over
the fallen form of another Tattooed Man – the biggest
and meanest looking specimen Tom had ever seen. The
man was conscious, grumbling about the pain in a
good natured way while the Thaistess worked. Mildra
looked up and for a moment her gaze locked with
Tom's, then she gave a slight smile and a shallow nod,
indicating the wounded man before her. She understood, knew that he had to go, but that look told him
that she wouldn't be coming with him. The realisation
came as a shock, though hardly a surprise. Here in the

Stain a healer was badly needed, and it was typical of
Mildra that she'd choose to stay where her talent and
training could be of the most use, putting the needs of
others ahead of whatever she might want. It meant a
parting of the ways, and after all they'd been through
together that saddened him. Memories of her caring
smile, of her easing away the aches in his muscles after
a hard day of walking, of her naked skin beneath his
hands in the meadow of flowers chased each other
through Tom's mind as he returned her smile. No point
in making promises; these were uncertain times, but
he resolved to seek her out once this was all over, assuming they both survived. Even if he did, though, he
doubted the closeness they'd shared during the long
journey together could ever be recaptured now that
they were back in the real world of Thaiburley and all
that entailed.

For the moment, none of that mattered, it *couldn't*
matter. Tom had to find the Prime Master. He focused
on the man's familiar face. The details came more easily this time, and he was determined not to be
distracted again. He felt the rushing sensation that heralded transport.

"Hey, kid," Kat said, grasping his arm, presumably to
get his attention, speaking for all the world as if she
hadn't been trying to pummel him into the ground just
a few moments before. "Where exactly did you..."

They jumped and were suddenly somewhere else.

"...pop up from?"

"What did you do that for?" he snapped, angry with
her for distracting him despite all his good intentions.

"Do what? I didn't do *anything*."

"Yes you did. You grabbed hold of my arm."

"Well pardon me, your holiness. I didn't realise you'd become so precious these days that no one's allowed to even touch you."

Somebody cleared their throat. Kat's eyes widened as she evidently took in their surroundings for the first time. "Where the breck *are* we?"

They were in a small room, dominated by a plain oblong table around which were clustered an interesting assortment of individuals: a Jeradine who might or might not have been Ty-gen – Tom never had learnt to tell one from another – plus five elderly men and three women, all bar one of whom were looking at him and Kat in obvious astonishment, presumably due to their untimely arrival. The exception being the Prime Master, who smiled at them as if people materialising in front of his eyes was something that happened every day and the most natural thing in the world.

"Ah, Tom," the Prime Master said. "Glad you could join us."

SIX

Everyone agreed that time was of the essence. Tom was anxious to get going and the Prime Master kept insisting that he was at least as anxious as Tom. So why were they still standing around discussing things?

It turned out that he and Kat had materialised in the middle of an emergency session of the city's Council. He got the impression that this very functional neutrally-appointed room wasn't their usual meeting place but a location dictated by circumstances. Tom had never met the other members of Thaiburley's ruling body before – apart from his namesake, Thomas, the newest of their number – and he studied those present with interest. There was the Jeradine, who did indeed prove to be Ty-gen, an arkademic – distinguished by her customary powder blue robes – and six other members of the Council beside the Prime Master. Evidently Thomas was busy elsewhere and the other four members of Thaiburley's ruling twelve remained unaccounted for. The uncomfortable glances that passed among those present at mention of this told Tom all he needed to know regarding their suspected fate.

The arkademic was introduced as Assembly Member Birhoff and she had apparently been the first person to encounter the Rust Warriors, or the first to survive at any rate. Tom didn't pay much attention to her initially, but she seemed to pay plenty to him. The intensity with which she studied him made him squirm. She might have been the youngest of the group but that wasn't saying much and to Tom she still looked *old*. He tried to get away from her as quickly as possible. He wasn't certain whether there was anything lustful in her gaze or not, but either way it struck him as predatory and he wasn't buying her false smiles for a second, let alone her friendly overtures.

Tom had sensed something odd since his arrival, and finally he realised what it was. The prevailing atmosphere in this room, which contained more of the great and the powerful of Thaiburley than he had ever encountered before, was one of fear. These men and women, so used to resolving issues with a flex of talent or the stroke of a pen, were suddenly confronted with a problem they had no answer to. Their dismay was almost palpable, as they contemplated the very real prospect of losing control, a control which they had taken for granted all their lives.

Evidently the spiky mood Kat had demonstrated when Tom first appeared in the Stain hadn't entirely gone after all. This time it was the Jeradine who felt the sharp edge of her tongue. "Ty-gen?" she exclaimed. "What in Thaiss's name are you doing here?"

"Hello, Kat," said the familiar, inflexion-free voice. "It is good to see you too."

"You can forget all that 'good to see you' oxshit, I want to know what's going on. I was your contact for selling khybul figures to the City Above, remember? You said you needed me because you didn't know anyone up-City, and now I find you cosying up with the brecking *Council*?"

The Jeradine seemed completely nonplussed, and it was the Prime Master who stepped in to respond. "The Jeradine are an ancient race who have been a part of this city since its founding," he said. "Ty-gen is here at my invitation because the current emergency threatens all of us, and it was felt that his people's knowledge and wisdom might be of value."

Tom could only admire the Prime Master's skill at diplomacy. Here he was, the single most powerful person in a city of tens of millions, yet he still had the time and patience to explain himself to Kat, a mere street-nick. And this wasn't just because of the situation, it was simply how the Prime Master was, *who* he was. Tom felt pretty certain that had he been in the Prime Master's position just then, with the responsibility of a city in crisis resting on his shoulders, he'd have summoned the guards and had this irritating girl clapped in irons, or gagged at the very least.

"Look, this has been fun and everything," Kat then said, "but I have to get back to my men." Ty-gen and his perceived duplicity had evidently been dismissed from her thoughts in an instant. "When I left, two of them were badly injured, maybe dying. All of them are stuck in the middle of the Stain and their leader's just vanished into thin air. Thaiss only knows what's going on back there."

"You *can't*..." Tom began, then he saw Kat bridle and decided on a different approach. "I mean *I* can't; take you back that is, not right now at any rate."

"You'd better be able to."

He shook his head. "This is too important. There isn't time. The fate of the whole city..."

"...can go to hell in a body boys' cart for all I care. My people, my tribe, they're what matters. The rest of you feel free to look out for the city all you want, but, in the meantime, *take me back to the Stain!*"

"Your people, Kat, are a part of this city just as much as Ty-gen's," the Prime Master interrupted, speaking gently, soothingly. "I know it hasn't always seemed that way," he added quickly, holding up a restraining hand as she went to comment. "I can't begin to express my regret at what you all suffered in the Pits. Thaiburley is vast and at any given moment there are myriad demands on our attention. Reacting to everything that goes on in a timely manner isn't always easy. We do our best." There were nods of agreement from the other Masters. "But we're human, and we make mistakes. The Pits was an abomination that should never have been allowed to exist for as long as it did. We closed the place down in the end but we were far too slow. I know that; we all do. It's a failing that still weighs heavily on each and every one of us." This elicited more nods and even an *mmm* of agreement.

"The fact remains that the Tattooed Men are a part of Thaiburley, and the threat that now faces us imperils the future of the entire city, from the Heights all the way to the City Below. If Tom has returned from wherever he's been with a way to combat this threat, then we need to hear what he has to say without delay."

Kat harrumphed but seemed to accept the situation with a good grace that surprised Tom. In the past he had felt the full weight of the Voice of Command, the strength of compulsion that arkademics could muster when they needed to, and Kat's acquiescence had him wondering fleetingly if there were other Voices they could call upon, perhaps a Voice of Reason.

Tom realised with a start that all eyes had turned to him. They were all waiting for him to explain himself. So he told them. He didn't dwell on the journey to the citadel and the trials they'd faced – the death of Kohn and the loss of Dewar – instead concentrating on the discovery of the ice citadel, the meeting with Thaiss and what he had learnt, explaining about the goddess's brother and the subverted core, the missed renewal and the cleansing that the city's heart required, why this was so urgent and so vital. Finally he came to the container strapped to his back and its precious contents. Tom spoke as quickly and concisely as he could, covering everything in a handful of minutes. Throughout, he stared directly at the Prime Master, not wanting to be distracted by the reactions of these people he didn't know, nor even Kat's.

His words were met with complete silence, which lingered on for a few seconds after he'd concluded. For once, even Kat had nothing to say. At length, the Prime Master – who had surprised Tom by remaining seated since their arrival, not even standing up to greet him – shook his head. "So much has been lost to us," he said, smiling at Tom. "Thank you, on behalf of those of us here and, indeed, the whole city, for all that you've achieved. We have no right to ask any more of you, but I'm afraid we must, and I fear that the worst may still lie ahead of you."

Tom nodded, reckoning the gesture to be as eloquent as any words he might have come up with. He'd already accepted that this wasn't the end of things, that reporting to the Prime Master was no more than a stepping stone on the journey he found himself on, but he was counting on his mentor for some wise counsel at the very least.

"Can we see it?" Assembly Member Birhoff – "call me Carla" – said.

Tom hesitated. He glanced at the Prime Master, who shrugged to indicate that he had no objection. Seeing no reason to deny the request, Tom wriggled out of his rucksack, opened it up and withdrew the cylinder entrusted to him by the goddess. The leather felt warm to the touch and he imagined he could feel the core material it contained throbbing, though that may have been no more than his fancy.

"Is that it?" Birhoff exclaimed. "Is that small tube really supposed to renew the core of the entire city and save us?"

"It wouldn't need to be enormous," one of the Councillors said – Tom couldn't recall his name.

"Indeed not," the Prime Master agreed. "This is all about replenishment and the flushing out of impurity rather than total replacement. Besides, I'm not sure core material is governed by physical constraints as we know them."

"What…" Birhoff said, pausing, her brows knit as if her next words were of the utmost import and needed careful selection. "What if we didn't just use this to replenish the core?"

"How do you mean, Carla?" the Prime Master said, an ominous note in his voice.

"Think about it," she said. "The Rust Warriors have seized significant territories within our own city, despite the best efforts of our arkademics and guards and the Blade. They've done so because the core that we rely on, that we draw our powers from, is the very thing that spawned them. The core is corrupt, compromising our abilities and supporting our enemies. But here, come to us quite literally as a gift from the goddess, is a source of pure untainted core material, which has arrived in our hour of greatest need. Can that really be coincidence? And what do we intend doing with it? Entrust it to the care of this poor lad from the City Below and send him into the very heart of enemy territory. Forgive my impertinence, but am I the only one to see that this is madness? Instead of throwing away such an unexpected but glorious gift, why not utilise it? We could draw upon the uncompromised power it contains and drive the Rust Warriors from our city and, once we've done so, *then* worry about cleansing the core."

"Very eloquently put, Carla," the Prime Master said, "but you're not in the Assembly now. This isn't a debate. Our priority, above every other consideration, is to restore the core. Once we've done that, the Rust Warriors and even bone flu itself will cease to be a threat."

"I'm sorry if I presumed too much, Prime Master," Carla said quickly, displaying a facile humility which wasn't about to fool anyone. "I merely thought the case worth making."

"Which you have done and done well, but the core must be replenished and the sooner we do so the better."

Tom could only agree, relieved that no one seemed swayed by Carla's speech.

"Physical access to the core is limited, for obvious reasons," the Prime Master explained, turning towards Tom. "There are two communion platforms, one on this Row, the other two Rows beneath us. Both are in areas of the city we've lost to the Rust Warriors. This was one of the matters we were set to discuss at the meeting before your most welcome arrival. We'd assumed that this was pure coincidence – these aren't by any means the only sectors of the Heights the Rust Warriors now occupy – but after hearing what you've said, I'm inclined to believe it's deliberate. That being the case, it seems likely that the two platforms will be heavily defended."

"All well and good," Kat interrupted as he paused for breath, "but this still doesn't get me back to my men."

The Prime Master turned to her with a regretful smile. "Tom isn't exaggerating, Kat. From what he says, every second is indeed vital. If the city should fall, anarchy and death awaits us all – you, me, the Tattooed Men. So I'm asking this for all our sakes: help Tom. Work with him as you did before. By doing so you'll be helping everyone, including your own people, and I guarantee that afterwards you will be returned immediately to wherever you wish to go."

Tom stared at Kat, willing her to agree. Somehow whatever awaited him wouldn't seem so daunting with her prickly presence beside him. She in turn stared at the Prime Master, chewing her bottom lip for a thoughtful second before asking, "What's in it for me?"

Tom thought he knew Kat and that nothing she might do could surprise him anymore. He'd been wrong. He stared at her, astounded at her audacity. This wasn't some market stall holder she was addressing, ripe for a bit of bartering. This was the Prime Master of all Thaiburley for Thaiss's sake. Didn't she realise that? He held his breath and waited for his mentor's response, not entirely sure what to expect.

"Apart from saving the city and your people along with it, you mean?" the Prime Master said with arched eyebrows and the hint of a smile.

"Yeah, exactly; apart from all that. Look, you've got soldiers and guards, right? I'll bet none of them fight just for the warm glow of knowing that they're serving the city. Doing the right thing and saving all those innocent citizens won't put bread on the table or clothes on their backs now, will it. You *pay* them for what they do, right?"

The Prime Master nodded. "Indeed we do." The smile was definitely there now.

"So why do you expect me to put my life on the line here purely from a sense of duty? I mean, no one's talked about paying me and you don't even ask for that sort dedication from your own men."

"A point well made," the Prime Master conceded. "Now, let me see... would a sum of gold sufficient to keep you and your Tattooed Men in comfort for a full year satisfy you?"

Kat didn't hesitate. "Deal!"

Tom finally let out his breath. "*Now* can we get going?" he asked.

The answer, it emerged, was no.

Deciding on details, that was what delayed them. One thing Tom had learned since he'd arrived up-City was that things tended to take longer in the Heights than he was accustomed to. In the City Below, he'd have checked his knives, adjusted his backpack, and then set out; simple as that. Here, everything had to be *planned*.

Taken individually, everything made sense. Of course they would need protection: both the Blade and a contingent of Council Guards would accompany them. "The guards' weapons have been primed by arkademics," he was told. "They should be effective against Rust Warriors." Of course, Tom needed to know where they were going. "The Blade know," the Prime Master assured him, "but in case you get separated..." He then touched Tom's thoughts in a way that he had before and suddenly Tom *did* know. He could sense the core beating at the city's heart just as he could feel the restless coil of power at his back. Of course they needed all the help they could get. "I would come with you," Assembly member Birhoff said. "But I have to report to the assembly on the outcome of this meeting." Tom was grateful for small mercies. Of course everyone wanted to wish them luck and offer them brave words. He could understand all of that; it was just that the combination of all these things took time.

He tried to avoid Kat's gaze, realising that he could have whisked her to and from the Stain a dozen times before all was ready. Mercifully, she seemed unconcerned by the fact, though she did corner him at one point, evidently as tired of the delay as he was, and say, "Can't you just zap us there the way you brought us both here from the Stain?"

Tom shook his head. "I have to be able to visualise a person or a place clearly, or it doesn't work, and I've never been to the core."

"Well, can't the Prime Master go there and then you can visualise him?"

Again he shook his head. "The Prime Master can only jump to very specific places within the city, not anywhere the way that I can."

"Hey, so you're more powerful than the Prime Master now?"

"No, of course I'm not."

But she wasn't having any of it.

The final delay was an unexpected one. It came from the Council Guard, or rather their commander, a Captain Verrill. The Prime Master had assigned seven of the Blade and a dozen of the Guards under Verrill's command to accompany Tom, and the captain seemed none too pleased at the prospect.

Tom had met Verrill before. The tall, powerful-looking officer was never far away when the Prime Master was around. He'd always been civil to Tom and, on occasion, had even threatened to crack a smile. In fact, he gave every indication of having a personality beneath the professional veneer, which was something Tom couldn't have said with any certainty of the others he'd met among the white-and-purples.

Verrill had always struck Tom as unfailingly loyal, yet now he hesitated, as if uncomfortable with what was being asked of him.

"Is there a problem, captain?" The Prime Master asked, presumably sensing the same.

"No, sir, not a problem, but… our sworn duty is to safeguard you and the other members of the council, not anyone else. No offence intended." This last was said with a quick glance in Tom's direction.

"Indeed it is, Captain," the Prime Master said with a smile. "Your diligence does you credit, as ever, but these are unusual times. By accompanying Tom you *will* be safeguarding me, and all the council members. If you stay here and Tom fails in his endeavour, Thaiburley will fall. What then of your duty? Should Tom succeed, we'll all be safe. So, you see, protecting him protects us all. There's no conflict in what I'm instructing you and your men to do, captain; safeguarding Tom will not represent a dereliction of duty but rather its strongest prosecution.

"We'll still retain a pair of guardsmen each and a contingent of the Blade, but, to be frank, should you fail, it won't really matter how many there are to safeguard us. We're no longer of any consequence in this, not compared to Tom. So please, Captain, do as I ask with a clear conscience."

That seemed to settle it, which meant that all the obstacles were cleared and they could finally set off, though, on reflection, Tom wasn't really sure why he was in such a hurry. *Rust Warriors*. The very thought of those silent, inhuman killers sent a shiver coursing through his body at least as chill as anything Thaiss's ice tanks had ever delivered.

At Pilgrimage End he was mistaken for a prophet, a wild man returned from the mountains of Thaiss enlightened by the goddess. His appearance doubtless contributed to this misapprehension. After narrowly surviving his fight with Bryant – or whatever the man's real name had been – and escaping the Jeeraiy, Dewar had become obsessed with catching up to Tom and Mildra. Though, looking back now, he couldn't have said why. Perhaps the Prime Master had touched his mind with more than merely the threat of blood magic reprisal in that interview back in Thaiburley. The obsession had driven him relentlessly forward, overriding awareness of his own body's needs and appearance. He'd eaten little and slept little, while his thoughts never strayed to such trivial concerns as hygiene and grooming. So it had been an unkempt and decidedly dishevelled figure that arrived at the abandoned temple, and the days spent unconscious in its ruins since hadn't exactly improved the situation either.

Strange, Dewar could see all this clearly now, when at the time he'd been oblivious to any aberration in his mental state. With the benefit of hindsight, he recognised that sanity had deserted him during the trip here, and, indeed, that he and it had been less than fully acquainted for many years. His time in Thaiburley's under-City, his servitude to Senior Arkademic Magnus, his determination to better himself by moving ever forwards and upwards, all of this had been motivated by one thing: the need to prevent his past from ever catching up with him. The torment and horror he'd inflicted on others, both at Magnus's behest and before, had been a safety valve, his way of sharing the pain and unfairness of his life – all the injustice the world had ever dealt him. His suffering had been constant, why should others be spared?

The pleasure gained from such deranged interludes had proven ephemeral and unsatisfying, driving him to ever greater lengths to scratch an itch that could never be reached. He had abandoned all restraint, allowing the darker side of his nature to flourish unhindered. It had always been there, but at the start of his career had turned this to his advantage, channelling such urges into his work and earning significant sums in the process, not to mention notoriety and appreciation for his inventiveness. Few of the victims in those early days could ever be described as innocents; though he doubted the same was true of those he'd dealt with in Thaiburley.

Not that he was ashamed of this period – Dewar was far too pragmatic for that. Nor did he feel any remorse for the people who had suffered and died at his hands. It had happened; nothing he could do about that now, so best to accept that period for what it was – the past – and move on.

It struck Dewar as ironic that during all those years nobody had ever treated him as a madman. Dangerous, evil, cruel, untrustworthy – yes, all of those things; but never mad. Yet now, when perspective had returned and he was able to think with logic and clarity, he was being mistaken for a prophet left mentally unbalanced by an encounter with a goddess he didn't even believe in. He didn't lie to the Thaissian priests when they took him into their temple to bathe him, shave him, feed him, anoint him with oils, and provide warm soft bedding for his comfort. He didn't need to. They saw in him a man touched by destiny, and they were right. They saw before them a man fully focused on a mission beyond their ken, and they were right in this too. Where they erred was in thinking that either the mission or the man was in any way holy.

Dewar now knew what he had to do. For the most part he was willing to dismiss the threat held over him by Thaiburley's Prime Master as pure bluff. Perhaps it wasn't, perhaps the drop of blood drawn from Dewar's pricked finger really could be used to bring all manner of retribution down on his head, but he doubted it, and there was nothing he could do about the situation in any case. Besides, by his reckoning he had done more than enough to discharge his duty where the boy and the Thaistess were concerned.

No, high time he stopped bothering with the affairs of others – he had his own life to put in order.

From Pilgrimage End Dewar walked the mountain paths to Pellinum, encountering little along the way apart from two small groups of pilgrims headed in the opposite direction, and some miserable weather. Fortified by the ministrations of the priests and enjoying the benefit of a full stomach for the first time in many days, he used the walk to build up lost muscle and regain a degree of fitness.

Pellinum liked to boast that it was the largest settlement this side of the vast floodplain known as the Jeeraiy, and indeed it might have been, but the place seemed little more than a village to someone accustomed to the vastness of Thaiburley. In fairness, though, it was a sprawling metropolis when measured against Pilgrimage End.

On his second night in Pellinum, Dewar saved a wealthy man from a mugging, chasing away the attackers before helping the victim home. Though badly shaken, the man showed little sign of injury but every sign of gratitude and relief. So it was that Dewar gained access to one of the largest and notoriously secure dwellings in the town's most affluent district. Once inside, he slit the man's throat, robbed him, and then used some of the proceeds to pay off the two muggers.

The next morning found him on a boat bound for Stoutford, a settlement on the easternmost edge of

the Jeeraiy. He was by no means the only passenger
and soon fell into company with a portly, wheezing
fellow whose laugh was even more expansive than
his waistline. This larger-than-life character proved
to be the agent of an ambitious trading company out
of Kathay, seeking new markets. As the day wore on
the two shared a bottle of wine Dewar had brought
along for the journey, and then another. After the
second bottle had been emptied of all but the dregs –
with the assassin drinking considerably less than he
appeared to – Dewar's new friend was, it had to be
said, slightly the wrong side of sober. This didn't stop
the fellow from producing an ornate silver hip flask
from an inside pocket and offering it to Dewar. The
assassin sniffed at the open mouth, detecting nothing
beyond the unmistakable alcohol-laden caramel of
Kathan brandy; and a very decent one it proved to
be at that.

By the time their boat nudged up against the quay
at Stoutford, the trader was snoring soundly, the
empty silver flask lying on the seat beside him. Or it
was, until Dewar pocketed it for safe keeping. He slid
out from the seat on his transient friend's other side
and left him there, confident that the fellow would
awaken with a heavy head but lighter pockets, cour-
tesy of the substantial purse the assassin had just lifted
from him, a comfortingly heavy weight now ensconced within the folds of his own clothing.

Once ashore, Dewar wasted no time in spending
some of the purse's contents, replenishing supplies
and then acquiring a sound horse and some good

quality tackle to match. Within an hour of stepping off
the boat he set out for Eastwell, a town that straddled
the great trade route which bisected the continent. As
he left Stoutford behind, Dewar spared a thought for
his inadvertent benefactor, wondering if he were
awake yet.

The horse served him well and they made good
time. Dewar judged his mount's strength and stamina
with precision and so avoided riding the beast into the
ground while getting the most out of it. Nonetheless,
the horse was exhausted by the time they arrived at
Eastwell and he rewarded it with two nights' rest at a
good stabling facility, where it was able to rest and
feed and regain its strength, ready for the last stage of
the journey.

It had taken a little over two days to reach Eastwell,
a town he had passed through before and whose taverns he knew well enough to engineer an encounter
with fellow travellers. On the second morning following his arrival, Dewar reclaimed his horse and joined
a trade caravan as it trundled out of the town on the
road to distant Deliia.

Deliia was perilously close to familiar territory, and
he didn't want to run the risk of his arrival being
noted; far better to merely be one of a crowd rather
than a lone horseman riding through the gates. Once
at Deliia his plan was to sell the horse and seek passage
on a boat. One bound for the Misted Isles.

No, Dewar didn't for one moment regret the ex-
cesses he had perpetrated in those dark, fear-ridden
days in Thaiburley. He did, however, acknowledge that

during that period his talents had been employed by the wrong people for all the wrong reasons. He fully intended to put that right. Dewar was going home.

SEVEN

Initially their party passed through populated corridors, though Tom barely noted the fact. He spent the first part of the journey lost in thought. The sounds of movement, of conversation, the laughter of children and the scolding of worried parents – all the accoutrements of a living, bustling metropolis – washed over him to leave only the briefest of impressions. Afterwards he would recall people's faces: an elderly couple staring, two young children being held back by an anxious mother, and a smartly dressed youth looking puzzled, but he wasn't really paying attention at the time.

Kat's bartering with the Prime Master had made him feel uncomfortable and he was trying to work out why. It brought a number of matters sharply into focus, causing him to question things he'd previously taken for granted. First among them, what was *he* doing here?

Kat's reasons for coming along were clear enough. The leverage the Prime Master had applied was not so very different from the methods Ty-gen had used in persuading her to take Tom across the City Below: both boiled down to bribery. Was she really so materialistic, and was that a true reflection of how little their friendship meant to her? Or was he being naïve?

If Kat's motivations were so obvious, his were anything but, even to him. Throughout all that had happened he'd trusted in the Prime Master, who was undoubtedly a lot wiser than Tom, confident that the older man knew best and was happy to do whatever he advised. Kat hadn't.

It now seemed to Tom that all his life he'd been happy to let others make decisions for him, passing on the responsibility of his own life to somebody else. First it had been his mother, then Lyle and the leaders of the Blue Claw, and now the Prime Master. Maybe that was the real difference between him and Kat. Maybe that was why she always looked for the angle while he just went along with whatever others recommended. He'd been in a gang of one kind or another from the very first, and had never learned how not to be.

If so, maybe it was high time that changed. Thanks to Kat's example, he found himself wondering for the first time what *he* was likely to gain from all of this. Sure, he was trying to save the city, but that hadn't been enough for Kat. Was he a fool for not standing up for himself a bit more? He hadn't *wanted* to leave the streets and be taken under the Prime Master's wing, but it had been taken for granted that he'd go along with the process. He hadn't *wanted* to leave the city and go in search of the goddess Thais, but the Prime Master had been insistent, arranging matters without paying heed to his own concerns or desires. He hadn't *wanted* to return to Thaiburley with the weight of the city's survival resting on his shoulders, but the goddess had never allowed for any other course of action, and he didn't *want* to be heading off now into corridors infested with Rust Warriors to save the city and everyone in it, but no one seemed to consider the possibility that he might do anything else. And here he was, doing exactly as expected.

Of course Thaiburley's survival mattered to him, it was his home, but it was a lot of other folk's home as well. Shouldn't saving the place be down to *other* people? Tom felt a familiar sense of the inevitable, of life rushing past beyond his control. There had been times along the Thair's course when he'd felt swept along by circumstance in much the same way that a piece of flotsam is propelled by the river's current. If anything, events had only gathered pace since then, attaining a momentum that felt unstoppable, inevitable. Not that digging his heels in at this stage would have been a realistic option in any case, hemmed in as he was by Council Guards and the Blade. But, assuming he survived this, Tom determined that things were going to change. He'd make his own choices from here on in, no matter what others might expect of him.

"We do what we must, Tom," said a familiar voice. "Life doesn't always follow the path we expect, and we all make sacrifices. Some more than others, granted, but that's simply the way of things."

He looked up, astonished to see the goddess walking beside him. "You came back," he said.

"In a sense."

How could she possibly be walking here? Where were the Blade that moments ago had hemmed him in? "You're not real," he said, as hope that the burden of responsibility might be lifted from his shoulders evaporated as rapidly as it had blossomed.

"Oh I'm real all right, just not physical. Matters proceeded far more quickly than I would have liked. You're not ready. The information you need is still being assimilated, so I sent part of me back here to help you, to guide you."

"How?"

"Inside your head, of course," as if that much should have been obvious.

"So only I can see and hear you?"

"Exactly, and don't worry, I'll remain dormant most of the time, only emerging when I'm needed."

"Thanks a lot."

"For what?" Kat asked. The goddess had disappeared and he realised he must have spoken that last phrase out loud. "Are you still sulking with me for grabbing hold of you back in the Stain and hitching a ride?" Kat said.

"What? No, don't be daft."

"So what's with the silent treatment?"

He shrugged. "No reason."

"That's all right then, if you're sure."

He forced a smile and nodded. "Yeah, I'm sure."

Inside he was seething, wondering how much of his thought processes were now laid bare to the goddess, and whether that information was being shared with the real Thaiss back in her citadel, or was this aspect of her self-contained? Either way, he didn't like it and felt used yet again. With an effort, he stopped worrying about the goddess, reckoning there was nothing he could do about her presence no matter how much he resented the intrusion. To distract himself from fretting about this unwanted passenger, he turned his thoughts on Kat. It felt odd travelling with her again. Not awkward, just a little odd. He supposed it was because he'd grown accustomed to the reassuring presence of Mildra beside him – her warmth, quiet wisdom and gentle words. "Warm and gentle" were hardly the words he'd use to describe Kat. She was all spiky darkness and pointed steel to Mildra's comforting pastels and softness. He'd spent a lot longer with Mildra, of course, but somehow having Kat here felt more natural and, given what they were likely to be facing, he wouldn't have had it any other way.

Presumably she'd been giving matters a bit of thought as well, because as they walked she said, "So, when did you become such a POP?"

Person of imPortance: not a phrase Tom had expected to ever hear said of himself. "Beats the hell out of me," he admitted. "It sort of crept up on me when I wasn't looking. But it doesn't mean anything. I'm still the same nick you took halfway across the City Below."

She laughed. "Yeah, right. Don't seem to remember any Council Guards coming with us that time around, let alone the Blade. And what do you mean halfway? It must have been at least two thirds."

Tom grinned. "More like three quarters, but only because you took us so far in the wrong direction."

"Hey!" She cuffed his arm. "We had demon hounds after us, remember? Anyway, you were the one who wanted to avoid Blood Heron territory."

Tom's good humour soured slightly as he took in the towering ebony figures around them. "Wish we were back there now," he muttered. "Thaiss, Kat, when did everything get so complicated?"

"Know what you mean. We didn't have much of a clue what was going on then, either, but at least we were still in the streets. All these corridors, they're just plain wrong. Makes me feel I can't breathe in here."

Tom had almost forgotten how unnatural the enclosed world of the Rows had felt to him when he first encountered it. Until Kat's comment he hadn't realised how quickly he'd adapted to this environment. "You get used to it," he assured her.

She snorted. "I don't intend to be here long enough to get used to anything, thanks all the same."

The comment brought home to Tom how much he'd changed. Kat was still very much a part of the City Below, but he wasn't certain he was, not anymore. If he didn't belong on the streets, where did he belong?

The thought sat uncomfortably, which must have shown on his face. "You okay?"

He made a point of gazing again at the Blade and Council Guards surrounding them. "What do you think?"

They lapsed into silence.

• • • •

The longer Tom had spent in Thaiss's citadel, the more sense the initially random images and histories had begun to make, a process that continued after he'd left. As things came increasingly into focus, one particular piece of information stood out; not because it was obvious or recurring, but because it was completely absent. He'd meant to ask the goddess about it before he left, but in the end their departure had been so rushed that he'd forgotten to do so. Only now, as he marched through the corridors of the Heights towards goodness knew what fate, did the matter resurface.

The thing that his ever-inquisitive mind kept picking over was the fact that nowhere, in all that he'd seen and heard, had Tom discovered any mention of a name for the goddess's brother. It was as if someone had deliberately purged every trace of his name from the records, *all* records. In fact, the more he thought about it, the more Tom felt certain this had to be the case.

"I hope you're not gonna go all moody on me," Kat said. "Because no one else around here is exactly a barrel of laughs." She glanced towards the stone-faced Council Guards marching beside them.

"Sorry. Just thinking."

"I noticed." Then, after a slight pause, "Tell me something. What did it feel like, killing the Soul Thief?"

Tom kept walking but inwardly he froze, wary of discussing the matter given how sensitive Kat had proven to be on the subject. "You won't hit me?"

"Not this time."

"It was..." He hesitated, trying to find the best way of expressing the experience. "It was unlike anything I've ever felt before. At first there was this numbness that crept over my head, then it was as if everything was stretching, pulling upwards, and it *hurt*. For a split second as I fought back, before she was gone, I saw her; I mean *really* saw her for what she was."

"Go on," Kat said softly as he fell silent.

"There were all these scraps of personality, tiny bits of those she'd killed, I guess, which she'd kept a hold of. I had the sense that there was something desperate in the way she clung on to them, as if they might replace some of what she'd lost... not real *whole* people, not by a long shot," he said quickly, remembering what Kat had once told him about the Soul Thief taking her mother. "Just their distant echoes."

"What was it she'd lost, then, her humanity?"

"No, nothing like that, she was never human."

"What then?"

He took a deep breath. "She was a Demon, one that had fallen from the Upper Heights a long time ago."

"You're kidding me. A *Demon*?"

"Originally, yes, like I said, a long, long time ago." Tom couldn't believe this; he was sounding like the Prime Master talking to *him*. "You see, Demons aren't alive in the same sense that we are. They're spawned straight from the core and linked to it far more directly than anyone – you do know that all the talented in the City Below and the arkademics and healers draw their abilities from the core?"

"Yeah, I picked that much up as we've gone along."

"Well, whenever the core is renewed…"

"Which is what we're on the way to do now, right?" she interrupted.

"Right. When that happens, the Demons are reabsorbed, they become part of the core again, and then a whole new generation of them is born. The Soul Thief must have been a Demon that somehow got left behind – not from the last generation, she's been around for too long, but the cycle before or even the one before that. Somehow she must have missed or resisted the call to return to the core with the others, fleeing down to the City Below and hiding out in the Stain instead. And she's been there ever since, living on the scraps of core material she's been leaching from the talented, using their link with the core to survive."

"Why, though? What made her different? I mean if that's what her kind are supposed to do, why didn't she simply line up with the rest of them and get reabsorbed?"

He shook his head. "No idea. Cowardice? A stronger drive to survive than the others?"

"And she's been preying on us ever since."

"Yeah, raiding the streets at intervals, whenever she's had to, picking off a few of the talented each time and draining them before vanishing back to the Stain; until the next time she gets hungry. So many people die on the streets, who's going to notice a couple more?

"And because she was so careful, people tended to dismiss her as an old wives' tale," Kat murmured. "A myth that was useful for scaring disobedient kids into bed." She shook her head. "What changed this time? Why did she attack so openly and take so many?"

Tom shrugged. "The core's corrupted. Everything's screwed up. Maybe she had no choice – maybe she couldn't get whatever she needed from just a few; or maybe the corruption fed through and drove her to greater lengths."

"A breckin' Demon." Kat shook her head. "Thaiss, who'd have thought? And what does that mean for us right now, do you reckon?"

"In what way?"

"Well, you say this core thingy is corrupted, what would that have done to the rest of the Demons, the ones still living in the Upper Heights? If they're so closely linked to the core, won't they have been corrupted too? Are we going to end up facing a whole army of Soul Thieves trying to stop us from doing whatever it is you're supposed to do?"

Now there was a disturbing thought. Tom hadn't even considered how the corruption and the hundred years of delay in the core's renewal might have affected the Demons. "I don't know," he admitted. "I honestly don't."

She snorted. "Seems to me there's a brecking lot you don't know."

"That's what I keep trying to tell everybody," he assured her, "but no one ever wants to listen."

They came to a large, sealed door blocking the entire corridor. A pair of the Blade stood sentry before it. At the party's approach, one of the obsidian figures moved, pressing something in the wall, and the door swung ponderously open.

"We're crossing into hostile territory," Verrill said, speaking to them for the first time since they'd set out. "Everyone needs to stay alert and please, keep the noise down."

Tom nodded. Kat just raised her eyebrows, as if to say "oh yeah, and what are you going to do about it if we don't?"

She kept her mouth shut though, as they crossed the threshold into a lighter, brighter world. The corridors here were wider, airier, and even Tom felt he could breathe more easily. Their party adopted a new formation. The Blade clustered tight around Kat and Tom as before, but the Council Guard spread out, some staying close while others provided both an advance and a rear guard – four ranging ahead of them, checking every branching corridor, and four lagging several paces behind.

This wasn't the only difference. The whole atmosphere of the city had changed. Gone were the voices, the bustle – the background noise of living so easily taken for granted and now noticeable only by its absence. Silence surrounded them. It was as if when passing through the door they had stepped into a completely different realm and were now moving through a city of ghosts, which, Tom supposed, in many senses they were. The sound of their footsteps reverberated through the stillness, so loud that each and every slap of leather on tile might almost have been a deliberate act of defiance.

Tom wanted to say something, just to hear a noise that was indisputably human, even if it was only his own voice, but at the same time he felt reluctant to break the pervading spell of silence. He willed Kat to make some irreverent remark, but she remained un-characteristically quiet, perhaps heeding the captain's words or perhaps simply daunted by the eeriness that surrounded them.

In such unnatural stillness any sound was bound to be magnified, its significance exaggerated by unlikely portent. So it was with the peculiar series of noises that reached them from somewhere ahead, steadily rising above the *karumph* of collective footfalls.

A series of pronounced clicks and then a louder snap, as if something was being wound up and then released to smack against a wall. The pattern repeated constantly. Tom tried to picture what could possibly be causing such a sequence and drew a blank.

The way ahead opened into a large quadrangle. The ceiling rose to twice its former height, clearly claiming space from the Row immediately above. The floor changed abruptly from plain and functional to a mo-saic of brightly coloured tiles. Corridors led from each of the four sides of the square while black-painted wrought iron stairways dropped down from a balcony above, presumably leading to the higher Row.

In the centre of this open area stood one of the most bizarre things Tom had ever seen. It was a square glass booth, the bottom part of which revealed an interlinking array of different sized cogs: some bronzed, others sliver, while a few of the smallest were jet black. In addition to these cogs there were coupling rods, metal strips, rubberized wheels and cyclical chains. The whole thing looked so intricate that Tom wondered whether it served any real purpose at all or was just there to provide decorative entertainment. The mechanism had obviously been active for a while and continued through its cycle as they traipsed through.

The Council Guards in the lead of their group split as they came to the machine, two passing on either side of it, while the Blade and those Guards who remained close to Tom and Kat moved as one to the left of the booth.

Tom slowed down, fascinated by the way motion in the visible workings was transferred from one cog to another as the various components interacted.

In doing so, he caused the party's formation to stretch, giving him a clearer view of the booth and allowing Kat to slip through the ranks of their guards.

The top part of the booth featured four painted mannequins – two male and two female – all sawn off at the waist. They stared forth from alternate facets of the kiosk, so that the four formed an outward-facing cross. Brightly painted with long-lashed eyes, rosy cheeks and vacuous smiles that were doubtless intended to be endearing, but Tom found them vaguely sinister, particularly in these unnaturally still corridors.

The series of sounds which had so intrigued him as they approached were caused by the mannequin facing them, one of the female ones. Somehow, the mechanism must have become jammed in the "on" position,

because her right arm, bent at the elbow, was in the
process of thrusting out towards them. As it reached
the wall of the kiosk a small slot opened, at around
chest-height for a child, to disgorge a handful of
brightly coloured tablets – presumably sweets – which
cascaded down the face of the kiosk to join the growing
mound of similar objects on the floor, spreading
steadily outward from the machine to form a glistening
rainbow pool.

The slot clicked shut and after a few seconds the arm
moved slowly backward to repeat the process, presumably over and over again until either the sweets ran out
or its power did. Each movement of cog against cog
was accompanied by a theatrical ratcheting sound and
the dispensing slot closed with an audible snap.

Kat bent down to pick up a couple of the sweets,
popping them into her mouth. Tom stopped to watch
her, and the whole party ground to a halt. "Hey, these
are all right," Kat said, scooping up a large handful
which she then stuffed into various pockets. "Want
some?" She held out a few towards him, ignoring
the guards.

He shook his head. It felt disrespectful, somehow,
like robbing the dead. Sure, he'd done that himself
alongside others from the Blue Claw in the past, but
that had been in the City Below, where a corpse's pos-
sessions were no more than a resource to be recycled,
where it was all about survival, and corpse frisking
was an accepted part of the routine. This was a different world, though, and those sweets were intended
for bright-eyed clean-faced kids in freshly washed

clothes, kids who'd never had to face the things he had, who didn't even know they existed – until recently at any rate. Taking their sweets just seemed wrong, as if in doing so he would somehow be contributing what had befallen these unknown children and the robbing of their innocence.

Kat shrugged, oblivious to any such concerns. "Suit yourself," she said, giving him a curious look as she brought her hand back and shoved the sweets into her mouth instead.

She then sauntered back to join him and, following a scowl from Verrill, their little party was able to set off again, like some multi-limbed caterpillar. As they left the quadrangle, the sounds of the machine churning out its sweets receded with every new step.

Shortly afterwards, they encountered their first body.

The corridor on the far side of the square took on a different character to the one they'd walked through previously. Doors lined either side at staggered intervals, many brightly coloured, bearing decorative touches and ornate numbers which ran in sequence – 387 followed by 385 and then 383 – while doormats sat before several. They had entered a residential sector.

Most of the doors were closed, a couple stood ajar and a few were broken in, smashed apart as if made of eggshell, while some of the doormats had been kicked askew. Tom resisted the temptation to glance into any of these open dwellings, afraid of what he might see there, though they all seemed wreathed in darkness in any case. One, an all-white door, bore a patina of dried, russet stains which he definitely didn't want to think about. He noticed Kat studying this intently and guessed she was imagining the deathblow that had caused it.

These were the first signs of actual violence they'd seen. The smashed doors, the dried blood, even the disturbed mats, combined to bring home the gravity of their mission and the dangers that lurked unseen around them.

If they didn't, the first body certainly did.

It was a man, lying half in and half out the open door to one of the dwellings, his face down, arm stretching across the hallway. A pool of dried blood spread outward from where his mouth must have been, like some perverse cartoonist's speech bubble. The Blade and the Guards on the left hand side were forced to move around or step over him. No one made any comment.

This proved to be the first of many.

Tom was used to bodies; they'd been an everyday fact of life for as long as he could remember, so he had no qualms in stepping over those sprawled across the centre of the passageway, and blood was hardly a novelty either, but he quailed at the sheer number they were coming across and wondered how many had actually perished up here in the Heights. It was clear that death had descended on these corridors suddenly and unexpectedly, and he could only hope that elsewhere there might have been more warning and fewer casualties.

There were no body boys up here to remove the dead so they simply lay where they'd fallen, and he presumed they'd stay that way, at least until all this was over.

The corridor opened into another broad square, this one far wider than the sweet machine's and with a higher ceiling. It went up four or five rows at least. As they entered, Tom stumbled to a halt. This time, nobody complained.

The quadrangle had evidently been designed as a leisure park of some sort. To their left stood a children's play area, complete with climbing frame, slides, swings, a tumble wall, and other items Tom could only guess at; to the left a series of tunnels, skating tubes, ramps and curved climbs, while ahead stood a tiered rockery of stone seats, steps, and plants. At the top of this array was what had clearly been a fountain, now toppled and no longer working. Several watercourses were cleverly interwoven with the flower borders and seats, leading to four curved ponds at the base of the arrangement. Currently bobbing on the surface of these ponds were a number of large and very dead fish, while the water around them was stained red.

Not that Tom spared these details anything more than passing notice, not even the dead fish. His attention was principally captured by the human bodies. They began at his feet, as the party entered the square. Closest was a woman, her abdomen ripped open; beside her lay a small child, perhaps her daughter, neck twisted at an impossible angle. The bodies and their blood carpeted much of the floor and rose to drape themselves over seats and pathways. They peaked where a man's form sprawled over where the fountain

used to stand. Arms were outstretched, limbs ripped
from their sockets, heads twisted and bludgeoned,
while eyes stared sightlessly up at him, as if in accusa-
tion or perhaps desperately beseeching.

Tom felt his stomach heave and fought to control it.

"Thaiss!" whispered Kat from beside him. The fact
that a survivor of the Pits was shocked by what they
found here spoke volumes.

The flies didn't help. There weren't yet enough of
them to be considered a swarm but there were more
than enough for Tom. Disturbed by the party's arrival,
the dark insects took to the air, the droning of their
wings providing a flat and disconcerting soundtrack to
the carnage around them. He swatted distractedly at
one that zigzagged too close, missing it completely.

The metallic, slightly sweet smell of fresh blood
seemed to have been with Tom since they passed the
first body, but here its cloying presence tainted every
indrawn breath and was accompanied by the stench
of something rotten. The massacre had obviously been
recent but enough time had passed for decomposition
to begin – a couple of days ago or perhaps three, Tom
judged; no longer.

He could picture it, people being herded and driven
from the corridors that fed into the square, running
from certain death until there was nowhere left to
run. A mob of frantic, terrified folk erupting from the
mouth of each passageway simultaneously, milling in
confusion and horror, four panicked streams of the
doomed colliding, to swirl together like water thrown
casually into a bowl. A mother's hand clutching tightly

to the smaller hand of a child, desperate not to lose that tiny strand of human comfort; her other arm reaching out to shove and pull people apart, to force a way through, to escape. Except there was no escape. Behind each knot of people a party of Rust Warriors entered the square, moving with efficiency and purpose, spreading out to form a cordon and then closing in, tightening that cordon with every step and killing as they did so.

Tom had no idea whether these vivid scenes were the result of his talent picking up on some echo of actual events or just his imagination working overtime. All he knew was that he was suddenly sweating and finding it difficult to breathe. His stomach convulsed again, and this time there was no stopping it. He bent forward and threw up. He felt somebody pat him on the shoulders, not in admonishment but in sympathy. Kat.

As he stood upright again she held out a small cloth. "Here."

He took it gratefully and wiped his mouth, before craning forward to spit out more sourness, not looking, not wanting to know where his vomit might have landed.

They started forward again, skirting the perimeter of the square, where the bodies were marginally fewer, picking their way with care. The Council Guards were grim-faced and even the Blade seemed more vigilant.

Tom found the best way to deal with this was to take it literally one step at a time and not think about how far there was to go or how many dead people he still had to pass. He half expected Rust Warriors to rush out of the side corridor and attack them at any moment, but their party crossed the open mouth without incident. Eventually they made it to the far side of the killing field, their passage contested only by the flies.

Kat summed up the sense of relief. "Thank the goddess for that!" she muttered as they stepped over the final out-stretched arm and into the clear corridor beyond; a sentiment Tom suspected many of the guards in white and purple around them would happily have echoed.

They still hadn't encountered any Rust Warriors, but no one could doubt the enemy were nearby, not after what they'd experienced at the playground. This lack of direct confrontation began to play on Tom's nerves. It wasn't as if he had a death wish or anything, he would have been delighted if they could reach the core without meeting any opposition at all, but that was never going to happen. At some point they'd have to fight, they all knew that. The only question was when. The anticipation was becoming an irritation, the constant need to be alert fraying Tom's nerves. He found himself peering into the depths of every corridor they passed and scrutinising closed doors as if he might somehow predict which one was about to burst open and disgorge deadly ambushers.

When the attack finally came it was almost a relief.

Without any warning Rust Warriors erupted from a side corridor, falling upon the rearguard. The ambush displayed the sort of cunning Tom wouldn't have expected from Rust Warriors – the one he'd killed beside the Thair had seemed lumbering and slow-witted, though he wasn't sure why he'd assumed that – since it required them to stay hidden while the rest of the group passed by.

The first Tom knew of the attack was when a man screamed. He whipped around to see one of the Guards enveloped in the same eerie nimbus of light that had spelled an end to Kohn. All the guilt he'd felt then at his failure to react quickly enough to save his friend came flooding back.

The stricken guard's colleagues tried to help, only to be forced back by the other Rust Warriors, and they were soon engaged in a desperate fight for their lives.

The Council Guard were more than just ceremonial decoration, for all the purple-trimmed whiteness of their gleaming uniforms. They were expert swordsmen, strong men at the peak of physical fitness, chosen for their courage and prowess and schooled in the art of killing; warriors disguised in popinjays' clothing. The other three guards engaged the enemy swiftly and efficiently. Steel flashed and stabbed, blades sank into their opponents. But not a single Rust Warrior fell.

Tom watched helpless as one Guardsman's sword struck his nearest adversary once, twice, piercing stomach and then chest without any effect. A scything blow from his opponent then cut the man nearly in two, slicing through armour, flesh and bone with equal ease. Whatever the arkademics had done to empower the guardsmen's weapons didn't seem to be working.

Tom's view was then obscured as Verrill rushed past him, leading the other four Guardsmen from the main party to reinforce their colleagues. As he went he called out orders, telling the four-strong advance guard to lead the party onward.

"Go!" he then yelled, either to Tom or the Blade. "We'll hold them off."

Kat looked as if she might be about to join the fight but Tom stopped her. "Don't," he said. "You heard the captain, and there's likely to be worse waiting ahead of us."

She nodded, but clearly didn't like running away any more than he did, though run they did, urged by two of the remaining white liveried guards who now dropped back to bring up the rear.

On reflection, Tom would have been more impressed by the Rust Warriors' ingenuity had there been a second group waiting to attack from the front, but it didn't happen. Unless, of course, the ambush was intended to simply cut off any retreat and their party was already heading exactly where the Rust Warriors wanted them to go, perhaps towards where their main strength lay in wait. Now that was a sobering thought.

The road to Deliia was busy, far more so than Dewar would have expected even given that this was the great trade route. Riders flashed past them, individually and in small groups, while the caravan he'd joined proved to be one of several headed for the coast. Business must be booming.

The traffic was too heavy for any normal circumstance, though, and he began to suspect there was more going on than he'd realised, suspicions that were confirmed when they stopped to rest and water their horses a little after midday. Dewar engineered a conversation with a rider who was also taking a break from the road – one heading in the opposite direction. Dewar didn't press the point, he didn't need to; the phrase "rumours of war" told him more than enough.

By late afternoon as their caravan hove into view of the sea and Deliia's low-rise dwellings appeared as a dark stain on the horizon, progress had slowed to a crawl. They had joined a long queue of those waiting to filter through the city's gates.

It occurred to Dewar that he needn't have bothered joining a caravan at all under these circumstances and that, with such a constant stream, he could have ridden straight through and made better time. Too late for regrets now but there was no point in compounding the problem by staying with the wagons without good reason. He made his excuses and rode forward, bypassing the long line of waiting carts that clogged the road to the envious glares of their drivers. Even so, he wasn't the only horseman anxious to enter the town and still had to bide his time.

Eventually, as the sun set and the rosiness of dusk tinted the skyline, he found himself passing beneath the old walls of the town that was just a quick skip across the sea from the island on which he had been born and raised. Nearly home, and nobody had a clue that he was coming.

EIGHT

Part of Tylus was actually relieved to see Kat go, not to mention Tom. He recognised the lad immediately as the street-nick he'd attempted to arrest on the city walls, the one whose escape had brought him to the City Below in the first place. Clearly there was more going on here than he'd been told.

Of course Tylus had been startled when Kat and Tom disappeared in the same abrupt fashion that the boy and the Thaistess had initially arrived, but not sorry, not by a long shot. Kat's presence had proved a distraction all morning, far more so than he would ever have anticipated. And that fact disturbed him.

It probably wouldn't have been an issue if not for the conversation with Richardson the previous evening. Kat had been a pain throughout the journey. Her abrasive attitude and stroppy mood were enough to make anyone give up trying to be civil and leave her to get on with things, but Richardson's announcement regarding his surprise betrothal had forced Tylus to consider his fascination with the Tattooed Men's leader in a different light.

Kat *was* intriguing, no question about that. Utterly different from any woman he'd ever met before. She was bold, edgy, thrilling – the free spirit Tylus had always yearned to be. And *that* was the source of his fascination. It was all down to novelty. How could he fail to be enthralled? But she was also young. A fact that was easy to forget when you saw her strutting before the Tattooed Men and wielding those twin swords with such skill, but she was probably not much older than Jezmina. It meant she was still a girl rather than a woman, despite her behaviour. Certainly in the light of his upbringing and the culture of the Heights, he couldn't consider her as anything but. Down here, he wasn't so certain. People tended to grow up much quicker on the streets.

So was he being a hypocrite? He'd been so discomfited by Richardson's talk of marrying Jezmina, even though the girl's demeanour belied her tender years, and more than a little embarrassed for his friend. How then did his own interest to Kat – his *attraction* – differ from Richardson's situation? Yes, she was older than Jezmina, but not by that many years, certainly not enough to make the thought a comfortable one.

For a surreal moment Tylus pictured what the future might hold in the unlikely event he and Kat were ever to develop a serious relationship – the reaction of his family and friends in the Heights. He imagined they would respond as he had to Richardson's happy news, with uncomfortable politeness and ill-concealed dismay, embarrassed for *his* sake. It would mortify his mother; she'd probably never recover from the shame. He could just see it now, as he stood in the cosy front room of the family home and introduced Kat to both his parents, the inevitable look of horror they'd share.

Actually, the relationship might almost be worth pursuing just for that moment. An unkind thought, but it brought a smile to his face when little else that morning had.

No, he was determined to be sensible about this, and forget his developing interest in Kat. It could only ever lead to disaster and significant embarrassment. Issie on the other hand, was a breath of fresh air. Even his mother couldn't fail to be impressed by an arkademic…

He shook his head, as if to dispel such thoughts, and turned his attention to the situation at hand, specifically to what Mildra was doing as she worked on the fallen men. He was suitably impressed by what he saw. She was obviously a highly talented healer and worked with competent efficiency. As he observed her, he couldn't help reflecting on how different people's lives were, all dictated by an accident of birth. Had he been born anywhere other than the Heights he could never have become a Kite Guard. There were no Thaistesses in the city's upper Rows, so if Mildra had been born there she would most likely have become an arkademic like Issie – a career that opened up the way to the Assembly, the administrative tier of the city's government. She might have been debating and implementing policy that affected millions instead of devoting her time and energy to a religion that few in the Heights even gave credence to.

This sort of disparity was something he would never have spared a thought for prior to his arrival in the under-City. He had never even realised that such institutionalised inequality existed in Thaiburley. All the more reason to bring the Kite Guards down from their lofty perches so that they could experience a taste of real life at the other end of the social scale. It reaffirmed his determination to get the new training school up and running as soon as possible.

Issie came over to join him. "The Prime Master has contacted me via the Blade."

Interesting; so the Prime Master was able to commune with the Blade at distance. Hardly a revelation, but not something Tylus had realised before. "We're to continue on and take out the second target," Issie said.

"Can you do that, lead us to this Insint thing, I mean?"

She nodded and showed him a crushed piece of mechanism. He recognised it immediately as the piece he'd recovered from the scene of the fallen sun globe during his early days on the streets. "This is part of the creature we're after. Once I attune myself, I'll be able to take us straight to it."

Tylus was duly impressed. "Is that something all arkademics can do?"

She shook her head. "No. Well, yes, to a degree. We all study the same disciplines but have aptitude in different areas of talent, and so tend to specialise in those. All arkademics have a basic grounding in resonance skills, but there are at most half a dozen or so who are as adept at it as I am."

He grinned. "Good for you."

"Why thank you, kind sir." Her smile in response turned sour almost immediately. "Mind you, look where it's got me." She glanced around meaningfully at the Stain.

"Don't dismiss the place so readily," Tylus advised. "The City Below has a habit of getting beneath your skin and surprising you."

The smile returned. "There speaks the voice of experience."

He laughed. "Guilty as charged."

"All right then, I'll reserve judgement, but this place is going to have to go some to change my mind."

Tylus grinned, his spirits lifted despite all that was going on around them.

"Mind you," she added, "at least this assignment has put us back in touch."

"So it has." And only then did he realise how grateful of the fact he was. His gaze slid beyond her. "I'm not sure the Tattooed Men will stick around much longer though, not without Kat to tell them they should."

"You never know. There was a little more to the message. Kat sent word that someone called M'gruth should take charge of the Tattooed Men and that they should continue working with us."

Tylus nodded. That made sense. "Anything else?"

"Yes, though it's a little odd. She said something about M'gruth not letting her down and making her wish she'd brought Shayna along...?"

Tylus laughed. "That sounds like Kat."

"Oh? Know her well then, do you, this Kat?"

"Well, I… that is…" The Kite Guard could feel his cheeks heating up as rapidly as his tongue turned ponderous and inarticulate. "We've seen a bit of each other lately, we had to in order to plan for this mission," he said, far more defensively than he'd meant to. Then he added, "I did save her life after all," before wondering why in Thaiss's name he'd blurted that out. Did he really expect it to impress a woman who spent her days approving and debating legislation which affected the lives of millions?

"Really? You'll have to tell me about that when this is all over."

"There's not really that much to tell," he said, silently cursing his big mouth. "Anyway, perhaps we'd better have a word with M'gruth before the Tattooed Men decide to up sticks and head back to the streets."

M'gruth took the news of his promotion with customary stoicism, but he could really have done without the responsibility just then. Having shot two of his closest friends in the heat of battle he'd have much preferred to keep a low profile, and being put in charge of the Tattooed Men was hardly the way to achieve that. He couldn't even question the authenticity of the instruction either, not when it came parcelled up with a quip about Shayna like that.

"Thaiss," Ox grumbled. "We must really be scraping the bottom of the barrel for leaders if she's put you in charge."

M'gruth was inclined to agree, but he wasn't about to admit as much.

"Promise me one thing," the big man continued.

"What?"

"If you decide to shoot me again, do it properly next time, will you? I don't want to have to go through this again. It hurt like frissing hell!"

"Don't worry, I've no intention of going anywhere *near* the flechette guns, not for the rest of this outing at any rate." M'gruth had taken the first opportunity to hand the borrowed weapon back to the gunner he'd snatched it from when he went charging in to rescue Kat. Some rescue.

Ox grunted. "Suppose we should be grateful for small mercies."

M'gruth felt mortified by what he'd done. Both his victims had survived, but only thanks to the ministrations of the Thaistess. He had no idea what he would have done if they hadn't. Ox had been hit by two darts: one in the arm and one in his side. The second had still been embedded in the wound, but the Thaistess had drawn it out as if her hand were magnetized, and then set about healing her patient.

Ox was as strong as his namesake and he was sitting up almost immediately, declaring himself fit and anxious to get going. His main concern appeared to be the fact that the wound on his arm had disrupted the pattern of tattoos covering the limb. Mildra's healing talent had knitted the two sides of the wound together, leaving a small ridge of pale skin: newly formed scar tissue, which naturally bore no tattoos.

"See that?" Ox had said, pointing at the break where

the scar line crossed his precious pattern. "You did that, M'gruth."

A fact he was all too well aware of, but, by M'gruth's reckoning, if a small breach of his tattoo was all the big man had to complain about after being shot he was doing all right. Unfortunately, the same couldn't be said for their second casualty. Petter had also taken two flechettes, but both in his abdomen, and he'd lost a lot of blood. The Thaistess had spent an awful lot longer working on him than she had on Ox, and by the time she'd finished she was clearly exhausted. As for Petter, he'd shown no signs of waking up.

These were anxious moments for M'gruth. "Is he going to be all right?" he'd asked as the Thaistess stood up, her work evidently finished.

She'd nodded, wearily. "Should be. I got to him just in time. Another minute or so and we'd have lost him, but failing any setbacks he ought to be fine. All he needs now is some sleep, the chance to recuperate."

"Sleep?" M'gruth glanced around at the deceptively deadly wasteland surrounding them. "Is that all?"

"Yes," she replied, evidently missing the irony. In fact, she staggered and looked fit to drop herself. M'gruth reached out to steady her. "By the look of it, he's not the only one. Thank you for all you've done," he added, suddenly conscious that he hadn't actually said as much before.

It was obvious that neither Mildra nor Petter would be going anywhere for a while. M'gruth and the other Tattooed Men were all for abandoning the mission, but then Kat's instruction arrived, telling them to continue under M'gruth's command; and that left them with a problem.

Kat's spectacular disappearance had nearly put paid to the mission in any case, but Mildra had calmed things down, explaining that Tom would have taken her to see the Prime Master. Doubtless M'gruth wasn't the only one who remembered the boy from the time they'd found him with Kat at one of the safe houses just before the sun globe came down so they knew the pair had history. Besides, this was a Thaistess offering them reassurances; one who went on to cement their respect by saving two of their own. Experience had taught the Tattooed Men the value of pragmatism. They couldn't do anything about Kat's disappearance, not right now, so they'd get on with what they could do something about; but they wouldn't forget.

In any case, Kat was a Death Queen. She could handle herself.

The Blade shattered spectacularly. A loud crack sounded and ebony shards exploded in all directions. To Tom they looked like glass, as if the Blade had been no more than a khybul sculpture, a fragile figurine of blackest crystal smashed apart by a giant hammer. He flinched instinctively, covering his eyes and turning away from the blast. At the same instant a lance of pain burnt across his upper arm. A razor-sharp piece of debris must have hit him in passing, slicing through shirt and flesh alike to leave a bloody red line as testament to its passage. He dreaded to think what that would have done had it caught him full on.

This time the Rust Warriors' attack had been more co-ordinated, the sort of thing he'd feared at their first encounter, the sort of thing they must have pulled at the playground. A force of glowing figures had blocked the way ahead. All bar two of the Blade had immediately surged forwards to engage them. As soon as they had, more attackers came from behind. Tom had seen at least four of the Warriors reduced to russet flakes before the glow from another successfully engulfed one of the ebony giants, which had led to the dramatic explosion.

Around Tom, the battle continued with ferocious intensity. The other Blade were still pouring munitions into the Rust Warriors, who were doing their best to fight a way through the deadly hail and come to grips with their opponents. The sound was deafening, the speed and intensity of combat bewildering. Tom felt lost, a midget cowering in the shadows and gawping as Titans clashed. He searched desperately for Kat and spotted her, leaping, ducking, her twin swords flashing in the glare of flickering fire one instant and violent explosion the next as they stabbed and cut. Death Queen incarnate. If the violent demise of a Blade had given her any pause it didn't show. She looked to be loving every vicious second of this. Tom braced himself against a wall, feeling the core carton press into his back and suddenly wondering what would happen if it were to be opened accidentally. He shifted position, his gaze still followed Kat. He knew deep down she was only here because of him, whatever the talk of reward, and that she could die at any second for all her skill and athleticism. That was one death he never wanted to have on his conscience.

Beside him a shape started to form. The goddess. He clamped down on his thoughts, willing her to disappear, refusing to let her manifest. This was one situation he wanted to deal with on his own. After a few intense seconds the shimmering form evaporated, the pressure eased, and he could concentrate on the fight once more.

Tom could scrap with the best of them. He was used to tussles with opponents armed with clubs, knives and chains, but this was something else. His knife remained in its sheath. It might as well have been a toothpick. Violence on this sort of scale would never come as naturally to him as it did to Kat, it seemed, but he was conscious of the fact that everyone else was pitching in and he was fed up with being little more than an impotent bystander. He had to try and do *something*.

Close by, a Rust Warrior was locked in battle with one of the Blade – impaled on a shaft of steel protruding from the Blade's wrist. The Rust Warrior glowed with silver light, as if it were attempting to overwhelm and mimic the Blade in the same way it might an unprotected human. The attempt was wholly ineffectual, the glow stopping where it met black metal, but the Rust Warrior was slowly inching along the dark shaft of the lance, apparently impervious to the fire being poured upon it from the Blade's other outstretched hand.

The Rust Warrior was almost in reach of its opponent's body, and Tom had already seen the likely result if that happened.

He focused on that one Warrior, closing his mind to all other distractions. He reached inside himself, feeling for the inner strength he'd drawn on when confronting that first Rust Warrior on the banks of the Thair, the one that slew Kohn. It came more easily this time, the welling of power, and he flung it towards the enemy. The Rust Warrior stopped in its struggles; the aura surrounding it seemed to dim and the fire pouring from the Blade's uplifted hand finally took hold. The Warrior caught fire, shrivelling where it stood. The flames collapsed in on themselves as if the towering figure they burned were nothing more than a hollow and insubstantial effigy.

Within seconds the fire had died and all that remained was a russet swirl of floating ashes.

Tom didn't pause. He concentrated on the next glowing figure, drawing on his hate and disgust and frustration, using the emotions to shape his power. This one stopped moving, convulsed, and then died as ebony blades swept through it. The third one simply exploded; a violent burst of light and heat that Tom flinched away from even though he wasn't that close. An instant before screwing his eyes shut the image of one of the Blade in silhouette, limned by the blossom of fire beyond, burned itself into his retinas. He opened his eyes again but was still partially dazzled, that image remaining with him. He tried to blink, to clear his vision, knowing that until he did he was going to be useless, not to mention vulnerable.

A figure loomed above him. Rust Warrior! Every nerve screamed the giant's identity. But Tom hesitated.

He remembered what he'd done to Dewar on that bleak mountainside by the ruined temple, how he'd struck out blindly with his power and damaged a companion, possibly forever. He didn't want to be responsible for that sort of mistake again. Before he lashed out he needed to know for certain this wasn't one of the Blade come to protect him but an enemy, but his vision just wouldn't clear. Then it did, enough for him to register the glowing hand reaching towards him. Enough for the realisation of imminent death to surge through his mind, the horror paralysing him. He couldn't think, couldn't move. The hand seemed to move in slow motion, as if to deliberately prolong his suffering. Still his limbs were frozen, his thoughts too sluggish to draw on the well of talent inside that might just save him.

Something flashed downward: the blade of a sword, intercepting the reaching hand, slicing through it at the wrist. The hand dropped away, losing its glow as it fell. There was no spurt of blood, no dripping ichor, nothing to indicate injury; just a severed stump. The reprieve freed Tom of his stupor. The weight of his doom lifted in an instant and he could breathe again, he could think. Though the eerie glow remained and the stump still advanced towards him, death no longer seemed inevitable. Instead, he defied it, he reacted. He attacked the Rust Warrior, finally unleashing his talent, not simply using it to crush and destroy but to repulse, to deny, to negate. The stump withdrew, the giant figure staggered backward. Still Tom kept up the pressure, forcing the Warrior away. He was vaguely aware of Kat being there, of her screaming something at him, but he couldn't spare the attention to decipher what. With a final effort he flung his enemy from its feet, sending the giant flying backwards. Now he did kill, reducing the Warrior to a burst of heat and light and a flurry of bloodied flakes. Realisation sank in that he was only alive thanks to Kat's intervention. He couldn't believe how close the touch of death had come and he was determined to make this reprieve count. Surviving such a close call had invigorated him, he felt more awake, more *alive* than he had in an age. And Tom hadn't finished, not by a long shot.

Kat's words came to him then, as his brain caught up and had time to process what she had shouted earlier. "What the breck are you playing at you dumb ass? Do something!" What indeed. Then, presumably as he reacted, she'd yelled, "Go, kid! Give it hell!"

Same old Kat. Tom drew strength from the familiarity of her presence. He allowed his ability to well up inside him, spurred on by the emotions that raced through him – fear, embarrassment, even shame at his need to be saved, but most of all there was anger; at the Rust Warrior for nearly killing him and at himself for nearly allowing it to. He felt the energy of his talent spread through his body like water rushing to fill a vacant vessel. Power sang through his veins, making his skin tingle and fingertips burn. When he couldn't contain it anymore, he let go, lashing out at his enemies. Not just at one Rust Warrior this time but at all of them. Tom could sense them, their presence appearing to his inner eye as dark yet amorphous nodes of being.

They possessed a porous, honeycomb fragility in comparison to the black solidity of the Blade. In a heartbeat he had reached out to touch all those in his immediate vicinity, crushing every single one of them in the process.

The moment passed, his talent receded, draining out of him as rapidly as it had risen, leaving behind only a sense of something missing.

Kat on the other hand was animated and still pumped up. "Woohoo!" she crowed. "Go Tom! When you get angry, kid, you *really* get angry."

The words sounded muffled, as if heard through a filter, his awareness still expanding from its deadly focus to encompass the outside world once more. "Will you stop calling me 'kid'?" he said, though more from habit than from any genuine offence.

"After seeing this, maybe I will," she replied.

The attacking Rust Warriors were gone. There were no bodies, no smouldering cadavers, just a few rusted flakes still settling to the floor like autumnal leaves.

Tom made a quick headcount of the survivors. Two of the Blade had been lost and three of the Council Guards had fallen, leaving just one of the white and purple and five of the towering ebony figures. There was still no sign of Captain Verrill or those men who had stayed with him to fight as a rearguard, and Tom doubted there ever would be.

"Sir, are you able to continue?" the lone guard asked. The man's Heights accent struck Tom as almost comical amidst so much carnage, and as for his composure – no outward sign of fear, no apparent shock at seeing his colleagues cut down around him. Thaiss, how Tom wished he could be more like that. The guardsman might almost have been one of the Blade.

"Yes," Tom assured him. "I'm ready. Let's get this over with."

The Blade seemed to draw even closer around them as they pushed on, two in front, three behind. The surviving guard stayed tight by Tom's side, Kat at his shoulder. If he'd felt uncomfortable with such close attention before, it didn't bother him in the least now. Something had changed; his attitude. Tom no longer felt like a precious passenger guarded by formidable bodyguards – the soft centre of the group. He now felt fully part of things, as formidable as Kat and as powerful as the Blade. Normally such a concerted use of his talent would have left him drained and weak, but not this time. The power had receded but not completely. He could feel it, primed and ready, a mere thought away. Instead of being exhausted after the fight he felt energised, alive, and itching to go again. His talent bubbled within him, barely in check. He didn't know whether this was due to carrying a cylinder of pure core material on his back or simply the adrenalin rush, but he wasn't complaining either way. The Rust Warriors were welcome to attack again. When they did, they wouldn't know what had hit them.

NINE

Tom's spirits were lifted by Kat, who had been in buoyant mood since the battle. Her confidence was infectious. Their mastery of the Rust Warriors, or rather *his* mastery, gave them every reason to hope that the worst might be over. Bone flu begat the Rust Warriors, and they were used to seize control of key areas in the city. That seemed to be the extent of the plan. If so, they'd now learnt to overcome their enemy's chief, perhaps *only*, weapon. All they had to do was keep sharp and focused and they couldn't fail. Tom wanted to get the core replenished as quickly as possible so that he could get on with the rest of his life, his *new* life, which would be lived on his terms. Yet a nagging corner of his mind worried that things couldn't be this easy – if the loss of more than half those sent to guard them could really be considered easy.

One thing that Tom was increasingly conscious of as they moved ever closer to the heart of the city was how pleasant the surroundings were. He recalled the dingy oppressiveness of the Swarbs' Row – the first of

Thaiburley's internal corridors he'd had any real experience of – and this was a long way removed from
that. Everything here was light, bright and airy. Since
they'd entered the residential areas even Kat seemed
to have forgotten her discomfort at being enclosed.

Tom wondered which Row they were actually in. The
Heights, certainly, but which one? He recalled the levels
verse – the rhyme that was supposed to enable a person
to work out exactly where in Thaiburley's labyrinthine
passageways they were at any given moment.

From the Medics' Row where lives are saved
To the streets of the Bankers where fortunes are made
From Residence Rows where Kite Guards patrol,
And learned folk study the soul,
Arkademics and Masters with wisdom to share,
The city's leaders, entrusted to care…

He snorted. Fat lot of good that did him. Where was
the verse that said:

From empty corridors and silent places
Where Rust Warriors wait to steal your faces…?

Okay, so maybe he'd never make a poet.

He guessed this had to be one of the Residences;
certainly he could well imagine they might look
something like this. Not that it really mattered, he was
just curious.

As if to emphasise exactly how pleasant life in the
Heights could be, they stumbled into a virtual park,

just a short while after the pitched battle in which Tom had frozen and so nearly died.

Due to the straight corridors, Tom could see the park long before they actually reached it. He could hear it too. Bird song. Tom had almost forgotten what that sounded like. Songbirds were a rarity in the City Below. Those few that had managed to establish themselves were likely to end up in the frying pan or the cook pot long before they reached old age.

The nearer they came, the more he was able to see of what looked to be a garden, and the more it struck him that those living in the City Below were provided with nothing like this. Once he would simply have been awed by something like this, not questioning why those up-City should have such luxuries when his own Row didn't, but he was increasingly coming to question such inequality rather than just accepting it.

The sounds that now washed over them reminded Tom of waking up beside the Thair to the feel of his cheeks gently warmed by the sun's early rays and the chorus of a hundred tiny voices raised in song as if to welcome the day – a celebration of the new dawn. People in the Heights really had no idea how lucky they were.

The open area the group then stepped into was much larger than the play park and had the added benefit of not being littered with dead people. On the contrary, everything here seemed very much alive, even when it proved not to be.

A small bright-breasted bird shot across the open square above their heads – a flash of brown and red.

As it flew, the bird squawked out alarm at their intrusion, its strident call rising above the background chorus. The bird looked so realistic and yet...

"It's a projection, isn't it?" Kat said, her voice quiet, as if she didn't fully believe her own words.

"Yes," Tom replied. "I think it is."

"But how...?"

"No idea."

A small brown creature – like a tiny rat but fluffier and somehow cuter – scurried across their path to disappear into the undergrowth. Kat laughed in delight, a child-like sound that surprised Tom coming from her.

The floor of the square was carpeted in close-cropped grass while around them bushes and even a few trees rose in a profusion of greens – bright, dark, glossy, matte – shades and shapes abounded. Here sat a bush of tiny leaves that veered towards yellow, there a bunch of spear-like grasses standing tall and straight and pale, while beside them was a plant whose long, pointed leaves were variegated and so shiny they might almost have been waxed. Where the grasses stood rigid with military precision, these leaves spread outward and curved towards the ground. Small low benches carved from white stone were dotted among the undergrowth, each one about the right size for two people, giving some indication of this small park's purpose.

One particularly tall flower caught Tom's attention, a single bud that stood proud at the tip; a rod-straight stem which emerged from a collar of spear-like leaves. He bent to examine it and as he did the bud rapidly opened to reveal a beautiful bright red flower, the petals curving upwards as if to suggest an elegant wine glass. At the same time the flower released a puff of air in Tom's face. He jerked back instinctively but needn't have worried. This was not an attack, but proved to be no more than a concentrated blast of what he assumed must be the flower's normal perfume. Sweet, floral, if a little sickly for his taste.

He reached out to hold the flower's stem, feeling the hardness of metal beneath the fibrous green. A device, not a living thing at all, despite the very convincing appearance. Curious to see if everything else was similar, he reached out to touch the broad, fern-like leaf of a taller plant nearby. His hand passed straight through its gently swaying form. A projection.

"None of this is real!" he said, feeling almost cheated.

"Some of it is," Kat replied as she lifted her hand to suck on the tip of a finger. "The brecking thorns on this one are at any rate."

The entire park proved to be exactly that: an ingenious blend of the real, the artificial and the completely illusory; and much of the time it was impossible to tell one from another.

"This whole place is trying to play mind games with us," Kat muttered.

Tom knew what she meant. The park was doubtless intended to relax people, to ease stress and inspire feelings of tranquillity; a retreat for city dwellers who might otherwise never experience the outside world. Maybe under normal circumstances that worked for him, but not today. When you were moving through hostile territory, constantly looking over your shoulder and suspicious of every shadow, a place where everything was geared to fool the senses took on a far more sinister aspect.

Even so, he couldn't help but be impressed by the artifice, the thought that had gone into planning all this.

"Gardens of Tranquillity, they're called," the lone surviving Council Guard supplied. So, Verrill wasn't the only one among the White and Purples capable of being human. "People come here to relax... Or they did."

Kat snorted. "Creepy."

The feature that most drew Tom's attention was the waterfall, though his initial impression was anything but favourable. The falls burbled down one wall – a dozen or so small pools in a descending series from which water bounced and tumbled, one to another, the whole set among rugged grey stones topped with mosses and tufts of grass. Tom might have been more impressed if he hadn't seen so many examples of the real thing during his time in the world outside. This seemed no more than a crude and clumsy imitation by comparison. At least, it did until he stepped to one side and was suddenly granted a view beneath the surface of the rock face.

A succession of small containers, like oblong buckets, were being carried on a conveyor belt to the top of the falls, where each tipped and deposited a basinful of water into the uppermost pool before heading back towards the ground on the opposite side of the belt, to be immediately replaced by the next container in line for a repeat performance. Huge toothed wheels turned ponderously in the background, keeping the buckets moving at a constant pace.

Tom took a step backwards and the rock wall appeared solid and rocklike again. Forward and it became translucent, like tinted glass, once more displaying the fall's inner workings. He repeated the process several more times, backward and forward, marvelling at the transition.

Kat was like a small child, running her hands through illusory leaves at different speeds to see how much disruption it caused the projected images, sniffing at the scent-laden flower mechanisms – which were scattered throughout the park.

She looked across at him and grinned. "Have you ever seen anything like this?" she asked.

"No," Tom admitted, "never."

One of the things he'd always admired about Kat was her maturity. It wasn't simply that she was a year or two older than him, she had about her a sense of having seen and experienced things far beyond his ken. More than once it had made him feel like a fumbling child in comparison, yet in this environment she was the one acting like a child. It was a side of her he'd never really seen before. He doubted whether many people had.

The Blade moved across this contrived pocket of the outside world unperturbed, walking through the projections as if they weren't there, causing Tom to wonder whether they could actually sense them at all. If so, they clearly weren't fooled by the pretence and could differentiate readily between the real and the illusory.

Tom couldn't, and he found himself enchanted by this whole virtual park, if not to the same degree that Kat was.

"These gardens are used for education as well," the surviving white-and-purple said. "Groups of children are brought here to learn about the outside world."

"Why not just take them outside?" Kat wanted to know.

The guard shrugged.

The educational element made perfect sense to Tom. Why else would you have artificial flowers puffing out exaggerated concentrates of perfume in such extravagant fashion? Kat had now triggered so many that the place was starting to smell like the sweetest apothaker's shop in the world. Tom could just imagine some aged sage instructing a group of attentive children on the colours and perfumes of the various blooms. Of course, if the kids in the Heights were even remotely like those in the under-City, the "attentive" part was never going to happen, but it still conjured up a comfortable image.

One patch in particular drew Tom's interest: long spindly stems growing taller than he stood, bedecked with broad, flat, serrated leaves which resembled opened hands. Why this apparently innocuous bush should appeal to him so strongly he wasn't sure, but there was something in the way the leaves gently danced, as if marking time by shifting from one delicate tip to another, and the burnished redwood stems bent grudgingly forward and back, that he found enchanting. He stepped forward, straining his neck and pushing his face in among the insubstantial stems as if seeking a whiff of elusive perfume.

"Snap out of it," a voice said; the goddess.

Tom ignored her, irritated at the interruption.

"It's a trap, can't you feel it?"

What was the old crone going on about? Then he remembered the meadow of flowers in the mountains above the Jeeraiy. He'd had no notion that his actions were being influenced then, could something similar be happening now? Once alerted, he found the intrusion, sensed the presence seeping into his thoughts. The hypnotic plant, he realised; somehow this invasive presence was leaching out of the projection and into his mind.

"Well, now that you've finally woken up, do something about it," the goddess said.

He did. He flexed his power, destroying the insidious tendrils of attempted control before following them to their source, to the very systems that generated the virtual elements of the park.

A dark form appeared at his shoulder, towering over him. A black lance shot out, punching through the illusory plant, through the floor and into whatever circuits lay beneath. There was an arc of energy, the acrid smell of burning and a wisp of smoke. The willowy plant disappeared as did the presence which had attempted to invade Tom's mind. In fact, all the projections flickered out across the entire park, which suddenly seemed reduced and less magical as a result. The lance withdrew to reveal blackened and broken circuits. The Blade turned and walked away without saying a word.

Tom stared at the hole in the floor. It opened into the guts of the very systems that ran the city.

Thaiburley itself was turning against him.

It had been a trap, just as the goddess claimed. One not triggered by the Blade or by Kat or the Council Guard, but only by him. The realisation shook Tom. Up until now there had only been the Rust Warriors to contend with, but it was obvious their enemy was adapting, that it could utilise other tools when needed, and that they couldn't relax for an instant.

The broken park was now behind them and they continued through the bland, bright, and eerily empty corridors of the Row. It had been a while since they'd seen any bodies, and Tom wondered whether the citizens of this section at least had received enough warning to evacuate.

Tom's brief use of his talent in the park had done nothing to assuage it. The power still sizzled just below the surface, as if anxious for release.

It didn't have long to wait. A force of Rust Warriors appeared in the corridor ahead, half a dozen or more. Three of the Blade quickened pace and moved forward to meet them. Glad of this now familiar enemy, Tom didn't hesitate. He reached toward the Warriors with his mind and struck with bludgeoning force. The first two imploded in a shower of russet petals, and those behind followed in quick succession. By the time the Blade were able to engage the enemy, only a single Rust Warrior opposed them, and the trio made short work of that one.

Beside him, Kat was whooping and laughing. "That was amazing. Nothing's gonna stop you reaching the core now, Tom, you're invincible!"

He was almost willing to believe as much himself and laughed along with her, though he did so more in relief than anything else. The close call in the park had shaken him, and he worried what else might lie in wait for them.

TEN

Deliia hadn't changed much in the time Dewar had been away. That was both a comfort and a concern. There were people here who knew him and places he felt obliged to avoid as a result. Given the size of the reward that had apparently been posted on his head, even his own mother would have been tempted to turn him in were she still alive.

There were a few things working in his favour. The scent of war was in the air – even more prominent than the smells from the pickling factory and the fish smokeries that normally vied for a visitor's attention. With the spectre of conflict looming large, people had more immediate concerns than looking out for a man who had risen to prominence years ago, even if that man was the "King Slayer" – the assassin who had come so close to killing the ruler of their near neighbour and ally the Misted Isles.

If his intention had been to merely pass through the town, Dewar would have felt fully confident of doing so without being noticed. Unfortunately, he didn't have that luxury. There were things he needed to acquire; very particular items which were liable to raise awkward questions if requested in the wrong place or in the wrong way. Far better that he should assemble what was required here before travelling to the Misted Isles themselves. That community was too close-knit. It would be all but impossible to get what he needed there without drawing unwanted attention. Not that the process was all that simple in Deliia, complicated as it was by the need to avoid his former contacts and rely on less familiar sources.

He was already reconciled to not replacing the one thing he missed the most: the kairuken. His had been lost during the desperate battle in the Jeeraiy against another former member of the Twelve, and its absence had weighed heavily on him ever since; but the weapon was so much his trademark that any attempt to replace it would be asking for trouble.

As long as he was careful, it ought to be comparatively simple to go about his business quietly, assembling the various items he wanted and slipping across the channel without anyone being the wiser. All the activity helped, of course. With so many new faces in town, one more recent arrival was all the less noteworthy.

It would take a stroke of spectacularly bad luck to betray him. Of course, ever since the day that Inzierto III had so fortuitously escaped death at the expense of one of his courtiers, Dewar had been forced to admit that luck wasn't always the most reliable of companions, so he wasn't about to take anything for granted.

It all went smoothly at first. He was used to improvising and little of what he wanted was likely to arouse suspicion, particularly in the prevailing climate when weapons were far from a novelty. There was only one truly exotic item. He thought long and hard about alternatives but in the end decided it was worth the risk of raising an eyebrow or two. Discrete enquiry identified an herbalist who might just carry what he was after.

Now all that remained was to decide on the best approach. The herbalist in question was one Molivat Kraisch, said to specialise in the unusual and the outlandish, to possess a keen intelligence, and to be "odd". That last was the word that cropped up universally whenever Kraisch's name was mentioned. Evidently there was something about the herbalist that made folk uneasy.

This was enough to make Dewar feel the same, so he decided to make his approach as circumspectly as possible. To do so, he would need a proxy, an accomplice. It took him more than half the day to find her and, once he had, he would have been hard pressed to explain exactly why he settled on this girl in particular. Except that she was young, pretty in a waif-like way, and had about her an air of desperation. Also, she looked like a girl who might well have a much-loved but ailing mother.

He encountered her soon after midday at a coffee house not far from the town centre. It wasn't a place he was familiar with – one of many that had sprung up subsequent to his exile – and it proved to serve an excellent brew. The girl served him, and there was something about her appearance, her demeanour, that clicked instantly into place. He lingered for a second cup and then a third – strong, dark, lightly spiced but not enough to detract from the flavour, just enough to blunt the bitterness. Whoever blended this had an excellent palate. Three cups were no hardship at all.

Dewar was at his most charming, engaging the girl in banter, and discovering her name was Seffy.

He tipped her heavily. "Tell me, Seffy," he said after refusing a fourth cup as she cleared away the empty third. "Would you be interested in making a little extra money?"

Her smile dissolved into a look of wary calculation. "I'm not that sort of girl, sir," though she said it in a manner that suggested she might be but only if the price was right.

"And I'm not that sort of a man," he assured her; *at least, not today*.

She stared at him, clearly puzzled and waiting for him to continue. She appeared to be around twenty years old, with long, straight brown hair, big doe eyes, a sprinkling of freckles across her high cheekbones, a thin figure which was untroubled by curves and hinted at a lack of proper nutrition. Yes, she was perfect.

"I'm in need of a very particular kind of medicine. Don't worry, I don't have a disease," he added quickly as she recoiled slightly. "My condition isn't infectious. It's just that a part of my body no longer works as it should and requires a special supplement. The most effective supplement is extremely hard to find. Only one herbalist in all of Deliia is likely to have it. The trouble is that this man and I have some history and there's a lot of bad blood between us. He would never sell the medicine to me; in fact he'd delight in refusing to do so if he knew I was involved. So I need somebody with whom I have no obvious links to go and buy the medicine on my behalf, and for that I'm willing to pay, and pay well."

"How much?" she said instantly, suggesting he'd been right about her being desperate.

He named a figure, which he calculated to be higher than she was ever likely to earn in any given month of waitressing, even allowing for tips. He saw her eyes widen and knew that she was hooked. Now all he had to do was reel her in.

She then proved that she wasn't entirely stupid by asking one more question. "Why me?"

Dewar was ready for that one. "Because I like you, and if I'm going to hand over a lot of money to a virtual stranger, it might as well be to someone I like." He smiled, with what he hoped was enough warmth to allay any further doubts. "Besides, how could anyone resist a pretty face like yours, eh?"

No hint of a blush but she returned the smile and he knew then that they were in business.

Seffy finished her shift late that afternoon. Dewar met her a little way down the street – she didn't want to set tongues wagging among her work colleagues by walking out of the shop with a random man. The efficiency with which she spelt out the arrangement made him suspect this wasn't the first time she'd met a customer after hours.

"Where to?" she asked, which came as a pleasant surprise. He would have expected her first concern to be the money.

"This way."

The herbalist's shop wasn't far. As they walked, the assassin coached the girl in what he wanted her to say. She proved a pleasingly fast learner, and he congratulated himself on the decision to approach her. By the time they stopped, just around the corner from Kraisch's place, she had learnt her lines and could deliver them convincingly.

"What's your name?" he demanded.

"Kathy Wicks, sir."

"And why are you here, Kathy?"

"It's me mum, sir. She's in a bad way, and the doctor says that the only thing could help her is something called... zyvan berries?" It was actually zyvan berry juice, but too much accuracy might in itself be suspicious. Dewar nodded and she continued. "He said he knows how to prepare the medicine but not where to get the berries from. I've come to you because I've always heard you can get hold of anything. Is that right, sir? Can you, please? For me mum's sake."

He asked her several questions, such as the name of the doctor who'd tended her mother and where exactly she'd first heard of the herbalist's establishment. She responded clearly and without hesitation, thinking on her feet and delivering lie upon smooth lie with the face of purest innocence.

Dewar nodded his approval. "You should have been an actress."

She smoothed back her long hair. "Reckon I am, as it happens. I spend me life smiling at strangers every minute of every working day. What else would you call it?"

Ah, Dewar reckoned this was perhaps the first wholly unguarded thing she'd said to him since they met. She was beginning to trust him, whether she realised it or not.

Satisfied, he held out some money – not the amount he'd promised her but more than enough to pay for a few drops of zyvan berry juice. But when she took it, he didn't let go.

"Where did you get the money from?" he asked sharply.

"Saved it, sir," she replied without pause. "I work as a waitress, see, been puttin' aside what I could, for medicine."

He grinned and released his hold on the coins. "Good girl."

He peered around the corner, watching as the girl crossed the road and entered the herbalist's shop. Once she had, he stepped back out of sight, leant casually against the wall and waited. He was nonchalant, relaxed, glancing up at the sky one minute and down the street the next; a man waiting for his girl to finish her shift or perhaps for his mates, ready to go for a swift ale or two down the tavern after work. No one worth paying attention to, that was for sure.

There was a risk in what he was doing, though fortunately Seffy was taking most of it. What he hadn't told her was that zyvan berries, also known as death kiss berries, had no real medicinal benefit for any known ailment, though they were one of the gentlest and most pain-free methods of killing somebody. Their toxin also benefited from being virtually undetectable. That latter made them of interest to him and a favoured tool for many an assassin. Kraisch would doubtless know this. He would also know that the berries were once popular with medics for putting terminally ill patients out of their misery. Dewar was counting on the latter to allay any suspicions. It was perfectly reasonable that a kindly physician of a certain generation might seek death kiss berries to ease the passing of a favourite patient, and of course he wouldn't trust the patient's daughter with his real intent, not when he was relying on her to find the berries.

Yes, a risk, but a calculated one.

He had to wait longer than anticipated, and it was just reaching the point where he would have to go for a short walk before his lingering became suspicious, when the girl hurried around the corner.

"Did all go well?" he asked.

"Yes…" she said.

Her tone, though, prompted him to ask, "But?"

"He asked a lot of questions."

Kraisch was suspicious then, damn! Dewar gripped her arm and hurried her away from the corner and the shop. "Such as?"

"Oh, all sorts, like what was the doctor's name, what was my mother's name, what illness did she have, stuff like that."

"And you answered him each time?"

"Course I did; convincing as you like."

"Good. You have the berry juice, then."

"Well, not exactly."

"How inexact are we talking here?" He stopped walking, which meant that she had to, as well since he was still holding her arm.

"He says he can get some but that he doesn't have any at the shop. Wants me to go back an hour after dark and he'll have the berries for me then."

Three hours away. And where else would a herbalist keep his stock apart from on the premises? Either Kraisch was extremely suspicious, or he had designs on Seffy that had nothing to do with zyvan berry juice. "He took the money, I suppose?"

She shook her head. "Wanted to, but I wouldn't let him."

"Good girl." Three hours. Enough time for Seffy to consider the risks in going back to the herbalist. Enough, perhaps, for her to decide to take the money intended for the berry juice and not come back, cutting her losses.

"So what now?" she asked.

"You go to his shop an hour after nightfall, as instructed."

"Oh, I do, do I? I'm not so sure about that. I mean, it isn't what we agreed on, is it? You never said nothing about *two* trips, nor about skulking around in the dark."

"True." His smile was a thin one, "which is why I shall of course be paying you double the sum agreed, once you deliver the zyvan berry juice."

She stared at him for a moment, as if mulling over the new terms. "All right, I'll do it, then. *Double*, mind."

"Double," he assured her.

"And where will you be?"

"Close by throughout. I'll meet you on the corner where I waited for you just now, and will give you back the money for the berry juice just before you go into the shop." He held out his hand. "I'll take care of it for now, though, just in case you lose it."

She stared at him, her nostrils flaring, but obviously thought better of arguing, settling on a smile instead. "Fair enough." She handed across what was, after all, his money, and said, "Later, then." With that, she flounced off.

"Yes," Dewar said quietly, watching her go. "Later…"

A man was staring at him, trying not to be obvious and failing miserably. Damn! That herbalist was one suspicious brecker. He must have had Seffy followed from the shop. Not that Dewar could blame anyone other than himself; he should have been more careful.

Best to get this sorted out now, see what damage had been done and then adjust plans accordingly. He strolled off in the same direction the girl had taken but walking far more slowly. The man followed. Dewar took a side road Seffy hadn't and his shadow did the same. Two shadows now; the first had been joined by a friend. Neither looked to be the intellectual type, though the newcomer was a great deal bigger, broader, and meaner-looking than the original.

Now that support had arrived his pursuer grew bolder. The pair hurried to catch up with Dewar, who

was happy to let them, anxious to let events play out.
They reached him, one on either side, and bundled
him into an alleyway, where they backed him against
a wall.

The smaller, stubble-chinned fellow – his original
stalker – took the lead, standing directly in front of
him and glowering.

Dewar flinched before an onslaught of fetid breath
as the man said, "Hand it over."

"Hand what over?"

"Don't come the innocent with me. The money that
tart gave you I watched it. Bold as brass you were.
Well listen, and listen good. Gunnell Street is *my*
manor. If any girl earns so much as a farthing on that
stretch it comes straight to me. Not to you, not to anyone else, to me! Got it?"

It was all Dewar could do not to laugh. These two
weren't connected to Kraisch at all. This was just a
pimp and his muscle trying to protect their territory.
He relaxed and, given that there were no implications
to his mission, determined to let off a bit of steam and
enjoy himself.

A man walked across the mouth of the alley,
glanced in, looked immediately away and kept walking. Thank Thaiss; the last thing Dewar needed was a
well-meaning passer-by getting in the way.

"Now, hand the money over nicely and I'll just have
Mitch here give you a few gentle slaps to see you on
your way. Of course, if you'd rather be awkward about
it, I'll let him really go to town and you'll find yourself
waking up in the infirmary. So, what's it to be?"

"No, please, I won't argue." Dewar lifted his hands in apparent surrender, palms open, clearly empty. In doing so, he moved his thumb, tensing the flexor muscles of his right forearm in a specific way, simultaneously twisting the arm slightly at the elbow. He'd been hoping for a chance to try out the new spring-loaded arm holster before crossing to the Misted Isles, and here was the perfect opportunity.

The knife shot forward into his hand. He clasped the warm hilt automatically as it landed and followed the weapon's momentum, plunging the blade into the pimp's neck. He struck from the side, so that any blood spurt wouldn't come straight at him, and was already sliding his body in the opposite direction as he pulled the blade free. He took a few steps backwards, going deeper into the alley and away from Mitch, who, predictably, was coming for him. The enforcer had to side-step the collapsing form of his dying employer as it slithered down the wall, but, judging by the murderous expression, that wasn't going to stop him wreaking revenge.

Dewar studied the big man's approach. It wasn't blind, it wasn't mindless. Mitch clearly knew a thing or two about fighting. But then so did Dewar. The thug had produced a club from somewhere – a crude baton of polished wood. Not as sophisticated as a razzer's puncheon, perhaps, but it still meant he had the advantage of reach over Dewar's knife.

The assassin crouched, both hands before him, his right hand holding the knife ahead of the left, which was ready to hold, deflect, defend.

With a quick roll of the arm, Mitch attempted a swipe at Dewar's blade with his club, but the assassin was ready for that, twisting the knife out of the way and attempting a strike of his own as the arm sailed past. He missed. Dewar danced a few steps further back. Mitch advanced, following him warily, but the assassin had counted on that. His steps back were a feint. As soon as he completed the second Dewar sprang forward, taking the enforcer by surprise and instantly stepping inside the natural striking arc of the club. His right arm drove the knife into Mitch's exposed side while his left hand grappled to hold off the arm wielding the baton. He struck a second time and a third, quick piston-like blows, before Mitch managed to swat him aside.

Dewar rode the force of the blow, disengaging but staying on his feet and, most importantly, keeping hold of the knife.

The big man was standing awkwardly now with his free hand pressed to his injured side, blood leaking between his fingers. He was hurting and injured, probably severely.

"Your employer's dead, Mitch." Dewar nodded towards the livid red stain that marked one wall; a smear that led down to the pimp's lifeless body. "You're badly hurt. What's the point in fighting on? Let's both walk away from this while we still can, and you go and get yourself stitched up."

The look in the enforcer's eye told Dewar that it was never going to happen. For Mitch, the fight had turned personal. Understandable, the assassin supposed, after someone had punctured your side several times with a dagger.

Mitch was evidently a man of few words. "Breck you!" he growled, before straightening and lumbering forward again.

That was a mistake. He must have realised it as soon as Dewar did. His movements were hampered, made clumsy by the severe wounds. He didn't quite stagger but gave every impression that he might be about to at any second. Dewar easily avoided the crude swing of the club. He skipped aside as the roundhouse sweep whistled past him, to move behind Mitch and draw his blade across the enforcer's throat, all in one movement and without breaking stride. Dewar kept walking towards the mouth of the alley, not bothering to look back. His ears reported the choking gasps of Mitch's final breaths and then the sound of something heavy dropping to the ground.

Despite his best efforts at avoidance, his tunic was speckled with blood. Hardly ideal for keeping a low profile. He exited the alley and headed towards his lodgings for a fresh change of clothes and to review his plans for the evening.

It would have taken a man of rare paranoia to keep a constant watch on the street, but Dewar wasn't about to take any chances, so he walked past the herbalist's shop just once, paying no more attention to the target building than to any of the others around it. He saw all he needed to. Two storeys; the shop at ground level, living quarters above, probably a cellar as well – a fairly typical arrangement for Deliia. The building stood at the end of a small terrace, with a narrow road to one side. The upper storey projected out to over-hang the road slightly, while the roof was tiled and gently pitched.

He turned the corner and sauntered along the side road, climbing up a slight incline in the process. A small back yard was protected by a shoulder-high fence. No indication of any dogs, which was hardly a guarantee. The upper storey boasted a single window on this side; narrow, but he could still get through it if need be. Unfortunately, it stared straight into the matching window of the house opposite. Too exposed. He rejected the window as a potential entry point, which left only the back door.

Breaking in at ground level carried its own risks, so timing was going to be crucial; but that door was his best option. Decision made, he continued on his way, already rehearsing the moves in his mind.

The situation was far from ideal. His current strategy had been formulated in a hurry and Dewar hated half-baked schemes. All his professional life he'd re-lied on meticulous planning and precise execution. Before his exile he had been a senior member of the Twelve – the secretive society dedicated to assassina-tion which acted as counterbalance to imperial ambition and had been an integral part of the Misted Isles' system of government for centuries. In those days such discipline had come as naturally to him as breathing.

He was fast coming to the conclusion that the years spent hiding in Thaiburley had seen his standards slip. His former self would have been dismayed at the slip-shod strategy he had formulated. Still, there was no point in ruing spirits that had already escaped the bottle. All he could do was deal with the situation as it stood. He should perhaps be grateful for this oppor-tunity and treat it as a dry run. This undertaking had highlighted weaknesses that he couldn't afford once he reached the Misted Isles. It gave him the chance to tighten things up so that there would be no errors once the endgame began.

The girl was due to arrive any moment, so this was his last chance to review preparations and satisfy him-self that he hadn't overlooked anything. He did so quickly and could see no better alternatives. The flat but broad rucksack now hugging his back contained all the tools he was likely to need.

Seffy met him as arranged. She looked nervous, and he wondered how close she'd come to not returning at all despite the potential reward. He smiled reassur-ingly and handed over the money for the berry juice, the same sum as before.

Dewar went first, hurrying past the shop with his head down – who but a burglar or mugger would loiter in the shadows after dark? He turned into the side road and paused after a few steps, crouching to fiddle with his boot, as if dealing with a loose buckle or perhaps a stone that had worked its way inside to trouble his tender foot.

A moment later he heard rather than saw Seffy ap-proach, her clipped footfalls sounding loud in the still

of the evening. Three knocks, a slight pause, and the
door creaked open. A man's voice bade her enter. As
soon as he heard the door close again Dewar moved,
vaulting the fence and crossing quickly to the back of
the house. He stood for a moment, back pressed to the
wall, waiting to see if his intrusion had been noticed.
No sign of a reaction, so he sidled along the wall to the
door, conscious of how vulnerable he was to a casual
glance out the window by anyone in the house opposite. The lock proved to be a decent one but nothing
special. He had it sprung in seconds and slipped inside
the dim interior of the house.

He was in a small room – an ante room, rest room,
preparation room, kitchen; he neither knew nor cared.
Two voices reached him through the open door leading to the larger room beyond – presumably the shop
proper: Seffy's and that of a man.

Dewar moved with calm efficiency, crouching and
slipping off the rucksack. When it came to distance
killing his weapon of choice would always be the
kairuken – such an elegant instrument, its razor
sharp discs equally as deadly as a crossbow bolt and
far quicker to reload. However, he was nothing if not
adaptable. He removed the two elements from his
bag, deftly fitting and securing the bow-section to
the stock, careful to make no noise. He was operat-
ing in near darkness, but that was no hindrance. He
had practiced this manoeuvre many times blind-
folded, so the dim light filtering in from the shop was
a bonus. Ideally, he would have liked to have completed the assembly before setting out, but that

would have made the weapon awkward to carry and too obvious.

He finished in under a minute, the resultant bow by no means the largest or most powerful he'd ever used but it would still pack a punch within the confines of a room and was unerringly accurate. A good weapon.

He cocked the bow but didn't load it yet, though he did take out three bolts before stashing the bag against the wall beside the door. Only then did he continue forward, crouching low as he entered the main area of the shop. During the short time it had taken him to assemble the bow he'd continued to listen with half an ear to the two voices, which had grown ever more strident: the man's aggressively so, the woman's defensive. There was something naggingly familiar about the man's. Dewar was certain he'd heard it before, further justifying his caution in not approaching the herbalist directly. The name Kraisch was unfamiliar to him, but, as he well knew, names were malleable things and easily changed.

His view of the shop's interior was blocked by a solid counter, which made sense – his entry point being via what was clearly a back room, not accessible to the public. This was both a blessing and a hindrance. It hid his approach even more effectively than the darkness would have done, but at the same time prevented him from getting a sense of the room's layout and assessing with any certainty how many people were present.

The quickest way to remedy that was to raise his head carefully and peer over the top of the counter, but he resisted the temptation. Movement at that sort of height was too likely to be spotted, being close to the natural eye line of anyone standing in the room's interior. So instead he moved to the end of the counter and peered around its edge. Slow movement this close to the ground was far less likely to be spotted.

From his slightly skewed vantage point Dewar could see three people. A single lamp illuminated the scene, its low position on a shelf casting long shadows, creating a surreal form of shadow play enacted against the wall behind the principles in exaggerated gestures and movements.

The assassin's gaze was drawn first to Seffy. She was being held by a much larger man, both of her arms gripped in his ham-sized fists. In front of her was another, shorter man, his back to the assassin.

"I told you, I don't know!" Seffy was whining now. Either she really was a consummate actress or this wasn't acting. Dewar suspected the latter and couldn't blame her. For all she knew at this point he'd sent her in here to die.

"Come, come," the shorter man said. "The story of your poor sick mum, all very touching, I'm sure, but a complete fabrication, no?"

Dewar froze. He'd been right. He did know that voice. He'd been unable to place it earlier but, hearing it more clearly and now that he was able to match voice with phraseology and to the stance and build of the speaker, he recognised who this was all too well. He didn't need to see the man's face, he could picture it still: heavily lidded eyes, slightly sagging jowl that invariably leant the man a hang-dog expression, receding hairline, and ears that jutted out... Prosman the Poisoner. So this was what had become of him. Not a member of the Twelve as such, but Prosman had been very much a part of the organisation, supplying tailored poisons for the assassins' every need. His downfall had been unexpected and swift. He'd perpetrated some indiscretion or other – Dewar never had been privy to the details – and had disappeared overnight. This was about a year before Dewar's own misfortune. No one spoke of his fate and it was assumed he'd been quietly killed, but evidently not; he'd merely relocated to Deliia and reinvented himself as Kraisch the herbalist. Hardly the most opaque of disguises, but effective enough it seemed, because he was still here and evidently thriving.

No wonder Kraisch had such an uncertain reputation in the town. Dewar never had trusted the poisoner and doubted the herbalist was much of an improvement.

"Perhaps I've been too gentle with you," Kraisch was saying. "Perhaps you think a few sharp words and a slap or two are the only rewards that await your silence. Is that it? Well permit me to enlighten you."

Dewar couldn't see the whole room from his current position so didn't know if there was anyone else close to the counter, out of his line of sight. He decided to risk a quick look. The guard holding Seffy might be facing this way but his vision would be limited beyond the range of the lantern. Lying flat to the ground, the assassin pushed himself out beyond the counter, seeing a single pair of feet before he drew back. One man, three targets in total.

"On the shelves around you sit a wealth of subtle potions and elixirs," the herbalist continued.

Dewar slid two throwing knives from their sheaths, placing them carefully on the floor beside him.

"With them, I can escort you through the most exquisite levels of pain. Each time you think it can't possibly get any worse, it will."

Two of the three crossbow bolts were placed carefully next to the two knives.

"I shall pluck each and every nerve in your body, individually and in concert, composing a symphony of torment especially for you, an opus that will build gradually, by the gentlest of degrees, taking days to reach the ultimate, poignant crescendo of death. Of course, you will have been driven quite mad by this point."

The third bolt he loaded into the still-cocked crossbow.

"Trust me, long before the end you'll have told me everything you know about anything I might ask and will be begging for the blissful release of eternal rest."

Dewar stretched out on his stomach, crossbow held before him.

"And we'll start with a drop of this, your precious zyvan berry juice." The herbalist held out a small bottle, waving it in front of the terrified girl's face.

Seffy jerked her head away. "All right, all right, I'll tell you everything," she blurted. Not that Dewar could blame her. This wasn't exactly what she'd signed up for.

"Oh, I know you will," Kraisch assured her.

In some ways, the man holding Seffy posed the least threat, because he already had his hands full and would take precious seconds to react in any meaningful way. At the same time, he was standing completely still directly in front of the assassin, and might try to use the girl as a shield later. While Dewar had no compunction about killing the girl, why complicate matters?

The man stood head and shoulders above Seffy, which meant a narrow target, but the possibility of missing never even entered the assassin's mind. There is an art to using a crossbow, or rather a technique that, once learned, prevents you from using the weapon poorly. The knack lies in the ability to combine aiming and shooting in a single smooth process. Were a bowman to concentrate on taking aim first and then think about shooting as separate stages, the minute pause in switching focus from one to the other would invite a jerk of the trigger finger and increase the likelihood of slight tensing of the muscles in anticipation of the shot. Either could mean the difference between success and a near miss. A well-made crossbow was invariably accurate. Its wielder often wasn't.

Dewar had learnt all this while still an apprentice. He took aim and fired in one seamless flow of thought and action. The bolt punched into the target's forehead between the eyes. The man was thrown backwards, taking Seffy with him. She screamed but Dewar wasn't paying attention. As soon as the bow fired he discarded the weapon and snatched up one of the throwing knives. Half rolling and half pushing himself beyond the counter, he flung the knife. Its blade sank into the throat of the man standing by the counter even as he began to react. Dewar was on his feet in an instant, snatching up the other throwing knife and charging at the startled herbalist.

He could see Posman's podgy features now, a face that was instantly recognisable for all that it was older and even saggier.

Dewar saw Posman's eyes widen in recognition. "King..."

The assassin's knife buried itself to the hilt in the poisoner's chest, and the rest of the hated phrase died with the man.

Suddenly all was still. A sparse handful of seconds had passed and three men lay dead. Not bad, if he did say so himself.

"Wow," Seffy said, coming forward. "That was... amazing!" Her face was flushed and she was breathing deeply, the pronounced rise and fall of her chest granting her the suggestion of shape where none had been apparent before. He realised abruptly that the danger, the violence, the close brush with death, perhaps even the threat of torture, had excited and aroused her.

"He called you 'King'," she said. "Are you some kind of royalty, an exiled prince or something?" Her voice was soft, seductive.

Dewar said nothing, knowing there was still a job to complete. He bent down to prise the innocent-looking and oh so costly bottle of zyvan berry juice from the dead man's fingers.

Seffy continued her slow advance towards him, her eyes gazing into his as he straightened up. "You don't really have a medical condition, do you?"

"No, I don't." He moved away, deliberately turning his back on her as he quickly reclaim his bow and the unused bolts, and finally the rucksack from the other side of the doorway, but she was still there when he turned around. His throat seemed tight and he felt his manhood stir in response to her suddenly very sexual presence. He tried to remember when he'd last been intimate with a woman. Before he'd set out from Thaiburley, certainly.

"Presumably you've got a place in town where you're staying?"

"I do."

"Far from here?"

"Not in the least."

"Good, only all this violence has unnerved me." She was no more than a step away now. "I really don't want to spend the night alone."

"Well, after putting you through such a traumatic experience, it would be rude of me not to make certain you slept well…"

"Thank you." Her head tilted towards him and they kissed, her lips soft and warm, the tip of her tongue briefly teasing his.

Dewar broke the embrace and frowned. "But what about this ailing mum of yours?"

"Oh, I'm sure she'll cope."

"In that case, if you're certain…" With a mock bow and a flourish of the arm, he ushered her towards the door. As he'd noted when he first saw her, Seffy was far from ugly, and it would be pleasant to scratch this particular itch.

He could always kill her in the morning.

ELEVEN

Tom knew they were getting closer to the city's core. That sensitivity which the Prime Master had either instilled or brought out in him had become an almost constant throb in his mind, impossible to ignore. If he was aware of the core, he reasoned that the core was probably aware of him, which meant they should expect attack of one kind or another at any minute.

Not that he felt any satisfaction when his assumption proved to be right; far from it, this was one instance when he'd have been happy to be wrong all the way.

When it did come, as their company turned a right angled corner, it proved that the stakes had just been raised dramatically.

Confronting them stood a trio of figures united in their magnificence: Demons. All were male, all were bare-chested – displaying muscular, toned physiques – all had handsome features crowned with blond or light brown hair. They stood before the party with their wings partially opened, looking haughty, regal and glorious. An enigmatic, winning smile graced their lips and their clear eyes held warmth, compassion and grace. It was hard to believe that the Soul Thief was descended from the same stock. These looked far more like gods than Thaiss ever had.

"Goddess!" Kat murmured. "So *that's* what a real Demon looks like."

"Yeah," Tom replied. Seeing the Soul Thief was no preparation, no preparation at all. This was the first time even Tom been able to get a good look at a proper Demon. Before, when the Prime Master had taken him up to the city's roof, he'd caught fleeting glimpses in the corner of his eye as the Upper Heights' denizens teased him, but seeing them in their full glory like this was something else entirely. It was all he could do not to abase himself at their feet and pay homage.

And they glowed.

A halo of light appeared around each of their heads, a rippling nimbus that swiftly spread to encompass their whole bodies, apparently emanating from somewhere inside them.

The Blade closed ranks, as if anticipating something dire. They blocked Tom's view of the glowing trio, but they couldn't shut out the light, which must have built rapidly in intensity, so that the Blade were suddenly limned by searing brilliance – a dazzling luminance which punctured every crevice and gap between the black bodies and limbs of the Blade's imperfect barrier. Tom shielded his eyes, but despite himself he continued to watch through the cracks between his fingers, unable to entirely look away.

To Tom's horror, the Blade started to disintegrate. There was no violent explosion such as when they had faced the Rust Warriors earlier – this was more a form of erosion, a stripping away of layers. Shreds of blackness seemed to peel off the Blade and fly backward, behind the cowering humans. It was as if the light acted as a powerful abrasive, scouring the Blade away bit by bit, like the grains of a sandstorm flailing the flesh from a living body all the way down to the bone. Nor was that the only effect. The walls around them started to tremble and crumble. A trickle of dust fell on them and Tom looked up to see a jagged crack opening in the ceiling directly above his head. It seemed the whole corridor was about to collapse.

The Blade weren't going down without a fight, though. Black light – that was the only way Tom could think to describe it – erupted from the towering ebony figures, denying the blistering golden glow, holding it at bay. One of the Blade turned its head slowly to look at Tom. It said a single word.

"Run."

He did, the Blade's command seeming to free him from paralysis so that his legs were suddenly his own again. Nor was he alone. All three of them ran. As advice went, this seemed well worth heeding.

Behind them they heard the groan of structure under pressure followed by the rumble of collapsing masonry. Tom didn't look back, even as the floor trembled and bucked and not even when a cloud of dust overtook them, he simply kept running for all he was worth.

His blind funk was broken only when the guard said, a moment later, "Are we going the right way?"

"Are you kidding?" Kat replied. "As long as it takes us away from those things, any way is the right way."

Tom could only agree, though he knew what the guardsman meant. Unless they could deliver what Tom was carrying to the core, all they were achieving by running away was to delay the inevitable; and right now they were heading in completely the opposite direction; he could feel it.

He slowed, considering options, which was when the second great upheaval came. Tom saw the guardsman ahead of him falter and fall against the wall and even Kat staggered, while Tom was thrown from his feet. A great crack appeared in the wall to his right, widening and lengthening at an alarming rate as it raced towards the ceiling. Chunks of masonry started to fall. The whole ceiling looked set to come down.

"Tom!" Kat's voice, from somewhere on the far side of the mayhem, he hoped.

Tom scrambled backwards on his hands and knees as the ceiling and walls began to collapse in earnest. He pushed himself to his feet and turned to run, when something struck him on the head. Searing pain obliterated every other awareness for a brief instant before everything went blank.

Tom wasn't sure how long he had been unconscious. He came to in a room, a big room, even though it was obviously part of a residential unit – a living room or lounge.

"He's coming round," someone said, a boy's voice.

His mouth was dry and his head was pounding. He tried to lift a hand to feel the bump which he was certain had risen just to the right of centre, where he'd been struck, only to discover that his hands were tied behind him, and his feet too – they were fastened to the chair legs.

A face appeared in front of him, startlingly close. Ginger hair, plump cheeks, clean, pale complexion with clear brown eyes. "Hello," said the same voice that had spoken before. "I'm Ryan."

"Ryan, leave him alone!" snapped another, older voice.

The face quickly withdrew, enabling Tom to get a clearer view of the rest of the room.

Chairs and sofas, soft and cushioned in a biscuit brown off-white colour, formed a false quadrangle, though the room extended well beyond that space; and it was all so bright. Was this how everyone lived in the Heights? He'd always imagined that the homes built deep within the city, with other walls and dwellings pressing in on every side, even from above and below, would be dark and claustrophobic. The corridors they'd been travelling through might have been wide and airy, but he'd somehow expected the residences themselves to be more akin to the oppressive closeness he'd experienced in the Swarbs' Row. This was anything but.

Unfortunately, none of the well-padded, comfortable softness had been spared for him. He was sitting on, and indeed tied to, a far more functional piece of furniture; a hard-seated chair of solid wood.

There were seven other people in the room, all of them boys – no girls allowed in this gang, apparently. Ages ranged from Ryan, the lad who'd said hello – he seemed the youngest at maybe nine or ten – to the boy who now dropped into a chair facing Tom. About the same age as him, maybe a year or so older; dark haired, well-fed, every feature showing the sort of arrogance that suggested a sneer was never far away from curling his thin lips.

They were all smartly dressed, all clean-looking and all very obviously Heights boys.

Tom continued to work at the bonds holding his wrist, but he wasn't getting very far.

"I'm Miles," said the sneer-faced one. "This is my gang. Who are you and what are you doing here?"

None of your brecking business, Tom thought and would probably have said if his hands and feet weren't tied to a chair. "I'm Tom, and I'm just passing through, not looking for any trouble. Why have you tied me up?"

Miles shrugged. "Cos we could."

This signalled an outbreak of sniggering which rippled around the group.

Kids, Tom thought, *real kids*; none of them with the maturity of a six year old, at least not the six year olds he was used to. This was the Heights. None of these boys had needed to grow up anything like as quickly as he had. "Where are your parents?" he blurted, regretting the question as soon as he'd uttered it. Why risk antagonising them? Him and his big mouth.

Fortunately, Miles seemed oblivious to the implications and just gave another shrug. "Dead, or gone."

Neither possibility seemed to matter to him. Tom felt initial dislike turning to disdain. Didn't the idiot realise how lucky he was to even *have* parents? Evidently not, for he continued, "It's just us now."

At least it explained what was going on here: these kids were flexing their muscles, enjoying the first taste of what they imagined to be freedom, not caring that the city was falling apart around their ears, probably convincing themselves that it didn't affect them, that they were smart enough and clever enough to somehow survive. Doomed along with everyone else in Thaiburley if Tom couldn't get out of here.

"Listen," he said, softly, as if sharing a secret with them, and he sat forward as best he could. "When I said I'm just passing through, that's true; I am but I'm on a mission, a really important one. I've been sent to save the city, and you can help me. Think about it. I'll make sure everyone knows that you helped me. You'll all be heroes."

He glanced around the group and could see that one or two of them liked the sound of that, but not Miles, it seemed. "And I suppose the Prime Master himself sent you."

"Yes, yes he did," Tom admitted, wondering even as he spoke whether truth was really the best policy here.

Miles immediately howled with laughter, the other kids following suit a fraction later. "Now we all know you're lying. You're obviously not from the Heights – the clothes give that much away – just some kid who, in all the confusion, has found his way up here into our part of the city, and is now trying to make us let him go by spouting a pack of lies." Miles sprang from his chair and came over to thrust his face at Tom, who instinctively shrank away. "You're making it up as you go along, aren't you? Well we're not falling for it, you hear?" Spittle landed on Tom's cheek. "We're not stupid. You're nothing. If the Prime Master was going to send anyone to save the city it would be one of us, not some oik from the lower Rows."

"Yeah, right. Stands to reason." There were nods from the assembled kids.

Miles strutted back to his seat and pulled something onto his lap. Tom froze. It was his rucksack.

"Now, Mr Saviour of the City, let's see what you're carrying in this little bag of yours."

"No," Tom said. "Leave that alone."

Miles paused and grinned wickedly at him. "Why, afraid we'll discover what a thief you are? I bet you've been looting the empty residences and taking whatever caught your eye."

"I haven't taken anything. Don't do that," Tom said, as Miles continued to undo the rucksack. "You can't. It's dangerous... part of my mission..." Still no give in the knots that held his hands, no matter how hard he tried.

"Nice try, but if it's dangerous for us, why has a kid like you been trusted to carry it?" Miles pulled the sack open. "Well, well, what have we got here?" He pulled out the core canister.

"Please," Tom said, desperate for them to understand, to believe him. "I need what's in that container to save the city." But no one seemed to be paying him any attention anymore.

They'd left him with no choice. He couldn't allow them to open that canister. Apart from the devastation raw core material would cause if let loose, this really was Thaiburley's only hope of salvation. Tom focussed and reached out with his talent. He hated to do this, remembering all too clearly what he'd done to Dewar, but he had to.

"Looks like the sort of thing they store documents in," someone said. "Maps and stuff like that."

Tom pushed against Miles's mind.

"Yes, and very fine it is too," Miles said. "Look at the detailing, the studwork. It's beautiful."

Nothing happened. Tom stared at Miles. He could sense the older boy; his consciousness was there as a solid, dense block, but Tom's talent couldn't penetrate, it just slipped around the surface without gaining any purchase, washing over it as an eddy of water might around solid stone. Perhaps it was the blow to the head, perhaps that had affected his abilities in some way. He turned his attention to one of the other boys, the one who had identified himself as Ryan, reaching out and tweaking, just a little.

"Ow!" The boy cried out immediately.

"What's the matter?"

"Nothing, just a headache, I'm fine now."

This elicited another juvenile snigger from the boy next to him.

So it wasn't a problem with his abilities, they were still working fine. It was Miles. Miles was himself talented, whether he realised it or not, and his talent made him impervious to others', or at least to Tom's. What could he do now?

"Clearly a discerning thief," Miles was saying. "Just the one thing taken by the look of it. Let's see what's inside this pretty little package, shall we?"

You mustn't let him open that cylinder, the goddess said, materialising, as was her wont, to stand beside Miles.

Don't you think I know that?

If he does, the energies released will kill everyone here and destroy this whole section of the city.

"No, you mustn't, you can't!" Tom wriggled in his seat, stood up falteringly, hands and feet still bound to the chair, and tried to frog-hop towards Miles and the canister. Two boys sprang forward and pushed him back down.

Miles made tutting sounds with his tongue, clearly loving every second of this. He reached for the first clasp on the core canister.

Tom relaxed, knowing that he had no choice. He hated to do this. The other boys were innocents really, they were just easily led. Without Miles they'd probably be perfectly reasonable, but he had to do something and he couldn't touch Miles; whereas he could touch them.

Miles fiddled with the first clasp, appearing to move in slow motion. Tom reached out with his talent towards the other boys, resigned to what he was about to do even as he regretted it.

"Well, well," said a familiar voice. "What have we got here? A bunch of cloud scrapers playing at being street-nicks."

"Kat!" Tom could hear the relief in his own voice. She stood in the doorway, twin swords drawn.

Miles looked up, startled, but he wasn't about to give ground. "Get her!" he yelled.

"Oh, come on." Kat laughed as three of the gang started towards her, brandishing two knives and a length of piping between them. Ryan, the youngest, was among the trio, clasping one of the knives. "Is that the best you can come up with, 'Get her'?"

"Don't," Tom said, reckoning these kids didn't need to die; they were just doing their best to survive in an impossible situation, latching onto the first authority figure that presented itself. "She'll kill you."

"What are you waiting for?" Miles said as the three seemed to hesitate, "She's only a girl."

"No," Tom insisted. "She isn't 'only' anything. She's a Pits warrior and a Death Queen, and if you attack her she'll kill you."

Ryan at least paused at his words. Tom saw the boy glance in his direction, fear in the lad's eyes, but it was already too late. Kat sprung forward, straight towards the centremost kid. Her twin swords were flickering blurs to either side which ended with one of them striking forward and stabbing deep into the middle boy's torso. His body slid off the blade and hit the ground a fraction after the other two.

Miles leapt to his feet, shock on his face, but he still kept hold of the canister. He backed away from Kat, in such a way that the chair he'd sat on was between her and him, as if that was going to stop her. The other three boys stood motionless, horror on their faces as they stared at this dark apparition who had walked in and so casually cut down three of their friends in the blink of an eye. Tom noticed a damp patch blossom on the crotch of one, clearly visible against the dark brown of his trousers.

Kat's gaze flicked over them. "You three, get out, now!"

None of them needed any further urging and all three scampered past Kat and out the door.

She continued to advance towards Miles, who had backed away as far as he could, his heels knocking against the wall. "You can go, too, if you put that canister down," she told him.

A cunning look entered the boy's eyes. "So this is important to you, is it?" His fingers again reached for the catches. "Stand back, then, or I'll open the canister and pour whatever's in here onto the ground."

"No, you won't," Kat assured him, still walking forward, her twin swords held at her side, pointing towards the ground, her hips swaying in a slow, slinky, almost seductive sashay. "You won't live long enough to do that."

There was an air of desperation in Miles' voice as he said, "Well what will you give me, to hand it back to you?"

What's in it for me, again. Was Tom the only person in the world who didn't put his own interests first and ask that question at every turn, even when the stakes were so high? He was beginning to wonder if there was something wrong with him.

"Your life," Kat replied softly, her gaze never wavering from the boy's eyes. The cunning there had gone entirely now, replaced by something that might almost have been panic.

Miles moved suddenly. "Well you can have it, then!" He flung the canister to one side. Tom watched in horror as it tumbled through the air, one catch flapping free. If the second burst open on impact...

Kat was moving almost before Miles. She ran a couple of steps, dropping both swords as she went, and leapt with arms extended, all in the blink of an eye. Tom saw her hands close on the core canister, watched her land and roll, coming up hard against the wall, back to the ground, one leg crooked against the wall, but with the canister cradled safely to her body. Miles had used the distraction to make a run for it, bolting not for the door but into one of the other rooms.

"Thank Thaiss!" Tom let out a held breath on seeing the canister safe.

Kat was on her feet in an instant and came over to cut him free. His hands tingled with returning circulation and felt clumsy as he resealed the dangling clasp and stashed the canister back into his rucksack. As he did so, his gaze fell on the three dead boys.

"Did you have to kill them?"

"Yes," she replied calmly, with no hint of regret. "To save the others, to save some of them at least... and to save you."

He wanted to believe that, wanted to believe that something dark hadn't reared up from within her and taken possession just for a moment; but then he looked into Ryan's sightless eyes and wasn't sure.

The room Miles had fled into proved to be a bed-room. A gaping hole in the back wall led into another dwelling, through which he had doubtless made good his escape.

"Pity," Kat said.

Tom made no comment.

"Come on!" a voice called urgently from outside. "It's coming."

They hurried out into the corridor, glancing to their left, in the same direction that the guardsman was anxiously staring. Tom sensed that this was where the Demons and the Blade had so recently fought, but si-lence reigned there now. Unfortunately, the corridor wasn't empty. Striding towards them came a winged, golden figure. Kat and Tom ran to join the guardsman, who was already at the foot of the mound of rubble where the corridor had collapsed. They scrambled up, pulling and crawling and forcing their way through, regaining their feet in the corridor beyond, where they started to run. None of them had much faith in a pile of rubble stopping a Demon.

Tom led them down a branching corridor to the right, if only to put the wall of rubble and the Demon beyond out of their direct line of sight.

Tom knew that his fitness levels had risen dramati-cally during the long journey to the Thair's source, but presumably the days of inactivity that came after had undone much of the good. His legs were feeling leaden and the warm air seemed increasingly difficult to breathe. Finally he had to stop, to lean against the wall, panting. He looked at his two companions guiltily, but was relieved to find them in no better shape than he was. Kat was covered in sweat, and she bent forward as he watched, hands on knees. She stood up again and smiled briefly, presumably not yet willing to spare the breath to speak. The guardsman was red-faced and panting worse than Tom. In truth he had no idea how the man had managed to keep up, weighed down by armour as he was. Tom knew that the armour was some sort of toughened polymer rather than solid iron, but it still weighed a fair bit.

After a moment they had recovered to the point where they could manage a brisk walk, Tom again taking them right almost immediately, so that they were now headed in roughly the same direction they had been before the Demons appeared.

"We don't even know your name," Tom said to the guardsman as they walked. It seemed to him that if they were all about to die, he might as well at least know who was sharing the experience with.

"Jayce," the guardsman said after the briefest of hesitations.

Tom nodded. "Good to have you with us, Jayce."

Kat was looking at him oddly. "What?" he asked, irritated by her unfathomable expression.

"Nothing," she replied. "I was just wondering when you grew up."

Her words surprised him, though his answer was quick enough. "Must have been somewhere on the road between here and the goddess's citadel," he said.

"Must have been," she agreed. "Did you actually meet her? Thaiss, I mean."

"Yes."

"Breck me! Got to admit, that's not bad going for a street-nick who couldn't even find his way across town when we first met. You'll have to tell me about it sometime."

He nodded. "Maybe I will. When this is all over."

She gave him a look which didn't need words.

"We will make it," he said quietly, as much for his own benefit as hers.

Tom's internal compass still had a fix on the city's core, and it told him that they were now heading towards it again. Hopefully the two right turns he'd led them through would take them past the Demon.

"Nice idea," Kat said, evidently recognising his intent, "but..." She nodded ahead, to where a glowing figure could be seen at the far end of the corridor.

"Shit!"

Another Demon, or perhaps the same one, seeking to intercept them. And this time there were no Blade to protect them.

"You two run for it," Jayce said. "I'll hold him off."

"Really?" Kat said. "Very noble of you, but the last time we saw these things they were whipping the Blade's collective ass. No offence, but you wouldn't even slow it down."

"Kat's right," Tom said. "No point in throwing your life away needlessly. Come on." He gripped the guardsman's arm and propelled him towards a somewhat plain looking door, but one that was wider than the residential door they'd passed and looked to be something else entirely. Afterwards, Tom would wonder whether he'd subconsciously recognised the deep bass vibration that must surely have been detectable had they not been distracted by the approaching Demon.

All he knew for sure was that when he pushed that door open he was immediately struck by a wall of heat and a familiar rhythmic sound that seemed to reverberate right through him, like the beating of a gigantic heart.

The goddess stood before him, her clear calm voice delivering information as precisely as it had in the citadel. *This world is a nexus, accessible from many others. As such it has become a melting pot for various races. Many – humans, kayjele, and skimmers among them – were already in residence when the founders arrived, and without detailed genetic analysis it's impossible to say which are truly native and which were themselves earlier settlers. The Jeradine, however, arrived with the founders. An ancient people, the Jeradine have called many worlds home, but this will be their last. Those resident in the under-City are likely all that remain of this venerable race. Their knowledge helped open the way to this world and helped to make the construction of Thaiburley possible. Their reward was a permanent home within the City of a Hundred Rows, sited in the City Below by their own choice.*

Tom blinked, banishing the image and trying to blank out the voice. He was delighted that so much of the knowledge he'd absorbed at the citadel was falling into place. He just wished there was some sort of filter, a means of consciously regulating the flow of information and even to turn it off at times. When he was fleeing for his life, for example.

If they'd found the corridors warm, this place was a furnace. It was also jarringly familiar. So much so that Tom might almost have stumbled back into his own past.

"Where the breck are we?" Kat wanted to know.

"In a pumping room," Tom told her.

The oppressive heat, the reddish light, and the deep rhythmic thrum of sound that reverberated through the air and the floor alike, were all just as he remembered. As was the great engine or perhaps gigantic organ that dominated the centre of the chamber. He was seeing it from a different perspective this time, from ground level rather than a viewing balcony part way up a wall, but the memories from that mad flight down from the Heights, when he'd stumbled into a room just like this, remained vivid.

They were much closer to the great engine than he'd been on that previous occasion, and from here its size was even more impressive. It was like a great sack – one that surely would have been large enough to hold scores of people – formed from an unknown material that might almost have been organic. The impression of something living was only enhanced by the network of wires and metal bands that encased it, which looked like veins, and the constant movement. As they entered, the pump was contracting, sliding across the floor and apparently climbing the great metal pipe that rose from its centre to pierce the ceiling. With a mournful sigh it began to relax once more, sliding back down the silver grey pipe as if the effort had all been too much and flowing out across the chamber's floor towards them.

"Breck," Kat muttered, shying away. "I don't want that thing smothering me."

Tom knew what she meant. There was a sense that this was in fact a living thing, or part of one, harnessed to unnatural purpose. Thankfully, the flowing mass stopped its advance well short of them and began the process of contracting once more. Tom wondered briefly where the kayjele attendant might be, but guessed it must have fled this sector along with everyone else.

"There's no other exit," Jayce said, emerging from the far side of the pumping mechanism. He hadn't stopped to ogle the thing as they had. "The only door's the one we came in by."

"Great," Kat said. She then stared at Tom. "Tom…?"

He nodded. "Yeah, I know, the Demon Hounds."

"They have *hounds*?" Jayce asked, looking around anxiously.

"No, a long story – another time, another place," Tom said. "Look, you're going to have to trust me, Jayce. Huddle together. Closer," he gestured towards the guardsman. "We've all got to be touching. Okay, now don't move a muscle and keep completely quiet. I mean *completely*."

"What…?"

"Shhh…" Kat hissed at the Guardsman.

Tom's talent, which he had believed was his *only* talent for much of his life, the ability to hide in plain sight, was their only hope now.

He began his litany as soon as all of them were set-tled. *We're not here; you can't see us, you can't smell us or hear us, we're invisible. We're not here, you can't see us...* As the repeated phrase cycled through his thoughts he felt his talent well up, far more conscious of the process than he ever had been before, as it unfurled to cover them all in its protective mantle.

No sooner had Tom felt his talent rise around them than the door burst open and the Demon strode in. Tom focussed on his litany, making sure it didn't falter and that there was no chink in the protection it was affording them. At the same time, he observed this creature from the Upper Heights, the highest level of all Thaiburley, noting that Demons weren't in fact un-naturally tall – certainly not toweringly so like the Blade. It was just that their physical presence made them seem so much bigger and imposing.

It's working! Tom thought, daring to hope that they might actually get away with this. The Demon strode into the room, his great white wings flexing as if the drafts of warm air were tempting it to take flight. For long seconds the creature stood just inside the door, head turning from side to side, clearly searching. *You cannot see us...* Tom stepped up the intensity, waiting for the Demon's gaze to fall on them and stay, but it didn't. Then the creature strode forward, passing close to where the three of them pressed against each other. Still it stared ahead and not at them.

Just a little bit further. The pump was about to relax again, which meant the vast mass of cables, pipes and tissue would flow outward to fill much of the floor. If the Demon followed the curve of the room around only a short distance further, the expanding mass of the engine would soon put him out of eyeshot, giving them a clear pathway to the door.

Just as he was about to step past the motionless trio, the Demon paused, cocked his head, and then turned slowly to face them. He looked directly at Tom, and smiled. "You didn't honestly expect your little trick would fool a Demon, did you?" His voice was light, high, with the hint of a sneer, like Lyle when he was showing off to the impressionable younger members of the Blue Claw. One thing was clear: the Demon had been playing with them, pretending not to see them and drawing closer in the process. "I am the core personified; you seek to use talent against *me*, when I am living, walking, *breathing* talent? You are an insect, and the meagre gifts you think to command are little more than conjuring tricks."

Tom felt his determination waiver. The Demon was right; he could feel the fundamental truth of its words. Who had they been trying to kid? They never stood a chance. The Prime Master, the Council Guards, the Tattooed Men, even the Blade, they were all powerless compared to just one single Demon. The being before them was glowing, golden, magnificent. How had Tom ever thought to defy such a one?

He slumped to his knees, knowing it was over. His life, his dreams, his future, they all ended here. He deserved no better.

From beside him came a strangled, tortured shriek that sounded more animal than human. A small figure leapt at the Demon, a dark wildcat starkly outlined by golden light. Tom watched aghast as two slender arms rose and fell, and twin blades flashed silver against the gold. *Kat.*

"Don't listen to it, Tom," she yelled, "it's sapping our will."

The silver became blurs as Kat attacked, her blades puncturing the golden nimbus and slicing into the body within. She danced and twisted and sliced and cut and thrust, while the Demon bellowed his rage and pain.

"Talent!" it shrieked "You have *talent.*"

Kat had talent? Of course she did. Tom had never really thought about it before this but how else could a small girl ever rise to prominence in the ranks of the city's toughest warriors? The lethargy and sense of hopelessness which the Demon had induced started to lift. Tom's limbs were his own again. He rose from his knees, as did the guard beside him. Two facts were suddenly crystal clear: Kat had talent, and despite the Demon's sneering dismissal, that talent was hurting it.

Tom gathered himself, drawing on the well of power which he still didn't understand but was beginning to accept as a part of him. This was no Rust Warrior. He knew that to best a Demon he'd have to muster more force than he'd ever called on before.

He was almost there, almost ready to unleash his fury, when disaster struck. Presumably tiring of fending off Kat's blows, the Demon fought back. Kat's scream sent a chill down Tom's spine. A blast of energy shot from the Demon's nimbus, catching her full on and sending her hurtling through the air. Kat struck the unyielding wall with an audible smack and then slid down to lie motionless on the floor.

"No!" Tom seemed to see it all happen in acute detail, as if Kat's limp form had moved in slow motion. In horror, he released the shackles restraining his talent and let loose with everything he had, feeling the energy surge through him but knowing he was too late, that he should have struck a split second earlier, when he still had a chance to save Kat.

Perhaps the Demon was distracted by having to deal with Kat's unexpected assault, perhaps he hadn't expected Tom to attack with such ferocity. Either way, Tom felt his power take a hold of his enemy, overwhelming defences and inflicting damage. But the Demon wasn't finished yet. He rallied, stalling Tom's attack before he could fully press home his advantage.

As Tom had expected, this was completely different from fighting a Rust Warrior or a human. The first time Tom had used his power in such a destructive fashion, when he had taken down the Warrior that killed Kohn, it had been a simple outpouring of hate focussed on the monster that had just murdered a friend. What he directed at the Demon was more intense, more sustained, more draining. This time the target didn't simply tremble and fall apart as the Rust Warrior had, it fought back; and Tom sensed that if he didn't prevail in this contest and do so soon, *he* would be the one doing the falling apart. The snag being that he wasn't at all sure he *could* prevail. The Demon was pure core, a construct fashioned from the stuff at

Thaiburley's heart, whereas Tom had never been more than a conduit for that same force. His initial success had been due to the element of surprise, and he'd failed to make that really count. The Demon had recovered, and Tom could feel his own efforts faltering, his grasp on his enemy's inner being slipping away. Attack slipped inexorably towards defence, as it became increasingly difficult to hold off the Demon's strengthening assault, let alone press on with his own.

The Demon clearly sensed as much. "Prepare to die, boy."

Sweat trickled down Tom's face. He squinted against its salty sting. He clenched his teeth and fought with everything he had, stubbornly refusing to admit the possibility that it wasn't enough. At that moment thoughts of Kat and of Thaiburley's fate were the last thing on his mind. He was fighting for his life.

At the last moment, as his strength began to falter, a towering figure loomed behind the Demon, seeming to have come out of nowhere. Tom was so focused on resisting the pressure that threatened to break through and crush him that he only saw it dimly, the arm that rose and fell, the solid metal object brought down so forcefully on the Demon's head.

The pressure disappeared. Tom wasn't in the mood to stop and wonder what had happened. He flew onto the attack, his remaining talent bludgeoning past the Demon's defences, only to find that he had penetrated something incomprehensible. Without meaning to, he found himself immersed in the Demon's mind, which itself was linked to the corrupted core. For a

disorientated second Tom felt that he was connected
to the whole city, that his sense of self had flowed and
stretched to touch every point of Thaiburley at once.
In that instant, Tom felt that he could encompass the
whole world.

Confused and overwhelmed, he panicked, desperate
to regain some sense of equilibrium, to feel whole
again. He lashed out, breaking and destroying, in the
hope of triggering a return to normality. His outburst
of blind violence ripped the Demon apart from within.
The golden figure, driven down to its hands and knees
by the blow to the back of its head, twitched and collapsed, hitting the floor face first.

Was it dead? Was it breathing? *Did* Demons breathe?
While Tom was considering these finer points of
Demon physiology, the felled figure started to shim-
mer. The Demon sparkled and twinkled and melted
away, fading as if seeping into the floor somehow, until
it had completely disappeared. The whole process only
took a couple of heartbeats, leaving no mark or sign
that anything had ever been there. Tom assumed that
the Demon had been reabsorbed by the core.

Only then did he really turn his attention to their
saviour. For a fleeting moment he thought of Kohn,
but instantly realised this wasn't the kayjele he'd
known. For one thing, the single cyclopean eye that
dominated the giant's forehead was bright with intelligence and vision, not milky with the rheum of
blindness.

"Thank you," Tom said, with a shallow nod of
gratitude.

The giant still clutched in his right hand what appeared to be a huge steel wrench, which was presumably what he'd hit the Demon with. Tom barely registered the details. He was already hurrying over to where a crumpled black form lay pooled at the foot of a wall. "Kat?" No response.

Tom crouched down and reached towards the still form.

"Don't move her," Jayce advised. "She might be injured. If you move her you're liable to make it worse."

Tom's hand hovered for a fraction of a second, but then completed the intended action and grasped Kat's arm. There was still no reaction. "We can't just leave her," he told Jayce. He'd left Dewar, he wasn't about to abandon Kat.

He adjusted his grip, to hold the bare skin of her wrist. Warm, but then wasn't everything in here? Closing his eyes, he reached out with his talent, gently, a feather-light touch. Yes, she was still alive, but hurt, badly hurt, her life energy flickering and uncertain.

Tom wiped his brow and licked his lips, tasting the saltiness of his own sweat. There was no one here to save her but him. Mildra had told him he could be a healer if he wanted, and Thaiss seemed convinced that he could do just about anything, but he'd never attempted anything like this and there was no one here to show him how. He sat back on his haunches and wiped the palms of his hands on his trousers. The bass boom of the semi-organic pump's latest inhalation vibrated through him like a mournful sigh.

Still he hesitated, hands hovering just above her small black form. Perhaps leaving her here would be the best option after all. But then she might die of her injuries or fall victim to a Rust Warrior. No, he couldn't shirk responsibility, not this time. Sucking in a deep lungful of the warm, inadequate air, he took hold of her wrist again, closed his eyes and concentrated, attempting to feel for wrongness in her body. He sensed… *something*, an apparent anomaly, which he gingerly caressed away with a whisper of talent, ever conscious of how destructive his power could be and indeed *had* been whenever he'd summoned it in the past. He tried to be restrained and delicate, tried to smooth out the wrinkles in the flow of energy he could sense within Kat's body.

Tom had no idea how much time passed before he sat back again. Nor did he know whether he'd achieved anything worthwhile. He wasn't a medic and had never aspired to be a healer. He hadn't received the sort of training that Mildra had and didn't know enough about anatomy to knit together bones or repair specific blood vessels the way that she was able to, but, in the absence of either training or direction, he'd done as much as he could.

His scalp itched with perspiration and his damp clothes clung to his body. He'd have given anything for a sip of cold water, but all he could really think about was Kat. He squatted there and simply stared at her, willing her to get up, to say something, to simply move…

Her eyes suddenly twitched and then shot open.

"Kat?" He grinned, relieved and more than a little pleased with himself. "You're all right."

"Says who?" she asked, tentatively pulling herself upright, wincing with pain. "If this is all right…" She sat with her back against the wall, breathing deeply. "… then life sucks. What happened to the golden guy with wings?"

"Our kayjele friend over here arrived in the nick of time and thumped him with a wrench and then I finished him off with my talent."

"Bully for you." Kat stared at the kayjele, eyeing him up and down. "Big brecker, isn't he?"

"Yeah, they do tend to be."

"Is he gonna come with us to the core?"

Tom hadn't even considered that, but he shook his head, knowing the answer. "Doubt it. He'd have to crawl through the corridors. Besides, his place is here, tending the pump. That's what the kayjele do in Thaiburley."

"Shame. I've got a feeling we're going to need muscles like that before we're through." So saying, Kat clambered carefully to her feet, face a study in concentration as she did so, one hand holding her side. "Broken rib by the feel of it. Where's Shayna when I need her?"

"Sorry, I did my best."

She stared at him, wide eyed. "*You* healed me."

He nodded. "Sort of, at any rate."

She grunted, still feeling her obviously tender rib. "I'd say you've still got a bit to learn."

"Don't worry I know." He bit his lip, reminded of his own inadequacies. "Are you going to be all right to go on?"

She gave a bitter laugh. "Trust me, kid, I've fought mire bears, dragon worms and murderers carrying far worse than this. It could do with being strapped up, though, if you want me to be much use from here on in. Have we got the time?"

Tom nodded. "Sure." Who knew how much time they had? It felt as if they were in their own world here, completely cut off from events elsewhere. What difference would a few more minutes make?

She obviously read his expression. "That'll be a 'no' then, but we'll make the time anyway, right?"

He grinned. "Right."

"Well… turn around then!" She shooed him away with her hands. "I'm gonna have to take my top off. You, too, soldier boy," she said in Jayce's direction.

Tom and the guardsman both hurriedly shuffled round to stare at the wall. Tom couldn't help but be amused at Kat's coyness. In the Blue Claw, the kids would wash and scrub each other and change clothes without any thought of modesty, the few girl members doing so as readily as the boys. Nudity had never been an issue for him, but Kat's asking them to look the other way had suddenly made it one.

After a short period of rustling and grunting, Kat said, "Kid, I'm going to need a hand here."

"I'll have to turn around."

"Of course you will, genius. I'm hardly gonna let you grope over my body without seeing what you're doing now, am I?"

As Tom spun quickly back towards her, he just knew his cheeks were burning. Thankfully, Kat didn't seem to notice. She had wrapped her chest and side in bright white bandage, with evident efficiency. "You carry *bandages* with you?" he asked, impressed by such foresight.

She looked at him, puzzled. "Doesn't everyone? Now, just hold this, where my hand is, and don't be afraid to press. If you let go the whole breckin' thing will fall apart and I'll have to start again." ·

Tom gingerly reached out to where Kat's hand held a section of pristine whiteness in place against her own side. His fingers lay over hers, which then slipped out from underneath as he took over. They'd held hands once, to escape from a group of nicks, but that was then and it had just been a ruse. This was somehow more intimate. Tom's breath caught in his throat, and he struggled to keep his hand from trembling.

"Remember," she said, "press hard."

He nodded, not trusting himself to speak.

The seconds seemed to ooze past with viscous slowness rather than flowing at their normal pace, but eventually, after what seemed to have been an age, she'd finished, fastening the final length in place with a pin. "Thanks. You can let go now."

"Oh, right." He pulled his hand away sharply, as if he'd just burnt it on something.

TWELVE

Tylus was beginning to wonder if he was really cut out for command. Oh, he appreciated the Prime Master's faith in him and still believed passionately in the Kite Guard School and all that it could achieve, but standing before a group of officers freshly arrived in the City Below and sharing the benefit of his experiences was one thing, leading a party of disparate components into the heart of the unknown Stain quite another. While Kat had stood beside him the responsibility was at least shared, but since she'd disappeared he felt that this was very much his expedition, for all that M'gruth was nominally standing in as her deputy. Which meant that if everything went horribly wrong, it would all be down to him.

Not that he was about to show his doubts, especially not in front of Issie. He concentrated on appearing calm, wise and totally in command, and was grateful that she didn't seem to question the performance, presumably accepting this as the norm. For her part, the arkademic had spoken little since their journey resumed, clasping the wrecked mechanism in one hand and focusing intently on it as if able to fathom its deepest purpose. Presumably this helped her to trace its source. She now walked at the front of the party, surrounded by her knot of dark sentinels, speaking only to provide him with occasional and in-variably terse updates.

Their group was somewhat reduced. After consult-ing with M'gruth, Tylus had agreed that they couldn't continue with one of the Tattooed Men unconscious and an exhausted Thaistess in their midst, and they certainly couldn't leave the two unattended in the Stain. Sergeant Whitmore and his surviving officers had lifted Mildra and Petter aerially back to the more clement environs of the streets, utilising the new ham-mock-like slings the Kite Guards were equipped with, each passenger suspended between two officers. Pet-ter, of course, was oblivious, but Tylus was impressed by how little fuss the Thaistess made in the face of what must have been a fairly daunting prospect. De-spite the passenger being strapped into the sling, comfort and safety still relied on some skilful and synchronised flying by the two officers supporting them. The straps of the sling had to be kept taut, and that required some precision flying. Tylus wouldn't have fancied trying it.

After the stress of the journey – the need to remain constantly alert and the series of small incidents that had dogged their progress, not to mention the van-quishing of the Soul Thief – the Tattooed Men had been glad of a break while they waited for the Kite Guards to return, as had Tylus and, he suspected, Issie. It gave them all a chance to catch their breath, to sip from canteens and munch on provisions. The Blade, as usual, stayed aloof.

The respite had been short lived, with Whitmore and a single officer soon returning – the other two men having stayed behind to guard and see to the needs of the Thaistess and her patient. As soon as the pair touched down the group set off once more, in search of the mysterious Insint.

Progress was steady; they were mercifully unhindered by any of the Stain's denizens. They might almost have been moving through a genuinely lifeless wasteland, although the experiences of the morning had shown otherwise. The only indication that they weren't alone came when a distant baying reached them, coming from the direction of the wall and the dark chamber that Tylus knew lay beyond. The Kite Guard looked to M'gruth for some explanation of the sound.

"Demon hounds," the Tattooed Man supplied. At Tylus's blank look he went on, "Dogs the size of a big ox and just as powerful. Vicious breckers, too. They've been known to raid the streets from time to time for food. You'll know if they've caught our scent; there'll be a lot more howling and it'll get nearer faster than you'd believe."

A comforting thought. Speaking of scent, the foul smell of the Stain seemed to be intensifying with every step, as Issie led them nearer to the river.

"Hope this thing isn't aquatic," M'gruth muttered. "Wandering around in the Stain is all well and good, but plunging into the Yellow Thair definitely wasn't in the brief."

The river at this point had gained the "Yellow" epithet due to the high levels of pollution and effluence its waters carried by the time they passed through the Stain. As far as Tylus could see the water wasn't actually yellow, the name intended as reference to the amount of urine it was said to contain, or so he'd been told.

They were getting very near the Thair now. Ahead of them, a lone blood heron took off from the bank, scalding them for the disturbance. Tylus always found the ungainly way these birds launched into flight comical, as their long necks strained forward and back, almost as if grasping the air in front of them in an attempt to pull their heavy bodies skyward. Only once their wings settled into a regular rhythm did the neck straighten and the bird adopt a more dignified dart-like shape.

They really were close to the river, and there was nothing obvious to suggest their target was on its banks. Suddenly M'gruth's glib comment seemed all too plausible. What would they do if the wretched thing was somewhere in the middle of the Thair?

The stench wasn't the only thing that had increased as they drew nearer the river. So had the number of insects. Tylus slapped at his neck, where another blood-sucking pest had just bitten him.

"It looks as if they even grow their insects bigger in the Stain," M'gruth commented from beside him.

Tylus looked in the direction the Tattooed Man indicated, to see a swarm of oversized bugs coming towards them from the direction of the Thair. Something about them didn't look quite right. Their flight was too direct, too purposeful, and the way the light from distant sun globes winked off their carapaces here and there suggested they might even be somehow metallic.

A number of things clicked into place. "Those aren't insects," Tylus said. "We're under attack. Kite Guards, with me!"

Tylus took a few hurried steps forward and sprang into the air, spreading his arms as he did so. Immediately he felt the familiar sense of lightness, and his feet lifted from the ground as if that solid surface had somehow slipped from under them. In the corner of his eye he saw Whitmore and the other remaining Kite Guard follow suit.

They didn't have much time, with the small swarm closing fast. Tylus climbed as steeply as he could, trying to get above them. Down below, others were reacting. He heard M'gruth shout for Ox to ready the flamethrower, and four of the Blade strode forward to meet the metallic insects, which Tylus suspected were the same as the crushed mechanism he'd recovered from the site of the sun globe disaster, the one that Issie clutched even now.

A pair of the metal beetles detached from the main group and started to climb to intercept the three Kite Guards. Terrific. Tylus had been intending to try out the other new weapon – aside from the bombs – that the arkademics had supplied them with, but using it against individual bugs was going to take a lot more accuracy than aiming for a swarm.

The problem with using any sort of weapon while flying was that in order to stay aloft you had to keep your arms out and the cape stretched taut between limbs and body. The moment you started waving your hands about doing something else, such as firing a weapon, you lost control and risked to plummeting straight down to a hard landing. Tylus had no idea *why* this was the case given that the supposed science behind the capes was decidedly suspect to say the least, but it was. This meant that the choice of weapons for a Kite Guard was limited and use of even their traditional equipment such as puncheons and net guns while on the wing took a lot of practice and involved an element of risk. So the arkademics had come up with something new especially for this outing, a weapon that didn't require the bending of the elbow or manoeuvring of the arm.

As Tylus saw the two metal bugs climbing towards him he stopped trying to gain altitude, levelling out and then banking, dipping his left shoulder, swivelling so that his right arm was above. He brought his left arm down slightly so that it projected straight out from the shoulder, and then gazed intently along it, using its length to aim by. As the nearest bug came into sight he balled his fist. A beam of pale, bright blue light shot from a small nozzle mounted on his wrist. Breck! He'd missed the bug by a fraction and the thing was closing fast. Resisting the temptation to panic, he shifted the arm downwards slightly, and the blue beam licked against the bubble of metal, which was now no more than a couple of arms' lengths away.

The instinctive adjustment almost spelled disaster, as in bringing his left arm down Tylus' right arm automatically went up and he started to roll. He quickly corrected but in the process lost sight of the bug. He had visions of the thing still coming straight at him and tensed, expecting to feel metal latch onto his leg at any moment and inflict who knew what damage; but then he saw the thing dropping back towards the ground, a wisp of smoke trailing behind it. In fact, both the bugs that had been arrowing in to intercept them were now heading groundward. Whitmore had evidently dealt with the second. Realisation struck home. The arkademics' weapon actually worked!

Tylus had no idea what the blue light was supposed to do, but he knew it was something the arkademics had developed after studying the crushed mechanism he'd recovered. He'd been assured that it would prove effective against similar technology, but such assurances were easily given by folk sitting comfortably back in the Heights. This was the first time the weapon's effectiveness had actually been put to the test. Thankfully, it seemed to have passed with flying colours.

Tylus was almost disappointed to see the main group of metallic bugs – a dozen or more – flare briefly and brightly as they drew close to the four Blade. He had no idea what the Blade were doing to them but it was as if the bugs hit some invisible barrier a few steps ahead of the four ebony figures. The bugs died in a ripple of tiny flashes and then dropped to the ground, depriving the Kite Guards of the opportunity to try out their new weapon on a larger group of targets.

With the immediate danger averted, Tylus flew on to the river, hoping to gain some clue as to where the

metallic bugs had come from. He scoured the bank
and the terrain between the group and the water but
there was nothing to see. He came back and touched
down, leaving the other two Guards aloft to watch for
any further threat. The bugs had surely been no more
than an opening salvo.

Following M'gruth's comment about hoping their
quarry wasn't aquatic and the direction the bugs had
come from, Tylus fell into the trap of assuming their
enemy lurked somewhere in the depths of the Thair.
As they reached the banks of the river – still a considerable waterway even if diminished from the great
river that flowed into the under-City – he found himself scanning the water, searching for a hint of
something breaking the surface. So the attack, when it
came, took him by surprise, though it shouldn't have
done. After all, it was hardly the first time this trip
they'd been ambushed from beneath their feet.

The thing that surged out of the ground almost at
the tips of the Blade's toes was very different from the
scorpion/snake/human hybrid that had attacked them
before. That one had looked to be a hotchpotch of
parts harvested from various creatures, stuck together
if not at random then certainly with little thought of
aesthetics. This one had far more the appearance of a
complete, planned entity; though whether the entity
was organic or mechanical was more difficult to de-
termine. Tylus had the impression, though, that this
might once have been human, that machine parts had
somehow been grafted onto and into a human body
to create an obscene fusion of the two. It was bigger

than the previous creature; broader, more powerful and less sinuous.

As soon as it appeared, the creature – presumably this Insint they were hunting – leapt upon the nearest Blade, grasping the black figure in metallic claws; and then it seemed to fall apart. No, nothing so dramatic, Tylus realised. The legs that gripped the Blade detached, or rather the part of the thing's body they belonged to did, leaving behind a spindly mechanism vaguely similar to the Maker's creations that had subverted the street-nicks so effectively, but bigger, much bigger. Nor was it alone. An identical contraption broke away from Insint's other side and latched on to a second of the Blade. It occurred to Tylus that these may perhaps have been the templates for the Maker's smaller mechanisms.

Everything was happening at once. Tylus had the impression of a broad back, metallic but resembling a beetle's carapace. It might have been gleaming and bright once, but was now tarnished and scratched, and it even showed a hint of rust at the edges. This creature was old, an impression only emphasised by a series of indentations that ran down the thing's back like symmetrical pockmarks. From some of these rose more of the small beetle-like mechanisms that had attacked them before – no more than half a dozen this time. The bugs sped straight towards the Tattooed Men who, reacting far more quickly than Tylus had even thought to, were advancing on the scene, coming to help the Blade.

Belatedly, Tylus remembered himself, spread his arms and took to the air, hoping to use the arkademics' weapons as they were intended, against Insint. Behind him, the other two Kite Guards did the same. Only as he took to the wing did he see four great forms rushing towards the party from behind. "Look out!" he yelled, just as the pack of demon hounds smashed into the ranks of the Tattooed Men. Tylus watched as two of the men went down, disappearing beneath impossibly huge canine forms. Another screamed as slavering jaws crashed together, tearing away an arm amidst jagged white bone and flying blood.

Insint was in constant motion, its movements surprisingly quick for a creature so large. The two detached elements of the creature were wreaking damage. The first Blade attacked had collapsed to the ground, the spidery mech poised above, its legs puncturing the Blade's tough hide. Energy crackled between and around them. The second Blade remained on his feet, arms clenched around the main body of the mech, holding it at bay while some of the spear-tipped legs latched onto the Blade's torso and others scrabbled for purchase. Again bolts of energy surged between them but it was unclear who had the upper hand; they had evidently fought their way to an aggressive stalemate.

Tylus took all this in at a glance, turned to Whitmore and called, "Help the Tattooed Men with the hounds. Both of you, move! I'll take care of Insint."

All of which sounded a great deal more confident than he actually felt.

The central part of the mechanism, or creature, or whatever it was, kept low to the ground. Despite losing spidery legs on either side of its body Insint remained highly mobile, using the disconcertingly human-looking hands of its foremost limbs to grip the ground and help manoeuvre. Other than those hands, the most human feature was its face. Embedded in metal, surrounded by corrugated tubes and odd receptors, the features were still unmistakeably human; nor was that face blank and inflexible as the earlier creature's had been. When appropriate, Insint grimaced with effort and his brow furrowed in concentration. Such emotions, so much in evidence, were what gave the impression that this was a person in an outlandish, oversized suit rather than a cunningly contrived construct. Tylus wasn't about to let that sway him though. He sighted along his arm and squeezed his fist, but Insint was gone, and the blue light played harmlessly across the ground. Cursing, Tylus relaxed his hand, banked, and prepared to come in for another pass, but the creature kept moving unpredictably, dodging ordnance thrown at it by the Blade. An ebony lance narrowly missed skewering him and then he twisted away from a black beam that struck the ground with explosive force, throwing up a cloud of debris, detritus and smoke, forcing Tylus to swerve sharply or risk being engulfed.

Peripheral images crowded in on Tylus as he persisted with trying to get a clear shot. He saw one of the Blade blast the spidery mech from its stricken colleague, glimpsed one of the demon hounds go down in a tangle of netting fired by a Kite Guard while another yelped as its back legs were hamstrung and Tattooed Men darted in for the kill. He watched as

Insint squirted a stream of liquid at one of the Blade
that had come too close. Whatever it was smoked on
contact – acid, perhaps? Still the infuriating creature
wouldn't stay still or even perform a predictable
movement. A master of evasion, no doubt about that.

He needed to be. The two spidery mechs lay smok-
ing and broken. The Blade were driving Insint back,
hemming him in. One of their number lay unmoving
while another stayed close to Issie, but the remaining
four Blade were working in concert, steadily squeezing
the space the creature had to manoeuvre in. They attacked and closed, Insint defended, dodged, and
occasionally fought back, but his options were increasingly limited. Tylus seized his chance. Dipping his arm
and banking, he triggered the blue light and watched
it strike the stretched and augmented human-mech
hybrid squarely on its dimpled carapace.

The effect was immediate and dramatic. Insint
screamed. Tylus had no idea what eldritch properties
the arkademics had instilled within this pale blue luminance, but its touch clearly brought agony to the
creature, having far more effect than anything the
Blade had thrown at him. The ebony warriors didn't
hang around to watch, though. As Insint writhed in
the blue glare a spear slammed into his body, perhaps
below the carapace – difficult for Tylus to see while
on the wing, but it lodged there – while black energy
licked at his back quarters, producing a cloud of acrid
smoke as the metal seemed to blister and wither.

Insint clearly decided that enough was enough. Voicing a wail of frustration and pain, the beetle-like body

sprung into the air, heading towards the river. Tylus
wasn't sure if this was a huge leap or a glide – though
the creature had no wings – but before he or anyone
else could catch him, Insint had dived into the water,
disappearing beneath the surface. The Blade were in
close pursuit, two of them plunging in after the creature. Tylus flew over the patch of water where Insint
had disappeared, but he could see nothing in the
murky depths. He landed on the bank, where the other
two Blade had stopped short, and was soon joined by
his fellow Kite Guards. It wasn't long before Issie and
even the Tattooed Men came across as well, the demon
hounds evidently having been driven off or killed.
Tylus made a quick head count. Besides M'gruth, he
made it six of the former Pits warriors still standing.
They'd be leaving a few more comrades behind for the
Stain's scavengers, it seemed.

No one spoke. The whole group of them simply
stood and waited, all eyes fixed on the water. For long
minutes there was nothing to see. The surface of the
Thair remained calm, with no indication that two of
the Blade and the creature responsible for so nearly
destabilising the whole of the City Below had disappeared beneath it.

Then, as Tylus was contemplating taking to the air
for another pass over the river in the hope of seeing
something – *anything* – he felt a deep vibration, a
rumbling that travelled up through the soles of his
feet to spread throughout his body. Even as this registered, the bubble of an explosion arose in the centre
of the Thair, a great dome of displaced water and

energy that burst to disgorge a boom of sound and spray them all with water. Issie shied away and Tylus moved instinctively to step in front of her, to protect her, even though one of the Blade still hovered at her shoulder.

The river subsided, though waves now lapped at their feet in the aftershock. A dark form began to emerge, climbing onto the bank: one of the Blade. Tylus watched, but no second figure appeared.

"Insint lives, though badly damaged," the Blade reported, its voice deep and resonant. "It has headed further into the Stain."

M'gruth and Tylus looked at each other. The Tattooed Man raised his eyebrows. "I suppose you're going to tell me we still have to go after this brecking thing."

"Yes," the Kite Guard replied, no happier at the prospect than M'gruth. "I'm afraid I am."

It would mean going on into the far cavern, the dark bowels of the Stain, where light from the sun globes failed to penetrate. Weren't they the lucky ones.

Morning had marched forth, chasing out that recurring usurper night to fully establish her dominion over the world by the time Dewar blinked into wakefulness. It was unusual for him to sleep so late, but then it had been an unusually active night. Memories of their energetic lovemaking chased through his mind: Seffy's soft kisses and expert hands, her long hair tickling his thighs, her firm and slender body pressed beneath his one moment and then writhing on top of him the next…

He reached out a hand, but aside from his own lethargic self, the bed was empty. He sat up sharply, to find the room likewise. The girl had gone, slipping away while he slept, which at least saved him from having to make one unsavoury decision. He couldn't pretend to be sorry.

Dewar sat up, rubbing his eyes, to see an empty bottle on the floor and a glass lying on its side close by. Red wine, a decent if over-priced Bexon rouge. Perhaps that explained the fragility of his head this morning. No, he hadn't drunk that much, and the wine certainly wasn't responsible for the bitter aftertaste lurking at the back of his palate. Valerion root! Doubtless mixed with something else for it to have been so effective. He didn't bother trying to discern what that might be, it didn't matter. Seffy had drugged him. *Him.* Realisation came as a shock. Did she routinely carry a sleeping potion with her or was this an impulse purchase made as a precaution during that late afternoon visit to the herbalist? Either way, it showed admirable resourcefulness and meant that he had severely underestimated her.

Concern chased hard on the heels of insight. He leapt from the bed and reached for his money belt, pulling it from the back of a chair where it lay buried beneath the rest of his clothes. Had she robbed him as well? The belt felt lighter than it ought to, but that might just be his concern colouring perception. At least it hadn't been emptied. He opened up the belt and poured the contents out, kneeling on the bed to count it. A quick calculation showed that all she'd taken was what he'd promised her plus a little more, presumably as payment for the night's frivolities.

Dewar sat back, looked at the money spread across the rumpled sheets and felt his shoulders tremble. He threw back his head and laughed. Clever girl, *resourceful* girl. She had surprised him, delighted him in truth, and very few people managed to do that. He couldn't begrudge her what she'd taken, not even the conveniently overlooked sum designated for buying the zyvan berry juice. She'd earned every copper.

If Seffy was as astute and resourceful as this suggested why had she cooperated in the first place? The danger must have been plain to her from the outset. Had it been out of curiosity, or perhaps for the thrill, even for the sex? Most likely a little of all those things, Dewar concluded.

He suddenly realised why he'd approached this particular woman in the first place. In so many ways, she reminded him of Marta.

THIRTEEN

Up until now the corridors had seemed overly warm to Tom, but as he stepped back into them after the claustrophobic swelter of the pump room they felt cool, even airy and refreshing by comparison; though he suspected this said more about the pump room than it did about the corridors.

Tom had done all he could in both words and thoughts to thank the kayjele for his help, trying to recall how he'd communicated in similar fashion with Kohn. Now, as then, he had a sense that his words were understood and accepted, and hoped this was more than just wishful thinking. As anticipated, the kayjele made it clear that he wouldn't desert his station to go with them.

So the same three exited the pump room as had entered. The corridors seemed eerily still in contrast to the constant thrum of that great engine. For a while, as they headed onward, Tom thought he could still feel the beat of that huge pump through the soles of his feet, but dismissed the notion as imagination, unless perhaps the memory of that powerful vibration still resonated through his body.

Initially they walked in silence, Tom guiding the way but distracted by his own inner turmoil.

He wasn't at all surprised to find the goddess walking beside him. "You must hurry," she said. "Time grows short." She appeared as a picture of vigour and vitality; the fragility he had sensed in her at times in the ice citadel nowhere to be seen.

"I know, don't worry," he assured her. *Where were you when I needed you, when a Demon came so close to killing us all?*

"You didn't need me." Thought and speech became a jumble with a goddess in your head. Again Tom worried that his most private thoughts were no longer private at all. "You just thought you did, when you already had the strength and resources to defeat the Demon without me. I would have intervened if it had become necessary."

"Easy enough to say that now," he said, but the goddess had gone, leaving an imperious command to "Hurry!" hanging in the air behind her.

"To say what, exactly?" Kat asked. He must have spoken that last retort aloud.

"Oh, nothing," he said quickly. "Just thinking out loud."

She seemed far more sensitive to his moods than she ever had when they crossed the City Below together. Half the time during that journey she'd acted as if she couldn't care less, now she seemed genuinely anxious for him. He wondered whether that was down to changes in him or in her.

"That figures," she said. "Mind you, about time you stopped looking so thoughtful all the time, I reckon. Trust me, it doesn't suit you."

"Thanks."

"So, what were you mulling over anyway?"

Realising that she wasn't about to let the matter drop, he searched for something plausible. There was no way he was going to admit that he'd been chatting to an invisible goddess in his head.

"It's nothing really. Except that, when I was fighting the Demon, there was a moment when we were tightly linked. I had to reach inside... which doesn't even begin to describe what that was like." He shuddered, remembering that indescribable thinning of his sense of self. "But the point is, I caught a glimpse of its thoughts. They're not evil, you know? The Demons, I mean. They're just trying to survive. In the century or so since the core missed being renewed they've become more independent, more self-aware. I don't know, perhaps the core's corruption had something to do with that as well, but they're not simply avatars anymore. They want to live, and they know that if I succeed they'll be reabsorbed into the core, they'll cease to be, and a whole new generation of Demons will emerge to replace them."

Kat stopped and grabbed his arm, jerking him around to face her.

"Hey!"

"Listen, you," she said. "Stop this right now. Their motives don't matter. Good, bad, divinely blessed or cursed, none of it means a brecking thing. They want to stop you at all costs. They'll kill you without giving it a second thought. *They are the enemy*, and you can't afford to sympathise with them or see their point of view. If you do, we're all in trouble. We're fighting for our lives here, Tom. It's kill or be killed, with no room for compassion or any of this 'love your enemy' oxshit."

"I know, I know," he assured her. "Don't worry. I'm not going soft, just can't help wondering how everything got so totally messed up."

She looked as if she was about to say something more but settled for a simple shake of her head. She let go of his arm and they resumed walking.

"Do you want to hear the stupidest thing of all?" he said as they hurried to catch up with Jayce, who had stopped a short distance ahead to wait for them.

"Go on."

"There are no such things as Demon eggs. I mean, this whole business started with me being sent up to the Heights to fetch one back... and they don't even exist. They're a myth."

"Seriously?" and she started to laugh.

"You think that's funny?"

"Yes," she replied. "As a matter of fact I do."

He found himself grinning in response. "Yeah, me too." Then the smile slipped away as a question occurred to him, one that he'd always wanted to ask her. "Why did you run away, Kat?"

"What?"

"After the fight with Rayul and the street-nicks, when the Blade came to get us, why did you run away? Was it from the Blade... or from me?"

She looked down quickly as if to hide her expression, but he caught a glimpse of the pain reflected there the instant before she did. "No, nothing like that. It's complicated. There were things I had to take care of, that's all." After a brief hesitation, she added, "Anyway, you were safe, you didn't need me. You had the Blade."

Of course I needed you, he whispered inside his head, though this time he made sure the thought didn't escape into the world at large where anyone else might hear it.

Inzierto IV and sleep had become infrequent and unreliable companions of late.

The king had occupied the throne of the Misted Isles for a full decade and a half now. While this was by no means unprecedented – history claimed that Cenulous the Penniless had ruled for a full decade longer – it was still an achievement he was proud of. In truth, he had never been allowed to sit comfortably on the throne in all that time, but then he doubted many of his predecessors had either. There were five Isles in total – seven if you counted Porquita and Chicol, which he tended not to; the pair of them being little more than rocky outcroppings, home to thriving colonies of screeching seabirds, a flock or two of hardy sheep, and a scattering of stubborn crofters who refused to relocate. The only things the two minor isles were remotely good for were wool and guano.

The five major isles, of course, were another matter entirely. Each had their own rich history and set of traditions, complete with their own royal family, at least in historical terms. Unfortunately, historical families had a habit of throwing up unlooked-for descendants at the most inopportune moments, no matter how many times you wiped them out to the last babe in arms – thrice in the case of Media's royal line, the second largest of the Misted Isles.

A surfeit of families with claim to the throne was always likely to cause... complications. Intrigue, scheming, clandestine alliances, plots and counter plots were common. Indeed, it was said that the court positively thrived on them. All well and good if you were some minor noble looking on from the sidelines, but when you were the king seeking to keep hold of your throne it was a different matter entirely.

None of this explained the king's insomnia. He was used to such pressures. No, it was the imminent campaign that had unsettled him. That and the spate of recent deaths. Oh, he knew that all were perfectly explainable, accidents and illness each and every one. Count Ruben was no longer a young man, and heart attacks struck without pattern or prejudice, while General Hayt would insist on wearing such heavy armour, which was never advisable when overseeing manoeuvres in the harbour that involved the embarkation and disembarkation of so many warriors from troop ships – all too easy to get knocked overboard. The good general sank like a stone, apparently, before anyone could attempt to rescue him. As for Captain Vargas, he and alcohol were notoriously firm friends and there were plenty of witnesses to confirm how deep he'd sunk into his cups that night. It was hardly surprising he should fall off a bridge on his way home and break his neck.

Yes, all were understandable, all were fully plausible acts of misfortune, but even that was a cause for concern. At the start of such a major military campaign, misfortune was the very last thing he needed. Whispers that the expedition was dogged by bad luck would dispirit the troops almost as much as defeat in battle. Was he doing the right thing? Was this too bold a move?

The army was ready – assembled at five key points along the western coast of Indryl, the largest contingent immediately outside Indryl city itself. A sea of tents had sprung up beyond the city boundary – a vista of canvas waves as impressive as anything the sea herself could muster – while many of the warehouses adjacent to the docks had been hastily converted into barracks and were now bursting with men. The fleet of ships that would ferry the troops to the mainland were practically all in attendance; awaiting only final confirmation that the time was ripe. Confirmation which he so far had hesitated in issuing. He was loathe to begin the campaign until the Demon gave him the word. Over thirty thousand men, the cream of a generation, stood ready for war. An impressive force, certainly, and yet Inzierto knew this to be little more than a drop in the ocean compared to Thaiburley's millions. If the City of Dreams stood firm and untroubled, his armies could dash themselves against its walls like waves against an implacable rock face, perishing without purpose. Only if Thaiburley were a city already in turmoil, its political infrastructure tottering – or better still collapsed – its civil order overturned and systems inoperative, would his plans have any chance of succeeding. This much the Demons had promised him. With their help he would establish a new order, with mighty Thaiburley a mere vassal state to the Misted Isles. United, they would be formidable indeed; perhaps not ruling the world as such, but they would certainly dominate a good portion of it. And from there, who knew what else would be possible?

For now though, the army waited, and Inzierto knew the dangers inherent in keeping them inactive for too long. Discipline had largely held firm for now, but it had only been a couple of days. Before long, impatience and boredom would set in. With so many men, primed for action stuck in a confined area with nothing to do but drill, disobedience and violence waited in the shadows to pounce. The Demon *had* to come through soon.

Once it did, once Inzierto felt confident enough to unleash his armies, the real headaches would begin. Even with the expansion work carried out at the other departure points, only so many ships could dock at any one time, and there were only so many men each of these ships could carry. They'd been rehearsing for weeks to make the process as slick and fast as possible, but it would still take two days for the entire army to disembark. The general hadn't been the only casualty of those rehearsals. Inzierto had made a point of finding out. Forty-seven men had either drowned or been crushed during the weeks of preparation, twenty-five in a single incident involving the capsizing of one troop ship that had collided with another, larger, vessel.

His thoughts returned to the three important deaths, the ones that concerned him so much. No, individually none of them was suspicious. Not the general who was to lead operations in the field, the Count who had helped organise and plan it, nor the captain who was to command the home guard in the absence of the army's main strength.

And yet – *and yet* – the coincidence of three such prominent figures falling foul of cruel fate in quick succession, especially at this crucial time, made Inzierto distinctly uneasy. It was almost as if somebody conspired against him, *but who*?

Not in several generations had the main strength of each isle's military been concentrated so close to the capital. There was a certain logic in one of the four princes launching a coup now when their military strength was so conveniently on hand, but it would take a brave man indeed to make a move with so many still-loyal troops also in attendance. Frankly, Inzierto doubted whether any of his potential rivals had the balls. Besides, why would they strike on the very eve of the campaign, when the governance of Thaiburley had been dangled before them to counter just such a temptation? No, he simply couldn't see it.

Inzierto sat up in bed, his head woolly from tiredness but alert with concerns that refused to relent. He reached for the small crystal bottle and glass tumbler that stood in attendance on his bedside table. The bottle contained water infused with various herbs and vaguely minty in flavour. This was the creation of his court physicians and designed to encourage sleep. A new glass and bottle were delivered fresh each evening before he retired, the latter sealed to safeguard against tampering – one could never be too careful, and Inzierto was ever conscious of his own mortality.

He broke the seal, poured out a generous mouthful of the liquid, lifted the tumbler and swallowed. It wasn't unpleasant to the taste, if a little sweet, and he could have done with it being slightly colder. Perhaps he'd demand some ice next time.

Now wide awake, Inzierto rose from the bed, flexing his toes as they sank into the deep pile of finest Asturian carpet. Hideously expensive to import, but worth every copper at moments like this. He wandered towards the window, intent on gazing out over the rooftops of his city. How had that poet Larken described the scene?

Those elegant, regal spires, rising beside the sea,
Not reaching for the stars but content to let them be.

A simple stanza but one he'd always liked, feeling that it said something noble about both the city and its citizens. Not for the first time he worried that current ambitions flew in the face of the verse's wisdom, that he was indeed reaching for the stars and over-extending himself. It was too late for such regrets, though, he was committed. The whole nation was committed.

The king rubbed his neck absently. Odd, the water hadn't seemed especially cold but it had left his throat feeling numb, as if he'd swallowed a mouthful of coldest ice; and the effect seemed to intensify with every breath. Not yet alarmed but certainly disquieted, he stopped halfway to the window and turned back towards the bed, intent on examining that bottle.

"Zyvan berry juice," a voice said quietly from the shadows.

Inzierto spun around, very much alarmed now. *An intruder? Here in his private quarters? Impossible!*

He peered into the room's furthest corner but couldn't penetrate the stygian gloom.

"Distilled while the berries are still green, just before they ripen," that detestably calm voice continued. "It paralyses the vocal chords even as it numbs and constricts the throat. The nasal passageways stay open for a while, so you'll still be able to breathe for now, but calling out becomes... problematic."

He could see the man now, though not with any clarity; a darker form moving within the blackness. Moving towards him, Inzierto presumed, since the shape gained definition before his eyes and was now discernibly human.

Who are you? he wanted to say, but all that emerged was a whistling croak, no louder than a whisper. The king's eyes dropped to the bottle. Surely the seal had been tight and not tampered with. How then had the assassin administered the poison? Assassin: now there was a term guaranteed to stir memories and raise troubled ghosts from the past.

"You're wondering about the bottle?" the intruder asked, evidently following the king's gaze. "Yes, it was sealed. The tumbler, however, wasn't. A drop of the juice smeared on the bottom of the glass is all that was required. Quite a delicate job, actually. Too much and it would kill you far too quickly, too little and you'd still be able to make some sort of noise audible beyond this room, and that would never do, would it?"

Inzierto's hand fell casually onto the bedside table, as if he were thinking of examining the glass. In fact his thumb reached beneath the rim of the top and pressed a concealed button: the silent alarm. Within seconds his loyal guards would come swarming into the room. The way this buffoon appeared to like the sound of his own voice, he wouldn't have finished the job before then. The king felt hope rise anew. He might yet survive.

"Oh, by the way, I've cut the wires leading from that alarm of yours. We wouldn't want anyone interrupting us now would we, my king? No, far better this way: just you and me.

Inzierto slumped. He could almost see his tormentor now, as the man emerged from the shadows with such a deliberate lack of haste. Was there something familiar about this figure, or was he imagining it? A thought he'd entertained earlier refused to go away: *assassin*. Suddenly everything fell into place and he knew who this man was, an instant before his features became discernible. Realisation made the king's blood run cold. "King Slayer!" he wheezed.

"Ah," said Dewar, stepping into the light. He smiled broadly. "So *now* you remember me."

Leaving Deliia had proven to be a lot trickier than Dewar anticipated. Most of the ferries and cargo ships and even many of the fishing boats had been commandeered or hired for military use, and it seemed that every captain in the port had some commitment to somebody. Eventually he managed to bribe his way aboard a small cargo vessel bound for Indryl.

If the king was counting on the element of surprise for his campaign, the assassin feared his Highness was destined to be disappointed. No official announcement had yet been made as to why the army was being mobilised, but the objective was an open secret and it didn't take long for Dewar to hear the rumours. The whole town was buzzing with anticipation. A few drinks bought in an unremarkable tavern in the shadow of the city walls on his first day in Deliia had found the conversation soon turning to the imminent arrival of the Misted Isles army. Advanced elements were already ashore, it seemed. Oh, not in the town itself. They'd built a staging area a few leagues up the coast and had landed there, but every tradesman in Deliia looked set to turn a profit on the venture. An army needed provisions and equipment and weapons and horses and transport. No point in ferrying all of that across from the Isles when most of it could be purchased just as readily on the mainland and stockpiled against your arrival.

As for the army's purpose, nobody seemed in any doubt about that. There were few places on the continent

that justified amassing the sort of numbers that were
expected to come ashore near Deliia. Thaiburley, the
City of a Hundred Rows. Inzierto could only be
marching on the City of Dreams itself. Dewar had evidently arrived just in time. The man had clearly lost
his mind.

It was strangely moving, coming home again. As he
stepped off the boat at Indryl, both feet planted on
home soil for the first time in far too many years, he
took stock. He hadn't expected the experience to affect
him so deeply. Now that it had, he gave himself a few
moments to absorb that fact, and then moved on.

It took him a while to track down the people he was
interested in and longer still to plan their demise. The
king was still the king and Count Ruben was still a
count, but Vargas was now a captain and Hayt a general. Fortunately, their promotions were a matter of
public record and one thing Dewar had always admired about such things was that they lived up to their
name: they were public. Accessing them required no
guile whatsoever.

Vargas, the guard who had been paid to lie about seeing Dewar at the scene of the failed assassination, so
confirming his guilt, was always a drunkard. He was
also predictable, and the assassin soon identified his regular watering hole. All it took then was a nondescript
stranger perched at the bar next to Vargas, a powder
surreptitiously dropped into a tankard of ale to enhance
the effect of the alcohol, and the rest was child's play.

As for Hayt, the man had grown even more portly
and pompous than Dewar remembered. He wore

enough armour to make a war horse stagger. An inadvertent nudge from a distracted sailor who was soon lost in the crowd of horrified troops that rushed to the quayside was enough to send the oaf to a watery grave. It was the least he deserved. This was the man whose overzealous interrogation of Dewar's sister while leading the search for the assassin had killed his last surviving relative.

Ruben was a man of fastidious habit. His routine hadn't varied since Dewar's exile. Poisoning his midafternoon beverage had been the simplest job of the three. A fitting if overdue end for the man who had orchestrated the public outcry that saved the First's reputation and ensured that the chosen scapegoat – Dewar – became the Isles' most hated fugitive.

Three down, two to go, of which the king was of course the most prominent but by no means the most important, not in Dewar's eyes. He reserved that accolade for the man who had ordered the king's assassination and then denied all knowledge, robbing Dewar of legal recourse and hanging him out to dry: Brent, the First among the Twelve.

Since returning to Indryl, Dewar had searched in vain for some sign of his former commander. Oh, he knew that man had become a close advisor to the king and was doubtless at the heart of palace intrigue, but nobody seemed to have seen him in a good while. It was as if he had vanished off the face of the world at around the same time the Misted Isles started gearing up for war. Coincidence? Dewar didn't believe in coincidence, not where Brent was concerned.

He'd find him, wherever he was, but first he must deal with the matter at hand. Dewar watched on dispassionately as the king felt around his throat, as if that might somehow free the passageways and vocal chords. It wouldn't. Such an elegant poison, zyvan berry juice, so economical.

"Of course, none of this is necessary. It's not you I want to see dead at all," he lied. "After all, I did try to kill you, even though that act was fully authorised within the terms of the political system underpinning our society. No, I can't blame you for wanting me dead or exiled after that. You're not the one who turned a legal act into an illegal one by denying sanction."

Without warning, Dewar closed on the startled king, grasping him by the front of his nightshirt – nice material, silk by the feel – and glowering into his face. "Where is he, Inzierto? Where's the First?"

The man gaped like a floundering fish, trying to suck in air, trying to speak.

"If I walk away now, you'll die," Dewar told him. "A slow, horrible, painful death, and no one but you will even hear the screams. If you tell me what I want to know, I'll administer the antidote. All you have to do is tell me where the First is. Where is he, hmm? Where's Brent?"

Wheezing and straining, the king managed to frame a single word, more breathed than spoken.

Dewar stared at him, hearing the wheezed syllables and seeing the shape of the lips but not quite able to believe either. "Thaiburley? You sent him to *Thaiburley*?" The assassin stifled the urge to laugh. The city that had become his adopted home, which had also been the second state to exile him. The irony was delicious. All the years Dewar had spent living in that city, trying to secure a future when he should have been claiming his revenge, and when he finally returned home it was to discover that the chief object of his revenge had gone to where he'd just been.

"You sent him there as a spy, as an agent provocateur, didn't you…" Who better?

Inzierto was gesturing, pointing towards his throat. "Oh, of course," Dewar said. "Forgive the distraction, my king. I promised you the antidote, didn't I?" He stepped in closer and drove his right arm forward in one fluid motion. The spring-loaded knife leapt into his hand and he buried it in the king's torso, deftly slipping the blade between two royal ribs until it pierced the heart. He clutched the older man to him and whispered, "Farewell, my liege, consider the antidote delivered and all debts cancelled."

He held the twitching body of Inzierto IV close until all life had fled. Only then did he ease his lifeless form onto the bed, making sure to place the king at the very centre, so that he was lying on his back, head cushioned by a single pillow. He then brought the hands up to cross at the chest, and closed the wide, staring eyes. Dewar treated the body with an uncharacteristic degree of tenderness, respect even. After all, this man had been his king.

Satisfied, he stood back, staring at the peaceful-looking body. He'd expected to feel something more significant at this moment, but in truth little had changed. There was no real sense of triumph, while the hurt at the core of his being didn't seem lessened; perhaps because the First still breathed.

Thaiburley. Dewar sighed. No matter what detours he took or the distractions that arose along the way, it seemed his path was always destined to lead back to the City of a Hundred Rows. With the faintest of bows in the direction of the dead monarch – little more than a shallow nod of the head – he turned and stepped back into the shadows.

FOURTEEN

"What's that?" Whitmore was looking towards the great dark maw of the second chamber, that stygian hinterland of the Stain which they'd all doubtless been hoping to avoid.

Something moved in the depths, a pale agitation that coalesced into a great loping shape.

"Demon hound," somebody muttered – one of the Tattooed Men – yet in many ways this was unlike the beasts that had attacked them earlier. Canine in form, certainly, but this creature was lean to the point of being scrawny and its hide as pale as fresh-churned milk. It looked almost to be made of bone, as if any flesh that might once have covered that emaciated frame had dropped away years ago.

For long seconds the beast stood there, just within the furthest chamber, its head swaying from side to side as if questing for them, trying to catch their scent. Then, without uttering a sound, it turned and slunk away into the darkness, its alabaster shape vanishing by rapid degrees.

Tylus stared after the thing, unable to shake the irrational feeling that they had just encountered some guardian of this entrance to the further cavern.

"So, we're to go in there, are we?" M'gruth said.

"Indeed." Tylus tried to keep his voice steady, determined not to betray any of the disquiet he actually felt, particularly as M'gruth had spoken in a tone that suggested acceptance of the inevitable rather than any genuine trepidation.

"Great," the Tattooed Man said. "I suppose we'd better get some torches organised then."

They stood in a world of deep twilight, the rays of the nearest sun globe barely reaching this far and making no impression at all on the darkness that faced them.

"No need," Tylus replied.

He reached to his belt and unclipped the compact, battery-powered torch that was a part of every Kite Guard's equipment. A click of the single button and a beam of silver luminance stabbed forth. A pair of identical beams joined it as the other two Kite Guards followed suit.

"Impressive," M'gruth allowed. "But unless those things last forever, shouldn't we perhaps turn a couple of them off? I'd hate to get stuck in there with no light whatsoever."

Tylus bit back a testy response, resenting the way the older man had so casually seized the initiative. This was *his* expedition now, not M'gruth's. Even so, he couldn't fault the man's logic. The beams would in fact last for hours and each officer had a spare set of batteries in their belt, but there was no telling how long this was likely to take and no point in taking any chances. Not that he intended to comply entirely with the Tattooed Man's advice.

"We're too big a party to rely on just one torch," he declared. "We'll keep two on at any one time and rotate between the three to extend battery life for as long as possible."

M'gruth nodded. "Makes sense."

So, with his status as commander duly reinforced, Tylus led the way forward. Within a few short steps they were crossing into the second chamber and leaving the comfort of the sun globes' luminance and the world they knew behind. Issie and her quartet of guardian Blade were at his shoulder, followed by the two Kite Guard officers – one active torch between them – with M'gruth and the Tattooed Men bringing up the rear.

Tylus' first impression was of cold; not in the sense of a chill breeze striking his face but more as an absence of warmth which seemed intent on sucking the heat from the air, leaching sustenance from the front chamber, the City Below. This impression was soon brushed aside by the sheer wonder of the landscape around them. They might almost have been entering an alien world, or so it seemed to Tylus, so different were these surroundings from any he'd encountered before.

In the beam of his torch he saw great teardrops of rock descending from the ceiling, held in place by solid strands as if something gelatinous had oozed downward only to become frozen or calcified, while great tapering turrets rose from the ground to meet them in apparent greeting. Not just turrets, Tylus realised as he played the beam to either side. In places the grounded part of these odd pairings were squat and bloated, like the melted wax of a poorly made candle, and elsewhere they resembled nothing so much as wonky phalluses. He moved the torch away quickly, a little embarrassed by his own observation, especially given the presence of Issie close behind him.

"Great Demons," someone muttered in a distinctly up-City accent. "Where in the world have we come to?"

"Welcome to the depths, laddie," M'gruth growled in response. "Please leave your flying cape at the door."

Judging by the chuckles the comment elicited, the Tattooed Men were enjoying themselves at least. Tylus only wished he could say the same. This place didn't just look strange, it *felt* strange too; colder and damper than the City Below he was used to, and then of course there was the sound. A great bass rumble that seemed to emanate from the very air itself, like the overlapping beat of a million drums all of which were keeping different time. Water, he realised; a mighty cascade of water, pummelling rock and stone to roar out a challenge that boomed forth across the cavern.

"We need to head to the right," Issie said. It was difficult to be certain with the way sound here seemed to fill the whole cavern, but he thought that would take them towards the source of the roar.

They stayed close to the cavern wall and their way led downwards, steeply enough that Tylus was forced to stop admiring the bizarre scenery and concentrate the torch's beam on where he was treading. There was no clear pathway and the order of their company, which he had so carefully arranged as they entered the dark chamber, soon disintegrated, though the Blade still managed to stay close to Issie. In places, the rock of the wall gave the impression of being in motion, albeit slowly; of flowing down towards the ground in a multitude of small runs, like over-wet paint from a child's watercolour held upright before it had dried, or perhaps a cauldron heated too vigorously and bubbling over.

There was a fair bit of banter, particularly among the Tattooed Men, perhaps designed to keep their spirits up. "It'd be nice to know where that ghostly demon hound went to," somebody said.

"I wouldn't worry," another voice replied. "It was probably frightened off by your smell."

"Thaiss!" somebody exclaimed suddenly.

"What?" Tylus stopped, so abruptly that he nearly lost his footing. He swung the torch beam around, anxious to see what new menace confronted them.

Ox's broad face was caught wide-eyed in its glare.

"Nothing," the big man mumbled sheepishly. "Just stubbed my toe."

Sniggers surrounded him and one of the other Tattooed Men shoved him good-naturedly.

"Try to tread more carefully," Tylus snapped before turning forward once more. He instantly regretted the words. It wasn't as if Ox had *meant* to stub his toe.

"It's all right for you, you've got the torch," a voice muttered.

The Kite Guard ignored the comment, but he tried to keep the beam trained closer to his own feet and not so far ahead from then on.

They'd said all there was to be said, those who remained of Thaiburley's council, having discussed every conceivable matter ad nauseum. In the end it didn't matter; none of it mattered. Everything rested on an innocuous-looking street-nick with power beyond his understanding. If Tom should fail, then the city was lost and all their contingencies and future plans amounted to nothing. They might as well all have saved their breath and spent what time remained with their loved ones. An uncharacteristically fatalistic thought but, under the circumstances, he felt he could forgive himself for that. The meeting did have one thing in its favour. It had provided those present with welcome distraction and enabled them to forget, or at least ignore for a while, the way in which the city they'd all served and overseen for so long was falling apart around them. The surviving council members were all quartered nearby, within the "safe" sector maintained by the Blade, and eventually they had left, one by one; even Ty-gen, who was staying in the Heights for the duration of the crisis.

The Prime Master wilted into his chair as the door closed behind the last of them, glad to be left to his own devices. It meant that he could relax and not bother with the charade that there was nothing wrong with his health. Jeanette knew, or at least suspected. They skirted around the subject, not mentioning it by mutual consent. Thankfully, there was plenty to occupy the minds of his fellow councillors, and he benefited from the myth of his own durability – people assumed that he would go on forever and were blind to any indication that he might not.

With a sigh, he stood up and shuffled from the makeshift meeting room into his home proper. The pain was becoming increasingly hard to manage, and he'd all but lost the use of his left hand, while the right was growing progressively arthritic. He dropped into his favourite chair – the comfortable leather one behind his desk – and pulled his left glove off, to stare at the hard, scaly skin beneath. Soon, perhaps within a few hours, any semblance of a living, breathing epidermis would flake away to leave the hard white bone of his self-grown tomb. The speed with which bone flu progressed varied from victim to victim, but the Prime Master felt increasingly certain that he wouldn't last the night, which meant he couldn't afford to fall asleep. At least, not in any natural sense.

Slowly and very precisely, having only his right hand to call upon, he removed the stopper from the decanter on his desk and poured himself a glass of red wine. Next he took out a small bottle of clear liquid from a drawer, placing it beside the glass. He stared at the two vessels for a second, appreciating the asymmetry of their size and shape which still somehow managed to complement each other. With a snort, he decided, *not yet*.

He would savour one final glass of good untainted wine before he attempted the fatal dose. This was simply delaying the inevitable, perhaps, but he was only human and he kept hoping that Tom would yet win through and save the day. It was a slim hope, he knew that, but it was what he'd been reduced to. His talent was failing him. Abilities he'd taken for granted since he was a young child were gone.

Long sight was now beyond him, and when he'd lost contact with the last of the Blade sent to guard the boy his frustration was complete, his confidence shattered; but he hadn't despaired. As time passed, though, and nothing changed, his lingering hopes grew increasingly forlorn. The point was fast approaching where it would be too late for him in any case, even if Tom did succeed in cleansing and replenishing the core. At least if he went now he could do so believing there was still a chance that his beloved city might be saved.

He was frustrated by the clumsiness of his stiff fingers – his own body betraying him – but persevered with the attempt to pick up the glass, until he was able to take a sip, savouring the deep full flavour and the liquorice overtones. If this was truly to be his final drink, he could have chosen a lot worse.

The small bottle on the desktop monopolised his gaze. He set the glass down beside it once more and started to compose himself in preparation. Despite the city's predicament, at a personal level there was much for him to feel content about. He had done a great deal in his life and seen so many things. More than most men, certainly. And here and there he'd been able to make a difference; a positive one, he liked to think.

That thought provided a crumb of comfort to carry with him into the darkness. His greatest regret was that he hadn't found the right words to say goodbye to the one person he most wanted to. He hoped she'd understand, and that she could forgive him. For leaving her again.

FIFTEEN

They passed through an area where the walls and ceiling were blackened by the fierce passage of now-dead fires and the flooring became bubbled and uneven underfoot, as if it had melted and flowed in the raging heat before resetting in newly irregular patterns upon cooling. The walls remained sound, however, and while a number of the ceiling lights were dead, enough still functioned for them to see where they were going; until, that is, they came to the section where the lighting had failed entirely.

The three of them stood side by side, staring uneasily into the gathering gloom ahead.

"If ever there was ever a place that offered the perfect site for an ambush, this is it," Kat observed.

No one chose to argue.

"I take it there's no way around, we have to go through this section?" she added.

Tom nodded. "Afraid so." They hadn't passed any intersecting corridors in a while and the pressure of the core's proximity wouldn't be denied. It had become a growing ache in his head, driving him on.

"Okay then, I'll go first." Somewhere along the line Kat seemed to have taken charge, but then she'd been doing much the same for pretty much all her life and if her leadership was good enough for the Tattooed Men it was certainly good enough for him.

"Jayce, you take the rear, with Tom in between us." She drew one of her swords. "We'll stick close to the left side of the corridor, weapons in our right hands, fingers of the left brushing the wall all the while. That way we can be certain one of us won't go stumbling off in the dark and get separated. Listen out for the person in front or behind you, make sure you can always hear them. If at any point you can't, say something, and don't be afraid to answer."

They proceeded as Kat had described, Tom clutching his knife ferociously, having accepted he was never going to be a swordsman during the trek along the Thair. All the while he worried that he might trip on something in the dark, fall forward and stab Kat. Of even greater concern was the thought that behind him Jayce might do exactly the same and stab *him*.

They were tense moments, those spent in total darkness. Tom didn't need Kat's encouragement to listen out for the others. He strained at every step to hear his two companions, to draw comfort from any confirmation of their presence, and he suspected both of them were doing the same. Thankfully, the period was brief. A single light flickered erratically in the ceiling ahead, dispensing irregular pulses of illumination in a stop-start manner that strobed their world with twilight, allowing Tom to glimpse Kat's movements in broken jerks. As they drew nearer, the light grew starker, her presence sharper. She glanced back and grinned reassurance, though none of them spoke. Then they had passed beneath this isolated beacon of light and were walking forward again into greyness and shadow, until the dark swallowed them once more.

That flickering beacon proved to be a harbinger, however, and their return to total darkness was a brief one. More lights appeared ahead, this time neither isolated nor flickering. First a pair with little space between them, then a continuous line, restored once more as normal service resumed. They abandoned the wall and were able to walk confidently again. Tom saw clearly where the last lick of sooty blackness stained the wall and then stopped. All three of them had made it, they'd come through the pitch black corridors without attack from Rust Warrior, Demon or even rebel kids, though Tom had no idea how they would have coped if any such had materialised. He saw his own relief mirrored in the eyes and smiles of both his companions. Kat even chuckled.

Her good humour didn't last long. Their nervousness at walking blindly might have passed but the tension of their situation mounted at every turn. Kat's sword had been returned to its scabbard but her hand never seemed to be far from its hilt.

"Where *are* they?" she muttered.

Tom knew how she felt. The lack of recent opposition was growing almost sinister. Perhaps there were no more runaway kids, perhaps they'd passed through the main strength of the Rust Warriors, but where were the Demons? The very future of their race depended on Tom's failure, so why weren't the denizens of the Upper Heights – the core's avatars as the Prime Master had called them – flinging themselves against him in feather-winged droves?

It suddenly occurred to him that he had no idea how many Demons there actually were. More than the few they'd seen to date, surely, but if the primary functions of this elusive race were to defend the city's roof – which hadn't come under attack in centuries, if ever – and to provide a physical manifestation for the core, would there need to be that many? Probably not. So if the Blade had accounted for a few and he'd seen to another – with a little help from the kayjele – these could very well represent significant losses. Perhaps that explained why no more attacks had come. Perhaps the Demons were saving themselves for one final effort at a time and place of their choosing.

"Your logic is sound," said the goddess, who now walked beside him again. "The specific number of each generation varies, but there are usually around a score and never more than three dozen. You're close to the core now and an attack *will* come, make no mistake. Stay focussed. Whatever happens, you must stay focussed." With that she vanished, as abruptly as she had appeared, to leave Tom staring at Kat.

"What?" she asked, noting his attention.

"Nothing."

"No, you saw something didn't you. I'm not letting you get away with 'nothing' again. What did you see?"

"The goddess," he said on impulse, tired of hiding the fact.

"Sorry? As in Thaiss herself?"

He nodded, knowing how ridiculous it sounded.

"You mean like a visitation, a religious vision or whatever?"

"Something like that, yes."

"Wow, that trip up the Thair really messed with your head, didn't it."

"Trust me, you don't know the half of it," he assured her.

The pounding in Tom's head, the lure of the core, grew to dominate his thoughts. They were right on top of it, he could sense it. The very last he anticipated was a dead end – the first they'd encountered. They were no longer in any of the residential areas – Tom felt certain they'd left those behind a while ago. The corridors had become bleaker, blander and more functional, as had the doorways, which were far fewer and, where present, were simple utilitarian oblongs, lacking any hint of adornment or personalisation. Even so, it came as something of a shock when the corridor simply ended in a blank wall.

"The core's ahead of us, just the other side of this wall," Tom muttered, unable to keep still. "I know it is."

Jayce had stepped forward and was feeling the surface of the wall, standing on tiptoes and reaching up to run his fingers along the ceiling join, as if hoping to find a gap that might indicate the presence of a door.

It was obvious his search had been in vain even before he stepped back, pursed his lips and shook his head.

Kat had been staring at the wall intently, as if it might offer some clue under close scrutiny. Clearly it hadn't as she sighed and said, "We'll have to go back, then."

Tom shook his head. "It would take too long. We're here. Now."

"With just a solid brick wall to get through," Kat pointed out.

"Perhaps I can visualise the core enough to take us there," Tom said, almost to himself. He'd caught a vague glimpse from the Prime Master's mind but wouldn't really want to rely on that.

"Then why have we just traipsed halfway across the brecking city?" Kat exploded.

"Because I *can't* really visualise it." He was pacing in circles, the need to get past this wall gnawing at him.

"What happens if you try to visualise it but can't?"

"I've no idea," he admitted.

Kat shook her head. "It's a no go then. We can't take the risk."

Tom knew she was right. He didn't much fancy the idea of trying only to end up stuck in some limbo because he couldn't see the destination clearly enough, or worse still risk materialising halfway through a brick wall or whatever... but there had to be a way, he simply wasn't seeing it.

Jayce thumped the wall with the flat of his hand. "It's solid," he said. "This is going to take some knocking down if it comes to that."

"There must be *something*…" Tom stepped forward to run his hands across the barrier that was keeping him from his goal, almost as if he doubted Jayce's findings, though in truth he did so merely for want of anything better to do and to stop himself from pacing.

The moment his fingers touched the surface he felt a surge of energy, which seemed to run rapidly through his arm and ripple outward to encompass his entire body. Right then, he didn't need the goddess's guidance or the homing instinct the Prime Master had stimulated, he could *feel* the core burning in his mind. It was as if a switch had been flicked somewhere inside him. He, the core, and the wall, they were all connected by a stream of energy, which flowed constantly between them. They were a circuit, which had sat dormant and waiting, broken until his hand touched the wall and closed the loop, enabling the energy to flow.

"Tom!"

He barely heard Kat's exclamation and certainly didn't need it to tell him what was happening. He could feel the wall accept him, welcome him even. It was as if this inanimate barrier chose to step aside and usher him within. The wall melted from sight. He felt it fade beneath his fingertips, disappearing as it simply took itself elsewhere. As easily as that they were granted access to the core.

Tom hadn't known what to expect. The Prime Master had described the core's portal as a "platform", which meant nothing to him. In the event, it proved to be exactly as the name suggested: a large, flat section of disconnected flooring that stood proud of the main floor and seemed to hover in the air unsupported. Quite why it did so, other than as a statement of its import, was beyond Tom.

He barely noticed the platform however; it was the far wall, from which the dais projected, that demanded his attention.

"A bit of a let-down, if this is it," Kat said.

No it wasn't, not for Tom. He couldn't focus on that wall, couldn't decide quite what he was looking at. It was as if he were staring at two different walls, both existing in the same place at the same time, one overlaying the other, flip-flopping in and out of focus constantly. The first was a featureless blank, just another unremarkable wall, but the second was something else entirely. Tom was instantly reminded of a memory absorbed while he was in the immersion tank. He saw again in vivid detail the enormous column of core material being lowered into Thaiburley's heart. This was it. *This* was what he remembered from those newly acquired memories. Phasing in and out of focus, of existence, as if jostling for attention with the mundane wall it shared space with, was a section of that vibrant, swirling, impossibly bright energy. This time though, it was different. This wasn't someone else's memories – images in which he had no emotional investment – this was physically in front of *him*, in person. It had instant impact in a way that the planted memories could never convey. The core pulsed with vigour, seeming almost alive.

It reached out to him and Tom felt his body respond. The core's energy touched every part of him simultaneously, seeming to stimulate every cell, evoking a sense of euphoria such as he'd never experienced before. Tom felt a shiver run up the back of his neck and his hair tingled, as if every strand was stretching upward to attention. He wanted to laugh, to sing, to share this exulted state with the world.

He grabbed Kat's hand, perhaps to dance with her, though afterwards he couldn't be certain. She instantly pulled away, snatching it out of his grip.

"Tom, what the breck are you doing?"

"Can't you see, can't you *feel* it?" *How could she not?*

"No, so you're going to have to tell us poor blind folk what's got into you. What are you seeing that we can't?"

"The light… the colours… the *core*!" and he was laughing now.

Suddenly he stopped as a sense of dread washed over him. "Oh no."

"What?"

He felt them coming – when he was this alive, this connected, how could he fail to? Streaks of individual sentient core energy zeroing in on his location, racing towards him like arrows loosed by a company of expert archers converging on the same bullseye.

The Demons. Tom might have anticipated their arrival but to Kat and Jayce it must have seemed as if Thaiburley's most elusive citizens materialised out of nowhere. One instant they were on the threshold of a vacant space, the next a host of winged, serenely smiling, achingly beautiful Adonises filled the room. No women among the lot of them, Tom noted in passing. How could anyone ever have believed in Demons' eggs when the Demons themselves were all male?

"Thaiss!" Kat exclaimed. "We had trouble enough dealing with just one of these breckers, what are we supposed to do about this lot?"

Good question, and there would be no kayjele to help them this time.

The assault began almost immediately. There was no attempt at violence, no physical threat from the assembled host at all; the demons were far too subtle for that. They played to their strengths.

It was impossible not to be impressed by such physical perfection, the aura of health, of vitality, of *goodness* that surrounded them. It was only natural to feel a sense of awe at these visions of angelic perfection; and love and devotion were little more than a few quick steps away from awe.

Why was he trying to destroy them, these wondrous, perfect beings, what was he thinking of? They had a right to live just as much as he did.

Tom, don't listen to them. The goddess, nagging him again, as she always seemed to be. Why wouldn't she leave him alone? *Fight it Tom.*

"Be gone, old woman," said the Demons. "You no longer hold dominion here."

Tom… But the image of the elderly woman distorted, flickered, and dissolved, like some victim of the Rust Warriors. *The Rust Warriors!* That memory stirred anger, hatred, and resistance. Tom wriggled free, just a little bit, free of the Demons' insidious influence;

enough to remember, enough to question, enough for a seed of free will to take hold. From that seed, clear thinking spread, causing the Demon's hold on him to falter.

People had died. A lot of people. Directly or indirectly the Demons were responsible; they were in league with the Rust Warriors and the blood of Thaiburley stained their hands. Tom kept telling himself this, running through it again and again as if it were his litany for hiding. He was determined to fight them, to remain free of their will.

The Demons inevitably sensed his struggles and must have realised that he was slipping away from them, because they switched tactics. Tom felt the change but it took him a while to work out precisely *what* had changed, because it wasn't directed at him. The Demons were focusing their efforts on his friends.

"Tom...!" His name emerged from Kat's lips as a strangled gasp.

He looked to see her drawing one of her short swords and turning towards him, her movements jerked and stuttering in marked contrast to their usual fluid grace. It was as if she were a marionette being operated by some inexpert puppet master. Tom realised immediately what was happening.

"Fight them, Kat, fight them!"

"What... the breck... do you think I'm doing?"

Yet still the sword drew free of its scabbard. Nor was Kat the only tool the Demons were attempting to wield. Jayce, drilled for much of his life in discipline and the honour of duty, reacted to their manipulations somewhat differently. As Tom watched, he stood rigidly for a moment and then convulsed, collapsing to the floor to writhe and twitch. The internal conflict between what he knew he should do and what the Demons were compelling him to do evidently triggering a seizure of some kind.

Kat's sword was now clenched in both her white-knuckled hands, as she took a stiff-legged step towards him.

"For Thaiss's sake, Tom, kill me!" she urged.

"No!"

"If you don't... I'll kill... myself."

"No, Kat!" He watched horrified as the sword lifted in her shaking hands to point upwards and then, with agonising slowness, began to turn inwards towards its wielder. He saw this with only part of his awareness, however. The rest of him was elsewhere, skirting around the Demons, not joining with them, not plunging into that vast mass of their combined consciousness, just feeling around its edges, searching for a weakness. He sensed something surprising about them, a nebulous emotion that was wholly unexpected and which he was frantically trying to understand.

The Demons were afraid, which meant they must be vulnerable. If he could only work out what of, he might yet find a way of saving himself and Kat, of saving everybody.

"Trust me, Kat," he said. "Don't harm yourself, just concentrate on not harming me."

"Easy... for you... to say."

Sweat trickled down her face. The trembling blade continued to reverse, lowering by ponderous degree towards her shoulder.

It wasn't him. The Demons weren't afraid of his much vaunted talent... so what was it?

As if sensing his quest, a calm, almost musical voice spoke soothingly, "You can't beat us, Tom. Not this close to the core, the source of our strength. Nothing can touch us here, at the seat of our very being."

Was it just imagination that dressed his next thoughts in the voice of the goddess, or did some vestige of Thaiss still reside within him? *Listen to their words*, the voice seemed to whisper. *The clue to defeating them is in their own words.*

Tom thought frantically, analysing the Demons' gloating pronouncement, taking individual words and considering their implications, discarding the irrelevancies and unspecifics, concentrating on the truly important ones. They quickly boiled down to just three: Demons, source, core. They were the essence of what was going on here. In the blink of an eye he expanded his thoughts in a manner that would have been impossible before his stay with Thaiss, to consider the relationship between those concepts, and as quickly as that he had it: what the Demons were trying so hard to distract him from; what they were afraid of.

In order to stop him, the Demons had congregated at the one place where they were at their most powerful, but it was also where they were most vulnerable: yes the core was the source of their strength, but that same core had been calling to them for more than a century, attempting to reclaim them. They were programmed to heed that call, their nature demanded they merge with the core when summoned, yet they had resisted that imperative throughout and continued to resist it even now. Every day since must have been a constant struggle for them, a fight not to succumb; and never would that call be stronger than it was here and now, at its very source.

Despite their apparent confidence, their air of assumed infallibility, coming here was an act of desperation, a gamble they were driven to take; one in which the odds were stacked in their favour only for as long as he failed to recognise their peril.

The gamble had just backfired.

"Hang on, Kat, he yelled. "For Thaiss's sake, hang on!"

He could feel it immediately once he knew what to look for; that summons: a relentless insistence that tugged at them. Now Tom knew exactly what to do, how to beat them. He didn't attack, he didn't fling his talent impotently against the unyielding might of the Demons' combined magnificence; he simply grasped the bond that tied each individual Demon to Thaiburley's core, the tether that even now sought to reel them in, and held fast while he summoned his talent. Feeling it burn, feeling it swell within every last corner of his being until he could contain it no more. Only then did he let go, pouring everything he had into that link, strengthening it, boosting it, until the summons ripped through the Demon's fragile indifference, battering at their carefully constructed resistance.

And they did resist. At first. For desperate seconds they clung on. Futilely. First one and then another succumbed, their defences shredding as they were sucked into the vortex of the core. Two more followed immediately and the trickle became a rush. Tom felt them go, each parting scream a testament of despair and frustrated ambition, every single one of them indistinguishable from the last.

Finally it was over. He came back to himself and discovered he was on his knees, without any recollection of how he came to be there. Kat stood beside him, her sword lying on the ground, both hands held stiffly open at her sides. She looked petrified, her face as white as a freshly starched shirt.

He climbed shakily to his feet and drew her into his arms, hugging her close, an instinctive act which he would have suppressed if he'd stopped to think about it. She didn't resist but instead hugged him back, clinging to him until the trembling stopped. "It's okay," he said. "They're gone." He said this as much to reassure himself as her.

After a few ragged breaths exhaled against his shoulder and neck – their warmth a tickle on his throat – she pulled away. There was a little more colour to her cheeks now. "Thaiss, that'll be something to tell folks on a cold dark night!"

Tom grinned. "Should be worth a drink or two."

"You're not kidding." She stooped to reclaim her sword.

Jayce was in the process of pushing himself up from the floor, one hand spread on the ground for support, the other clutching his head, finger and thumb either side of his eyes as if to hold them in place. Flecks of drying spittle marked his cheek and chin. He lowered the hand, blew out his cheeks and gave Tom a shallow nod to indicate he was all right. Tom realised that, bizarrely, he was probably in the best shape of any of them.

"They've really gone?" Kat asked from beside him.

He nodded. "Sucked back into the core, where they belong."

"Remind me never to get on the wrong side of you."

"Oh I will, don't worry."

"Now what?"

"Now we do what we came here for. We replenish the core." Interesting how Kat was deferring to him all of a sudden. He reckoned he could get used to that.

Despite his confident words, Tom wasn't entirely clear *how* he was supposed to replenish the core, but there was no point in admitting as much just yet.

The room was unchanged, which struck Tom as wrong; there should have been some disorder, scorch marks on the floor, a hole, or at least some slight difference to mark the fierce, brief struggle that had just taken place here. But the impassive walls and logic-defying platform remained the same. As did the dual-nature of the core wall, alternating rapidly between functional neutrality and the writhing energy of the city's heart. Even the core looked no different. It had just swallowed an entire generation of Demons without even belching.

Tom walked slowly forward, mesmerised. He felt that he was being offered a choice of two different realities. Inevitably, he chose the core, concentrating on those shifting energies, until they stabilised and became permanent, the mundane blandness of solid masonry no longer interfering.

"Wow," Kat said. "Did you do that?"

"No, not really," he replied. "It was there all the time."

Tom knew what to do now. It was obvious. He clambered up onto the platform. Kat and Jayce followed, though he was barely paying them any attention now.

Calmly, almost reverently, he took the rucksack from his back and eased it onto the floor. He lifted the canister free of the bag, his hands tingling at the touch, a sense of pins and needles running in ripples up his arm. He placed the cylinder on the ground and flipped open both catches. Holding it with one hand, he tilted the tube towards the core, as if aiming a stunted canon. With his other hand, he lifted open the lid.

Tom had braced himself, not knowing what to expect. In the event there was no recoil, no physical reaction from the canister at all, as blinding light erupted from its mouth. Tom cried out, screwing his eyes shut and instinctively lifting his free hand to shield them. In doing so, the edge of his hand – perhaps his little finger – must have brushed the stream of escaping energy. In a panicked instant he was gone, his consciousness sucked from his body and propelled into the core.

Tom felt abruptly huge – not in a bloated, physical sense, rather it was his mind which seemed to be expanding at exponential speed in every direction at once. He panicked, certain that he was being pulled apart, that his awareness – that element that defined his sense of self – would be stretched to breaking point and simply shred apart to be absorbed by the seething energy around him, but it never happened. There was no collapse, no dissipation of thought or mind. Instead he seemed to be everywhere all at once, and everyone simultaneously. He was

– a scrawny boy crouching barefoot by a bin, scraping cold beans from a discarded can and sucking greedily at his fingers

– a Thaistess deep in concentration beside her temple's pond

– a master cobbler bawling out an apprentice who had stretched the leather too tightly and so ruined a pair of expensive shoes

– a young woman astride her husband, rocking her hips and groin backwards and forwards, uttering the occasional moan for effect while her thoughts focused on the beautiful pink dress she had bought earlier that day

– a bank worker dithering over whether or not to report a colleague whom he suspected of thieving, concerned in case the allegations should prove to be unfounded

– an arkademic worrying about her closest friend who had been missing since the earliest days of the Rust Warriors' attacks

– a mother boasting proudly to a neighbour of her son's success

– an elated office worker debating whether to celebrate an unexpected promotion by taking his wife out for an extravagant meal or making a beeline to the nearest whorehouse

– an old man ruefully reflecting on how swiftly his youth had slipped away

– a shopkeeper tempted to close up early after a particularly quiet day

– a healer banishing a child's stomach pain while an anxious mother looked on

– a bargeman bent over and vomiting into the Thair as his gut rejected the volume of ale he had steadily been pouring into it since lunchtime

a young girl laughing as her hands touched the wall, signalling safety in a game of chase

– a guardsman standing nervously at his post, wondering when rather than *if* the Rust Warriors would attack again...

Every Row, every situation, he was there – young, old, male female, rich or poor – he was there. In some ways it was like the immersion tank but taken to the ultimate extreme. Tom knew that he was primarily sensing the talented – those who had a link to Thaiburley's heart, a conduit which allowed his consciousness to flow out through the core to touch the privileged few, even those who were oblivious to their talent. He knew too that the talented formed only a small minority of the population, but in a city of tens of millions they still numbered tens of thousands and, for that moment, he was there, with each and every one of them.

Somehow, his mind coped. It didn't shut down or collapse, perhaps because of his experience with the immersion tank. That had been nothing compared to this but it had, in a sense, been preparation. The tank had taught him how to let images and impressions wash over him without attempting to grasp and interpret each and every one. Afterwards, he would feel certain that it was only this preparation that enabled him to cling on to his sanity amidst the kaleidoscope of impressions that threatened to overwhelm him. Had the goddess known? Had she suspected that he might find himself here? He wouldn't have put it past her.

Eventually, after what seemed an eternity, Tom began to regain some coherence and resume a sense of self. He felt a huge sense of energy coursing through him, of vitality and strength, of power and destiny beyond human ken. This was the core, this was so far removed from anything Tom had ever experienced, and yet beneath all that was a hint of something familiar. He isolated that hint and recognised it: Thaiss. The core energy was somehow of her in a way he didn't understand. Did the goddess actually generate the energy? She was linked to it at a fundamental level which she'd never hinted at, had hidden from him. Was it core energy that sustained her, kept her alive?

Suddenly, all his previous assumptions about the goddess were ripped to shreds. No matter appearances, she and her brother weren't human, he knew that now, could feel it as a certainty. How could he not have seen it before? These two beings had led a civilisation from one world to another, built the mightiest city humankind had ever seen, and they somehow controlled and manipulated this elemental, beautiful yet brutal force known as core energy. How could he ever have dismissed them as merely human?

Perhaps they truly were gods.

He could sense something wrong, an anomaly within the core; not rotten as he'd expected, not overtly evil – not wrong in that sense, but unquestionably out of place. Thaiss's brother, it had to be. Tom reached for that presence, attempted to explore this taint of something foreign, but it fled, recoiling from his touch. He pursued it, not with malice or even that specific intent, but in joyous sport, riding the vigorous wave of energy that washed through the core, driving the anomaly before him. It contracted, withdrawing into the farthest fringes of the core, and then it left. He felt the moment the taint departed and knew that it had fled into the City Below. To some degree, in some sense, Thaiss's brother survived. Replenishing the core hadn't killed him as anticipated, the process had merely driven him to a new vessel, a new host.

Had Tom wanted to, had he possessed the will, he might have followed then, might have seen where the taint had fled to and perhaps even finished it off for good, but the moment the anomalous presence deserted the core he lost interest. Instead he revelled in the vibrancy, the purity of the cleansed core, allowing it to wash around him and through him.

There was work to be done. A new generation of Demons to prepare and install. The latest group had been fully integrated. Lessons would be learned, improvements made. Slowly, increment by small increment, they were drawing closer to perfection, each new generation of avatars an improvement on the last.

At that instant, he felt something pulling at him, taking him away. *No!* This was where he wanted to be, this was where he belonged. But his protests were ineffectual. He was aware of something holding him back, tugging at him. The core seemed to be receding, or he was drawing clear of it. Not uniformly but by ragged degree. The energy still clung to him, like viscous toffee clinging to a slice of apple that had just been pulled through its heart, reluctant to let go.

Suddenly the world contracted. In one great surge, like water draining into a plughole, everything flowed back into Tom, leaving his mind reeling under the assault of more impressions than most people would experience in a lifetime. As awareness began to seep outward again, he realised he was sitting down. He felt human again; disorientated, but human. Kat was immediately behind him, reaching forward, almost sprawling, with one hand clasping his wrist, and the shoulder of that arm ached as if it had recently been wrenched.

"What… what happened?" he mumbled, remembering how to speak.

"Wow." Kat let go of his wrist and rolled into a sitting position, looking a little dazed. "I mean, just wow! I think I caught a glimpse of what you just saw. It was…" and she shook her head.

"But what *happened*?" he persisted.

"I grabbed you," she said. "You started to… I don't know, *stretch*, as if you were being dragged into that mass of energy, so I grabbed hold of your arm and pulled you back. That was when the world went weird, or at least my head did."

"I pulled you both out," Jayce said quietly.

"What?"

"You were both being pulled in there," Jayce explained.

Of course, Tom thought. Kat was talented too, so the core would want to absorb both of them if it had the chance. Jayce, though, wasn't. It had no claim on him, so he had been their anchor.

"I grabbed Kat, then grabbed you, and pulled you both out," Jayce continued.

"Thank you," Tom said, which was far from adequate, but it was all he could offer just then.

Kat frowned. Tom had regained his feet but hadn't otherwise moved. He just stood there, the now-dormant core cylinder lying discarded at his feet, as he stared at the curtain of energy which formed the room's back wall. The pulsing, flowing thing was pretty amazing, no question about that, but Kat had no intention of getting any closer to it. Yet Tom seemed completely lost in the flickering patterns and for a second she was afraid he might dive back in. If he did, she might just let him go this time.

Kat stood up, wary in case Tom made to move nearer the core. As she straightened, something fluttered from her pocket – a folded sheet of paper. For a moment she stared at it, not able to place what it was. Then she remembered. The apothaker's sketch. It had survived all this and stayed with her throughout. She bent down and picked it up, a little crumpled but still all there. She carefully smoothed the sheet out and opened it. To stare at her own image. *Bet I don't look this good right now*, she thought. Cute but with attitude. Exactly the look she aimed for but had a feeling she never quite achieved.

"Can I see that?"

Kat hadn't realised Jayce was behind her. She clutched the picture defensively to her chest, reluctant to show it to anyone. But he had just saved her life, so she relented and thrust it towards him.

He took the sheet and stared at it for a second, before saying, "Where did you get this?"

"A friend gave it to me."

"Was she the artist? I mean, do you know the woman who drew this?"

"Hey, I never said it was a woman."

"You didn't need to," he said. "This told me." He pointed to a small stylised "A" in the corner of the image, so artfully integrated that it could easily have passed as part of the design.

Kat snatched the picture back, folded the parchment and pocketed it once more. Only then did she reply. "Yeah, like I said, she's a friend of mine."

For long seconds the young guard didn't say anything. Kat found his expression difficult to fathom, until a single tear leaked from the corner of his eye to trickle down his cheek.

SIXTEEN

"It isn't over, not yet."

"What?"

Tom realised this wasn't exactly what either of the others wanted to hear, but it was the truth and he had to say it before they relaxed, before the urgency disappeared. "The presence that was corrupting the core, Thaiss's brother, it didn't die, it merely fled into the City Below. I've got to go after it and finish things."

"Why?" Kat asked. "You came here to restore the city's core, and that's what you've done. Job over."

Why indeed. Not for his own gain, not for some personal advantage, but for the sake of Thaiburley: the city that was his home, the city he loved, the city he belonged to heart and soul. For the good of everyone, not just himself. There, he'd admitted it. He was doing this, all of it, because somebody had to and he was the one in the right place at the right time; the only person who could. Simple as that. If it made him a hero in some people's eyes and a fool in others', that was their problem, not his.

He shook his head. "I have to see this through, that's all."

"Where are you gonna look? The City Below is a pretty big place, in case you've forgotten."

"I know, but the taint didn't just go anywhere, it went into a host, I could sense that much; someone or something that had been prepared in advance. I just have to figure out who or what."

"Insint," Kat said, as if struck by sudden realisation.

"What?"

"The expedition into the Stain, it wasn't just the Soul Thief we were hunting. I made a deal with the Prime Master. He helped us track down the Soul Thief and in return we agreed to help him take down something he called 'Insint', a left-over from the war apparently, some sort of creature or mechanism that's still around and working against the city."

Tom stared at Kat, reckoning that her suggestion might just be an inspired one. If this Insint had fought against the city in the war, then it was already an ally of Thaiss's brother. The natural place for him to flee. "All right, that settles it. I'll take us back to the Stain."

"At last!" Kat said. "That'll be *one* of the Prime Master's promises fulfilled." She gave a wry smile. "I guess the gold can wait."

"No, stop!" Jayce said. "First we have to report to the council, the Prime Master, to let them know what's happened."

Tom hesitated, loathe to lose any more time.

"That's where my duty lies," Jayce added, not quite pleading, but definitely heading that way.

Tom nodded, reluctantly, but both he and Kat did owe the young Guardsman their lives. "All right, I'll take you to the Prime Master and then Kat and I will head for the Stain, leaving you to make your report."

"Thank you."

Tom had Kat and Jayce stand close to him, each gripping one of his arms. He cleared his mind and summoned an image of the Prime Master, concentrating as the goddess had taught him, honing in on that face, drawing it to him and him to it and... nothing happened. He tried again, but still nothing. He thought about the process, trying to work out what he was doing wrong, and concluded that he wasn't doing anything wrong.

He felt Kat adjust her grip on his left sleeve. "Anytime you're ready," she said.

"I know," he assured her. "It's not working, and I don't know why."

"Maybe all the fiddling around with the core is to blame, affecting your power in some way," Kat suggested, as she and Jayce relaxed, letting go of his arms. "Maybe it has to settle into a new pattern or something."

"Maybe," Tom agreed, but he didn't think so.

"Try someone else," Jayce said. "Perhaps something's blocking your connection to the Prime Master but it'll work with someone else."

Good idea, but who? The Prime Master was someone he knew well, but the other council members he'd only caught brief glimpses of and they were just hazy impressions. "Thaiss!" he said at length. There was one other person he could picture clearly.

"What?" Kat wanted to know.

He sighed. "The only person whose face I can see in enough detail to try this is… Carla Birhoff."

Jayce snorted, which, Tom suspected, provided ample comment regarding his opinion of the assembly member.

"Really?" Kat said. "She obviously made quite an impression."

Tom glared in response to her mischievous smirk.

"Go for it, kid," she then encouraged. "It still beats walking back."

He supposed she was right.

He waited as they shuffled closer to grip his sleeves again before taking a deep breath, hoping he wasn't going to regret this. He pictured the insincere smile, the avaricious eyes that marred the almost-attractive face of this slender older woman, who struck him as someone past her prime but determined to keep age at bay. This time there was no problem. He felt the increasingly familiar rush of energy, and the anonymous blank-walled corridor they'd been standing in disappeared.

He trusted the core energy, trusted that it would deposit them safely in a position free of obstructions, and it did. They materialised in what was obviously a bedroom, where a semi-naked Carla Birhoff was in the process of changing her clothes.

The assembly member shrieked, snatching up a garment and clutching it defensively across her torso while at the same time turning away from them in a cowering crouch.

"Dear goddess, what… how… how *dare* you!"

Kat sniggered. Tom averted his eyes instantly and felt his cheeks burn. He wasn't too certain what he'd seen but he knew it was flesh, *her* flesh, and fervently wished he could be somewhere else just then – *anywhere* else.

Only Jayce seemed unperturbed; as cool and professional as you'd expect from a Council Guardsman. "Assembly Member Birhoff," he said, stepping forward and suddenly all business. "Apologies for the intrusion, but we're here on a matter both grave and urgent. We'll wait in the next room until you're able to join us. I would urge you, though, to please be prompt."

With that he herded Kat and Tom from the bed chamber into a well-appointed lounge that, if Tom's memory served him right, pretty closely matched the size of the one in which he'd been held prisoner by Miles and Ryan and the gang of renegade boys.

Kat flung herself backwards into one of two comfortable-looking sofas, arms outspread. "Hey, this is nice," she approved, wriggling a little. "Think I might get one of these for the new home... when I've got one." Tom made no comment, anxious to be on his way.

They didn't have to wait long, Assembly Member Birhoff joined them within moments, now fully clothed.

"Right," she said, clearly still angry, "would you mind telling me what the hell you think you're doing popping up in my bedroom like that?"

"I'm sorry..." Tom began.

"So you should be!" Birhoff snapped. "You have extraordinary talents, Tom, that's obvious, but they should be used wisely, not in some childish prank or for the sake of cheap thrills."

"I wasn't…" he began.

"Hey!" Kat interrupted, now on her feet and generating the sort of menace that Tom knew only too well. "Don't talk to him like that. He just saved the whole breckin' city!"

To her credit, the assembly member didn't flinch, though she did blink a couple of times before replying, in a much calmer voice, "For which we're all grateful, I'm sure, grateful to all of you." She graced them with a politician's smile. "But there are still such things as privacy."

"Let's all calm down," Jayce suggested; more for Kat's benefit than the assembly member's, Tom suspected.

"Sorry for bursting in on you like this," Tom said. "But I had no choice."

She looked at him quizzically.

"I couldn't reach the Prime Master for some reason, and…" He stopped, seeing her expression, which conveyed, shock and discomfort at the same time, her mouth forming an *oh* without any sound emerging. "What?" he said, though, with sinking heart, he already guessed what was coming.

"I'm so sorry, Tom." She lifted a hand to rest gently on his arm. "Of course, you wouldn't have heard. The Prime Master is dead."

"What?" Tom was stunned. Even though this was what he'd feared but had tried so hard not to consider, his brain still refused to decipher meaning from what his ears reported. "What do you mean he's dead? He was safe, here, with all of you."

"After you left the attacks intensified," the assembly member explained. "It was almost as if the Rust Warriors or the guiding intelligence behind them realised they were running out of time. There were so many of them, more than we'd ever imagined... the Blade, the Kite Guards, the Council Guard, arkademics, watch officers reassigned from other Rows, hastily organised militia drawn from ordinary citizens, we needed every single one of them just to hold our own. I don't think any of us imagined how many of our people had fallen victim to bone flu. They just kept coming. It was horrible."

Tom still couldn't believe it. "And the Prime Master fell defending the Row." What was someone of his importance doing on the front line anyway?

"No," and she shook her head. "That was the worst part. While we fought, he faced his own battle, alone. He had bone flu, Tom, very advanced. How he held it at bay for as long as he did we'll never know."

"The gloves," Tom murmured, suddenly understanding. "Didn't anyone guess? You were around him a lot more than I was."

She sighed. "We were all so busy. There were so many other things to think about, to worry about, and the Prime Master always seemed so..."

"Permanent," Tom supplied.

"Yes, exactly; permanent."

He drew a ragged breath. "So what happens now, for the city?" *For me.*

"We go on. We rebuild. We celebrate our survival and the lives of all the wonderful, brave folk we've lost. We assemble a new council, promoting the most worthy of the senior arkademics to replace those members who have passed away or can no longer serve. That's what we've always done, if not generally replacing so many at one time… in short, we go on."

Tom had only known the Prime Master a brief while but this wise and generous man had his respect and, yes, his love. He could cope, though; he'd suffered losses before. News of this latest one only strengthened his resolve regarding the future. The Prime Master had been Tom's only strong tie to the Heights and the world of arkademics and councillors, and now that tie was severed. In a strange way, this news of the Prime Master's death freed him. A final unwitting gift from a man to whom he owed so much.

Tom's gaze fell on Kat. He saw the concern haunting her eyes. "Do you still want to do this?" she asked.

"Yes!" Even more so now. For the Prime Master's sake as much as anything else, he was determined to see this through. "Are you ready?"

She nodded. They held hands this time. Tom had no trouble summoning the face of the Tattooed Man, M'gruth, and the familiar rushing feeling swept over him.

Tylus still led the way. Their company was hardly silent as they stumbled through that deep and dark second chamber, but the further they ventured the more they found that any noise was muffled by the omnipresent roar of what had to be a waterfall.

Conversation became difficult and they lapsed into the habit of silence. For no discernible reason one of the torches had packed up within minutes of its being switched on, so they were reduced to using just one at a time, which Tylus held. The resultant cone of illumination that fanned out before him provided a welcome tether to reality in these extraordinary surroundings. He sensed the others behind him but wondered if that was only because he knew them to be there. Part of him suspected that if they should disappear one by one he might never even notice they had gone.

Although by no means level or even, the ground had at least stopped dropping ever downward, for now at least, though it had taken Tylus a little while to recognise the fact. With no real visual clues and hearing all but negated by the thunder of rushing water, the mind took to playing tricks, and judging anything as subtle as gradient became a challenge.

Droplets of water drifted onto Tylus' face – nothing obvious, more in the nature of condensing mist. He lifted the torch's beam away from the ground to find the light reflected back at him from myriad such drops floating in the air like ephemeral jewels. Beyond this curtain, he thought he could glimpse more concerted movement – something rushing downward – which could only be the waterfall. As if to confirm the assumption, he nearly slipped over; the rocks beneath their feet were becoming damp and treacherous.

Tylus was just trying to work out whether he really had heard someone call out his name when he felt something land on his shoulder, startling him, but it was only a hand; Issie's to be precise. She was making a valiant effort to shout and make herself heard above the roar. He leaned towards her, trying to catch the words.

"The Blade are saying we should stay here," she yelled. "They've sensed something up ahead."

"Insint?" he asked.

She shrugged. He wasn't about to argue either way. Who knew what senses the unsettling ebony colossuses could call upon? Tall black shadows slipped past them, three of them, catching the edge of the torch's beam. This left just one to safeguard the arkademic – two of their number having been lost beside the Thair. Despite having encountered the Blade on more than one occasion, Tylus still wasn't sure whether to think of their fallen as dead or broken.

He became aware of the Tattooed Men gathering in the gloom around them and managed to catch hold of M'gruth's arm, leaning forward to explain what was happening.

"Hell of a place to call a halt," M'gruth observed. "We'll be drenched through in no time at all."

It was a fair point but not one Tylus could do much about.

M'gruth leaned closer to say something further. "Did they give any idea of exactly…"

Whatever he'd been about to ask was cut short as the world lit up with no warning, dazzling Tylus, while the sharp crack of an explosion boomed out to momentarily override the noise of the waterfall. At the

same time the ground beneath their feet shook, causing M'gruth to lose his balance and grab hold of the
Kite Guard to stop himself from falling over.

In the bright flash, a split second before he was dazzled, Tylus caught a glimpse of their immediate
surroundings; no more than a snapshot perhaps, but
it was enough to show him the waters of the mighty
Thair cascading down the rock face in a spectacular fall
not far from where he stood. The water plummeted
into a swollen pool, at the lip of which a battle was
being fought.

The three Blade had engaged something that could
only be Insint, though Tylus couldn't see enough to
identify their enemy for certain. Nor could he be sure
exactly what had exploded.

M'gruth had evidently grown tired of hanging
around waiting on the Blade's instructions. As Tylus's
vision cleared, he saw the Tattooed Men's adopted
leader speaking in the ears of his fellows, clearly intent
on organising them to join the fray. The Kite Guard
wasn't surprised. These were Pits warriors after all,
and, from what he knew of them, sitting around and
waiting wasn't in their nature.

Even without the flash of an explosion the site of
the battle would have been easy enough to locate. Energy crackled and sparks flew, clearly marking the
spot. Tylus was loathe to fly, not trusting the limited
scope of the torch's beam to identify any obstructions,
but he was hanged if he was going to stand by and let
the Tattooed Men and the Blade carry the fight.

He turned to Issie. "I'm going to try to help…"

"You can't fly, not down here," she said instantly.

"I've got to. Would you hold the torch for me, try to follow me with the beam as I fly…?"

"I can do better than that."

"Sorry?" He thought he must have misheard her due to the roar of the waterfall.

"This won't last for long and I can't generate too many of them, but here."

A silver glow started to form between Issie's cupped hands, a glow which built and strengthened until it became an orb of dazzling light, far too bright to look upon directly. Issie tossed the ball into the air, where it floated upward and outward, drifting towards the battle and bathing the scene in pale luminance. Tylus could see the uneven ground, the combatants, and he could see where the treacherous ceiling sent its sharp, hard teeth of rock downward to snag the unwary flyer.

"Go!" Issie urged.

He was already clipping the torch to his belt. With a mouthed "thank you" in her direction, Tylus took to the air.

He had no clear plan beyond wanting to contribute *something* – to dignify the vague notion of dousing Insint in the arkademics' blue light by describing it as a "plan" would have been to stretch the concept to breaking point. In the event, he hesitated to do even that, uncertain of how the arkademic's weapon might affect the Blade. The battle was being fought at super-human speed and it proved impossible to get a clear shot. Beneath him, everything was a blur of black and silver and steel, of flash and spark punctuated by the hammer of impact and shriek of metal rising above the thunder of the falls. Tylus was reduced to circling above in a tight figure-eight, alert for any opportunity. He nearly panicked and lost concentration as the light from Issie's flare started to fade, but held it together by reassuring himself that he could probably keep up this tight pattern even in the dark, especially with the sporadic bursts of energy from the fight below as guide. Fortunately he didn't need to, as a second silver sphere floated out to replace the first before the luminance died completely.

Below him, one of the Blade took a heavy blow from a metallic limb that sent it spinning out over the pool to splash down into the water and disappear. The pool's surface, already in constant motion due to the proximity of the falls, seemed to froth and boil oddly where the Blade had struck. Curious, Tylus widened the loop of his flight slightly so that he could take a closer look.

As decisions went, this proved not to be one of his better ones.

It all happened in the blink of an eye, far too quickly for him to react. He had the impression of something erupting from the water straight towards him – like a thick plant stem bursting from the ground at surreal speed. Before he could even think to manoeuvre, the thing struck and wrapped itself around him with crushing force. Pain lanced through his side and he couldn't breathe. Then he was being dragged down-ward, to hit the surface of the pool. The force of impact and the abrupt cold would have been enough to knock

the breath out of him if he'd had any. The tentacle continued to pull him downward into the cold, stygian
depths. He'd had no chance to draw a deep breath and
knew that if he couldn't free himself he'd drown in a
matter of seconds, never mind the cold or the fact that
he might well be crushed to death before that. On top
of everything else, his ears started to hurt acutely with
the rapidly increasing pressure.

Despite the death grip around his torso both arms
were free, which offered a faint glimmer of hope.
Frantically, he reached for his knife, drew it, and
stabbed at the tentacle, feeling the blade bite home
and the grip loosen slightly. Encouraged, he stabbed
again and again, frustrated at how feeble the blows
seemed, slowed as they were by the water. The tentacle loosened a little more under his assault, but as he
raised his arm to strike again another tentacle, or perhaps the tip of the same one, snagged his wrist and
knocked the knife from his hand. He clutched at it in
despair, his hand closing only on water.

His body cried out for oxygen, his lungs demanded
that he breathe. He fought hard not to, knowing that
there was no oxygen to be had, but he felt increasingly
light-headed and it was becoming hard to concentrate.
The grip around his body tightened still further. He
needed to breathe, to gasp for air became unbearable.
He wanted to scream. He tried to prise the tentacle off
with his hands. He kicked and wriggled, dimly realising that this would use up his precious oxygen all the
quicker, but knowing that if he didn't somehow escape *now* he never would.

After a mere handful of frantic twists the effort became too much, the energy drained from his limbs and his kicks became little more than feeble twitches. His head lolled as if his neck no longer had the strength to support it, and everything started to fade. Except the pain. *This is it*, he realised, with more curiosity than fear or even regret. *This is death*. And then he stopped thinking at all.

They emerged into a surreal world, made all the more so by the unexpectedly uneven ground, which caused Tom to overbalance and nearly fall over. Silver light emanated from a miniature sun, its radiance totally unlike the light from the sun globes or anything else Tom had experienced. Long shadows and eerie rocks surrounded them.

"About time you got back," said a man's voice; M'gruth, Tom realised, and the comment wasn't addressed at him.

"Having fun in my absence?" Kat responded, having to shout above the roar of the nearby falls.

"Not exactly."

A short distance away a fight was taking place, the combat conducted at incredible speed. A group of Blade were locked in battle with... a *thing*. It seemed to be all writhing body and jointed legs, with metal predominant.

"Is that Insint?" Tom asked.

"Yes," a woman replied – an arkademic, who was in the process of fashioning another mini-sun between her hands. She released it just before the first sputtered and died.

A Kite Guard flew in loops above, doing little else as far as Tom could see. As he watched, things took an unexpected turn. A thick tentacle shot from the water to wrap itself around the circling figure.

"Tylus!" the arkademic cried out.

"That's Tylus?" Kat said.

"Yes."

"Breck!" Kat started to run towards the pool.

"What are you doing?" Tom called.

"What do you think I'm doing? He saved my life," she shouted back, as if that explained everything. With that, she dived into the water.

Tom stared after her, stunned, while M'gruth and the Tattooed Men rushed past him.

There had to be *something* he could do. Not jump into the water perhaps, but... he still felt invigorated by his encounter with the core, its energy sang through his veins. He felt more powerful, more in command of his talent than he ever had before. Tom reached out, not knowing if this would work, but he couldn't think what else to do. His thoughts connected instantly with an ancient mind lurking somewhere beneath the water. Not intelligence as he knew it, this was something so focused on the need to feed, to satisfy its hunger, that few other considerations got a look in. Tom wasn't sure he could have done this at any other time, without the core energy burning so freshly, but the important thing was that he could do it now. The simplicity of the creature's motivations helped. He saw at once where to apply pressure, where to suggest that this morsel wasn't nourishing or tasty but that one was.

His tampering had two results. The most obvious being that two further tentacles shot out of the water, one wrapping itself around Insint and plucking him up high into the air, scattering the two Blade as it went. The two tentacles then literally pulled the creature – this last retreat of Thaiss's brother – apart. An agonised scream tore through the thrum of the waterfall – uncomfortable proof that whatever Insint had been, he wasn't all machine – before his bloodied remnants were dragged down into the depths.

The second consequence was a spluttering, bedraggled Kat, who surfaced at the side of the pool dragging an inert Kite Guard with her. "Give me a hand, will you?"

Tattooed arms reached down to pull both figures free of the water, where one spluttered and coughed and spat, while the other lay still.

By the time Tom got there, Kat had recovered enough to start pressing rhythmically on the Kite Guard's chest with the heel of her hand.

"Do you know what you're doing?" he wondered.

"Vaguely. Wasting my time, though, aren't I?" She paused. "He's gone."

"No." Tom could sense a spark, a flickering remnant of life's energy on the very cusp of expiring. Desperately he tried to fan that spark, drawing on his own energy to feed the fragile ember, and was rewarded by feeling it stabilise and strengthen a little, though not nearly enough and it threatened to fade again almost at once. "He's still with us, just."

"You can save him then, like you did me?"

"I'm trying…" But no matter how hard he tried, the spark grew no stronger. The man was dying as quickly as Tom was reviving him. Tom grew increasingly frustrated. *Why wasn't the man recovering?* "We need a proper healer," he said at last. "Someone who knows what they're doing."

"Shayna!" Kat said at once.

"Mildra," Tom said at the same instant.

Tom put his hands on the motionless Kite Guard, feeling Kat take his arm.

"Not again," he heard someone – M'gruth, most likely – mutter as the familiar rush of the jump swept through him.

Even after so short a time in the depths of the rear cavern, the full glare of the sun globes took a little getting used to – the light so much stronger than that produced by the arkademic's silver suns. Only belatedly did Tom wonder if Mildra might be asleep. She wasn't. They found her instead chatting to Councillor Thomas.

"Help us," Kat said. Tom was still busy holding death at bay.

Mildra was there in an instant, squatting down beside Tom. She assessed the situation at a glance.

"He was submerged in water, yes?" At his nod, she started rolling the supine figure onto its side. "We've got to clear his lungs of water," she explained. "No matter how much you strengthen him and bring him back, he's constantly drowning all over again."

Of course, why hadn't he thought of that?

Within seconds of her expert ministrations, the Kite Guard's chest heaved and he was coughing up water.

Tom felt the spark finally take hold and flare to life.
Soon Tylus was able to prop himself up a little; enough
to be sick on the ground rather than over himself.

Tom reckoned this a good time to step back. He saw
the relief on Kat's face and felt a pang of jealousy.

"What?" she asked, looking up to catch his expression.

"Nothing…" But he couldn't stop himself. "You really do care about him, don't you?"

She rolled her eyes. "Of course I brecking do. If you
mean by that 'do I want to have his babies?' Thaiss no!
But yeah, I have feelings for him. He saved my life.
Why, you jealous or something?"

"No," he said, far too quickly. "Of course not."

Kat's fleeting smile was enough to tell him that she
wasn't fooled for a minute. Breck!

It felt odd, simply sitting and talking, sipping on a
chilled drink without the pressing need to hurry anywhere or save anything. All very civilised. The rest of
the party had made it back from the Stain unscathed.
Mildra had gone to report to her order on all that had
happened; Kat had gone off with the surviving Tattooed Men to see what the rest of their tribe had been
up to in their absence, and even Tylus recovered
enough to lead his Kite Guards away. Only once the
man was on his feet again had Tom recognised Tylus
as the same Kite Guard who had so nearly caught him
on the walls as he fled the scene of Thomas' apparent
murder. Funny how these things came around.

Tom was left in the company of Thomas and Isar
– the arkademic with a knack for making silver suns

– which made him feel a bit like a privileged child who'd been allowed to stay up with the grownups. Deciding that they were all thirsty, the three of them relocated to a nearby café and were now enjoying a refreshing drink – or drinks in Tom's case; he was already on his second.

Stopping and simply relaxing was more enjoyable than Tom would ever have thought, even though much of the ensuing conversation bored him rigid. He let the others' words wash over him, and reflected on all that he had been through.

Touching the mind of that river monster, manipulating it, had been merely the latest in a string of new experiences, but it was one of the oddest yet. He imagined the creature had been washed over the waterfall when much smaller, and had been living there ever since, feeding on everything else that came over the falls, whether alive or dead, growing bigger and more formidable all the while. How long it had been there was anyone's guess, but Tom sensed it was a long, long time.

Another aspect of the incident gave him ongoing satisfaction, since it provided proof that Kat was a fraud. She might act tough and pretend that she was only ever interested in number one, but in the Stain's darkest corner she had shown her true colours. She stood to gain nothing whatsoever by leaping into the pool to rescue Tylus. It was an act of complete selflessness, putting her own life at risk for the sake of someone else. Proof positive that Tom wasn't the only one who could do that sort of thing after all.

He clung to that crumb of satisfaction during the days that followed, as Thaiburley gradually recovered and learnt to deal with the aftermath of all that had befallen her.

SEVENTEEN

Tylus still couldn't understand how he was alive. It appeared he owed the fact to the actions of Kat, Mildra... and Tom. The irony didn't escape him. The same boy he'd let fall off the city's walls and nearly die during his fumbled attempt at arrest, was responsible for saving his life. He'd found it hard to meet Tom's eyes when he came round.

His uniform was soaked through and soon turned cold and clinging. Mildra came to his rescue, producing a set of plain, worn clothes. He later learned that she'd simply knocked on a nearby house and bought them from the inhabitants. They'd wanted to give them to her despite their evident poverty – what with her being a Thaistess – but she had insisted on paying generously. The clothes were a little too small for him, but at least they were dry. He didn't want to think about how clean or otherwise they might be.

At least they gave him the opportunity to look reasonably presentable by the time the survivors emerged from the Stain.

Issie made a valiant effort not to laugh when she saw him, though there was a twinkle in her eye as she asked, "Is this what passes for casual fashion here in the City Below?"

"It's what passes for dry," he told her.

Her smile melted into a look of concern. "Thank goodness you're all right."

He felt awkward and changed the subject. "I suppose you'll be heading back up-City now."

"For a while, at least."

"Oh?" She wasn't seriously considering coming back here, was she?

Issie grinned. "You didn't think you were getting rid of me that easily, did you? Not now we're back in touch after all these years. The assembly intends to appoint a liaison to keep them informed on how this Kite Guard training school of yours is doing. I was thinking I might volunteer, so you're likely to be seeing a great deal more of me from now on."

"Really? That's... wonderful."

"Glad you approve."

He grinned. "I told you this place gets under your skin."

"Well, something certainly has, though I'm not sure it's the place, but I'm willing to give it a chance to."

"I'll have to introduce you to its charms, then."

"I was rather counting on that."

This seemed a good note on which to leave. Issie aside, Tylus was anxious to be off – and not only because he wanted to know how the building work was progressing. The sooner he could get into a change of uniform the happier he would be; not to mention the need to get his cape dried out. In its absence, he was reduced to being carried back to his makeshift head-quarters in the new sling arrangement by two of the other officers, which proved as uncomfortable as it was embarrassing. Despite the skill demonstrated by the two carriers, the sling inevitably swayed discon-certingly and occasionally jerked as the tension between sling and officers proved impossible to keep entirely uniform throughout. Each sudden tip had Tylus clinging to the sides. The flight was brief but not brief enough as far as he was concerned.

Having arrived safely back at the Pits and shed the too-closely fitting clothes in favour of a fresh uniform, it was time to say farewell to Sergeant Whitmore and his surviving men, who were set to return up-City. Prior to doing so, however, the Kite Guard sergeant approached Tylus with a request that both astounded and delighted him. He wanted permission to apply for a post on the staff at the proposed training school.

"This one mission has been more rewarding than seven years' worth of service in the Heights," the ser-geant had explained. "The City Below just seems so much more... *alive*, sir." Exciting was what he un-doubtedly meant.

"Despite the smell?" Tylus couldn't resist asking.

"Yes, sir, despite the smell. Daresay I'll get used to it."

The exchange heartened Tylus more than anything else that had happened since he set out to establish the Kite Guard School. So, despite nearly getting him-self killed, he was in good spirits when somebody else appeared: Richardson. Tylus's heart sank. The last thing he felt like doing was feigning joy at the officer's planned nuptials. So deflated was he at the prospect that it took him a moment to realise that Richardson looked anything but joyful himself.

Oh, he smiled and said, "Welcome back," readily enough, but there was a brittleness to his good humour. It didn't reach his eyes. The two of them were alone in Tylus's office; the Kite Guard at his desk, the guardsman before it, managing to look wretched despite standing to attention.

"Is everything all right?" Tylus asked, wondering as he did so whether someone shouldn't perhaps be asking *him* that, given where he'd just returned from and all that he'd been through.

"Yes, sir."

Sir again. Now Tylus knew something was up. "Really?"

His subordinate drew a ragged breath. "No... not really. It's Jezmina, sir. The wedding's off."

"Oh, I'm sorry to hear that," the Kite Guard lied. "What happened?"

Richardson's entire body slumped, any semblance of standing to attention forgotten. "It looks as if she was leading me on the whole time."

Now there was a surprise. Tylus gestured towards a chair, sensing this might take a little while. Richardson reached backwards and pulled the chair closer to the desk before dropping into it, his face a study in dejection. The Kite Guard waited patiently for him to continue.

"Remember I told you that my sister, Bren, makes dresses for a few of the high-end boutiques up-City?"

Tylus nodded, vaguely recalling something of the sort.

"Well, she landed a big new client a couple of months back – a slimy little toad of a man by the name of Birch. Middle-aged, always impeccably dressed, full of his own importance; you know the sort. Apparently he's got a nice little business set up supplying a load of the more exclusive stores in the Shopping Row. He's put a lot of work Bren's way. Anyway, she mentioned that he'd been calling around a lot lately, more than seemed necessary. She didn't mind, of course, how could she while he kept sending new orders her way? Turns out that the orders weren't the real reason he kept dropping by, though. He was finding excuses to sniff around my Jezmina. Bren told me he'd been flirting with her and she told me I should keep my eyes open, but Jezmina laughed the whole thing off, claiming it was nothin', and I believed her. But turns out it *wasn't* nothin' after all.

"He seduced her, turned her head with all his up-City airs and promises of a better life. Even if I'd known, how could I compete with that? Seems they've been seeing each other on the sly. Here we was, making plans for our wedding, and all the while she's been slipping away into some other man's arms." He shook his head slowly from side to side, and tears threatened the corners of his eyes. "I've never even touched her, you know… not *really*…"

"She's actually gone?" Tylus asked quickly, to forestall any further candidness.

Richardson nodded dolefully. "This morning. Birch, the skinny little spill dragon, turned up early and whisked her away to live in this flash house of his in the Tailors Row. She's run off with him. Can you believe that?"

Only too well. Predict it, no, but believe it? Most certainly. Tylus doubted the girl's ambitions would end there, either. This Birch character was most likely no more than the next in a long line of stepping stones, of which Richardson had been the first. A true opportunist, Jezmina would doubtless work her way through the city's Rows, maybe all the way up to the Heights before she was done, leaving a trail of broken hearts and misty-eyed lovers in her wake.

Despite his friend's obvious distress, the Kite Guard was finding it difficult to suppress a grin, one that threatened to crease his face from ear to ear. The pain that Richardson was currently suffering would soon pass and there was no doubt that he was better off without that scheming little harlot. Her running off like this was the best possible outcome as far as Tylus was concerned; particularly as it saved him from having to intervene himself and avoided any awkwardness that might have resulted. No, Jezmina had done them both a favour, even if he was the only one who recognised as much at present.

"How could she *do* this to me?"

Very easily, Tylus imagined. "I'm truly sorry for your pain," he said, able to say at least that much with complete sincerity.

Richardson pushed himself to his feet, rubbing a finger quickly beneath his right eye, as if to sooth an itch.

"Don't worry," he said. "I won't let any of this affect my work."

"I'm sure you won't, but if you'd like a few days off…" Tylus said.

"No, keeping busy; that's the best thing for me, I reckon. I'll be fine."

Richardson visibly pulled himself together and, giving a wan, brave smile, he then turned smartly and left the office. As the door closed behind him, Tylus leant back in his chair and allowed himself a heartfelt sigh of relief.

Kat was tired. She was glad to be back in the City Below and among the Tattooed Men again but news of the losses suffered in the Stain had hit her hard. She'd known the risks when going in, but had reasoned they were acceptable for the chance to hunt down the Soul Thief. Had it been worth it? No, not given the casualties, but hindsight was a wonderful thing. All of this only reaffirmed her determination to establish a more stable existence for the group – tribe; she supposed they qualified as such. For years the Tattooed Men had lived by their own rules, a separate society within Thaiburley's lowest level, but those days were gone.

Shayna had made a start in her absence, and a good one, though Kat couldn't help but have reservations about the place chosen as the new permanent centre of operations, their "home". Iron Grove Square: where the Soul Thief had killed her sister.

"I know we all have history here, especially you," the healer had said, "but this is the only place that makes any sense. All our other safe houses are just that: houses. None of them are large enough to hold all of us, not on a long term basis. This is the only one that can be segregated into separate dwellings, and here we can all stay close together rather than being spread across half a dozen or more locations. I promise you, Iron Grove Square really is the best, the *only* choice."

Kat had nodded, accepting the argument. She trusted Shayna implicitly, and knew she wouldn't make such a decision lightly. "Iron Grove Square it is then." The name a bitter taste in her mouth. "But we rename it. As of today, nobody is to call this place Iron Grove Square again. From now on, this is Charveve Court."

Shayna nodded and smiled. "Good. Yes, that's very good. I'll pass the word to the men."

They hadn't wasted any time, those who had remained behind when she headed off into the Stain. Already work had begun on rebuilding and repairing the fire damage. Kat stood in the courtyard with Shayna, surveying progress. "I don't want the upper floor rebuilt over there," she said, pointing to the far side of the quadrangle, where Chavver had died. "Leave that wing as a single storey." She didn't want any ghosts troubling them in their new home.

"Fair enough. We were intending to leave that one until last, just in case…"

"In case I said something like that," Kat finished for her.

Shayna nodded.

"You know me too well, old friend."

"Less of the old, if you don't mind."

It was familiar banter but Kat needed familiar just then. She missed Chavver and wondered whether simply failing to rebuild the floor her sister had died on was going to be enough. It would have to be, she supposed. Not just Chavver; she was also missing Tom, which came as a surprise. She hadn't before, not really, but this time… he'd changed. Matured a little, perhaps. Still the same Tom but more so, as if he was starting to grow into the potential the Prime Master had obviously seen in him from the start. It was hard to think of him as "kid" anymore. Funny, but on the rare occasions she contemplated such matters she'd always taken it for granted that she'd end up settling down with one of the Tattooed Men: Rayul most likely; but Rayul was gone and the Tattooed Men needed new blood. Of course, she was a queen, so any partner of hers would have to be someone special, but Tom *was* special, no denying that. Besides, he was kind of cute, not to mention vulnerable one minute and all-conquering the next.

She shook her head as if to banish such daydreams. They'd save for later. Right now there were more pressing concerns to deal with.

Crosston provided a natural point at which to break his journey back to the City of a Hundred Rows. After slipping out of the palace, Dewar had headed straight for the docks, boarding a ship on which he'd arranged passage in advance. It set sail just before dawn and was overtaken by the sun during the brief trip to Deliia, making port in the early hours of morning. He broke

the night's fast at a dockside eatery, an establishment
he recalled from his former life. It opened at such
unsociable hours specifically to cater for the sailors
from ships making early arrival. It was a rough and
ready place but clean, and the cooking was adequate
and honest. He ordered a hearty plate of crisp-fried
salted fish topped with a duo of fried duck eggs and a
round of blood sausage, with some lightly toasted
bread and a generous pat of butter on the side; all of
which went down a treat. The over-stewed coffee less
so, but that was his fault for chancing that an establishment like this might know how to make a decent
cup. He should have stuck to the watered-down ale
that most of the folk around him were drinking.

Breakfast completed, the assassin took a leisurely
stroll through a town still in the early stages of waking
up. He enjoyed the sight of others rushing around
when he had no immediate cause to – there was little
more he could do until the horse traders opened for
business. The important thing had been to escape the
Misted Isles as swiftly as possible. Barring a stroke of
extremely bad fortune, Inzierto's death would not
have been discovered before morning and, even once
it had been, he doubted the authorities would react
quickly. The murder would leave the palace with
something of a dilemma. Doubtless they would want
to manage the situation, considering their options
before releasing news of the royal death. An announcement would be made at a time of their
choosing, once they'd reached a consensus on what to
say. Even so, Dewar preferred not to take any chances.

Rolling up to the docks late morning only to discover that he had miscalculated and the port had been closed with rumour of assassination rife would have been frustrating to say the least. No, a quick, quiet exit had been essential.

After securing a horse at Deliia he rode straight through, not stopping at Eastwell as he might have done in other circumstances. By doing so, he hoped to keep ahead of any news that might be filtering through from the Misted Isles. His reward on arriving at Crosston the following day was to hear not a whisper of the king's death, an event which surely would have been on everyone's lips were it known.

Dewar couldn't have said why, having made it this far, he decided to venture once again through the doors of the Four Spoke Inn, except that it had proved to be a decent enough tavern on his previous visit, Seth Bryant aside. Good ale, good food, murderous landlord. Two out of three wasn't bad by his reckoning. Besides, the last time he'd seen Bryant the man had been face down in the waters of the Jeeraiy, dead or close to it.

Under the circumstances he should perhaps have been more surprised to see the familiar figure keeping station behind the bar, but he wasn't. The Twelve were universally tough; Dewar wasn't the only one who was difficult to kill, it seemed.

At first the assassin wasn't sure Bryant had spotted him, but as he drew closer to the bar the landlord finished serving a customer and glanced up. Their gazes locked.

Dewar very deliberately claimed one of the barstools, easing himself into the seat. "A pint of your strongest ale please, landlord."

Bryant hesitated for an instant and then nodded, almost imperceptibly. "Back here again, traveller?"

"So it would seem. I'd hazard we're both a little surprised to find ourselves back at the Four Spoke Inn."

"Perhaps," Bryant conceded. "Perhaps we are at that."

Dewar watched carefully as his would-be nemesis poured out a tankard of dark ale and placed it on the bar before him. At no point had the landlord's hand passed over the top of the glass. Surely it would have been impossible to introduce a powder or potion. Dewar couldn't have done so, and if *he* couldn't… Unless Bryant kept a doctored glass to hand against just such a circumstance – the same way he had so recently dealt with a king. Dewar stared into the man's eyes but gained no clue.

Deciding that Bryant had spent too many years as a humble landlord to entertain such devious forethought, he took a sip. His educated palate detected nothing untoward, though that was hardly irrefutable proof. He took another sip. A gamble, no question, but a calculated one, and he'd prefer not to leave this place knowing that a mortal enemy stood at his back. A gamble was necessary if trust was to be established. If not trust, then he might at least hope to establish understanding.

"Join me?" Dewar said.

Without saying a word, Bryant produced a second flagon from beneath the bar and poured himself an ale. He raised his glass in salute and quaffed.

"I've just come from Indryl," Dewar said casually.

He saw the other man freeze. "Really?" But he recovered quickly enough, to say, "I hear rumours of imminent war drifting from the Misted Isles."

Dewar nodded. "Indeed, though my understanding is that recent events may have superseded such ambitions."

"Oh?"

"Mm. It seems that his royal highness has suffered a misfortune."

"What sort of misfortune?"

"One of the fatal variety."

Another frozen instant, then, "That... is interesting. I'm surprised we've heard nothing about it here on the great trade route."

"It happened very recently," Dewar told him. "I'm sure word will reach you soon."

"Doubtless you're right." Bryant's expression was unreadable.

"I imagine there'll be a lot of changes in the aftermath of the sovereign's passing."

"Bound to be. Inzierto IV will be remembered as a great king. He's occupied the throne for a long, long time, and there aren't many down the years who can claim that."

"A great man, no doubt," Dewar agreed. "His passing will have far-reaching implications, including perhaps the Misted Isles' plans for war."

Bryant nodded. "A bad omen, certainly. What soldier would want to embark on a campaign when the king who ordered it drops dead on the eve of battle?"

Dewar's turn to nod. "It's enough to make any man wonder whether the gods disapprove of the notion."

"Even those who don't really believe in gods."

"Quite. A great deal is set to change in the Misted Isles, I'd fancy. Grudges once held will be discounted and yesterday's news will no longer seem as important as it once did."

"An interesting notion," Bryant conceded. "Though I'd venture that it'll take more than the death of one man, even a king, to effect such sweeping changes."

"Ah, but I hear tell that more than one poor soul has met with misfortune in recent days."

"You appear to be singularly well informed," Bryant remarked dryly. "Who else, pray, has suffered from fate's cruelty?"

"Well, for example, it seems that the commander who was set to lead the coming campaign, one General Hayt, took a careless step and fell overboard during a training exercise – sank without a trace, I'm told – while that tireless servant of the crown Captain Vargas staggered drunkenly from a tavern one night too often. He never made it home – fell off a bridge, by all accounts, breaking his neck in the process."

"How tragic. Two such sensitive souls, and Vargas now a captain!"

"Indeed, and there's more. Evidently, after so many years of whispering wise counsel into the ear of the king, Good Count Ruben succumbed to the strains of office and fell victim to a fatal heart attack."

"My, my, fate has been busy." A smile threatened to spoil Bryant's grave demeanour. "It sounds as if much will indeed have to change beneath the dreaming spires of Indryl."

"My thoughts exactly. It occurs to me that there would be ample opportunity for a man of your proven talents to find a position in the new order. After all, there will always be work for a... landlord."

"It would certainly seem to offer some interesting possibilities," Bryant said. "Ones you might perhaps be tempted to explore yourself?"

"No, no, not I." Dewar waved a denying hand. "I still have some unfinished business to attend to. First things first."

"And afterwards?"

Dewar shook his head. "Not even afterwards. Indryl's not for me, not anymore. My recent visit has convinced me of that much. I'll make my home elsewhere and do my best to forget about the Misted Isles, just as I hope they might forget about me."

"Anything is possible, I suppose," Bryant said.

Dewar took one final mouthful of ale and then placed his near-empty flagon down firmly onto the counter. "Right, I must be off."

"You're not going to stay the night this time?"

Dewar grinned. "I think best not to. After all, fate has been busy enough of late. No point in putting temptation in her way."

"Perhaps you're right at that."

Dewar climbed off the stool. Again their gazes locked. "I do wish you well, though," he said.

After only a fractional hesitation, Bryant nodded. "Likewise."

Dewar then left the Four Spoke Inn for the final time. In the process he turned his back on Seth Bryant, an act he performed with far more confidence than he would ever have done before.

EIGHTEEN

The stranger stepped boldly off the final step. There he paused, taking in his surroundings. This was the very first time he had ever set foot in the City Below. In some ways the place was exactly as he'd expected, in others it was far, far more. He'd been warned about the smell, and it didn't disappoint. He knew too that much of the under-City was derelict, though that didn't automatically mean unoccupied, but he was surprised at the pervading appearance of age down here, the sense of weariness and of things being worn out, even the buildings. He'd dressed down as much as his wardrobe would allow but quickly realised that even in his oldest and plainest clothes he stood out; but that was okay. The aim wasn't to blend in, but simply to be a little less conspicuous. After all, if things went to plan he wouldn't be here long enough for it to become an issue.

Nothing, though, could have prepared him for the sense of pressure from above, the feeling that an immense weight was resting on him, that the entire city and all its populace was bearing down on this one

Row, intent on crushing him along with everyone else. It made him want to hunch his shoulders and hunker down a little as he walked, even though the ceiling here was far higher than in any Row of the city proper. It was psychological, he knew, but he couldn't entirely escape the feeling.

He checked his sword and knives for reassurance, adjusted his belt, and set out. He knew exactly where he was going, having called up the under-City's schematic on the screen before setting out and memorising the address and route. Straight ahead should be Unthank Road. He walked down its centre, conscious of the curious stares of some and the apparent disregard of others.

No one spoke to him, but on the other hand no one challenged him either, which he reckoned to be a fair trade off.

Third turning on the left: Coskermile Street, then immediately right into Tylers Lane. The houses here were at least habitable and looked to be reasonably well maintained. Small, single storey buildings, crammed side by side as if whoever built them had been determined to squeeze in at least one more property than there was actually room for. The novelty of individual dwellings took some getting used to for a Heights-dweller like him – "cloud scrapers" he believed the grubbers down here would have called him. The arrangement struck him as unnatural. There was no way he could ever have lived like this.

One more left turn and he was almost there. Just a case of counting down the door numbers now.

If his information was correct, this was the right one. He stopped before it; a simple plain door, cheaply made – a fact that the veneer of green paint failed to disguise. No knocker; he'd have to use his fist. Yet he hesitated, suddenly nervous, suddenly afraid that the only thing waiting for him beyond this flimsy barrier was disappointment. He delayed a few more seconds, reluctant to bring an end to hope. Then, he straightened his shoulders, drew a deep breath, and knocked.

"Coming," called a voice from within. After a few seconds during which he tried to calm his breathing, there came the sound of a bolt being drawn back and then the door opened partway, to reveal the wrinkled face of an elderly woman. "Ah, you're a fine looking lad and no mistake," she said. "What can I do you for? A love potion, is it? Some young maiden's head you're desperate to turn? Or a luck potion; perhaps you've suffered a run of bad fortune of late and would like to turn that around… No, not luck I don't think. Stamina! Young fellow like you, I'll bet you take part in plenty of sports and are seeking an edge… unless it's stamina of a more intimate nature you're worried about, eh? I can help with that too, if that's what you're after."

He stood silent, trying to decide how best to reply. He'd rehearsed this meeting and what he was going to say a hundred times in his head, but none of his imaginings had featured such an opening barrage and, now that he was actually here, he couldn't remember the lines anyway.

The woman had stopped talking for a second and was considering him, scratching her chin and frowning.

"Though to judge by the cut of your clothes, you're not from round here, are you? You're from up-City, maybe even the Heights." She seemed suddenly suspicious. "What's someone like you doing here in the under-City, calling on a simple apothaker?"

"Arielle?" he said uncertainly, thinking that perhaps he could see in this aged apparition the ghost of the vibrant, beautiful woman he remembered, but not quite believing she could have changed so much.

The instant he spoke the name she started as if slapped, and then whipped a knife from under her robes, pointing it towards him menacingly.

"Who are you?" she hissed. "Some agent of Birhoff's come down here to finish the job, or are you just here to gloat, to see how I've suffered? Well you can tell the spiteful bitch that I've suffered plenty. Is that what you want to hear, eh? Is it?"

"No, nothing like that, I promise you… Aunt Arielle, it's me, Jayce."

Her mouth opened slowly, though no words emerged, and her eyes widened. He thought he saw recognition dawning in their depths. "Jaycie," she said at length, "*my Jaycie*… is it really you?"

"Yes, aunt, it's me."

The knife tumbled from her fingers. The hand that had held it rose uncertainly towards his cheek, perhaps to stroke his face, but then stopped short, as if afraid that should she touch him he might disappear. "Look at you, you're all grown up." A single tear trickled from the corner of her eye. "Jayce… *my Jaycie*…" She spoke his name as if the repetition might somehow make this all the more real. "How did you find me? Why... what are you *doing* here?"

He felt his own eyes welling up. His beloved aunt, whose presence illuminated so many childhood memories; he'd found her again after all these years. He could scarcely believe it, and his voice was far from steady as he said, "I've come to take you home, Aunt Arielle. I've come to take you home."

There were two people Tom was determined to see. He wasn't sure what it said about him that both were girls, or rather women, or maybe a bit of both. Actually, it might easily have been three. He still felt a twinge of guilt that he'd never checked up on Jezmina, the girl he'd been besotted with when he ran with the Blue Claw, but he understood she was settled now, working for a seamstress and even *engaged*, which he found hard to believe: the timid young girl he remembered blossoming into a bride-to-be in such a short time. Even so, he concluded it was probably best for both of them if he didn't call around raking up the past. So that just left two.

He decided to start with Mildra.

He found her in the same temple he'd been brought to the first time they met, when the Dog Master's creature had latched onto his back and tried to infect him with the parasite that was subverting the will of the street-nicks.

"Tom!" She looked genuinely delighted to see him and didn't seem at all surprised, almost as if she'd been expecting him to pop out of thin air at some point. Perhaps she had.

He'd been a little worried about seeing her again now that she was back in her normal environment and they were no longer constant companions. Part of him had expected her to be formal, aloof, reserved at the very least. The way she immediately rushed forward and hugged him dispelled any such concerns.

"I've missed you," she said, breaking the embrace.

"Me too," he replied. "Missed you, I mean, not me."

She laughed, and led him to a chair. Were these her private quarters? If so, they were more modest than he would have anticipated. Plain walls, two leaded sash windows that looked out onto a small courtyard, a hearth – not lit, but clean and looking as if it hadn't been used in a while – a low table and a few chairs. Arrangements of fresh flowers decorated the mantelpiece and the table; flowers were never cheap in the City Below so they were something of an indulgence perhaps, but a minor one given her status.

Mildra produced a pair of finger cymbals and clashed them expertly, producing a single pure note that resonated throughout the room. Within seconds there came a knock at the door and a grey-robed acolyte entered.

"Ah, Sian, would you fetch a jug of fruit juice and two glasses?" She turned to Tom. "Are you hungry?"

He shook his head and held up a denying hand. "No."

She smiled at the acolyte. "Thank you."

The girl bobbed her head in acknowledgement and scurried from the room, without once meeting Tom's gaze.

After she'd gone, Mildra leaned forward and giggled,

saying in conspiratorial tone, "I think you've startled her. She has no idea how you came to be in my private rooms without her seeing you arrive."

"Will it cause a scandal?"

"Almost certainly."

They both laughed. It felt relaxed and comfortable seeing Mildra again, which came as a huge relief to Tom. During the short time they now spent together, sitting and chatting, he came to realise that the friendship they'd developed during their journey to Thaiss's citadel was a strong one, an enduring one. He had a feeling they would always be friends, no matter what the future had in store for them. The brief intimacy they'd shared in the meadow of flowers seemed a distant memory, though one he recalled with a degree of wistful fondness. Mildra was still the only woman he'd ever touched in a romantic fashion; a strange thought when he considered her now, in a Thaissian temple, dressed in her priestly robes.

He wondered if she ever thought of their moment of aborted passion, but knew that this was one question he would never ask.

Eventually he felt able to say what had brought him here, the thing he'd been determined to tell Mildra. "About Thaiss," he began. "Don't be fooled by what we saw at the citadel. I think she almost wanted us to underestimate her, to dismiss her as human, but she isn't, she's so much more than that."

Mildra smiled but didn't say a word.

Tom shook his head. "But you didn't need me to tell you that, did you? You already knew."

"Of course I did. I'm a Thaistess, Tom, how could I not? But I'm still delighted to see you, for whatever reason. And thank you for wanting to tell me that."

They hugged again when it came time to leave. Even through her robes, the gentle pressure of her body against his briefly stirred memories which were better left alone.

"Don't be a stranger," she said.

"I won't be," he assured her, and meant it.

Tom could have simply closed his eyes, pictured Kat, and jumped, but he chose not to. He'd been away from the City Below for too long and was grateful for the chance to reacquaint himself with the feel, the smell, the sounds of the streets. For the first time he began to understand why the Prime Master had delighted in wandering the streets incognito. It wasn't simply a matter of keeping an eye on things and monitoring the mood of folk, it was more fundamental than that.

He passed two kids, a boy and a girl, squatting and playing flip. After a great deal of shaking in her balled hands, the girl tossed a pair of flat stones down onto a grid that had been crudely drawn in chalk on the ground before her. Tom walked on, remembering the many times he'd played the game in just the same way. He stepped out into the road to avoid a woman who emerged from a doorway ahead, clearly struggling with a pale of water, before she tossed the contents onto the ground and disappeared back into her home. A pieman stood on the corner, selling his wares. They looked good and smelt even better. Tom paused to pay more than he needed to for a meat pasty, biting into it as he walked. It *was* good. Flaky pastry and a filling of minced beef and root vegetables in a rich gravy. Still warm, too, though not so hot that he burnt himself on the first mouthful.

As he continued to stroll and eat he acquired a new friend. A scruffy looking dog appeared from nowhere to trot beside him, craning its neck upward towards his hand, nose twitching. White fur with a mottled patchwork of browns, a terrier's face, and the sort of forlorn expression in its eyes that only a hungry dog can truly master. Tom ate two thirds of the pasty and then tossed the remainder to his canine shadow. The mutt caught the offering, turned, and scampered off with the prize, doubtless to consume it somewhere in private.

This was the real reason the Prime Master had roamed the streets, Tom realised; not to gather information but to stay connected, to make sure he never forgot what it meant to be human.

Tom knew where to find Kat, or at least where to start looking for her: Iron Grove Square. He didn't recognise the Tattooed Man on the gate, but the fellow obviously knew him. He was allowed in and Kat appeared moments later.

"Suppose I should be honoured," she said.

"Don't see why, it's only me."

She snorted. "Yeah, right: 'only'. I suppose this is the big goodbye, is it? Guess you'll be vanishing off to live up-City now." She said this without looking at him, as if to emphasise that the topic was of no more than passing interest and the subject was already beginning to bore her.

Tom frowned and then said. "I doubt that, somehow." Already much of what he'd been through in recent days had taken on a surreal, dream-like quality, and this wasn't at all how he'd imagined the meeting with Kat would go.

"Oh?" Now she did turn to look at him. "I thought, what with you being such a POP nowadays, that you'd be looking forward to a life of comfort and luxury up in the Heights."

He shook his head, wishing he could start the conversation again and trying to find the right words. "Remember when we first met?"

"Sure, at Ty-gens."

"What did you think of me?"

"Trust me, kid, you don't want to know."

"But you saw a street-nick standing in front of you, right? Just like any of the hundreds of other nicks living throughout the City Below."

"Sure, but an awful lot's happened since then, and that was before I had the faintest notion what you could do."

"I know, I know…" he rubbed his forehead, realising that he wasn't explaining himself very clearly, and Kat was the one person he really wanted to understand. "What I'm trying to say is that in here," and he pounded his chest, "I'm still that same street-nick you met in the Jeradine Quarter, the one that Ty-gen bribed you to take home."

Kat grinned. "Yeah, bribed is the word, though Thaiss knows what I thought I was ever gonna do with that great chunk of a khybul statue in any case, even if it was the most beautiful thing I'd ever seen."

Tom knew what she meant. The crystalline representation of Thaiburley had been stunning, but that wasn't the point. It felt as if Kat was deliberately steering the conversation away from where he'd intended. "Are you listening to me?" he said. "Are you really hearing what I'm saying?" Thaiss, she could be frustrating sometimes.

"Okay, stay calm. I'm all ears."

"I know a lot's happened, and I've seen things and done things I never dreamed I would, but it's all taken place in such a short space of time. I've changed, of course I have, but I don't *feel* any different, not really, not where it counts." Everything came tumbling out, all he was desperate to tell her. "What do I know about the Heights and the people who live up there? Their fancy ways and their la-di-da lives, that's not me. I'm a street-nick."

"You could learn," she said, more softly than he'd ever heard her say anything before. "You'd be amazed how quickly people can get used to things, especially nice things."

"Maybe, eventually, given a few years, but I'd still be a freak; always would be to them up there, no matter what: 'the Kid Who Escaped from the City Below'. I'd never simply be accepted as *me*."

"You make that sound as if it's a bad thing."

"What else could it possibly be?"

She shrugged. "Whatever you want to make it. Sure, you'd be different, you'd stand out; live with it. I've been different all my life. Turn it to your advantage. Different doesn't have to mean inferior, it just means you're something that everyone else isn't – something they can never be; which can mean *better*. Make them envy your difference. Talk up your life down here. You could become a hero in no time, a rugged adventurer. I'm sure the girls would be queuing up just hoping you'd notice them. I bet every pretty little thing up there would be desperate to welcome a genuine bit of rough between their legs after all the namby-pamby ponces who've been boring them to death for years trying to get there."

"Kat!" Tom laughed; he'd never heard her speak so candidly before.

"Well, it's true."

Tom hadn't thought of it like that. Was she right? He had to stop himself grinning at the image she'd planted in his head. If Kat had been a lad and in his shoes, he could easily believe that everything she'd just described might happen, but he wasn't Kat. He'd never had her front, her brash self-confidence, and he could never imagine any of that coming true for him. "On the other hand, I could stay in the under-City," he said, "and wow all the girls down here with tales of all the exotic places I've been, the wonders I've seen, and the adventures I've had, not to mention the time I spent with the goddess, Thaiss. Do you reckon that might work?"

She shrugged. "You never know. There'll probably be a few girls whose heads would be turned by that sort of thing. Of course, they'd have to believe you first."

"There is that," he conceded. "So all I need to do is be on the lookout for a pretty girl who's gullible and easily impressed."

"You and most men, I reckon."

"Lucky for me you're not any of those things, then."

"Thanks!"

"Except for the pretty part, I mean," he said quickly, inwardly kicking himself.

To his relief, she was grinning. "Kid, you might have seen all sorts of things and done a whole heap of stuff, but you've *still* got a lot to learn."

He spread his hands, helplessly. "See? How could an idiot like me ever hope to make it in 'polite society'?"

"I don't know, I guess you'd just have to try and get by on your cute good looks."

He stared at her. Did she mean that or was she still joking around? Kat's smile faltered and she looked a little embarrassed, as if she wasn't entirely sure herself.

"I'll never be a cloud scraper, Kat," he said to break the slightly awkward silence. "This is my home. I don't belong up there." His gaze flicked towards the cavern ceiling.

"They're bound to try to keep you," she warned.

"Let them. It's a free city and I'll live where I want to."

She grinned. "That's the spirit. If you do end up staying down here, maybe I'll see you around."

"I'd like that, I'd really like that." He hadn't meant his voice to tremble in the way that it did.

Without preamble she suddenly leant forward and kissed him on the lips, a quick pressing of hers to his. "Yeah, me too," she said quietly, with a twinkle in her eye. "Now, I'd better get back to my men before they start to forget who their queen is." She swivelled around and strolled away.

Tom stared after her, reaching up to touch his lips, as if by doing so he could somehow make what had just happened seem more real. Then he found himself grinning, a broad smile that stretched from ear to ear. One day that girl was going to stop surprising him, but he doubted it would be any time soon.

Jeanette returned home exhausted. As Thaiburley's senior physician she had all too few opportunities to do the job she'd spent half her life training for. Admin, coordinating resources, policy making and lectures swallowed up the vast majority of her time, while research claimed what little remained. Dealing directly with the sick and the injured had almost become a novelty. Today had been one of those rare occasions when she actually got to roll her sleeves up and get stuck in, treating real, live people. The Rust Warriors might have gone, bone flu might no longer be a threat and the Demons might finally have done what they should have a century ago, but recent events had left an enormous amount of damage, to the structure of the city and also its citizens – both mentally and physically. Everyone with medical experience and healing ability was being called upon to do their bit, including her. After so many years chained to her desk by the shackles of bureaucracy, it was oddly satisfying to get some "hands on" experience again, to deal directly with patients as something other than test subjects.

She arrived home with a feeling that this had been her most honest day's work in years.

As she opened the front door, Jeanette was assailed by the rich aromas of braising meat and spices. She smiled, relieved that at least here was one job she wouldn't have to do today; cooking had always been a chore to her rather than a pleasure, perhaps because she'd never really found the time to enjoy it. Sharing her home with somebody else would take some getting used to, but the advantages were many; especially when the guest could cook. Her partner emerged from the kitchen, smiling warmly. They embraced, the novelty of such greetings still fresh.

The horror of nearly losing him – for good this time – shot through her anew, and she wondered how long it would be before she could forget, before this wasn't the first thing she thought of whenever they hugged. It had been so close. If she hadn't called around to see him when she did... With an effort of will she suppressed the thought, not wanting it to haunt her face when he looked at her. In the event, she even managed to smile as they separated.

"Had a good day?" she asked brightly, as if no dark thought had troubled her.

"Yes, thank you. As a matter of fact I have."

"What have you been up to, then?"

"Absolutely nothing," replied the man who had served Thaiburley for so many years as its Prime Master. "And it felt wonderful."

NINETEEN

Life was good. Thaiburley had survived its darkest hour in more than a century and there was a palpable sense of relief among those who had lived to tell the tale. The very air seemed redolent with the heady scent of optimism; society was in the mood to celebrate. By all means grieve the fallen, but not today. There was no room for sombreness or regret at this event. It marked a fresh beginning, and the survivors of the recent horrors saw themselves as the buds of a new spring, intent on bursting open to brighten the world.

Carla Birhoff studied her image in the restroom mirror and liked what she saw. She ran her hands down the sides of her figure-hugging dress, taking in the trim tuck of her waist and the blossom of her hips. For her age, she looked magnificent. The latter part of that sentence delighted her, while the first was something that couldn't be helped. Given that one caveat, she could not have been happier. Her star had risen dramatically during the crisis, her position as liaison between the council and the assembly gaining her enormous credibility, while the way she'd survived the massacre at her own party against all odds and alerted the authorities to the Rust Warriors' return had caused many to revise their opinion of her. She was now seen as something more than merely the supreme socialite, the decorative fluff at the Assembly's periphery. To cap it all, the survivors of the mission to the city's core had reported first not to the council, but to *her*. All of which meant that people were taking her seriously for once and her opinion carried weight. She loved this newly acquired status and revelled in the limelight. This was her time and she intended to grasp the opportunity fate had presented with both hands.

Affirmation of her newfound celebrity came when she was invited to present the honours at this, the official celebration of the city's triumph. Naturally she'd accepted, allowing herself to be persuaded after a suitably brief moment of feigned modesty. Who was to say that one day, if she made the most of current opportunity, she might not be in line for a position on the council itself? Imagine that: Councillor Birhoff.

Odd how cyclical life could be. For her this whole business began with a society event at which she was the star; and here it was about to culminate in another such gathering at which she was, if not *the* star, certainly *a* star. So much had changed in the interim. Little had she known as she crawled on her hands and knees among the dead and dying of her autumn ball how propitious ensuing events would prove to be.

She was seated at the top table, not so very far from the new Prime Master, Thomas; the youngest man to

hold the position in centuries. Carla remembered
Thomas from his time with the assembly; handsome
enough in a soft-faced sort of way but he took life far
too seriously. The man was so dedicated to the job that
she doubted he had room for much else. Relaxing and
having fun seemed alien concepts to him.

The Council Guards on the other hand tended to
know all about having fun. They were renowned for
working hard and playing hard, as she'd learnt to her
considerable delight over the years. She always did
have a weakness for a man in uniform, and only men
in their prime ever made it into the Council Guard.
Take the second officer she had to present a medal to
today – the guard who had accompanied the street-
nick Tom all the way to the core, the same man who
had been among the party that materialised so unexpectedly in her bed chamber. Tall, well-muscled,
ruggedly handsome, with a chiselled jaw and the sort
of strong features she favoured… so dashing in his
white and purple dress uniform. She would happily
melt into those arms any day. And he'd already seen
her semi-naked. She'd love the opportunity to remove
the word "semi" from that statement. She smiled
warmly at him and made a mental note of his name,
which she hadn't really paid attention to before: Jayce.
She determined to seek him out later. The third officer
to stand before her received a far more perfunctory acknowledgement. She'd met Captain Verrill before – a
cold-faced, rigidly formal man, a total bore who
seemed impervious to her flattery and wiles. Apparently he had triumphed in some pitched battle with a

force of Rust Warriors and then brought a wounded
man – the only other survivor of the skirmish – back
safely. So what? Wasn't that the sort of thing an officer
was supposed to do?

The meal that followed the ceremony was sumptu-
ous: a wild duck terrine served in a cradle of
crystallised ailie-bloom petals, with a piquant chutney
on the side and still-warm rolls which smelt wonderful
as they were broken open. Next, tiny wine glasses, no
taller than a finger, which proved to be fashioned out
of tiger berry sorbet. Each "glass" held a drop of a clear,
potent spirit. Next came a dainty selection of smoked
and pickled river fish, mere slivers of each, arranged
tastefully around the small, halved egg of a ketzal bird
– boiled but with the bright orange-yellow yolk still
soft at the centre – which itself was topped with beads
of oily black caviar that exploded like salty bombs on
the tongue. The fish selection wasn't entirely to Carla's
taste but she recognised several to be rare delicacies,
including a smoky mouthful of claw meat from the
mighty blue claw, the giant crab that was one of the
Thair's most formidable and elusive denizens. The
main course was beef baschelle – prepared by a chef
from the Familé Perdan. Carla detected the trademark
touch with her very first mouthful. That infusion of
herbs and spices and the way the meat melted on the
tongue but remained succulent and packed with
flavour was unmistakeable. She had been trying to
wheedle the recipe out of the family for decades.

Dessert consisted of an assortment of fruits, delicate
patisseries and ices. Mouth-watering no doubt and

certainly colourful, but Carla rarely found room for such things. Besides, while the meal may have been of the highest quality, the conversation around her proved to be anything but. It was the price one paid for such a swift elevation in social rank, she supposed.

She breathed a discreet sigh of relief when the final crockery was cleared away by attentive serving staff, which heralded the start of the less formal part of the evening.

Able to leave her seat and mingle, she made a beeline for the young officer she'd noted earlier. What was his name again? Jayce; yes, that was it.

He was deep in conversation with some elderly woman, being polite, no doubt. Perfect. The poor man was most likely as bored as Carla had been during dinner and would surely welcome being rescued.

"Ah, Jayce, isn't it?" she said as she joined them, adopting her most dazzling smile.

"Assembly Member Birhoff!" The lad looked startled that she'd addressed him. Flattered, perhaps?

"Please, call me Carla."

The old crone was still standing there. Couldn't she take a hint? Carla prepared to take the young officer's arm and steer him away, when he said, "I believe you know my aunt, don't you, Assembly Member?"

His aunt? Oh great. Carla spared the woman a glance. Perhaps she wasn't as old as she'd first assumed, and there was something vaguely familiar about her now that he came to mention it, though Carla couldn't place where from. Couldn't be bothered to, truth be told. She was more concerned with taking this handsome young officer away from prying ears to somewhere she could charm him unhindered.

"Aunt Arielle?"

Arielle? Carla's head whipped around again and she looked at the old woman more closely. Impossible. It *couldn't* be, surely, not after all these years... but it was. Here stood the one woman in all of Thaiburley who knew enough scandal to ruin her. *How?* Carla had dismissed the artist from her life, hadn't thought about her in years until she stumbled on that old painting, and had supposed the artist dead when she did, or at least banished forever. What was this woman doing *here, now*?

Carla was suddenly conscious of the strident beat of her own heart, so rapid, so insistent – as if trying to burst free of her ribcage – while the room started to draw away from her. It was as if she viewed the young guardsman and this vengeful ghost from her past through a telescopic, distorted tunnel, which grew longer by the instant. Her perspective tilted and she caught a glimpse of startled onlookers and then the ceiling, as her knees buckled.

Words came to her from a long way off, as the world dimmed and darkness closed in. "Oh dear," said the last voice she'd ever wanted to hear again. "I do believe the assembly member's fainted."

Night had settled over the City Below. The streets were all but deserted, fear and superstition keeping folk indoors at this hour. Only those with good reason to be abroad dared to venture out. Twin wrought iron gates

creaked open in the squat, solid block of the under-
City's principle gaol, allowing a small coach pulled by a
team of four burley oxen to exit. They made slow
progress, the coach evidently heavy despite its compact
size. The coachman held the reins loosely, giving every
impression he'd rather be somewhere else. Not that Kat
could blame him. She stayed motionless in the rooftop
shadows, but he didn't once glance up towards her.

Kat studied the main body of the coach: lacquered
wood braced by a lattice of iron bands and bolts, no
windows. No getting out of there without help.

The oxen made their plodding way up the street,
paced by the uncertain shadows cast by the street
lamps. At the junction it turned left, heading for the
docks. Kat followed, using the rooftops as her high-
way, easily keeping pace with the prison cart on her
right, conscious of the looming presence of the grand
conveyor to her left. The place where she'd so nearly
died. *One* of the places, she corrected herself.

The cart made its ponderous way down Chisel
Street, passing the conveyor's terminal before turning
into North Wharf Road, which skirted the Runs. Soon
after, it came to a halt, having evidently reached its
destination. The driver stepped down wearily and
strolled around to the back of the coach, where he fiddled with a bunch of keys attached to his belt, selecting
one and using it to unlock the carriage door.

Fittingly, the hinges of the wooden slab creaked
ominously as the guard pulled it open. Kat watched
impatiently as the set of concertinaed steps slid from a
slot in the carriage floor to unfold in staggered stages

to the ground. A guard stepped down, one foot on a middle step but otherwise disdaining to use the short flight. He turned to face the door even as he exited. Behind him came a tall, slender man, hands cuffed before him. The prisoner took advantage of every single one of the four steps, as if to demonstrate how it should be done. He trod carefully, almost daintily, taking his time, and, on reaching the bottom of the steps, he paused to look around, assessing his surroundings. Kat pressed further back into the shadows. She didn't want to be seen, not yet.

The man said something she couldn't catch from her vantage point, the voice carrying through the still night but the words themselves lost to the air. Neither of the guards responded, though the driver stepped forward and, finding a smaller key from among the bunch tied to his belt, released the man's cuffs. At the same time, the guard refolded the small flight of steps and closed the cart's door.

Both men then climbed onto the driving board and, with a flick of the reins, the oxen started forward.

"Hey!" This time Kat could hear the man's shout plainly. He stood with feet firmly planted, hands on hips, staring at the slow moving cart. "What about my sword?"

After a brief pause, the guard flung a belt supporting a scabbarded sword out onto the roadway. Muttering to himself, the man strode after the cart, snatching up the weapon and tying the belt in place.

Kat was glad. At least now she wouldn't have to kill an unarmed man.

As the cart turned a corner and disappeared from sight, the man straightened his shoulders, adjusted his clothing, and started walking the short distance towards the wharf at the end of the road, where a barge waited, lights still burning bright.

Night sailings were rare but hardly unheard of. Presumably this was one such, clearing the scum from the city before the sun globes warmed up. The City Below was used to scum, and Kat for one had no objection to this particular piece staying in Thaiburley, so long as it was no longer breathing.

She stepped from the shadows and strolled out to stand in the centre of the road, between the man and the barge. She stood with arms crossed.

"Leaving us already, Sur Brent?"

He'd stopped walking as she appeared, and now smiled. "Sadly, I have little choice." He pulled down the neck of his shirt to display a thin, snugly-fitting metal band which encircled the base of his neck. "I'm told that if I'm not a significant distance beyond the city walls by the time the sun globes start to warm, this charming piece of jewellery will sever my head from my torso."

"And you believe this nonsense, do you?"

He shrugged. "I don't think I'll bother putting it to the test; particularly as my work in the city is done. They want me to leave, I want to leave; why fight over it?"

"Ah yes, and you doubtless have to report back to these mysterious 'employers' of yours."

"Exactly so."

Kat nodded. "So that's it, is it? After all you've done, the powers that be are just gonna exile you, are they? Rather than tying you down, cutting your body open from throat to balls while you're still alive and letting the spill dragons feed on your innards."

He laughed; a loud, brief exclamation. "A colourful punishment, no doubt, but presumably your authorities don't have the, ehm... shall we say *stomach* for that sort of thing. Now, it's very kind of you to come to see me off, but this collar is itching a little and I'd hate for it to get any tighter, so, if you don't mind...?"

He stepped forward as if to brush past Kat, but she moved quickly across and continued to block his way. "Maybe you're right, maybe they don't have the stomach for that sort of thing, but then I'm not the authorities, am I."

"Get out of my way, Kat."

She did step back then, hands straying towards her sword hilts. "That's never going to happen."

"You don't really want to fight me," he said. "I was more than a match for your sister, remember, and they tell me that of the two of you, she was comfortably the best."

Kat's smile was thin-lipped and cold. "Thank you so much for mentioning my sister, not that I needed any reminding." She drew her blades, moving with deliberate slowness so that the sound of them sliding from their scabbards spread through the night like a protracted sigh.

With a resigned look, Brent drew his own, longer sword. "You'll forgive me if I make this brief, only I have a boat to catch."

Kat smiled. "As brief as you like. I wasn't planning on hanging around long myself."

His blade flickered out, like the silvered tongue of a serpent. She blocked it with ease but this had only been a feint. The very instant steel struck steel his sword turned to attack from another angle, only to be met by Kat's other blade. As those clashed, Kat struck with her free sword, but found only air as Brent danced out of the way. He stepped back, seeking to create some room and thereby give his longer reach the advantage. Kat followed, determined not to let him.

Kat knew what to expect – she'd seen him fight Chavver, after all – but watching someone and actually facing them were entirely different things. During these initial exchanges Kat took his measure, as he doubtless did hers. He was strong, fast, confident and well-balanced, never overextending. His footwork was as proficient as his swordplay, the co-ordination of hand, eyes and feet apparently faultless. In short, this wasn't going to be easy.

Good. His death would be all the more satisfying, then.

Kat moved onto the attack, launching a rapid series of strikes, first one sword then the other, in a familiar pattern that had overpowered more than one opponent in the past. Not this one, though. He moved and swayed and blocked and parried with a nonchalance she couldn't help but admire. She felt certain that Brent was fighting within himself, and put enough effort into her own swordplay to hope that he wouldn't suspect the same of her.

Their swords locked, leaving them glaring at each other over the crossed blades. Kat's second sword had been stopped in mid-strike, her wrist gripped in Brent's free hand. It became a wrestling match between a wiry man and a teenage girl, each attempting to overpower the other.

He might have been bigger than her but Kat was stronger than she looked; not as strong as Chavver, perhaps, but strong enough to surprise him, she hoped. For long seconds they struggled, Kat straining to hold him, feeling that her arm was about to pop from its socket and knowing that she couldn't keep this up for much longer.

Then he did something she'd never seen before; a twist that looked impossible and must surely have dislocated his wrist. Suddenly their blades unlocked and his longer sword flicked out towards her. Taken by surprise, her own effort nearly carried her forward onto the tip of his blade; but speed of reaction saved her, enabling her to twist out of the way. Instead of being impaled, she felt steel rake across her front, slicing through her tunic to cut a bloodied gash in her skin, running in an oblique line from somewhere between her neck and chest to her left shoulder.

She jumped back, both swords raised.

"First blood to me," Bryant said, eyes gleaming.

Brecking obviously, so why waste the breath to crow about it?

He was quick, he was clever, he was skilful and he was confident. No wonder Brent had given Chavver such a hard time. But Kat was all of those things too, and she was only just getting started.

Spurred on by the piquant sting of her wound she moved to the attack again, feet dancing, twin blades weaving intricate, synchronised patterns as she probed for an opening. Brent matched her move for move, his single blade seeming almost alive as it blocked a thrust here, parried a cut there, and arced round to deny her again. Kat was impressed. Not many would have been able to live with her at this speed. So she started to work harder, steadily winding up the pace of the attack while sacrificing none of her skill or aggression.

Through the shifting veil of steel formed by their blades Kat saw Brent's eyes widen. She'd surprised him, unsettled him. He'd thought that he had her measure, that she'd shown him all she had. More fool him. She ramped things up still further and finally breached his guard, her hand twisting past his blade, her own sword inflicting a shallow cut to his forearm; at the same time her other blade struck, slashing into his other arm, cutting deep enough to damage the triceps muscle – Kat knew about wounds, knew about damage inflicted and taken. She heard his sharp intake of breath as he stepped quickly back, disengaging.

She let him, giving him the time to doubt, perhaps enough to take the edge off his reactions. She wanted that arrogance to fracture, to let a little fear seep in, along with the realisation of how severely he'd under-estimated her.

"Much better; now we've both been bloodied," she said. *Now who's pointing out the frissing obvious?* But she couldn't resist, and upped the ante of their verbal sparring by promising, "For every cut you land on me, I'll pay you back double."

Before he could reply she attacked again, not holding back anymore, wanting to keep him off-balance and determined to finish this quickly. He was quick, but not this quick. The attack sent him stumbling backwards, his defence becoming more ragged, more desperate. She sensed the end was near. He knew that too, she could see it in his eyes.

Again one blade slipped through, even as the other was parried, cutting Brent in the side before he could dance out of reach. She grinned and pressed forward, her twin blades a blur.

He was weakening fast. Whether this was due to his recent time in jail or the wounds, Kat couldn't say. Perhaps he would have been tougher before his imprisonment; she couldn't have cared less. Life didn't deal in might-have-beens. Hers didn't, at any rate. A thrust with the left hand, a twist with the right. She felt one sword scrape his ribs while the other sent his own weapon flying from his hand and clattering to the ground.

Brent stumbled back a pace, sweating, panting for breath. "Enough," he gasped, holding up a defensive hand. "I yield. You've bettered me and I'm at your mercy." Perhaps he saw it in her eyes. For the first time, she saw a hint of fear in his. "You wouldn't kill an unarmed man, surely."

"Really; you think? Not the man who distracted my sister long enough for the Soul Thief to sneak up and kill her; I wouldn't kill him, you reckon?"

"Look, I had to," he burbled. "My orders were to keep the Soul Thief alive... she was a Demon, you see..."

"You *knew* she was a Demon? Breck, why am I always the last one to know anything?" Kat took a menacing step closer. "Who are you working for?"

"I don't suppose it matters now. The Misted Isles... the Demons contacted us offering..."

As he spoke, his hand came up again as if to ward her off.

No! Too late she caught the glint of something is his palm as it shot forward to punch into her upper arm. The pain was excruciating. She cried out. At the same time, she reacted. Instantly, instinctively. He tried to grasp her good arm but she was too quick, his fingers slipping away from their attempted hold as she struck at him, her sword lashing out once, twice and a third time, doing damage at every turn.

For a split second Brent stood before her, blood pumping from the slit in his throat, hand reaching, struggling futilely to stem the flow. He might have tried to speak, to tell her something, but any final words emerged as nothing more than incoherent gurgles.

"Sorry, I lied," Kat said. "For every cut you make, I'll pay you back *more* than double."

Brent collapsed to the ground, though Kat was no longer paying him any attention. "Shit... Shit... *Shit!*" She examined her wound, which was bad, she'd realised that straight away. There was a lot of blood – it must have severed something important. The "it" in question was a homemade blade, not a proper knife at all but the shard of something pilfered and sharpened.

She could testify to exactly how sharp the result was. The offending article was currently embedded in her arm, just above the elbow. The sensible thing to do was leave it there, she knew that. Removal would only risk further injury. But as well as hurting like mad this crude makeshift blade offended her, and she wanted it out of her body as soon as possible. Common sense be hanged. Wrapping a cloth around her good hand to give her better purchase, she grasped the shard, took a second to brace herself and then pulled, yanking it out in one firm swift movement. Another scream escaped from between her clenched teeth and yet more blood welled forth, but she ignored the pain, knowing she had to work swiftly.

She wrapped the same cloth around her arm just above the wound, using her teeth and her good hand to pull it as tight as possible, forming a tourniquet. Not perfect, perhaps, but it was the best she could do.

She straightened up, sheathed both her swords and – turning her back on Brent's corpse, dismissing the bastard from her thoughts – walked away, cradling her injured arm. She headed towards Iron Grove Square – *Charveve Court*, she corrected herself – and the Tattooed Men; she headed towards Shayna. Had she been fit and healthy, the distance would have been nothing, but in her current condition this was going to be a challenge, no denying it. She couldn't afford to stop, couldn't afford to rest. This was the City Below; if she fell down the chances were she'd never get up again but would instead become just one more corpse for the spill dragons to pick over and the body boys to collect come morning.

But that wasn't going to happen, not to her. She was Kat, leader of the Tattooed Men, last of the Death Queens, and she was going to make it. She *had* to make it.

> *...To the topmost Row, the Upper Heights,*
> *Where stars and Demons frequent the nights,*
> *The end of this verse, fair Thaiburley's crown,*
> *From which lofty peak you can only fall down!*

He loved it here in the Upper Heights, the roof of the world. It was morning and Tom had arrived early, to stand by the city's outer walls and gaze out across the mountains. He had travelled a long way of late – in more senses than one – and he'd seen any number of wonders, things which the street-nick he'd been a mere month ago could never have conceived of; but nothing he'd encountered could compare to this. Thaiburley's crown, the very place he'd been trying to reach on that day which now seemed a lifetime ago, when he'd scaled the city's walls and witnessed what appeared to be a murder.

He still recalled the first time he'd been brought up here by the Prime Master – the *old* Prime Master. Then the sight had taken his breath away, and it still did.

The wind today was stronger than on that first visit and the air colder, though not enough to cause him to regret choosing this as the venue for the meeting. It seemed fitting.

He turned to consider the city's roof. A panorama of decorative spires, artful crenulations, slender towers and elegant chimneys opened up before him, stretching away as far as the eye could see. According to the Prime Master, one man had conceived all this, someone called Carley. For a while Tom had wondered if this might be Thaiss's brother, but it wasn't, he knew that now.

A number of things had tumbled into place in the aftermath of his renewing the core, almost as if some part of his mind had deliberately held back a welter of information gleaned from the goddess, knowing that he needed to concentrate on the job at hand and only releasing this final flood once the work was done. Perhaps it wasn't his mind, perhaps this delayed knowledge had always been the goddess's intent. So many things that had puzzled him or that would have puzzled him once he'd found the time to think about them now made sense. Not everything, unfortunately.

The Jeradine, for example. He knew that they were an ancient race whose civilisation had once spanned the stars, now reduced to a dwindling population content to live out their days in the shadow of others. Why had they settled for such placid obscurity? Their ambitions and their motivations were completely alien to Tom, beyond his ability to understand. The more he discovered about them the more he became intrigued by his own ignorance on the subject. He determined to learn all he could about these enigmatic neighbours, hopefully with Ty-gen's help, but he couldn't do that from up in the Heights.

His attention returned to the inspirational vista before him, slipping back to that first time he'd been brought here. Seeing the city's roof had fulfilled a life-long dream, though there had been one disturbing element; he'd found the Upper Heights haunted by elusive will-o'-the-wisp figures intent on teasing him. The Demons.

They were gone now, of course, and the new generation had yet to establish itself, but if anything the place felt more haunted now than it ever had then. Tom kept expecting to glance around and find the familiar face of his mentor beside him, to hear that gentle voice offering him insights and wise words. Instead, he had just the wind for company.

That was set to change, though, as Tom spied the Prime Master's successor striding towards him. The man's brown hair was being blown into ragged wisps by the wind, as if mussed by some gigantic invisible hand.

Thaiburley's new de facto ruler smiled as he approached. Tom felt a lurch of loss at the sight. He still couldn't believe the Prime Master he'd known was gone, and it felt odd addressing anyone else by the same title, especially someone he knew.

"The view is extraordinary, isn't it?" Thomas said as he reached Tom.

His younger namesake could only agree. The cloud cover was high this day, giving a spectacular view over the mountain peaks. Tom could even follow the course of the Thair for a little way. It was odd to gaze down upon a stretch of river which he must have travelled along while aboard Abe's barge. The Thair seemed so small from up here. He wondered whether the Prime Master might have come up here to watch the barge the day he'd left. He didn't dwell on the view, though, not wanting to risk a return of the vertigo that had troubled him in the past. Instead he returned his attention to the city's rooftop.

"There's still a place for you on the council, you know," Thomas told him. "You'd make history: the youngest councillor the city's ever seen, by a decade or three."

Tom smiled but shook his head. "Thank you but no. That's not for me and we both know it. Just thinking about it scares me worse than the Rust Warriors ever did. Whatever powers I can or can't call upon, I don't know enough to make decisions for the whole city. I'd only end up making a mess of things."

"You have good instincts, Tom. I believe you'd do a lot better than you suppose."

Tom snorted. "I doubt that. Besides, where's the fun in being stuck in stuffy meetings the whole time?"

"You've got me there," Thomas agreed with a wry smile. "Where indeed?"

"Look, if you meant what you said about plans to regenerate the City Below, let me get involved in that. I could do some good down there. I know the streets and what's needed for the people in them. At least that way I wouldn't be sitting around wondering what the breck everyone else was talking about, which is what would happen if I sat on the Council."

"Yes, I *am* serious about rebuilding the City Below. It's been sorely neglected over the years, and this seems the perfect opportunity to do something about it. So much major work is going to be needed in different parts of the city, especially the Heights, that we might as well expand that to include the under-City as well, to roll everything up into one big redevelopment project. Your help with that would be greatly appreciated, thank you."

Tom felt as if a huge weight had been lifted from him. The prospect of spending the rest of his life in the Heights had grown ever less appealing as time went on. He knew that some people would be expecting him to do exactly that and had almost been willing to go along with those expectations, particularly given his own growing sense of alienation from the streets. The more he considered the possibility, though, the more he realised that it simply wasn't what he wanted. In fact he hated the idea. As he'd determined en route to the core, it was high time he shed the mantle of others' expectations and started determining his own destiny. Tom wasn't a street-nick anymore, but nor was he a cloud scraper, and the streets were still his home.

"I hear you met Thaiss herself," Thomas said, a little too casually. "How did you find her?"

By walking a brecking long way, Tom felt tempted to reply. Instead, after a moment's thought, he simply said, "Odd."

Thomas smiled. "I'm sure. Living that long must be… difficult; I mean, it must have a profound effect on who you are. What I suppose I'm getting at is, did you think her entirely sane?"

Tom considered the question for a moment, largely because he didn't really know how to reply. "I'm not sure I'd have any way of knowing," he said at last. "How do you judge the sanity of a god?"

Thomas laughed. "There is that, I suppose." After a slight pause he added, "One thing I don't understand is why she didn't come back with you. I mean, if Thaiburley means so much to her and she knew the city was in such deadly peril, why didn't she return here in all her glory and sort the situation out herself?"

She did, Tom thought, *if only in my head*. "I don't know," he replied. "I've wondered about that myself and, well…"

"What?"

"I'm not honestly sure she could. She's lived in that citadel for so long, relying on her machines to keep her alive… I wonder whether she can live anywhere else anymore."

"Dependent on the machines, you mean… in effect confined within her own citadel? Now there's a thought."

A strange look passed across the Prime Master's face just for an instant and then it was gone.

"What?" Tom asked.

"Oh, nothing. I was just thinking that perhaps it's as well Thaiss never visits her city these days, that Thaiburley might be better off with a goddess who only wakes up once every century or so, allowing our society to develop without constant interference. That's all." He smiled at Tom. "Anyway, I've a meeting with the reconstituted council to prepare for. So, if you'll excuse me." With that, Thomas left him.

Tom reflected on what struck him as a strange conversation. He thought back to the questions that had troubled him during his time at the ice citadel and the suspicion that he wasn't being told everything. He'd learnt a lot since then but still didn't have all the answers by any means. However, he was young, he was powerful, he had access to the city's core and knew how to reach Thaiss's citadel. The answers wouldn't elude him forever.

He watched Thaiburley's new and vigorous Prime Master walk away and couldn't help but wonder... would it really have mattered who had won here? After all, from everything he knew, Thaiss's brother had never sought to destroy Thaiburley as such, merely claim it as his own. He'd used some pretty nasty tactics, true, but perhaps he'd needed to in order to stand any chance of success. From the point of view of those living in the city, particularly in the City Below, would one god be any worse than the other?

When Tom had replenished the core, he'd felt the corrupting influence – the essence of Thaiss's brother – flee to the City Below. Everyone assumed that it had fled to Insint, a natural ally, but Tom wasn't so sure. After all, it now emerged that Insint had been linked with the Maker in some way and ultimately been responsible for sending Tom up-City in search of a Demon's egg, which Thaiss's brother would surely have known was a myth. So perhaps the two were never actually allies in the first place.

Someone else, though, had been in the City Below at the time.

Tom had done a lot of thinking in the past few days, about Thaiss, her brother, the city, and the core.

Everything he'd learned had been fed to him through the filter of the goddess's own prejudices, and one thing he'd learned from a life spent on the streets was that there were always two sides to any story. Memories of his merger with the core still troubled him, and he realised this was far more than just an energy source. How much influence did it have on events? Had it got what it wanted? Had the core decided that Thaiburley was due a change?

One thing Tom had come to realise about Thaiss and her sort was that they played the long game. It seemed to him that if an intelligence as old and cunning as her brother was supposed to be had gained controlling influence over the core, that intelligence would have made contingencies, preparations in case its grand scheme failed.

There were many in the streets who maintained that a name held power. Certainly Tom had felt a kinship with his namesake, the arkademic now the Prime Master, ever since he heard Magnus call his victim "Thomas" and realised that he and this man shared the same name. Yet he could have sworn he'd witnessed that Thomas being murdered, stabbed to death and then flung from the city's walls – the event that changed his life forever. He'd been told afterwards that only the skill of Thaiburley's finest healers had saved Thomas. But healers drew on the core for their talent. A core which, by that time, had been corrupted by the intruding essence of Thaiss's brother and which, Tom was becoming increasingly certain, had a will of its own. What if it wasn't the healers' skill alone that so spectacularly brought a man back from the brink of death?

Thaiburley's new Prime Master looked back, smiled and waved as he entered a stairwell and disappeared from sight. Tom reflected on something, one of the tit-bits of information that had bubbled to the surface as all the knowledge and history he'd assimilated at Thaiss's citadel finally settled into place. Buried within so many other facts was a detail that had otherwise been conspicuous by its absence.

He now knew the name of Thaiss's brother. His name was Thomas.

About the Author

Ian Whates lives in a comfortable home down a quiet cul-de-sac in an idyllic Cambridgeshire village, which he shares with his partner Helen and their pets – Honey the golden cocker spaniel, Calvin the tailless black cat, and Inky the goldfish (sadly, Binky died a few years ago).

Ian's first published stories appeared in the late 1980s, but it was not until the early 2000s that he began to pursue writing with any seriousness. In 2006, Ian launched independent publisher NewCon Press. That same year he also resumed selling short stories, including two to the science journal *Nature*.

ianwhates.com

THE CITY OF A HUNDRED ROWS VOL. I

CITY OF DREAMS & NIGHTMARE

IAN WHATES

"Born story-teller Ian Whates takes us on a gripping, terrifying trip-of-a-lifetime." – TANITH LEE

WELCOME to the city of a hundred ROWS.

You won't want to LEAVE.

THE CITY OF A HUNDRED ROWS VOL. II

CITY OF HOPE & DESPAIR

IAN WHATES

"A born storyteller." – THE GUARDIAN

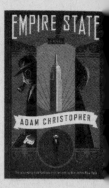

YOU DESERVE THE BEST
Grab the whole Angry Robot catalog

DAN ABNETT
- [ ] Embedded
- [ ] Triumff: Her Majesty's Hero

GUY ADAMS
- [ ] The World House
- [ ] Restoration

JO ANDERTON
- [ ] Debris

LAUREN BEUKES
- [ ] Moxyland
- [ ] Zoo City

THOMAS BLACKTHORNE
(aka John Meaney)
- [ ] Edge
- [ ] Point

MAURICE BROADDUS
- [ ] King Maker
- [ ] King's Justice
- [ ] King's War

PETER CROWTHER
- [ ] Darkness Falling

ALIETTE DE BODARD
- [ ] Servant of the Underworld
- [ ] Harbinger of the Storm
- [ ] Master of the House of Darts

MATT FORBECK
- [ ] Amortals
- [ ] Vegas Knights

JUSTIN GUSTAINIS
- [ ] Hard Spell

GUY HALEY
- [ ] Reality 36

COLIN HARVEY
- [ ] Damage Time
- [ ] Winter Song

MATTHEW HUGHES
- [ ] The Damned Busters

TRENT JAMIESON
- [ ] Roil

K W JETER
- [ ] Infernal Devices
- [ ] Morlock Night

J ROBERT KING
- [ ] Angel of Death
- [ ] Death's Disciples

GARY McMAHON
- [ ] Pretty Little Dead Things
- [ ] Dead Bad Things

ANDY REMIC
- [ ] Kell's Legend
- [ ] Soul Stealers
- [ ] Vampire Warlords

CHRIS ROBERSON
- [ ] Book of Secrets

MIKE SHEVDON
- [ ] Sixty-One Nails
- [ ] The Road to Bedlam

GAV THORPE
- [ ] The Crown of the Blood
- [ ] The Crown of the Conqueror

LAVIE TIDHAR
- [ ] The Bookman
- [ ] Camera Obscura

TIM WAGGONER
- [ ] Nekropolis
- [ ] Dead Streets
- [ ] Dark War

KAARON WARREN
- [ ] Mistification
- [ ] Slights
- [ ] Walking the Tree

IAN WHATES
- [ ] City of Dreams & Nightmare
- [ ] City of Hope & Despair
- [ ] City of Light & Shadow